By Pamela Hill

Published by Juliana Publishing

Book cover design and print by
Hillside Printing Services

i

Published by Juliana Publishing

Copyright © Pamela Hill 2011

British Library Cataloguing in Publication Data.
A catalogue record for this book is available from
the British Library.
All the characters in this book are fictitious and any
resemblance to actual persons living or dead is
purely coincidental.

Juliana Publishing
Highview Lodge
Oulder Hill Drive
Rochdale OL11 5LB

Printed and bound in Great Britain by Hillside
Printing Services, Rochdale Tel:- 01706 711872
www.hillsidegroup.co.uk

ISBN 978-0-9559047-3-8

Akina

1

Mattie Henshaw was roused from sleep by a blaring taxi horn at seven o'clock. She opened the curtains and watched the driver packing the boot with cases and bags as the couple's two young children darted about excitedly. The initial leg of their journey was about to begin and Mattie's eyes followed the taxi until it disappeared from sight. She tried to imagine their ultimate destination and sighed pensively. She too would be filled with euphoria when it was time for *her* family to head off to the airport. *Her* family! It sounded so strange...strange yet nice. Nice? That word didn't even come close to the way she felt; no superlative could express those emotions. The long-awaited day had arrived...her wedding day. In a few short hours she would walk from the church as Mrs. Mark Wyndham and mother not only to her soon to be adopted ward, Akina, but also to Adam, Mark's seven-year-old son from his first marriage.

A gentle tap on the bedroom door interrupted her thoughts. 'Are you awake yet?' Steph called. 'Can I come in?'

She crossed the room and opened the door. 'Yes, I've been awake for some time. I've been watching your next-door neighbours who have just driven off in a taxi. The children looked very excited.'

Steph nodded. 'I heard the horn. They're all going to Spain for two weeks. It's the first foreign holiday they've ever had and the children have been manic these past few weeks. Seth called yesterday to give them some spending money and couldn't get away quick enough. He said it was absolute bedlam.'

Mattie chuckled. 'I can well imagine. I can hardly wait to go to Florida on Tuesday but my excitement pales into insignificance when compared to Akina's and Adam's. They're forever asking about rides and other attractions at Walt Disney World. Having said that, it's to be expected when they've never been on a foreign holiday before.'

'And neither have you!' Steph reminded her. 'It'll be incredible. You'll see. I really envy you.'

'Why? That thick wad of money Bill gave you on your wedding day would have paid for a wonderful honeymoon and you'd still have had plenty over.'

'Yes, and *you* know *your* brother better than I do. He's so tight with money. He insisted we keep it in the bank earning interest, his point being you didn't know what you might need in the future. It's pointless arguing with him for he's as stubborn as a mule but as things have turned out he was right. We've a fair bit of expense ahead of us now.' She patted her huge bump and grinned. 'Just four weeks to go and will I be thankful when that time comes! I look like a house-end; I can hardly get into maternity clothes now and I have to fasten all my outsize trousers and skirts with a nappy pin. How disgusting is that?'

Mattie's lips stretched into a beaming smile as her sister-in-law grimaced. 'I'm just hoping you've got the dates right and that the baby doesn't come early whilst we're on honeymoon.'

She smiled. 'I'll tell it to hang on! Besides, a first baby's more likely to arrive late.'

There was a further knock at the door before Seth ambled in. 'I thought I heard footsteps. I'm sorry to interrupt your girl talk but your breakfast will be on the table in a few minutes. I'm making bacon, eggs and toast. I've already had mine.'

He wandered across to Mattie and gave her a hug. 'How are you doing big sister? Are you nervous?'

She kissed his forehead. 'No, not in the least; I'm excited and counting the minutes.'

'You've got a damn good bloke there you know. There's none better.'

She sighed. 'I don't need reminding Seth. I know how lucky I am.'

'Hey, he's lucky as well! No wonder he persisted when you kept knocking him back. He phoned me earlier to ask if you were okay. He wouldn't admit it of course but he's an absolute wreck. I could tell.'

'Oh dear! Shall I call him?'

'*No!*' Steph howled. '*It's your wedding day!* You can't have *any* contact with him until you arrive at the church. You know it's bad luck. Come and get your breakfast and try not to think about it or you'll be as nervous as he is.'

Mattie dutifully followed her from the room. She wasn't in the least hungry but knew she should try to eat something. She took her place at the table and momentarily her thoughts transferred elsewhere. It had been a long and hectic six months since Sam's

3

death and Mattie missed her very much. If only she could have held on long enough to see Akina in her pretty bridesmaid's dress…if only…

'Penny for them,' Steph interrupted, sitting down beside her. Recognising the distant look in her eyes she guessed what was on Mattie's mind.

'I was just thinking of Sam. She once said it was her one true regret that she wouldn't be here for our wedding, after *she* had been instrumental in getting the two of us together. Life's so cruel,' she sighed.

With a nod, Steph agreed.

Seth placed their breakfast plates on the table and poured their tea. 'I'm off upstairs now for a shower. I'll not be long. Make sure Mattie eats it Steph.'

'I will,' she promised him. 'So, how's Akina been of late?' she enquired of Mattie.

'Amazing. She just takes everything in her stride. She did make reference to Sam when we chose her bridesmaid's dress, saying her mummy would have liked to have seen her in that and I had to fight back the tears. It was an agonising moment for me. For such a young child she's so level-headed. I forget at times she's only six.'

'Yes, Akina's had to grow up quickly hasn't she? She's had to come to terms with things no six-year-old should have to face but I suppose, learning from a very early age that she'd only have her mother for a short time, she dealt with Sam's death more easily and she had you of course to take Sam's place.'

'*Oh no* Steph, I'd *never* try to take Sam's place. I'm her guardian and I love her as a mother would but Akina would never accept me as a replacement

4

for Sam, nor would I expect her to. No one would ever fill that void and take *my* mother's place. She never shuts me out though. I think she has feelings for me but in a much different way. When we went to collect the bridesmaid's dress, the shop assistant, assuming Akina was my daughter, made reference to me as her mother but she corrected her instantly stating I wasn't her mother; I was her *guardian*, she told her firmly but politely.'

'Ouch! Didn't that hurt?'

'No, not at all. I had foster-parents as a child and I thought the world of Olive and Richard; in fact I still do but never once did I think of them as Mum and Dad. I'd have thought you'd understand, your father having died but then maybe not because you never knew him did you? Your mother told me how he died in the war just before you were born.'

Steph's face turned red and tears filled her eyes. Hastily changing topic she asked, 'And what about Emily? Do you two get on okay?'

'Yes, Emily's a sweetie. We've never had a cross word. I think she's just relieved that I was there for Akina. She's too old now to cope with a boisterous grandchild full-time and Norman's in failing health so she has more than enough on her plate attending to his needs. By the time we'd packed up the house, a *colossal* task, we were thoroughly exhausted. We had to get rid of so much stuff. She'd have needed a whole fleet of removal vans to transport everything from Devon and where would they have put it? It's only a three-bedroom bungalow.'

'Is their new house ship-shape now?'

'More or less and being close, Emily can walk to ours in fifteen minutes so has regular contact with Akina. She's fond of Adam too and he likes having his new grandparents close at hand.'

'I've kept meaning to ask, are you happy moving to the house Mark shared with his first wife?'

She smiled at her obvious concern. 'I'm perfectly happy; it was my idea. During the time Emily and I were packing up in Devon, he was redecorating his house ready for sale. I'd not seen it and it was kind of assumed we'd have a fresh start in a house of our own but when Mark brought me up for a day or two for my birthday, I was thrilled when I saw it. It has four bedrooms; it's in a beautiful location; it met all our requirements for a family of four and it seemed senseless buying another with all the upheaval and expense that entails. Adam was able to continue at the same school and I didn't really want to uproot both children. I love it there. It feels like home. It's also easy for Mark to get to the hospital, especially when he's on call. We changed some furniture and curtains that weren't to my taste and Emily gave us a few antiques she couldn't accommodate. I think it helped Akina adjust to her new surroundings with familiar things around her. In any case, I wouldn't want to eradicate all her former memories.'

Steph nodded in agreement. 'You're right. You're such a caring person. I'm pleased things worked out for the two of you.' She laughed before continuing, 'Seth was *mortified* when you moved in with Mark. He couldn't believe that *you* of all people…'

'Er…what's *that* supposed to mean?' she cut in.

'Hey, *I'm* not criticising you Mattie. I wanted us to do the same when we were saving to get married but Seth wouldn't. He's rather puritanical.'

She grunted. 'Well I'm not, in fact I suggested to him that you should move in together prior to your wedding so he could save the rent when I moved to Devon but he wouldn't hear of it.'

'Huh! Is that right? When I suggested that to him, he said you'd be horrified and I didn't want to upset the apple-cart so I didn't mention it anymore. You were soon to be my sister-in-law and I didn't want any family arguments. The cheek of him! Just wait till he comes downstairs! Fancy him blaming you!'

'Seth had his reasons Steph and I intended telling you at some point. There are things you don't know that Seth would never divulge, bad things I couldn't talk about at the time he and Jack found out but as soon as we're back from honeymoon, I promise I'll tell you then, so please don't say anything to Seth. He's only kept quiet out of loyalty to me.'

She decided not to labour the point. She'd always known there was something *different* about Mattie, something relating to her past and something so bad that even Seth would never discuss it with her and then there had been that incident last Christmas but one when Jack, Mattie's younger brother, had been on leave from the Navy and they had gone out for a meal where Mattie had been dragged from her chair by a vile woman who had screamed that Mattie was a filthy murderous whore who should have got life for what she'd done. That terrifying experience still prayed on Steph's mind. No explanation had been

7

proffered then or later, the issue having been simply laid to rest and Steph had had to respect everyone's silence. It had been a family matter and Steph knew only too well how family matters could impact on one's life. She too had a secret she hadn't divulged to Mattie and her secret could never be revealed.

Mattie checked the time. 'I'll have another cup of tea and then I'm going to get ready. I really enjoyed my breakfast. I don't often have a cooked breakfast. Seth's quite domesticated now isn't he?'

'He is; he's been a big help during my pregnancy. He really takes care of me. He's one in a million.'

'I told you he was worth waiting for when he kept delaying your wedding. Seth's a thinker, rarely impulsive but his heart's certainly in the right place. I found him irritating at times and he and Jack were always at each other's throat but he's a good sound guy who'll always look after you. How's he getting on with your mum these days?'

'They're okay now. It was just the wedding thing when she thought he was putting it off. She wanted to see us married, speaking of which, have you met Mark's previous in-laws?'

'No, not yet; that pleasure's still to come. When Mark last took Adam to spend the weekend there, he went alone. He wanted to tell them about us and didn't want to embarrass me.'

Steph's ears pricked up. 'What did they say?' she asked breathlessly. 'Were they shocked?'

'According to Mark they were delighted and expressed surprise he'd waited so long following their daughter's death. They asked him all about me and

8

then they told him they'd really like to come to our wedding and...'

'You're *joking*!' she cut in. 'Are they coming?'

'Well, yes. I could hardly say *no* could I? When all said and done, they're Adam's grandparents and neither the death of their daughter nor our wedding changes that. They'd feel ill-at-ease if they'd never met me when bringing Adam home after he'd spent the weekend there, besides which, I have to think of Akina. Emily treats Adam and Akina the same. She doesn't favour one above the other and so naturally, I expect Mark's in-laws to reciprocate likewise.'

'How do you feel about meeting them?'

She shrugged. 'I don't know really. Suspicious I suppose. I feel I'm about to be closely scrutinised. They're bound to make comparisons aren't they?'

'Just smile sweetly and let the day take its course. Don't let them spoil your wedding day.'

'Mark says they're nice so I don't think I've any-thing to worry about and trust me, no one is going to spoil this day. I'd better get ready.'

As Mattie stood up, the telephone rang and Steph was quick to answer it. 'Let me. It might be Mark.'

It was Jack. 'How's my soon-to-be-married older sister?' he asked affectionately as Steph handed her the receiver. 'Are you ready for your big moment?'

'It can't come soon enough Jack. I've started the countdown now. More to the point, how's Mark?'

'For a man who faces his doom, he's not *too* bad. I've just poured him a stiff whisky.'

'*Jack!* Don't you *dare* get him drunk!' she cried. 'Let me speak to him.'

'*No!*' Steph yelled, grabbing the receiver. 'Jack, behave and stop winding her up.'

'I were only having a bit of fun with her. Mark's fine…really. He's only thrown up twice,' he stated, followed by a raucous guffaw. 'Put Mattie back on. I want a word with her.'

They chatted for a few moments and Jack put her at ease about Mark. 'I can hardly wait to see you in your dress,' he said softly. 'I thought the day would never dawn that you'd be getting married. You've no idea how happy me and Seth are for you.'

'That makes three of us Jack. I'm very happy too. What's Adam doing?'

'He's watching the telly. Have you been in touch with Meredith this morning?'

'No, not yet; I'll call her shortly. She's more than enough to contend with. You'd think Akina was the Bride. She intended getting up at six to get ready so Meredith has her hands full. I'm glad she offered to get Akina ready. She was as high as a kite last time we spoke. I could do with a dose of whatever she's on. The nerves *are* starting to kick in a little now.'

'You'll be fine. Remember we all love you.'

'I know that Jack. Give Mark my love. Tell him I'm counting the minutes now. Don't be late and *no* funny stuff in your speech, do you hear?'

'Loud and clear. See you soon. Bye Mattie.'

It became a lovely clear sunny day as the morning progressed towards midday and Mattie was pleased that Easter had fallen in April. Easter Saturday was a perfect day for a wedding. When first arranged, it

10

was to have been a simple close family affair with only a handful of people in attendance but the guest list continued to grow until numbers exceeded fifty for the main meal with others arriving later. Mark's work colleagues had assumed those not required for hospital duties would be invited, as was the custom when a Consultant was getting married. Those were grand weddings, providing the ideal opportunity for a free 'booze-up' as Mark apologetically explained to Mattie. In his case there had been special interest with combined emotions of joy and curiosity.

For several years his colleagues had encouraged him to start dating again after the tragic death of his first wife only weeks after Adam was born but their words had fallen on deaf ears and so Mark's unexpected announcement of his forthcoming wedding had been the talking point at the hospital for weeks. Everyone wanted to attend and whilst that was impossible because the hospital had to remain viable, there had nonetheless been a certain amount of duty switching by his close colleagues to guarantee their attendance. Mark had expected nothing less than a furious outburst from Mattie but to his surprise she had remained calm. She was in fact grateful that his colleagues would be coming because apart from his parents and Adam, no other guests were listed from his side until his former in-laws invited themselves.

For the umpteenth time Mattie checked her watch before calling Meredith to ask if all the flowers had arrived.

As expected, Akina answered. 'Sutton residence. Who's calling please?' she asked courteously.

'It's Mattie. How are you darling?'

'Okay,' she said sullenly. 'I wanted to get dressed but Aunt Meredith wouldn't let me in case my dress got creased or dirty. It's not fair.'

'Well, I happen to think she's right. After all, you want to look pretty don't you?'

'Of course I do. Are you dressed Mattie?'

'No, not yet. I don't want to spoil *my* dress either. Do you know if the flowers have been delivered?'

'Yes, they're here and mine's really lovely. Uncle Andrew's just getting the car out to bring yours and he's calling at our house afterwards to take Mark's, Adam's and Uncle Jack's…er…'

'Buttonhole?'

'Yes, buttonhole. That's a daft name for a flower. I've never even seen one. What does it look like?'

Mattie laughed. 'It's called a buttonhole because it's worn in the buttonhole but I agree; it *is* a stupid name. It can be any flower but it's often a rose or a carnation. Posh people call them *boutonnières*.'

'Then why don't they call it by its proper name? It's no wonder I've a lot to learn,' she remonstrated.

Mattie howled with laughter. 'Listen, you know a lot more than other children aged six.'

'I'll be seven in two weeks,' she reminded her.

'I'm well aware of that and you know much more than most seven-year-olds too!' *Far* too much, she mumbled to herself. 'Is Aunt Meredith there?'

'I'll just call her. She's upstairs.'

Mattie was about to tell her not to call her if she was busy but it was too late and Meredith picked up the bedroom extension. 'How's it going Mattie?'

'Fine. I was just checking the flowers were there.'

'Stop interfering in things that don't concern you. I'm in charge at this end. How do you feel?'

'Rather tense. I'm chomping at the bit now; I can hardly wait for the taxi to arrive. What time are you leaving for the church?'

'As soon as Andrew gets back when he's dropped off the flowers…half an hour or so I imagine.'

'Dare I ask how you're coping with *Madam*? And before you blast me, just remember it was *you* who volunteered to have her stay with you.'

Meredith cackled audibly. 'She's a character isn't she? She's had the two of us in stitches. I've never known a child ask as many questions. We've had to explain everything about the ceremony, who makes speeches at the reception and what they talk about. I think she'd be a marvellous wedding planner now, though Andrew had to explain most of it as he's the only one with hands on experience.'

'It'll be your turn soon Meredith, just a couple of months before you're Mrs. Andrew Sutton. I hope you'll manage okay at the office without me for the next couple of weeks.'

'Er…nobody's indispensible Mattie. Forget about the office and enjoy your honeymoon. There are no cases listed for hearing until the end of the second week and everything non-urgent can be put on hold. I managed all the time you were in Devon didn't I?'

'Yes you did, but don't forget you had help then,' she countered.

'Help? That useless dimwit? I'd have had every-thing done in a quarter of the time without her help.

How she could describe herself as a Legal Secretary is beyond me. Akina at six would have done better.'

'Jack called earlier and Mark's okay, not that I'd be told if he wasn't. I hope the day runs smoothly. I want everything to be perfect.'

'Everything *will* be perfect; you'll see. Shouldn't you be finishing off the final touches now?'

'I'm ready apart from my dress. There's nothing else to do. I've done my make-up and my nails.'

'Well I for one can't wait to see you.'

'Will you remind Andrew he's taking Steph and Adam back with him? I don't want him to leave the flowers and forget about the two of them.'

Meredith screeched with laughter. 'For heaven's sake stop worrying! I'm hanging up now. That way you can't blame me if you're not ready when your taxi arrives. Good luck!'

'*Good luck?* Why, am I going to need it?'

'Shut up! It's merely a figure of speech. See you in church and remember, keep your head held high as you walk down the aisle.'

Seth walked round the black limousine and opened Mattie's door, smiling proudly as he relieved her of her flowers with one hand and helped her out with the other. Tears filled his eyes. 'Mum would have been so proud today. You look radiant Mattie.'

With a lump in her throat she replied, 'Don't you *dare* make my eye make-up run Seth Henshaw. It's not like you to be sentimental.'

'It's not every day I give my beautiful sister away in marriage,' he said emotionally.

'I expected Jack being outside to meet us.'

'He rang whilst you were upstairs. He were upset. You don't need me to tell you what a soft bugger he is. He'd definitely have mucked up your eye make-up so I told him to stop inside with Mark. He'll see you when we go in. Besides, somebody has to keep an eye on Mark in case he tries to clear off through the back door,' he jested.

Akina appeared in view on the church steps. She had been instructed to wave to the usher when their limousine arrived and the usher in turn would alert the organist.

'Doesn't Akina look amazing Seth? If only Sam could have been here for this,' she sighed.

'Aye, she does. It's a crying shame. Right, come on before he starts playing your tune. Let's not be maudlin. This is supposed to be a happy day.'

Seth escorted her up the half-dozen steps into the church foyer and Mattie gave Akina an affectionate hug. 'You look beautiful darling.'

'So do you Mattie. You look like a sugary angel. I like the sparkly bits on your dress.'

'Thank you. You know what to do, don't you?'

'Of course I do. I have to walk slowly behind you and not too close in case I step on your dress. Then when you hand me your flowers I move to one side quietly and I mustn't speak until it's all over.'

'Right,' she said softly.

The usher appeared and addressing Mattie asked, 'Are you ready or do you need a moment?'

She exhaled noisily but when Seth squeezed her hand she smiled and nodded her head. 'I'm ready.'

15

He disappeared from view and moments later the organist pounded on the keys when all members of the congregation leapt to their feet.

Seth kissed her cheek. 'I'm so proud,' he sighed as she took his arm and then with a wink of the eye added, 'Come on; let's get this show on the road.'

Mattie sensed everyone's eyes were upon them as they slowly made their way down the long aisle but she only had eyes for Mark, who awaited her arrival with a broad beam lighting up his face. As she drew close he murmured, 'You look magnificent darling. I love you so much.'

'I love you too,' she whispered. At that point she caught Jack's eye and tears were rolling down his cheeks. No words were spoken; none were needed. Mattie knew how emotional he felt. She had been a second mother to Jack, the youngest, and more than anything he wanted her to be happy. Inclining her head in Jack's direction, she beamed with utter joy. Akina dutifully relieved her of her bouquet and the wedding service began...

Once outside, the guests gathered around to impart their sincere wishes to the Bride and Groom. Mark introduced all his colleagues to Mattie who thanked them for attending. The majority were unknown to her but as the long line was drawing to an end there were two people she recognised from the hospital. The first was Lucille, a friend of Steph's, who had unwittingly been responsible for a certain amount of antagonism between Mattie and Mark through-out their turbulent courtship and the second was Dr.

McAndrew who held Mattie warmly for some time before saying, 'I'm rarely emotional but that has to be the most poignant wedding ceremony I've ever witnessed. It was so beautiful; *you* are beautiful and I won't even try to describe the joy this day brings me because there are no words to suit the occasion. It's an understatement to say how thrilled I am my dear but I think you understand, don't you?'

Mattie nodded. 'I certainly do Dr. McAndrew and I thank you for your part in this because you taught me how to believe in myself again.'

'Nonsense! Anyway, enough about that! Today is a momentous wonderful day, the beginning of your future with Mark and I for one know you'll be very happy. I'll catch up with you later my dear.'

Lucille lost no time in delivering her predictable hackneyed remark, 'Well, what can I say Mattie?'

Mattie laughed. 'Knowing you Lucille, I daresay what *you'll* say has been very well-rehearsed.'

Lucille threw her arms around her. 'I'm so happy and I'll say this; if *I* couldn't snare Mark there's no one better to fill my boots. I'd hate that terrific guy to be wasted on anyone unworthy of such a catch.'

Mark roared with laughter. 'That's the first time I've laughed today Lucille. You're such a nutter but in a nice way. I'm delighted you could be here.'

'You're joking! Wild horses wouldn't have kept me away,' she quipped and turning to Mattie asked, 'Is it okay if I kiss the Groom?'

'You'd better ask Mark,' was her glib response.

She turned to Mark, raising her eyebrows and he gave her a friendly hug before allowing her to kiss

17

him on the lips. 'I really am overjoyed for you both Mark…truly and I hope you have lots of babies and live happily ever after.'

'Er…yes thanks Lucille but let's take it a step at a time please,' he responded with a throaty chuckle.

Looking flustered Seth approached. 'The photographer's going mad! He needs you both *now*.'

'Well, he'll have to wait a few moments longer,' Mark said. 'Tell him we'll be a couple of minutes.'

As Seth walked away, Mark sighed, 'Alone at last Mattie! I thought that line of folk would never end.'

'Er…who invited them?'

'I suppose you have a point. I just wanted a few moments alone with you to say how ravishing you look and I wanted to hold you. Thank you so much for agreeing to be my wife. They gazed deeply into each other's eyes and kissed tenderly. 'I think now might be a good time to introduce you to my ex in-laws, Adam's grandparents, if you're up for it.'

He took her hand and they wandered towards the elegant couple talking to Adam. 'I don't even know what they're called,' Mattie whispered.

'Rachel and Bob and don't worry, you'll be fine.'

As they approached, Rachel stepped forward and smiled. 'Hello, I'm Rachel and I'm very happy for you both. It was wonderful to hear Mark's exciting news. Bob and I are delighted he's found happiness at last. You look lovely and your bridesmaid is such a charmer. She's been talking to us.'

'Talking you to death, no doubt,' Mattie said on a laugh. 'Akina's my ward.'

'I know. She told me how you'd taken care of her

since the death of her mother. That must have been such a difficult decision for you to make.'

Defensively she countered, 'Not at all. There was never any question about it. She's a delightful little girl. I love her deeply and so does Mark and she's a welcome sister for Adam.'

Mindful of an awkward pause as Rachel digested her words, Bob thrust out his hand enthusiastically. 'I'm Bob. I'm delighted to make your acquaintance Mattie. It was a touching service and I wish you the very best for the future.'

'Thank you Bob. We're pleased you were able to join us today. Doesn't Adam look handsome in his morning suit?'

Affectionately he ruffled his grandson's hair. 'He does indeed. He's a very smart young man today.'

Addressing Adam Mattie said, 'Darling, will you find Akina please? The photographer's waiting for us and he's becoming rather impatient. You'll both join us for the photographs won't you Rachel?'

Hastily she said, 'We wouldn't want to intrude.'

'Nonsense! You have to be on the photographs.'

As Bob strolled off ahead with Mark, Mattie remarked sensitively, 'I know how difficult this must be for you today Rachel. Perhaps we ought to have met sooner. I'd never take your daughter's place in Mark's heart, nor would I try and it's the same with Akina; I'd never try to take her mother's place but I'll do everything I can for Mark, Akina and Adam to ensure their future happiness. Life must go on for those left behind so it's important we remain strong as a united family.'

Mattie understood her anguish, knowing only too well how she had felt to lose her mother but to lose a daughter had to be so much more painful. She had seen how deeply it had affected Emily to lose Sam, but at least they had been given time to prepare and say goodbye whereas for Rachel and Bob, there had been no opportunity to say goodbye. She had been an only child; her tragic death had been sudden and unexpected. The expression in Rachel's eyes made it abundantly clear they didn't wish to lose Adam as well, and having witnessed Rachel's unspoken plea, Mattie was determined that would never happen.

The venue chosen for their reception was known to most of Mark's colleagues at the hospital. Without being overly ostentatious, it was perfect for such an occasion and Mattie was soon to learn that information conveyed about the staff's professionalism and the outstanding culinary abilities of the chef had not been exaggerated.

Mattie had earlier expressed some concerns about the cost but Mark, shrugging his shoulders quipped, 'So? You only get married once!' and a silent few moments of thought followed as he regretted uttering those words. No doubt in the future, many such harboured memories would be evoked Mattie imagined but it was only to be expected. She knew better than anybody that certain memories could never be totally obliterated.

The guests wandered to their places at the beautifully adorned tables, patiently waiting behind their chairs for Mr. and Mrs. Wyndham to be introduced by the Master of Ceremonies. When they appeared in view, they were acknowledged by an unexpected cacophony of hand-clapping, whistles and cheers.

Following the enjoyable meal, it was time for the speeches. 'Remember what I told you Jack,' Mattie warned him.

Winking wickedly at his sister he smiled. 'You've already had *your* hour of glory. Now it's my turn.'

It was quite amazing she thought, how Jack, now aged twenty-one, had grown up over the past year. During the delivery of his speech, he was confident and witty and had done his research well, revealing more than a few embarrassing anecdotes from the past that Mark would have preferred to forget. No doubt his colleagues had been willing contributors, Mattie concluded.

Seth also said a few words but kept his comments brief and without the humour Jack had introduced into his speech but then Seth had always been more of a thinker than a raconteur.

Mark's response included a comment that he was the luckiest guy alive to have found such a wonderful wife and for a brief moment, Mattie's eyes met Rachel's but her countenance gave nothing away.

When the speeches were drawing to a close, there was an unexpected interruption by Akina who stood up and cleared her throat. 'I'd like to say something please,' she announced and the room became silent.

Mattie held her breath. Was there no limit to this child's confidence she wondered.

'My name's Akina and I'm the chief bridesmaid.' She giggled. 'I'm the *only* bridesmaid, actually.'

A shrill titter ran round the room.

'When I was at Aunt Meredith's earlier, she told me it was alright for *anybody* to make a speech at a wedding if they had something nice to say.'

When Mattie glanced quizzically at Meredith, she shook her head in astonishment and disbelief.

She continued, 'Well, I have lots of nice things to say. I don't know a lot about weddings because I've only been to one before. That was Uncle Seth's and Aunt Steph's last year and that was lovely as well. I didn't think I'd *ever* be coming to this one though. We learned at school that God created the world in six days - *the whole world* - but it took *much* longer than that for Mark to ask Mattie to marry him. I'm *amazed* at how silly grown-ups can be at times.'

Mark threw back his head, howling with laughter and Mattie joined in to conceal her embarrassment. All the guests were amused too but within moments there was silence once more with all eyes fixed on the intelligent young child who spoke with perfect clarity and self-confidence, breaking at appropriate places throughout her delivery to capture her audience's attention with the skill of a true professional.

'I'd like you to know why I'm very happy today. Mattie has been my guardian since September when my mummy died. Apart from Mattie, and Nana and Granddad Peters, I had nobody else but now Mattie and Mark are married, I've got a whole new family. I have my Uncle Seth and Aunt Steph, Uncle Jack, Grandma and Granddad Wyndham and today I met my new grandparents for the first time…Grandma and Granddad Foster and they're really nice. They were just Adam's grandparents before today but as Adam's my brother now, that makes them *mine* too. Adam's also my best friend. He's a year older than me. He takes care of me and we're looking forward to our honeymoon with Mattie and Mark. We're all going to Disney World. She glanced momentarily in Adam's direction and grinned before turning her attention to Seth. 'I'm happy for you as well Uncle Seth because you don't need to be cross with Mattie anymore now she's married.'

Seth felt some denial was warranted and looking confused stated, 'I've never been cross with Mattie. I don't know what you mean.'

He was soon to regret his contradictory response when Akina audibly argued, 'Oh yes, Uncle Seth. I didn't understand what you meant but I remember the words you said. You told Aunt Steph that you'd be thankful when they were married because Mattie shouldn't be living with Mark out of wedlock.'

For a split second there was absolute silence and then the room erupted with vociferous laughter.

Seth was horrified and stared remorsefully at his sister, while the guests, still howling with laughter, leapt to their feet to applaud the young speaker.

Through clenched teeth Mattie snarled angrily at Meredith, 'I'll talk to you later.'

Mark rose to his feet once more, drying the laughter tears from his eyes. 'Er...thank you Akina. That was...enlightening. I just wanted to add that I'll be taking bookings for Akina's services should anyone require a wedding speaker. I hope you all enjoyed your meal and the...er...what shall I call it, ensuing

23

entertainment. I certainly did. It just remains for me to say there's a free bar until eight if you'd like to vacate the tables so the staff may clear away.'

At the mention of a free bar, the guests dispersed within moments.

'I am *so* sorry Mattie,' Seth murmured contritely. 'I only meant…'

'Don't worry Seth. Truly, it's of no consequence,' Mark said. 'I actually found it quite amusing.'

'Well I didn't,' Mattie argued. 'I could have died. Why not go out and broadcast it from the rooftops? You should know Akina never misses a trick.'

'I've a great deal to learn about kids. It were just mentioned in passing and I didn't know Akina were listening. Besides, she's only six.'

'Six, going on sixty! I'm her guardian Seth so it's only natural she'd try to protect me. She obviously believed we were at loggerheads about something. I was at Mark's for less than three weeks. What did you expect me to do when I came from Devon with Akina? Move into a hotel? I was returning to work with Meredith; I had to finalise the wedding details; I needed a phone and people had to be able to contact me. You're so old-fashioned Seth. This is nineteen-seventy-seven.'

Punctuating his speech with sporadic sighs Seth pleaded, 'Don't let's argue Mattie, please. I've said I'm sorry. Besides, I'm the one who looked stupid.'

'I agree with Seth. I vote we forget it now,' Mark said firmly, shaking Seth's hand. 'No hard feelings mate. Go and get yourself a drink.'

As Seth hurried away, Meredith approached. 'Can

I just say I was as shocked as you were when Akina stood up to speak. We'd been discussing weddings in general and when the speeches were mentioned, she asked if the Bride made one too. I told her that sometimes the Bride wanted to say a few words but that it wasn't obligatory. She didn't understand that word *obligatory* so I explained what that meant and added there weren't any hard and fast rules and that any guest was allowed to make a speech if they had something to say. Never for a moment did I believe she'd give my words serious thought and make one herself. You have to admit it was hilarious and she definitely entertained everybody. Besides, there are always smutty innuendoes at weddings.'

'Yes, so you can expect plenty at yours Meredith. I'm working on it right now!'

Meredith grinned. 'So, do your worst. What could you possibly say that would rattle my cage?'

'That's for me to know and you to find out. Don't forget I spent six months with Sam and we did a lot of talking. You wouldn't believe the things she told me about your University days so you'd better learn to be exceptionally nice to me in the run up to your wedding or you'll be very sorry.'

Meredith recognised the glint of merriment in her eye. 'You weren't *really* upset were you?'

'Of course not. It served Seth right for being such an old fuddy-duddy. Besides, I already knew what he'd said. Steph told me earlier.'

'Let's get a drink girls,' Mark interposed. 'Where are the children?'

'They're outside with Andrew,' Meredith said.

'Mmm! Sounds like a good idea. I think I'll join them when we've circulated for a few minutes.'

'I want to speak to your mum and dad first Mark. I've not had chance to welcome them yet.'

Mattie had met them on two previous occasions. On their first visit they announced they were to be married when Mark, omitting to choose his words carefully, advised they'd be having another grand-child. Mark's mother immediately assumed Mattie was pregnant and although voicing no disparaging response, Mattie was quick to spot a critical glance. In a bungled endeavour to clarify the matter, Mattie inadvertently compounded Mark's shock revelation when advising Akina was six years old.

Suddenly aware of her error of judgment, Mark's mother stuttered apologetically, 'Oh...I didn't know you'd been married before. Mark failed to mention you already had a child when he said he was seeing someone. Are you divorced dear?'

'I'm single. I've never been married,' she replied mischievously, nudging Mark.

Judgementally, Mark's father peered over the top of his spectacles whilst Mark was left fumbling for words as he went on to explain about Akina and her mother's death, but they had laughed about it later.

Their second visit to his parents' house had been in October when Mark had brought Mattie up from Devon to celebrate her twenty-fifth birthday. They had taken the children to stay over with his parents and when they collected them the next day, Mark's parents eagerly reported that Akina was a polite and enchanting child. Akina had been equally delighted with her new grandparents and particularly thrilled with the ducks in their landscaped garden pond that she had been reluctant to leave behind.

Mark found his parents scrutinising the paintings that were hanging in the reception hall. His mother hugged Mattie fondly. 'You look exquisite my dear. That's the most beautiful wedding gown I've ever seen and doesn't Akina look enchanting? That was such a lovely service too. This is a perfect venue for a wedding and hasn't the weather been kind?'

Mattie nodded in agreement. 'I think we've been very lucky. It was miserable yesterday.'

'You know what they say...*the sun shines on the righteous.*'

'I know but I can't say I felt particularly righteous when Akina stood up to speak, Celia.'

'*The truth will out,* as Launcelot says in *The Merchant of Venice* and particularly so where children are concerned. I thought she spoke eloquently and she was very entertaining. Remember, times have changed and people aren't as judgmental nowadays. George and I already knew you were at Mark's as Adam had mentioned it. You're going to have your hands full now with two children you know. I know what it was like with one. Mark wasn't fit to know anything. I recall one occasion when he nearly cost George his promotion to Senior Orthopaedic Consultant when he related an amusing anecdote to one of his classmates, not knowing the person to whom he referred was the boy's uncle, a senior colleague and also Chairman of the Selection Board. Prior to George's interview he never said a word, biding his time until he sat down before them and then blasted him with both barrels about the need for diplomacy and respect,' she laughed.

'And despite that he got the job?'

'Yes he did, surprisingly, and Mark got an earful from his father but it wasn't really Mark's fault. He didn't realise he'd said anything wrong. That's why you have to be very careful about what you say and do in front of children if you don't want other folk to know. It's not enough to tell them to keep quiet. As I'm sure you'll recall from your own childhood, a secret is very hard to keep.'

Celia's remark had been made innocently but as Mattie digested those words, she felt a sudden rush of adrenaline as a terrifying vision of Albert Parkes appeared as a flashback. She staggered briefly and Mark grabbed her arm. 'What's wrong darling?'

She had to think quickly. 'It's these stupid heels! They're higher than I generally wear so I wobbled.'

Celia accepted her explanation but Mark wasn't at all convinced. He'd recognised that anxious look in her eyes he'd seen many times before, but now was neither the time nor place to question her.'

'Let's go outside,' he suggested. 'It's rather warm in here and it's been an eventful day. A breath of air would be nice. We'll catch up with you later Mum.'

As Mark led her away she sighed. 'I thought that was all behind me. I was talking to your mother and something she said triggered a flash-back of Albert Parkes. I wasn't expecting that today of all days.'

He held her in his arms. 'It'll get better. Time is a great healer. You're safe with me darling.'

The evening guests were beginning to arrive, each one bearing a gift that Mark and Mattie graciously received. The resident quartet was playing pleasant background music and a few guests were dancing.

Mark looked round the room as the line of guests came to an end. 'I think everyone's arrived now so would you like to dance with me Mrs. Wyndham?'

She laughed. 'I thought you were talking to your mother then. Of course I'll dance with you but only if you promise not to tread on my feet.'

The second they stepped onto the dance floor, the musicians stopped playing and changed their music sheets. Everyone sat down, watching attentively.

A colleague of Mark's approached and shook his hand, at the same time wishing them a prosperous, long and happy future. He then made his way to the podium where the musicians awaited his presence.

Mark explained. 'Chris is a fellow Consultant and under duress has agreed to sing for us. He's exceptionally good. He's a member of an all-male choir but till now has kept it under wraps at the hospital. I found out in theatre when he burst into song during surgery one day. Our marriage might be short-lived if he gets a ribbing from the others afterwards,' he laughed. 'He's threatened to kill me if he does.'

'It was kind of him to agree. What's he singing?'

'It's a special request from me to you, everything I've always felt but could never put into words.'

Mattie took a quick look around the room at the stunned faces of Chris's colleagues as the introduction was played and Chris lifted the microphone to his lips. In a voice as smooth as velvet, he began to sing the moving lyrics of Ewan MacColl; '*The first time ever I saw your face, I thought the sun rose in your eyes…*'

Blinking the tears from her eyes Mattie held Mark close as they shuffled slowly around the dance floor until the song came to an end, at which point there were cheers and a standing ovation for Chris. 'That was lovely Mark and so thoughtful. Let's go over. I want to thank him.'

'I think we'll allow his newly acquired fan-club to disperse first; he's surrounded. Meanwhile, we'll have a word with Meredith and Andrew.'

'*He* was fabulous,' Meredith told her as they sat down. 'Where did you find him?'

'He's a work colleague,' Mark said. 'He needed a lot of persuasion to sing, I can tell you. Although he sings in a choir, Chris *never* performs at functions.'

'I take it you chose the song Mark?' Andrew said and when he nodded Meredith added, 'That was an excellent choice…very appropriate. I've been making some notes today. I hope our wedding day turns out as well as yours.'

Mattie smiled. 'I know it will. Right, we're off on our rounds now. I've just spotted Olive and Richard and Sadie and Keith.'

Sadie hugged her affectionately. 'I was just saying to Mum I'd like this place for our wedding next year. It's fantastic and the meal was superb.'

'I have to agree,' Sally said. 'It's a splendid room and I love that quartet. This is such a happy day for us too Mattie. You'll always feel like a daughter to us, isn't that right Charles?'

He nodded. 'Always. May I give you a hug?'

'Of course Charles. Finally, I've been able to lay my past to rest. How's business?'

'Profitable, but not a word to Sally and Sadie,' he whispered, 'especially now I've a flaming wedding to pay for next year. I must talk to Mark about how to cut corners the way those two spend my money.'

Mark took her hand. 'Right, Chris is free and then we'd best continue making the rounds. There's still a few from the hospital you haven't met.'

After offering Chris their thanks, they meandered around the room, pausing to have a few words with each of the guests until suddenly Mattie was taken aback by the sight of a familiar face from the past.

'Well…hello! It's…er…a pleasant surprise to see you again Tom,' she stuttered. 'How are you?'

'Very well and may I say you look radiant.'

She couldn't resist but say, 'Like an Ice Queen?'

His cheeks turned scarlet and a forced laugh burst from his lips. 'Sorry! I can attribute *that* revelation to Lucille, no doubt.'

'Mark actually…but it was Lucille who told Mark what you'd said, so I guess you're right. It's alright Tom; your comment was justified and I'm pleased you're here. Did your shirt dry out alright?'

'Perfectly fine. I'm happy for you Mattie…really happy for both of you in fact.'

'Private joke?' Mark questioned touchily as they moved on.

'*No!*' she said defensively. 'It's another unwanted reminder of the past and if you'd think back to the hospital's London weekend, you'd recall you were

31

there when I accidentally knocked Tom's pint down the front of his shirt when he took hold of my hand. You offered to take me aside to talk to me because you knew something was troubling me.' She shook her head in disbelief. 'Really Mark, I can't believe you're jealous!'

'*Protective* is the word Mattie and I apologise for my insensitive remark. I do recall the incident now. That was the weekend I pined for you. I wanted you so much. I did everything in my power to win you over but still you rejected my every move.'

'Well, I'm here now,' she quipped.

He smiled fondly. 'Yes and I'm the happiest guy alive. I'm so glad we overcame all our difficulties.'

Gazing deeply into his brown expressive eyes she murmured, 'Hasn't it been a wonderful day Mark?'

'Yes and the best part's still to come.'

Mattie didn't fail to notice the twinkle in his eye. 'Before you get *too* excited, let me remind you the children will be there.'

'Wrong! I had a quiet word with Emily this morning and they're staying at their house tonight *and* I remembered to take their day-clothes for tomorrow so we won't be disturbed in the morning.'

'That's nice,' she sighed.

There was a vacant chair next to Dr. McAndrew and Mattie sat down beside her. 'Sorry it's taken so long to get to you but there are such a lot of guests and they all want to chat to us. Would you get Dr. McAndrew a drink please Mark and I'd like a white wine.'

'Certainly. What's it to be Helen?'

'I'll have the same as Mattie please.' Once Mark was out of audible range she said, 'I couldn't have been happier to hear you were to marry Mark when he gave me the news. You've obviously moved on.'

'With Mark's help and patience, yes I have. He's sensitive, caring and makes me feel safe. I love him so much. Meeting Mark is the best thing that's ever happened to me.'

'I was chatting to Meredith earlier. She's happy at the way things have turned out. She's next I hear.'

'Yes, in July. I've warned her that Akina will be making a speech at *her* wedding! Tit for tat!'

'Oh, what a wee canny lassie!' she screeched with mirth. 'To coin a familiar phrase, there are no flies on her. She's utterly delightful and she'll bring you so much joy. I gather from what she gave away and professionally speaking of course, that there are no problems in the bedroom department?'

'No, there aren't, I'm happy to say.' She giggled before disclosing, 'Between you and me, *I* was the one coming on to Mark when that time came.'

Again she burst into laughter. 'It doesn't surprise me and your secret's safe with me. Mark might be a little conservative but he's a jolly fine man.'

'He's the best! Right, he's on his way back so I'll say goodnight. Thanks for coming Dr. McAndrew.'

'I wouldn't have missed this day for anything and the name's Helen. Have a wonderful life Mattie.'

They wandered off together hand in hand. 'Let's find your parents Mark. I've hardly seen them and we only spoke briefly at the church. I'd hate them to feel neglected. They don't really know anyone.'

'Trust me; they're fine.' Earlier, he had arranged for the grandparents to sit together and as Mark and Mattie approached their table, they were engrossed in deep conversation.

'Are you all enjoying yourselves?' Mattie asked. 'I haven't seen you dancing yet.'

'There's plenty of time,' Celia replied. 'It's rather crowded on the dance floor but I imagine a few of your guests will be leaving soon.'

'We're making tracks shortly. I've phoned for our taxi,' Emily remarked. 'It's way past the children's bedtime and Norman keeps dozing off so if I don't get him home he'll be falling off his chair.'

During the following laughter, Mark's father rose and mumbled to his son, 'Did you remember to tell the staff that the free bar ended at eight o'clock?'

'Dammit! I forgot! I'll tell them now,' he snorted, looking at his watch. It was almost ten o'clock.

'Don't bother, I've seen to it. I nipped over a few minutes ago to pick up the tab. We couldn't decide what to get for a wedding present, so buy yourself a Daimler with what you've saved,' he stated dryly.

Mark was embarrassed. 'No Dad, I insist on paying. Please, tell me what I owe you.'

'It's sorted I tell you. I wouldn't have paid it had I not wanted to.'

'Thank you for that. Mattie and I appreciate your generosity.'

Emily stood up. 'I'd better find the children. The taxi will be here soon.'

'I'll find them,' Mattie insisted. She hurried away and returned with them a few minutes later.

34

'It's not fair. Why do we have to go? Why can't we stay till it's over?' Akina complained bitterly.

'Granddad's very tired now. He's a lot older than you,' Emily told her.

'So are you but *you're* not tired. I'll tell you what; we'll go home with Mattie and Mark and then you can go straight to bed.'

'I'll tell *you* what. We're going with Nana now,' Adam told her firmly. 'Just stop arguing and get all your things. You always have to argue!'

'Yes, come along darling,' Mattie said. 'It's way past your bedtime now. Mark will collect you both tomorrow. Besides, you can play with Poppy in the morning. Don't forget the little dog's been alone all day and she'll be missing everyone.'

'Alright, I'll make a deal with you Mattie. If we leave now with Nana, can we have a big duck pond like Grandma's?'

Celia hooted with laughter at her persistence.

'No Akina, you can't. Poppy would chase all the ducks and eat them and don't think of anything else as there are no deals to be made.'

It wasn't the answer she wanted to hear and intent on delaying their departure she gabbled, 'Then I'll just run round and say goodnight to everyone first.'

'*No Akina!* Have you been listening? Granddad's tired. Be a good girl now and kiss me goodnight.'

She threw her arms around Mattie's neck. 'It was terrific today.' She hugged Mark too before waving goodbye to her grandparents. Taking Adam's hand in hers she grumbled, 'Right, let's go Adam. I can't wait to be a grown-up. Have you noticed how they always send us to bed when they don't want us to know what's going on?'

Mark stifled a laugh as Mattie glared at him.

'Heavens above, you've certainly got your hands full there!' Rachel tittered. 'That child's a bundle of dynamite and absolutely adorable. I'm so happy we came today Mattie. We wouldn't have missed it for the world. We've really enjoyed ourselves.'

'We're delighted you came too,' and deliberately avoiding the word *honeymoon* added, 'You'll have to come round when we're back from holiday and see the photos of the children at Disney World.'

'We'd like that,' she said with a genuine smile.

Mattie was relieved that the ice had finally been broken and knew beyond doubt that the new-found friendship with Rachel and Bob would flourish.

Mark took hold of Mattie's hand. 'I think we can slip away now. I'll call a taxi and then make a short announcement to the guests.'

'Sounds good to me,' she said lovingly.

2

'Are you sure we've got everything Mark? Check again that you've got all the tickets and passports. I can't help but feel we've forgotten something.'

'Well if we have, we'll have to manage without it because there's sure as hell nothing else going to fit in our car. You didn't have that much paraphernalia when you moved from Devon. I manage with just a carry-on when I go abroad to conventions.'

'That doesn't surprise me. You probably wear the same underwear and socks for days like most men.'

'I'm shocked Mattie! I didn't realise you were so knowledgeable about men's dirty habits.'

'I raised two brothers Mark and had to check their underwear every day to make sure they'd changed.'

'In that case maybe you'd like to check mine,' he suggested with a mischievous grin. 'We've time.'

She chuckled. 'You never miss an opportunity do you? Behave yourself and ask the children to get in the car. Have they got their colouring books?'

'They've got everything they need and so have I,' he said holding her in his arms. 'You're amazing.'

'I know!' she quipped. 'Right, are we ready?'

'As ready as we'll ever be.' He went outside and called to the children, 'You two! In the car please. We're setting off shortly.'

Akina and Adam dashed to the car and scrambled in excitedly. 'Do you think it'll be a great big plane Dad?' Adam questioned optimistically.

'I expect so, Son.'

Quietly Akina muttered, 'I'm a bit scared.'

'It'll be fine,' Adam said reassuringly. 'Dad says it's like being on a bus. You don't feel anything.'

When Akina turned to Mark for confirmation, he nodded. 'Adam's right. You'll enjoy it Akina. You can walk about once you're above the clouds.'

'Really? Up there above the clouds you can walk about? Aren't you afraid of falling through them?'

'Not outside, dummy!' Adam scoffed. 'Inside the plane. Haven't you seen any pictures of planes?'

'I've seen *real* planes, in the sky, but I can't see the people so you can stop laughing or I'll nip you.'

Mark smiled. 'As soon as we've handed our bags in, we'll watch a few planes take off and land. I'm sure that'll make you feel a lot better.'

Akina felt more at ease for if Mark said they'd be safe, she believed that. *He* could make people better when they were very ill; *he* was really clever and *he* had been on lots of planes.

Mattie stepped in the car, a smile illuminating her face. 'Disney World here we come!' She turned to the children. 'Are you excited?'

'Not half,' Akina answered. 'I've never been on a honeymoon before. What does that mean Mattie?'

'Honeymoon? It's a special holiday so that newly married couples can get to know each other.'

'But you already know Mark. You've known him for *ages*. It sounds a silly idea to me.'

38

'Shall we turn back and stay at home then?' Mark intervened with a serious expression.

'*No* Dad,' Adam was quick to answer, elbowing Akina to keep quiet but her silence was short-lived.

'I'm buying a big Mickey Mouse with my pocket money,' she whispered. 'What will you get Adam?'

'I don't know yet. I'll see when I get there.'

Mattie overheard their loud whispers. 'Who gave you your spending money?'

'Our grandparents,' Adam told her. 'They gave it us at the wedding.'

'I think I'd better look after it. Will you pass it to me please and I'll keep it in my wallet.'

Akina was unhappy. 'But it's *ours*,' she protested.

'Just hand it to me. I'm well aware it's yours and you're becoming far too argumentative of late.'

'Yes, button it!' Adam said sharply.

'They're excited,' Mark commented in an attempt to end the dispute but Mattie wouldn't be silenced. 'I think some support from you would be preferable to the criticism obviously levelled *at* me.'

Giving her words some thought he was forced to agree. 'Hand it all to Mattie for safe keeping please. How much do you have?'

'We don't know; a lot I think,' Adam answered.

'Then Mattie can count it and you'll know.'

She counted Adam's first and there was forty-five pounds. 'You obviously have to share this.'

'No, we both got the same. They told us we could buy something nice with it.'

Mark was astounded. 'I take it you thanked them politely. That was very generous of them.'

'Is that a heck of a lot Mattie?' Akina asked.

Nodding, she reflected on her own childhood and brought to mind how her widowed mother, a seamstress, had been obliged to make clothes, do alterations and make soft furnishings for neighbours well into the early hours, merely to put food on the table for three hungry children while she had to make do with the leftovers. If only her mother could see her now, she sighed silently, happily married with two young children and making their way to the airport for the holiday of a lifetime in Florida. 'Yes, it *is* a lot of money Akina so please don't waste it.'

She felt a hot wet trickle on her cheek and wiped it away before anyone noticed.

Florida was baking hot but once Mark had figured out how to adjust the air-conditioning in their hire-car, the journey to their hotel was most enjoyable.

The children, who were tired, sat quietly in reception as Mark dealt with their registration. Unknown to Mattie, he was arranging an upgrade after giving much thought to the undesirable sleeping arrangements. The room allocated had two king-size beds that the four of them had to share but after advising the receptionist they were on honeymoon, for payment of a negligible supplement, she was happy to change that to a king-size room and adjoining self-contained annexe with two queen-size beds.

'Is this your first trip to Florida Sir?' she enquired with a pleasant smile as she handed him the keys.

He nodded. 'We're here to visit the theme parks.'

'You've come to the right place. You'll love Walt

40

Disney World, a wonderful experience the children will never forget. Enjoy the rest of your day Sir.'

It was one of those rare occasions when they entered their room that Akina was lost for words. She stared at the huge bed unable to believe her eyes.

Mattie too was astonished and more so disturbed by her mistaken belief they were all to share it.

Instantly reading her thoughts, Mark grinned and led her through the interconnecting door.

'Wow! This is terrific but I'm sure we were only supposed to have one room with two beds. Do you think it's a mistake? This looks *very* expensive.'

'Happy honeymoon darling. I got us an upgrade. I wasn't overly enthralled with the previous sleeping arrangements. I wanted time alone with my lovely wife. Do I assume it's to your liking?'

'That's an understatement if ever I heard one. I've never seen anything like this before.' Excitedly she summoned the children. 'Come and see your room. It's lovely *and* you have your own bathroom too.'

Akina's loquacity quickly resumed to be matched by Adam's avid enthusiasm as they squabbled over which bed each would have.

For once, Mark intervened without any prompting from Mattie and throwing Adam's rucksack on one of the beds stated irritably, 'That's yours, Son!'

Quick to spot an element of annoyance in Mark's voice, Akina sat down quietly on her bed.

'I'll start the unpacking,' Mattie said. 'Why don't you two get washed and when I find your clothes, you can change and then we'll go out for something to eat. You'll find what you need in the bathroom.'

'Me first!' Akina cried, jumping up.

'No, me!' Adam argued, elbowing his way past.

'*Quiet!*' Mark yelled crossly. 'I'm not putting up with your constant bickering for two weeks. Understood? If you can't behave properly you'll be going nowhere and that applies to both of you.'

Previously unaccustomed to Mark's intervention, they were as good as gold for the rest of the day.

Walt Disney World was a thirty-minute drive from their hotel and they made an early start the next day to avoid the long queues for the popular attractions. Although the children found it hard to control their excitement, they knew they had to avoid any repetition of the stern ticking off they'd had the previous day and sat quietly in the back of the car.

As they proceeded through the turnstile and made their way forward with the swarm of visitors, it was a truly wonderful vision along Main Street. Disney characters intermingled with everybody, posing for photographs with scores of mystified, overwhelmed children whilst Mark lost no time in capturing the vibrant mood with his newly acquired camera.

Akina and Adam barely slept a wink that night as they chattered and recalled many of the memorable aspects of their fun-packed day, the best part being that they had seen but a mere fraction of the theme park and the rest was yet to come.

They spent a few days luxuriating in their hotel's pool complex where Mark taught Akina to swim. It was the perfect setting in lush tropical gardens and whilst the children amused themselves in the water,

Mattie and Mark enjoyed a selection of cocktails.

There was much sadness as their memorable holiday drew to a close and with only two more days to go, they were determined to make the most of their remaining time by repeating the most thrilling rides and revisiting their favourite attractions. The children's first foreign holiday would not be forgotten and Mark and Mattie would take away memories of a honeymoon that had been perfect in every way.

'These have been the best two weeks of my life,' Mattie sighed as she climbed into bed on their final night.

'Mine too,' he said. 'I didn't intend to be hard on the kids earlier. I see the results of foolish accidents daily at work and often with irreparable injuries.'

'It was needed and they took note. Akina's been an absolute angel since you told them off.'

'Hasn't Adam too?'

'Yes but Adam's always well-behaved. He's very quiet and thoughtful like you.'

He wrapped his arms around her and held her to his warm body. 'I'm glad I upgraded the room. It's been great having you all to myself.'

She sighed with utter contentment and snuggled his neck. 'What did I do to deserve you Mark?'

'I could ask you the same question Mattie. I must have asked myself that a hundred times. Answer me this; do you believe in fate?'

She pondered for a moment. 'I don't know what I believe anymore. I used to go to church when I was little but when Dad died, I was needed at home and then when Mum was killed and the three of us were separated and taken into care, I lost whatever faith I had. I couldn't believe in a God who would permit such abominable things to happen to a decent God-fearing family. It felt like we were being punished for some terrible deed. Does that make any sense?'

He wrapped both arms tightly around her. 'I felt exactly the same when I lost my first wife and I was even angrier for Adam's loss, just an innocent baby who'd lost his mother. Every day I do my utmost to preserve life but I'm not a miracle worker and I lose a patient from time to time. Since *my* ordeal however, I often find myself thinking more about grieving relatives than the deceased, about the impact the sad loss of a loved one must have on *their* lives.'

'I know. I was told by Dr. McAndrew when I was a child to move on and leave the past behind but her shallow words meant little at the time. It's impossible to move forward because someone tells you to, but as time went by, I learned to channel my deep-rooted anger into other things, education primarily and although I eventually shrugged off all the anger I remained powerless to conquer my fear of men...'

He finished her sentence. 'Until you met me!'

With a further deep sigh she nodded. 'Thank God you were so persistent because I have everything I want now and I believe I'm gradually regaining my abandoned faith. I love Akina and Adam and I love *you* more than you could ever know.'

Clutching her much-adored Mickey Mouse, Akina struggled to climb over the additional bags and gifts that Mark had carefully piled on the back seat of his car. 'Move up and make room for Adam please,' he told her.

'But I'm *squashed*. There *is* no room for Adam. Look at all these bags,' she griped.

'Well, for a start you can take that Mickey Mouse off the seat and hold it on your lap. I told you it was too big to fit in our car when you were buying it.'

She grunted and heaved it onto her knee. 'I can't see a *thing* now.'

'I would see that as a problem if you were driving but as you're not, it isn't!' he informed her irritably. 'Squeeze in Adam and then we can be on our way.'

'We'll be home in forty minutes Mark and we can go straight to bed. I'll leave all the unpacking until tomorrow,' Mattie said softly.

By the time they arrived home, the children were fast asleep and Mattie had to wake them. 'You can go straight up and jump into bed,' she told them.

They carried the bags in and put them in the hall. 'Would you like a hot drink?' Mattie asked.

'No thanks darling. I'm going up. I'm shattered.' He kissed her goodnight and walked slowly upstairs and when Mattie joined him after checking on the children, he was dead to the world.

By the time Akina surfaced the following morning, Mark had already eaten a hearty breakfast and was reading the Sunday newspaper.

She kissed the top of his head. 'Do you feel better now? You were really grumpy last night.'

'Sorry darling. I couldn't sleep during the flight. I had cramp in both legs as there was little room for me to move about. I'm fine now. Is Adam awake?'

'I don't think so. His door was still closed when I passed. Where's Mattie?'

'She went up for a shower. Are you hungry?'

'Starving. Is that bacon I can smell?'

'It is. Mattie's cooked plenty so there's some left for you and Adam. Do you want anything with it?'

'No thanks. I'll just make a sandwich.'

He stood up. 'You go and wake Adam and I'll see to it. Tell him to hurry up please.'

She skipped away full of the joys of spring. Today was her seventh birthday, though it seemed no one had remembered. Mark hadn't mentioned it and there were no cards or presents to be seen. She was the same age as Adam now and felt very grown-up.

To her surprise, Adam was up and dressed. 'Your breakfast's ready. Are you coming down?'

'In a minute. You don't need to wait for me.'

Akina attacked her bacon sandwich eagerly, licking her fingers repeatedly to collect all the crumbs.

Mark smiled. 'You're enjoying that aren't you?'

'It's yummy and I was really hungry.'

'Hello darling,' Mattie said as she walked downstairs. 'I imagined you and Adam would still be fast asleep after all the travelling yesterday.'

'Adam got up before I did. He's already washed and dressed but hasn't had his breakfast yet. By the way, do you know what day it is today Mattie?'

She glanced over Akina's shoulder at Mark who winked. 'Er…let me think. You get mixed up when you've been on holiday. Today is er…Sunday. Yes that's right. It *is* Sunday isn't it Mark?'

Just then Adam arrived and sat down at the table and having caught the tail-end of the conversation, confirmed it was indeed Sunday.

'Is that all?' Akina asked sulkily.

'Well you know it isn't Monday,' Adam told her. 'If it was Monday you'd be at school wouldn't you? Don't worry. You'll be there tomorrow.'

Unable to contain her laughter any longer, Mattie hugged her. 'Happy Birthday darling. We hope you have a lovely day.'

'You're such a nit-wit,' Adam said, kissing her on the cheek, his hand mysteriously curled around the back of her neck. 'Happy birthday Akina.'

Mark gathered her up in his arms and twirled her round until she was giddy. 'I expect you're wondering where your cards are?'

She giggled. 'I really did think you'd forgotten.'

Mark looked serious. 'The one thing we have forgotten is where we've hidden them. We each chose a different hiding place downstairs and we hid them under something blue. That's all we remember.'

Equally sombre Mattie remarked, 'You'll need to feel under something black to find your presents.'

47

She squealed with excitement. 'Can I go and find them?' Without waiting for an answer, she ran from the kitchen and returned with a heap of cards. 'Just look at all these Mattie. There's a load here.'

Mark took a photograph as she tore open an envelope. 'I don't know who's sent this. I can't read the name.' She showed it to Mattie. 'What does it say?'

'It's from Grandma and Granddad Wyndham and there's a cheque inside. You must call them later to thank them.'

Most of the envelopes contained a sum of money or a cheque and Akina was delighted to find a gift-token inside Grandma and Granddad Foster's card.

'Come and help me Adam,' Akina said. 'When I looked for my cards I couldn't see anything black.'

Adam scoffed, 'Don't be such a numbskull. Just try to act like you're seven.'

She scampered all over the house with Adam but still found nothing.

'Do you want a clue?'

'Yes please.'

He removed a crumpled note from his pocket and handed it to her. 'Read that.'

She unfolded it and started to read aloud;

'Look in a mirror and you will find
Something black – now feel behind.'

She looked puzzled. 'I think it's behind a mirror. There's a big one in the dining room.' She ran into the room and stopped abruptly. 'That's stuck on the wall so it can't be behind there.'

'Read it again. It says *look* in a mirror.'

'I'm *looking!*' she said with an exasperated grunt.

'Can you see anything black?'

'No, stupid! I can only see *me*.'

'And what colour's your hair?'

'Oh right; I see now.' She read the note again and feeling behind her hair she found a second note that Adam had stuck to the back of her neck earlier. She giggled. 'I like this game.' That one read;

'*You might need a pair of socks*
To wear with what's inside this box.
Perhaps you'll find it on the floor
Maybe beside an outside door.'

Adam darted after her as she ran to the front door. 'Wow! What a big box. Help me lift it Adam.'

They carried it into the kitchen where Mattie and Mark awaited their return. 'I see you worked it out eventually,' Mark laughed. 'I wonder what it is.'

'Shoes I think,' Akina said, tearing frantically at the wrapping paper. 'No, they're long black boots. They're nice. Are they for when it's cold Mattie?'

'Do you recall what you asked me at Uncle Seth's wedding Akina?'

'No, not really. I'm always asking questions and sometimes you get annoyed with me.'

'*No I don't,*' Mattie protested.

Mark could feel an argument brewing. 'Perhaps if you open your other present you might remember.'

'There's another?' she cried excitedly. 'Where?'

'Look inside the box, on the lid.'

Another note had been fixed to the lid with tape;

'*I am something that you need.*
That's a warning you must heed.
To shield your head, your neck, your face

I must always be in place.
Find the study, look in there
To see what's sitting on the chair.'

Once again she screeched with excitement before hurrying to the study. 'This is the best game ever,' they heard her cry.

Only when she opened the box did everything fall into place. 'It's a *riding* hat! Thank you,' she cried with joy. 'I'm going to have riding lessons with you Adam and those are riding boots aren't they?' She ran towards Mattie and kissed her. 'Thanks Mattie. Now I remember what I asked you at Uncle Seth's wedding. I asked if I could have riding lessons. She hugged Mark fondly and an austere deathly silence followed her next words, 'Thanks Dad!' when even Adam looked up in surprise.

Mattie was shocked and it was Akina who broke the silence. 'What? What's wrong?'

'There's nothing wrong,' Mark told her. 'I'm glad you want to call me *Dad*, especially as the adoption is almost complete. We're a family now.'

Never in a million years could he have envisaged the subsequent repercussions from his next remark, made after catching a glimpse of Mattie who stared ahead ashen-faced and close to tears. 'Maybe now might be a good time to start calling Mattie *Mum*. After all, Adam does.'

The earlier deathly silence was nothing compared to what followed. Akina froze on the spot, her eyes fixed as if mesmerised like a deer in the headlights. Suddenly she began to blink rapidly when floods of tears gushed from her eyes. '*Never!*' she screamed.

50

'She's *not* my mummy and I'll *never* call her that.' She picked up her riding hat and flung it across the room before rushing upstairs to her room.

Mattie jumped up to follow. 'Stay where you are Mattie. I caused this so I'll deal with it,' Mark told her demonstratively.

When Mark left the room, Adam threw his arms around Mattie's neck. 'I'm really sorry Mum. I'm sure Akina didn't mean to make you cry.'

'It's alright darling. I'm not crying…well, maybe just a little,' she confessed, smiling at him through her tears. 'I hoped today would be special for her.'

When Mark entered her room, she was face-down on her bed crying bitterly. 'What's this fuss about? Come on darling, sit up straight and talk to me.'

'Leave me alone. Everybody's always cross with me. *That's* my mummy over *there*.' She pointed to the casket on her dressing table, a casket containing Sam's ashes. 'I know what you want. You want me to forget her but I won't!'

He gathered the child in his arms. 'No one wants that Akina. I'll definitely not forget her. She was a very courageous woman who loved you very much just as Mattie loves you very much too. It was most insensitive of me to say what I did.'

'I don't know what that word means.'

'Insensitive? It means I should have given more thought to what I was saying before opening my big mouth. The only reason I said that was because you called me Dad. I didn't want Mattie to feel shut out. She wants you to feel as if you belong to us.'

'I do but she agreed to be my guardian, that's all.'

He sighed. 'No, that's not strictly correct Akina. Your mummy hoped she would adopt you. She told her so and when it happens, instead of being Akina Peters, you'll then be Akina Wyndham as that's our family name but if you feel happier calling Mattie by her name, she won't mind at all, so don't worry.'

'Is Mattie angry with me?'

'No, of course she isn't. Like I said, she loves you very much. Dry your eyes. It's your birthday today and you have another surprise yet.'

At that her ears pricked up. 'What is it?'

'Well now, it wouldn't be a surprise if I told you would it?'

He took her by the hand and led her downstairs.

'I'm sorry Mattie,' she said, running to throw her arms around her.

'It's fine. I know how you feel. Don't forget I lost *my* mummy too. Why not call everyone now to say thank you for your birthday presents?'

'Would you like to see your other surprise first?' Mark asked.

'Oh, yes please,' she gabbled excitedly.

'Wait here then.' Mark left the room momentarily and returned carrying a birthday cake in the shape of a horse's head with seven candles. 'How's that?'

'Wow! It's great! Can we light the candles?'

'We can later,' Mattie said. 'Nana and Granddad are coming to tea, so you can make your wish and blow out the candles then.'

'Does that mean we're having a proper birthday party?'

'Kind of. You can help in the kitchen if you like.'

'I will when I've called everybody. Thank you for all my nice presents. I'm really looking forward to my first riding lesson. I can't wait.'

Whilst Mattie was making lunch the telephone rang and Seth in a high-pitched voice panted, 'Who've you been gabbing to for the past hour? I've tried to get through over a dozen times but your phone were constantly engaged. Steph's in hospital. The baby's coming! She started in labour this morning.'

'That's fantastic news Seth. Are you there now?'

'No, I'm at home. I've had to nip back for Steph's bag. I rushed out in such a wuther I forgot to pick it up. I'm a nervous wreck.'

'Anyone would think it was *you* giving birth. Try to calm down for heaven's sake or you'll be having another asthma attack. Where's your inhaler?'

'It's in my pocket and I'm fine so stop worrying.'

'Have they said how long she'll be yet?'

'It'll be a while yet otherwise I wouldn't have left her. Are you coming to the hospital?'

'Of course but not until later. The last thing Steph needs is an audience. We'll be here all day so call with any updated news and tell Steph to get a move on and your baby's birthday will be the same day as Akina's.'

'I still can't believe we're having a baby.'

She chuckled. 'You will next week when they're home and your sleep's interrupted every few hours. Your lives are about to change forever. Don't forget to call as soon as you become a *daddy*. Give Steph our love. I hope she has an easy time.'

53

'As if I'd forget!' he said on a burst of laughter. 'By the way, did you have a good holiday?'

'I thought you'd never ask. It was incredible and I'll tell you all about it when I see you.'

Mattie could hardly wait to tell Mark the exciting news when he returned from the supermarket with Akina. 'We'll have to make time to nip out and see them if only for a few minutes. Isn't it wonderful? I feel so thrilled for them. I wonder if we'll be lucky too and have a baby soon.'

Mark was shocked and his facial expression did nothing to hide his feelings.

'Relax Mark. I'm winding you up. I think we've enough to contend with at the moment. It'd be nice to think about in a couple of years though. I'd like a baby of my own, I mean with you, and *you're* not getting any younger.'

Their brief discussion ended abruptly when Akina appeared. 'Are we starting the party food or having our lunch first Mattie?'

'We'll have our lunch, tidy up and then make the tea. Uncle Seth rang whilst you were shopping and they might be having their new baby today.'

'On my birthday? Brill! Can we visit them?'

'Hopefully. Call Adam down please for lunch.'

As Akina ran upstairs, Mark grabbed Mattie from behind playfully. 'For your information, I'm young enough and fit enough to keep *you* satisfied so less of the Methuselah cracks! Besides, there's many a good tune played on an old fiddle.'

She laughed. 'I'll have to take your word for that, *Old Fiddle*. Mmm…suits you that!'

'Hey! Less of the lip. I'm not off to the knacker's yard yet. There's only nine years between us.'

'Ten actually, give or take a couple of months.'

'Age is merely a number Mattie. It's what's in the mind that counts. When I wake up in a morning and see you I feel like a love sick teenager. Don't worry about Akina. She'll settle down soon. She's a very intelligent girl; it's only seven months since Sam's death and also she's been uprooted from everything familiar to her in Devon and brought here to a fresh school and a new life with us. She's bound to feel insecure and I certainly didn't help matters with my insensitive remark earlier. When we were upstairs, she accused me of trying to make her forget Sam. I felt so ashamed. It was an error of judgment on my part, asking her to call you Mum. I just didn't think it through properly but we talked and I gave her my assurance that none of us would ever forget Sam.'

'Did she say anything further when you were out shopping?'

'No, not a word but she called me Dad twice, so I think that's here to stay. Does it bother you?'

'Not in the least. She never knew her father so it's not like she's turning her back on him. I'll keep my eye on her. Right, where are they? There's a lot to do this afternoon and we might have to fit in a short trip to the hospital too if the baby comes.'

'I'll nip up and fetch them.'

It was almost three o'clock when Seth called. 'It's a boy Mattie!' he screeched down the telephone.

She shrieked with delight. 'I'm so happy for you Seth. Are they alright?'

Proudly he yelled, 'They're great; both of them. I think Paul looks like me.'

'Well never mind Seth. Hopefully he'll change as he gets older. They usually do,' she joked.

'Don't be so bloody cheeky,' he laughed. 'Do you want to know what he weighs?' Before she'd time to answer he yelled, 'Eight pounds eleven ounces!'

'Ouch! Rather Steph than me! Are you sure she's alright?'

'Brilliant I tell you. We both are.'

'Yes but you haven't just parted with the equivalent of three bags of flour in one hit.'

He laughed. 'I never thought of it like that. Trust you! So, are you coming to see us?'

'Definitely. I can't wait to see my baby nephew. Emily and Norman are coming for tea so we won't stay long. We'll be with you as soon as we can.'

'Aren't you absolutely gorgeous?' Mattie cooed as she leaned over the sleeping baby. 'He's absolutely adorable Steph. Well done! Was it very bad?'

'No, not really. It was just a little scary with him being my first. It'll be better next time.'

'*Next time?*' Seth shrieked. Other visitors looked round to seek the cause of the commotion. 'Listen, I couldn't go through that again.'

'Hark at him,' Steph laughed. 'All Seth had to do was hold my hand and he was sweating so much he couldn't keep hold of it.'

Winking at Steph, Mattie announced, 'I've a bone to pick with you Seth after the embarrassment you caused me at my wedding. I might have spent three weeks with Mark *out of wedlock* as you call it but at least *Mark* didn't get me pregnant before we were married and don't argue; I'm good at maths.'

'Listen here Mattie! That baby came early as well you know. He wasn't due for another fortnight and we were always careful, every single time without fail before we were married, isn't that right Steph?'

Steph laughed heartily as did Mark. I'd button it if I were you,' Mark advised. 'Mattie will make you dig an even deeper hole and bury you if you go on. She's winding you up mate!'

'Oh, right!' he spluttered, looking embarrassed as Mattie joined in the laughter. '*As you sow, so shall you reap*, Seth Henshaw,' she told him. 'You might be a Librarian but I read books too.'

'Yes, well, take note of this quotation; *Our greatest glory is not in never falling, but getting up every time we do;* Confucius.'

Quick as a flash she quipped, '*The greatest griefs are those we cause ourselves;* Sophocles I believe.'

'Alright! Don't look so smug. Point taken.'

Akina looked anxious. 'Uncle Seth, are you angry with Mattie again?'

'Of course not. We're just having fun,' he said.

'I've brought a small Teddy for Paul. We'll buy you something you need when you're back home,' Mattie told Steph. 'Has your mum been yet?'

'Yes and she's thrilled to bits isn't she Seth?'

'Aye she is, so now we know all we need to know about raising a child till he's eighteen.'

'I'm sure all mums are alike Seth and you'll find she's more of a help than a hindrance.'

'Is that another quote from your...?'

'Ignore him,' Steph butted in. 'He doesn't mean it do you Seth? They get along fine now.'

'Er...I think we ought to make tracks now,' Mark interposed. 'We're having visitors for tea.'

'I thought we were having little party sandwiches and birthday cake for tea,' Akina giggled.

Steph gasped. 'I'm so sorry love. Happy birthday. We were going to come round later with your card and presents. We won't forget your birthday again though will we, with yours and Paul's being on the same day? Did you get some nice presents?'

'Yes and lots of money too *and* I'm having riding lessons with Adam. He knows how to ride a horse.'

Steph was impressed. 'Do you? I'd be too scared to ride a horse in case I fell off.'

'No you wouldn't. It's easy.'

'Like riding a bike?' Seth queried.

'That's harder. A horse with four legs doesn't fall over like a bike that only has two wheels.'

'Fair point,' Mattie said. 'It's great to see you all. Bye-bye Paul. Be a good little boy.' She gave Steph a hug and when they reached the exit, Mattie turned to give a final wave to the happy family.

'Aw! Look at the three of them together. Doesn't that make you feel broody?' Mattie sighed.

'*No!*' Mark told her emphatically. 'I'd rather walk on burning coals with bare feet!'

Mattie smiled inwardly. Before long she'd change Mark's mind.

4

'Will I be in trouble for missing two days at school last week?' Akina asked anxiously.

'No, of course not. I sent a note didn't I?'

'I don't think my new form teacher likes me very much. Every time I look up she's glaring at me.'

'You were only there a few days before the Easter holiday. I'm sure she likes you as much as the other children. It feels strange at first at a new school but you'll soon settle in and make friends.'

'I've got a friend already, Rosie. Her proper name is Rosemary but she hates that. Our teacher always calls her Rosemary though and that makes everyone laugh, so Rosie gets really annoyed.'

History repeats itself, Mattie mused, recalling *her* early schooldays when one of her teachers persisted in calling her Mathilda, much to the amusement of her classmates.

'Why can't I go to the same school as Adam? He says he likes his school.'

'For a start, you have to pass an exam to go there and it's also a fee-paying school.'

'I don't understand what that means.'

'It costs money darling…lots of money.'

'Well if we don't have enough I can ask Nana for some. She won't mind. *She* has *lots* of money.'

'Can we drop it please? I had to organize a school at short notice when we moved from Devon so let's see how you get on there. We have to leave now or you *will* be in trouble for being late!'

'Nice to have you back,' Meredith said with a wide beaming smile. 'How was the honeymoon?'

She sighed. 'It was superb…truly wonderful. We enjoyed every moment and seeing this pile of work on my desk, I wish I'd stayed there.'

She laughed. 'Trust me; it's not as bad as it looks. The way you fire through stuff it'll soon be gone.'

'I wish the jet-lag had gone! It's horrible. I hardly slept a wink last night.'

'Ah yes, but was it jet-lag or Mark getting tangled up in your nightie?' she smirked.

'Rest assured the former! We had a few problems with Akina yesterday. I think Mark was glad to get to sleep to shut everything out.'

'It's early days. She'll settle. Just give her a little time. There's a birthday present here for her.'

Mattie relieved her of the parcel and thanked her. 'I'll see she calls you this evening. Children are so lucky nowadays,' she sighed reflectively.

Mattie kept her head down for the rest of the day. 'I won't need rocking tonight!' she told Meredith. 'I just want peace and quiet, an early night and then hopefully, I'll be back to normal tomorrow.'

Mattie had barely walked into the house when the telephone rang. 'Change out of your school clothes and hang them up please Akina. I'll get the phone.'

'Hi, Mattie Wyndham,' she informed the caller.

There was a few moments' pause. 'Oh, hello Mrs. Wyndham, my name's Angela Simpson. We've not met but your daughter Akina and mine, Rosemary, are school friends. You may know of her as Rosie.'

'Yes, indeed I do. Akina told me she had a friend called Rosie at her new school.'

There was a further lengthier pause.

'The reason I'm calling Mrs. Wyndham…Rosie came home last Thursday, the day the children went back to school, with some rather disturbing news. I thought you ought to know about it.'

Mattie was becoming concerned. 'Please…please go on Mrs. Simpson.'

'I don't quite know how to say this so perhaps it might be better were I to come straight to the point. Akina's form teacher referred to her as, "*that half-caste child,*" in front of the whole class.'

Mattie was horrified beyond belief. 'But she was on holiday last Thursday and Friday. She only went back today. There has to be some mistake.'

'That was *my* first thought…that Rosie had mis-heard the teacher's remark so I spoke to one of the other parents I know quite well, who in turn spoke to her daughter. She confirmed what Rosie told me. Apparently it was during registration and when her name was called and she failed to answer she asked, "Has anybody seen that half-caste child?" I'm sorry Mrs. Wyndham but I felt you should be told. Had it been my child, I'd certainly want to know.'

'Of course and believe me, I'm grateful for your concern. May I take your number and call you back when I've had a word with my husband? I'm sorry; I really don't know what else to say or how to deal with it. Rest assured I won't disclose my source of information, whatever decision I make.' She noted her number and thanked her again.

She was in a quandary; she was close to tears and prayed to God that Akina hadn't been advised. Was there no end to the child's torment? More than anything she wanted to hold her, to make her feel loved and wanted. She also felt guilty. Akina had told her earlier that she believed her teacher didn't like her. Why hadn't she listened instead of brushing aside her concerns? Children had a sixth sense about such matters. Hadn't she felt the same from the moment she stepped inside her first foster-home when fear emanated from every fibre of her being and hadn't *she* had just cause to feel that way?

On the pretext of asking what she'd like for tea, Mattie went to her room where she was drawing a picture. 'I've just popped up to ask what you'd like for tea and here's a present from Aunt Meredith.'

'*Another* present?' she shrieked. 'I've never had *so* many presents before for my birthday. It's nice having lots of aunts and uncles. Is Adam home?'

'No but I think I hear Dad's car on the drive. So, what are you drawing?'

'Just a picture,' she answered impassively.

As Akina opened her present, Mattie studied the drawing carefully. There were four people holding hands, two adults; a male and female and two children; a boy and girl. 'Let me guess,' Mattie said. 'I reckon those two are you and Adam.'

'That's right and those two are you and Dad.'

Mattie could barely speak the words as she asked quietly, 'Why did you draw a line down the middle of the little girl?'

Without hesitation she explained, 'That's because Daddy was Japanese and Mummy was English, so I'm a half-caste.'

Akina's words rang round her head like a clanging bell and with an audible tremor in her voice she asked, 'Er...where did you hear *that* word darling?'

'At school. When I went back today, everyone in my class was asking about my *real* daddy... the one I never knew.' She chuckled. 'Have you seen this? You can make it do all kinds of things. Look, it sits down and dances if you pull the strings.'

She nodded. 'It's lovely sweetheart. It's a puppet. I always wanted a puppet when I was little.'

'And did you ever get one?'

Mattie sighed. 'No, we didn't get many toys.'

'I know. You told me you were poor. Well, you can play with mine anytime you want.'

She managed a feeble smile. 'Thank you. So, you still haven't said how you came to hear that word. I don't suppose you heard it from the children?'

'Yes, Rosie told me but all the class knew as well because the teacher told everyone and I've got a lot more friends now because I'm a half-caste. None of the others have a Japanese daddy so I'm special.'

Mattie was comforted by her words. It was clear Akina didn't feel stigmatised by the remark, quite the reverse in fact. She had formed new friendships owing to her classmates' curiosity but that didn't...

'Are you upstairs?' Mark called, interrupting her thoughts.

'I'll be down in a jiffy. What do you say to Spag Bol for your tea?' she asked Akina.

'Yes please! That's my favourite. Will you send Adam up? I want to show him my puppet.'

'I'll tell him. Don't forget to call Aunt Meredith.'

Mattie flopped down on the sofa beside Mark and emitted a huge sigh.

'Bad day?' he questioned with raised eyebrows.

'You wouldn't believe it!'

'Try me.'

She poured Mark a drink and got one for herself before reporting Mrs. Simpson's revelation and the ensuing discussion she'd had with Akina.

Mark was equally horrified. 'What do you intend doing about it? I'm behind you all the way on this.'

'I intend speaking to her tomorrow and I'd really appreciate you being there. Can you go into work a little later in the morning?'

'This takes priority over everything. What the hell is wrong with the woman? I can't for the life of me imagine a teacher saying such a thing.'

'Well she *did* Mark and whatever the outcome, I intend taking Akina out of that school. I'm going to speak to the Headmistress at Grange. There must be a way round normal entry requirements for children who relocate and if there's a vacancy, I'm sure the governors would welcome the additional fees.'

'We're going to be stretched, financially I mean. It doesn't end with the fees. They're forever asking for money for some new venture.'

'Mark! I'm not asking *you* to pay the fees. I have money put aside I've never touched…*blood money* as Seth calls it from Social Services, paid out to get Meredith off their backs when she threatened them with court action. It's still there, every last penny.'

He jumped up angrily. '*You're my wife,*' he yelled and that makes you *my* responsibility…that goes for Akina too. This isn't a question of *yours* and *mine*; we're a *family* for God's sake!'

'Shut up and sit down! You're being ridiculous. We *are* a family and I play my part too. We already pool our incomes so what's your problem?'

He gathered her up in his arms. 'I'm sorry Mattie. I don't know why I reacted in such a way. It always touches a nerve if you make reference to your past.' He brushed his lips against hers. 'Forgive me?'

'Of course. Listen, if you leave early with Adam tomorrow, you can be at Akina's school by the time I arrive and we'll go in together and confront her.'

Mattie dropped Akina outside the school gates and awaited Mark's arrival. 'They should have finished registration and gone into assembly now,' she told him when he arrived moments later.

'I'm not great at being confrontational,' he said.

'Is that so? I seem to recall you had little trouble yesterday when you bit my head off. Besides, I'm not expecting you to say anything. You're there for moral support and to intimidate her in your suit.'

He laughed. 'Why, what's wrong with my suit?'

'Nothing; nothing whatsoever. It's absolutely spot on for the occasion. It'll really intimidate her. Right this is the classroom I believe. Akina told me it was number five.'

They were just about to enter when a middle-aged woman approached. 'May I help you?'

'Thank you,' Mattie said. 'We're looking for our daughter's classroom. We have let's say, an *issue* to resolve with her form teacher.'

'I'm the Head. May I help with this...*issue*?'

'You're more than welcome to be present but we do insist on speaking with the teacher and we don't have much time.'

'Of course. May I have your daughter's name?'

'Akina Peters. She started here recently.'

'Oh yes. I know her well...a bright little girl. If I remember rightly, she came from er...'

'Devon,' Mattie prompted.

'Devon...yes.' She opened the door to the classroom and they followed. Sitting at her desk was the form teacher who looked up as they entered.

'Mr. and Mrs. Peters would like to speak to you,' the Head informed her.

'Wyndham!' Mattie corrected her. 'Our surname is Wyndham. Akina's surname is Peters.'

'How can I help you?' the teacher queried with a disingenuous smile.

Mattie walked to the front of her desk. 'You may start by explaining why, last Thursday, you referred to our daughter Akina as, "*that half-caste child,*" in the presence of all her classmates.'

For a moment she was stunned. 'No,' she laughed attempting to disguise her obvious embarrassment. 'There has to be some mistake. I certainly didn't...'

Mattie was furious and cut in, 'I'm not asking *if* you said it because I have several reliable witnesses who state categorically that you *did*. What I want to ascertain is *why* you would utter such contemptuous words about a seven-year-old child.' She awaited a suitable response and when none was forthcoming added, 'I'm waiting!'

The Head intervened. 'I'm sure there has to be a satisfactory explanation for this er…error.'

'I'm sorry. There *is* no error nor can there be *any* satisfactory explanation. It was crude and offensive and if I don't get to the bottom of this now, then I'll bring it to the attention of your Board of Governors and beyond if required. I'm a solicitor, specialising in Family Law so please don't trifle with me.'

The teacher was alarmed. 'I seem to recall I *might* have used that word. She has an unusual name that I couldn't remember. Yes I think that was it.'

'That's poppycock as well you know. At the time, you were doing registration. Her name was written down in front of you. You'd already called it out.'

She shuffled awkwardly and avoiding eye contact said, 'Well, I'm sorry then. I don't know why I said what I did. Besides I didn't know it was a forbidden word. I'm quite sure it's in the dictionary.'

Mattie snorted. 'Let's imagine you had the son of an unmarried parent in your class. Would you refer to the boy as, "that *bastard* child,"? You'd find *that* word in the dictionary too Miss…'

'Miss Smiley,' she advised reticently.

She laughed contemptuously. 'How appropriate! Almost the perfect oxymoron!'

'I don't know what you mean.'

'That hardly surprises me. My role however is not to pass judgment about your grammatical incompetence. Your verbal incompetence and the manner in which you conduct yourself in this classroom in the presence of my daughter is my only concern. Might I suggest you look up the definition of *oxymoron* in your previously referred to dictionary whilst enjoying some of your more reflective moments?'

'I'll apologise to Akina. I understand your anger.'

'No! You must say *nothing* to Akina…nothing at all! You'll merely make matters worse if you do.'

Mark stepped forward, placing a hand on Mattie's shoulder. 'In case this needs to be said, Akina will *not* be returning to this school after today. Having listened to your pathetic attempts at a cover-up, I'm all for taking this matter further. It is not the *word* half-caste that's the problem Miss Smiley. It's the manner in which it was used…derogatorily. Akina *is* of mixed-race and is civil and well-mannered but *you* on the other hand obviously have *no* pedigree worthy of mention as you certainly don't know how to behave in decent company. Good day to you.'

The Head smiled weakly as they walked from the room whilst Miss Smiley simply stared ahead with a concerned expression on her face.

Whilst walking to their cars Mark commented, 'I hope to God I never come up against you in a court of law. You were really scary in there…absolutely awesome.'

She smirked. 'You'd better make sure you behave yourself then, hadn't you? Hands off the nurses!'

'There's only one woman for me and that's you. Incidentally, what the hell's an oxymoron?'

She laughed. 'To be honest *that* wasn't though it should be. '"Deafening silence," is a good example. It's a contradiction of two words. "Jumbo shrimp," is another example. It infuriated me that the obnoxious old battleaxe's name was Miss Smiley. That's the reason I mentioned it.'

'I'm sorry about last night when I exploded. That was so out of character. I was wondering; are you free for lunch? I feel like taking you out on a date.'

Mattie recognised a familiar glint in his eye. 'As long as there's no groping in the car, you can pick me up around twelve.'

'Sorry, I can't agree to that. That's just what I had in mind. You really turned me on in that classroom. I quite like a powerful dynamic woman so let's live dangerously. I'll be there at twelve on the dot.'

Finally, after several abortive attempts, Mattie was connected to the Headmistress at Grange School...a Mrs. Jennings. She enquired about mid-term admissions in exceptional circumstances, outlining details of Akina's recent move from Devon.

'Let me make a note of your name and address. I need to check first to see if there are any vacancies. We have a long waiting list for the Prep School. We enjoy a fine reputation for our academic success.'

Mattie supplied the required details.

'That's an unusual surname Mrs. Wyndham but it sounds familiar. I'm pretty sure there's a pupil with the same surname in the boys' Prep School.'

'Yes, that's right. Adam is Akina's brother.'

'Of course. I do remember now. Your husband is a hospital Consultant is he not?'

'That is so and I'm a solicitor,' she made known, smiling privately. That should be worth a couple of extra Brownie points she thought, conscious of how independent schools functioned. She could almost hear the collection receptacle rattling and clanging at the other end of the telephone as the entire tone of the conversation suddenly changed.

'I do believe a girl had to leave us at Easter when her father sought employment abroad. There'd have to be a short written test and we always conduct an interview but it's nothing to concern yourself about. It's quite a simple test for a seven-year-old. Let me call you later and we'll arrange something soon...if we have a vacancy of course.'

'That appeared to go okay,' Meredith commented when Mattie hung up.

'Yes it's the old story...money talks. Immediately she recognised Mark's name, a vacancy appeared as if by magic.'

'Don't knock it kid. You worked hard for all your qualifications. Cash in wherever you can, that's my motto. It's not merely a better education she'll get; she'll also mix with a better class of student too and I don't mean that to sound toffee-nosed.'

'Well it does,' Mattie chuckled. 'But I don't care. I'll do what's best for Akina. I made that promise to Sam.'

'Yes, and what's more she knew you would. She held you in very high regard.'

'I've been meaning to tell you, I'll need the blood money to pay the school fees if Akina's accepted at Grange. Mark and I had words yesterday, our first real argument when I said *I'd* pay her fees. It's only fair when all said and done. I can't expect *Mark* to pay when he has Adam's to pay and I've got money sitting in the bank untouched and earning interest. What do you think?'

'I'll pass on that if you don't mind. Leave me out of your family financial squabbles. I'll look for the bank book later. I should have handed it over to you on your last birthday but you always threw a paddy whenever it was mentioned so I left it in the safe. I knew you'd ask for it when the time was right.'

'The time's right now and this is one argument I intend to win with Mark.'

'Good! So why ask me for advice if your mind's made up?'

'I didn't! I merely asked for your opinion so shut up Meredith! I *knew* you'd take Mark's side.'

She shrieked with laughter. 'I'm taking nobody's side. I just said I wasn't getting involved. Incidentally, what do you intend doing about Akina? Have you somewhere to send her tomorrow?'

'I'm sure Emily will be pleased to have her.'

'Why not ask if there's an old test paper she could see to boost her confidence. How's her reading?'

'Not bad. She's half way through Dante's Inferno at the moment.'

'*What?*'

'Joke, Meredith! You are *so* gullible. Seriously, I think she's okay for her age. She should do well at the interview; that's if they get a word in! She certainly doesn't need a confidence boost for that.'

Mrs. Jennings telephoned with good news later that afternoon. There *was* a current vacancy and she had arranged for both the entrance test and the interview to take place on Friday. A teacher would mark the test while the interview was ongoing and the result would be given to them before they left.

When Mattie enquired about specimen test papers she was asked to call on her way home to collect a sample that would be waiting for her.

She called Mark at work with the good news. 'I'll be home a bit later than usual so keep an eye on the casserole in the oven please. Don't let it dry up.'

'Did you get chance to speak to Emily?'

'Yes and she was delighted to have Akina there.'

'Did they give you any indication at Grange as to when she could start?'

'No, she has to pass the test first.'

'Don't worry. The interview carries more weight. It's more about attitude. Academic stuff is easy to teach to a child with the right social qualities.'

'I wish I shared your confidence,' she sighed.

'Mattie, do I *ever* lie to you?'

'Yes you do! You said you were taking me out to lunch today and you didn't. I was *so* disappointed.'

'No you weren't! Anyway, you'd left me with no choice. You'd already made it clear that there'd be no hanky-panky in the car and so I had to formulate plan B at home. I admit the take-away might have been mediocre but the afters were superb.'

She giggled. 'You're incorrigible!'

'And you're a temptress. See you later.'

It was after six o'clock when Mattie and Akina got home. 'I bet there's nothing left of that casserole,' she remarked, hurrying into the kitchen.

'Relax,' Mark said. 'It's fine. I did all the cooking for seven years until you arrived on the scene. I'm not an idiot. What took you so long?'

'We went to the school and the Headmistress was still hovering about…waiting to catch a glimpse of us no doubt. As she sidled past, she dropped some paperwork and Akina picked it up. She didn't know it was the Headmistress and they became involved in conversation about Japan. It seems Mrs. Jennings has spent some time there and Akina was naturally interested to hear about it. Within seconds I'd been drawn in too. She appeared impressed when Akina thanked her nicely and added she was very grateful to have learned a little about Japanese culture.'

'Akina actually said that to her?'

'Yes, she did. I've no doubt she'd heard Sam and I discussing the subject. Sam held a firm belief that it was vital for Akina to learn a little about Japanese culture as it was an equal part of her heritage.'

'Well done Akina. It sounds like you've already got a foot in the door. Did you like the school?'

'I suppose,' she sighed with mixed feelings. 'I've lost my new friends though. Mrs. Jennings seemed nice…much nicer than Miss Smiley.'

'You'll soon make more friends and it's a much better school. Adam will be there too, don't forget.'

'Food's up!' Mattie called. 'Come and get it. You seem to have done a good job Mark. It's perfect.'

After they'd eaten, Mattie tore open the envelope and read the test paper before showing it to Akina.

Akina sat down and read it. Most of the questions seemed easy but they became progressively harder towards the end.

'Let *me* see,' Adam said. 'Huh! Easy peasy! Just look at the two pictures and find four things that are different in that one.'

'I know how to read!' she told him impatiently. 'I can't see *anything* different.'

'Right dummy! Has that cat got a tail?'

'Yes, it has.'

'Has that one?'

'Er…no, that one hasn't. Right, I get it now. I've got to find three more though.'

Within minutes she'd answered all the questions and when Mark checked, most of the answers were correct. 'Look at those two again. You can do them all if you're careful. Take your time because you've made a silly mistake on the last one.'

'That says, "Look at the pictures and then draw a circle around four things you can find in a kitchen," and I found a pan, a fork, a cup and that thing there with holes in. I can't remember what it's called.'

'It's a colander.'

'So I found four things. There's a bed, a mirror, a comb and that's a Teddy Bear so they don't count.'

He nodded but said nothing and when she stared at him blankly, he pointed to the question. 'Read it again carefully.'

'I've read it twice *and* crossed out the things that aren't in a kitchen.'

'I can see that Akina, but does it tell you to cross anything out?'

'*Yes!*'

'Point to where it says that.'

'*There*! It says it *there*.'

'Read it aloud please.'

She began to read then halted mid-sentence. 'Oh, it says draw a circle around them. I didn't see that.'

'*You* have to learn not to be argumentative young lady when people are trying to help you. If you read the questions carefully on Friday you'll be okay.'

'It's alright Dad. I'll remember the answers now.'

'Akina, you won't get *this* test on Friday. This is to give you an idea of what's expected.' Turning to Mattie he said, 'I'll speak to our Child Psychologist at work. She'll have cognitive assessment tests for seven-year-olds. They won't teach you how to read the questions though,' he told Akina.

'Did you take a test Adam?' Akina asked.

'Yes and it was a doddle. I didn't need *Daddy* to help me,' he scoffed.

Glaring at him she yelled, 'Oh shut your gob!'

'*Akina!* I'm not having language like that and it's time for bed now,' Mattie said crossly. 'You go and get ready and I'll be up in a minute.'

Mark smiled. 'How do folk cope with *six* kids?'

'Search me,' Mattie said, winking mischievously. 'Another two would be great though.'

'Yes well, I'd put the odds on that happening the same as the odds on winning the top Premium Bond prize. You remember to keep taking the pill Mattie because we're perfectly alright as we are.'

She was shocked, 'What does *that* mean? Surely you're not serious about not wanting another child? What would you say if I *did* get pregnant?'

Mark shrugged disinterestedly. 'It's hypothetical because you won't get pregnant. The contraceptive pill is very reliable.'

'I'll see to Akina,' she said jumping up, but out of earshot mumbled to herself, 'It might be reliable if I were taking it.'

Mattie perched on the edge of her chair, trembling like a leaf whilst awaiting Akina's return. Checking her watch yet again, she sighed heavily. Barely two minutes had passed since the last time she'd looked. So much rested on Akina passing the examination; her whole future was dependent on that and the interview that followed. Adam had brought her one of his school books to read because Mattie was certain they'd question her about her hobbies and interests. Emily had been only too happy to help, that being less strenuous than charging around with a demanding seven-year-old all day. Mattie had coached her judiciously about the way she should behave during the interview. She should be courteous though confident from the moment she entered the room and only speak when spoken to.

Mattie glanced at the time once more. Forty-five minutes the test lasted she had been told. The flight time to Florida had passed much more quickly than this. Her palms were sticky and her mouth was dry.

Suddenly the door opened and Akina ran towards her wearing a wide beaming smile. Bouncing down on the chair beside her she said, 'It was really easy that test. There was only one question I wasn't sure about but I answered it anyway. What do you call a child who goes to school?'

'I'm not sure…a student maybe or a scholar.'

'That's okay then because that's the one I picked, *scholar*. I hadn't heard of that before but the others didn't sound right. I chose that because it looked a bit like *school*.'

'Good girl. You did okay then you think?'

'*Much* better than okay. It was really easy.'

Mattie gave her a hug. 'What matters is that you did your best. This school has really high standards so don't be disappointed if you haven't reached the required grade. There are plenty of other schools.'

A lady popped her head round the door. 'Akina, would you like to come in now dear?'

Mattie turned to face her. 'Remember what I said. Listen to the questions, speak very clearly and only when spoken to and don't be cocky. Good luck!'

Akina skipped away without a care in the world as Mattie checked her watch again.

Following Akina's interview they waited several minutes before Mrs. Jennings gave them the result.

'I'm sorry for the delay. I had to wait for the test paper to be marked. It's designed to provide information not just about the child's perception but it's an indicator too of the speed at which a child thinks and works. The average candidate would complete approximately two-thirds of the paper. You, young lady answered every single question so it took a bit longer to mark than usual. I'm afraid I can't divulge the standard you attained as we never disclose such information but I can certainly say, Akina, welcome to Grange Preparatory School. Well done!'

For a moment Mattie was speechless and then her face burst into a relieved smile and tears sparkled in her eyes. 'Your mummy would have been so proud of you today Akina.'

'Are you Mattie?'

'Of course I am darling. I'm *very* proud.'

Mrs. Jennings smiled. 'We had a chat about your mummy didn't we? You must continue to make her proud and do your very best all the time. Right?'

'Yes Mrs. Jennings.'

'When will she be able to start?' Mattie asked.

'Er…it's Friday today. How about Monday? I'll give you an information pack that tells you everything you need to know, the school uniform stockist and so forth. She doesn't have to wait until you've bought the uniform. Sometimes they have to order items that are out of stock. If you have any queries you can call my secretary. We like to have the girls here by eight-forty-five. I'm so pleased it was good news Mrs. Wyndham and now if you'll excuse me, I have lots of paperwork to attend to before I leave. My secretary will bring you the information pack. I hope you'll be very happy here Akina.'

'I reckon this calls for a celebration,' Mark declared on hearing the good news. 'How about we invite all the grandparents here for tea on Sunday?'

'Can we Dad?' Akina asked excitedly. 'Can I ask Rosie to come too? I'll never see her anymore now I've left that school and she was my best friend.'

Mark glanced at Mattie for her approval.

'I don't see why not. You can call her after tea.'

'Thanks Mattie,' she cried and ran upstairs.

'Why don't you check your parents are free first Mark? You should check with Rachel and Bob too. I said I'd have them over to look at the photos and it might be better to invite them the first time when the others are here. They know everyone now and I think Rachel would feel more comfortable.'

'I don't know what you mean.'

'Think Mark. This was their daughter's house and now there's another woman here running the show. She's bound to feel emotional. I know I would.'

Adam, who'd been sitting quietly remarked, 'Can *I* ask a friend to come too? I don't want to sit looking at photographs. It's boring.'

'I'll struggle to fit twelve round the table,' Mattie commented, counting up. 'It might be better if...'

'You'll struggle just as much with eleven,' Mark interrupted cuttingly. 'Adam lives here too!'

'Er...don't get on your high horse with me! *I* am not one of your junior doctors. I was about to say it might be better were I to do a buffet. People can sit where they want then. Of course Adam can bring a friend. I don't know what's wrong with you of late Mark. Does married life not agree with you?'

He jumped up and took her in his arms. 'Married life agrees with me just fine. I'm sorry darling. I've had a really bad day today.'

'Yes and I've had a really bad week. I returned to a fortnight's work piled sky-high on my desk. You don't return to a fortnight's patients piled sky-high on a trolley waiting for you!'

Mark inhaled deeply. 'I lost a child today Mattie. I can't explain how that feels. I felt so bloody helpless. He was about Adam's age and I had to go and tell his father. He clung to my sleeve as he sobbed. I wanted to weep with him. I've never seen anyone as distraught. I sat with him for fifteen minutes or so as he poured out his heart to me. A few months ago he lost his wife to cancer and this boy was his only child. Life's an absolute bitch at times.'

'I'm sorry. I shouldn't have snapped at you.'

'I started it. I should have let you finish what you were saying. I suppose I'm being over-protective of Adam. All afternoon I've been asking myself how one comes to terms with losing a child.'

'Had the boy been ill for a while?'

'No, his death was the result of a tragic accident. His father, a warehouse manager had picked his son up from school to take him to the dentist and afterwards, he called at the works to check if an urgent order had been despatched. He told his son to wait in the car but he wandered into the warehouse and was hit and crushed by a fork-lift truck. I could see there was little chance of saving him the moment I looked at him. The injuries were too extensive. No one could have saved him but still you have to try.'

'You did your best Mark. Don't punish yourself.'

'It was his father's eyes Mattie. I'll never forget the look in his eyes…the look of disbelief and pain when I told him. The Police had to be notified too and the HSE will have been informed by now.'

'HSE?'

'*The Health and Safety Executive*. They'll have to investigate the circumstances of the accident to determine whether anyone was negligent, so to add to his grief, the father could be in very serious trouble. In any event, he'll spend the rest of his days living with his guilt. That's why I chastise our two when they're acting the goat. They don't see the dangers. If only the boy had heeded his father's instructions he'd still be alive and sadly his father will now pay the price for his son's disobedience.'

'Are we having any tea?' Adam chipped in. 'I'm starving.'

As Mark glared at him Mattie jumped up. 'It'll be on the table in five minutes. Find Akina please.'

Akina had hurried upstairs to invite Rosie to tea before Mattie could change her mind. She was also keen to let her know that she'd passed her entrance examination for Grange Preparatory School.

'I told you to call Rosie *after* tea didn't I?' Mattie stated crossly when Akina reported she could come to tea on Sunday. 'It's time you started listening. A boy died today because he disobeyed his father.'

Adam burst out laughing when Akina looked up wide-eyed and asked, 'So am *I* going to die then?'

'Less of the lip Madam,' Mark yelled. 'And *you* young man, can wipe that smile off your face or the pair of you will be sent to bed without tea!'

The children ate their tea in silence and the question Akina had wanted to ask remained on her lips for a more fitting time, the question as to when her riding lessons would start.

After tea, as the children headed for their rooms Mark overheard the words *old grumpy* in an otherwise inaudibly whispered aside by Akina to Adam.

Mark was about to make an angry response when Mattie prevented him. 'Don't play into their hands. I'll talk to Akina later when she's alone. I suppose I should be thankful she's not withdrawn.'

'Meaning what exactly?' he asked critically.

'For God's sake, have you heard yourself? There was no inference or undertone in my remark about Adam if that's what you're thinking. I was referring to the fact that she's recently lost her mother. As for Adam, I wouldn't describe him as withdrawn. He's very much like Seth was at that age. Seth and Jack were as different as chalk and cheese. Jack was full of mischief, whereas Seth was the quiet, thoughtful one, never bored with his own company and at his happiest with his head in a book. All children aren't alike but I have to say I've seen changes in Adam's social behaviour since Akina moved in. He's more talkative and he isn't afraid to express his opinion anymore. There was no one but you to interact with till we arrived and let's have it right, you're hardly the life and soul of the party,' she jibed.

'What do you mean?' he laughed, grabbing hold of her. 'I'm a bundle of fun! Come upstairs and I'll soon put a smile on your face.'

'Well, you do look smart,' Mattie commented when Akina stepped out of the fitting room at the school uniform shop. 'Do you have everything she needs?' she asked the assistant.

'I'm just going to check on the sports clothes. We always seem to run out of sports items.'

Mattie looked at her sideways. It was on the tip of her tongue to ask, 'Then why don't you order more when you know you always run out?'

After a lengthy absence she returned with a skirt and one shirt. 'As I thought, we're low on stock but these will keep her going until new stock arrives. I can call you when they're in if you like.'

'Yes please,' Mattie stated irritably. A further trip to the stockist could have been avoided if only they had used common sense based on past experience. To further compound matters, the dim-witted sales-girl had three attempts at adding up the bill.

'Are you annoyed,' Akina asked as they hurriedly left the shop.

She grunted, 'No...frustrated. Everyone's coming to tea tomorrow and I've all the shopping to do yet. I've no time for incompetence!'

'That's another word I don't know.'

'It means er...ineptitude or lack of ability like the salesgirl who couldn't even add up the bill.'

The next day as the visitors helped themselves to the buffet food, Mattie apologised for overcooking the pastry on the fruit pie.

'That's *incompetence*, isn't it Mattie?' Akina said in earshot of everyone.

Mattie howled with laughter as Mark glowered at Akina. 'It's okay Mark. It's a new word she learned yesterday. She's simply repeating what I said about the shop assistant when we went to get her uniform. She's right though; I should have been more careful but don't say that word to your teacher Akina if she makes a mistake because it's not very polite.'

Celia and Rachel chuckled together. 'She's like a breath of fresh air. You're lucky Mark to have *two* intelligent children.'

The four children went upstairs after tea to play a game, leaving the adults to look at the photographs. At nine o'clock Mark took Rosie and Tim, Adam's friend, home. When he returned, Akina and Adam were watching television upstairs. 'Right you two; It's way past your bedtime,' he told them. 'Go and say goodnight to everyone. It's school tomorrow.'

When the others were ready to leave, Rachel took Mattie aside. 'That was a delightful buffet Mattie. Bob's a very picky eater but he certainly did justice to your food today. I'm not patronising you when I say you're a superb mother and wife. Mark's more relaxed than I've seen him for years; Adam seems happier too. He was saying he likes having a sister and that he calls you Mum.'

'I...well...er,' she stammered but Rachel silenced her. 'It's alright. Adam never knew Sarah. A child should have two parents wherever possible and Bob is with me in this. Sadly, we lost Sarah but Adam's still here and we firmly believe that a loving family environment is essential for our grandson. Mark's a good man and we feel he's made the perfect choice so don't feel ill-at-ease in our presence. That's what I wanted to say and your fruit pie wasn't burnt, Bob said, and praise from Bob is praise indeed.'

'Thank you Rachel. I'll see you get copies of the wedding and holiday photos. Have a safe journey.'

'Thanks and don't forget what I said. We'll have the children any weekend you feel like a break.'

She laughed. 'You might regret you offered; we'll be sure to take you up on that. Take care.'

Mark joined her at the door as they waved goodnight. 'That went well wouldn't you say?'

'Yes, it did...very well,' she replied, resting her head on his shoulder. 'They're such nice people and it was a pleasant change for Emily and Norman too. They rarely go anywhere together.'

'Did I tell you the food was a great success? Even Bob enjoyed it and he's an extremely fussy eater.'

'Rachel told me. She's such a genuine person *and* she's offered to have the children stay over anytime we'd like a weekend to ourselves.'

'Mmm! I'll look forward to that,' he said kissing her softly.

5

'Remember what I told you Akina. You'll find this school's much different from those you've attended previously,' Mattie said, straightening her tie. 'You look very smart and don't worry; you'll be fine.'

Adam took hold of her hand.

'*Let go of me!*' she protested. 'I don't need leading in like I'm your baby sister! I'm *seven* now!'

'Oh, one more thing,' Mattie informed her. 'Some of the pupils might ask questions about where you come from and I'd prefer you didn't say you were a half-caste. I don't like that word. It's alright to say you're half-Japanese or you can just tell them your daddy was Japanese and...'

'And my mummy was English,' she cut in.

'That's right and they'll be more than happy with that explanation. Don't forget to raise your hand if you wish to speak and wait until you're asked.'

'I *know*,' she sighed. 'You've told me already.'

Mattie decided she'd said enough on the matter.

'I'll wait at the gate with Adam for you to pick us up when school finishes. Bye Mattie.'

'I'll be here by four o'clock. Good luck and don't worry. You'll soon get used to your new school.'

Although left by Adam in the care of an older girl Akina felt conspicuous when led to her classroom.

'You have to be the new girl; Akina isn't it?' her form mistress queried with a hospitable smile. 'My name's Mrs. Davison. Listen up girls; this is Akina and I trust you'll help her settle in. Thanks Emma,' she said to the older girl. 'Davina, I'd like Akina to sit with you and will you show her where the cloak-room is as soon as I finish registration please?'

Quietly, Davina stood up and beckoned to Akina to take her seat and as Akina walked to the back of the room, every pair of eyes scrutinised her closely from head to toe. When the bell rang at break-time, she was immediately encircled and bombarded with questions by each girl wishing to be her new friend.

When Mattie arrived to collect her, Akina skipped towards her with a beaming smile. 'It's great Mattie and I understood most of the lessons. Davina, that's my new friend, explained things that were different from the old school and I really like this one. I can't wait to go back tomorrow. I've made lots of…'

'Shove up and make room for me,' Adam snarled, feeling left out of the conversation. Mattie, quick to recognise the cause of his hostility asked, 'So how was your day Adam? Was yours a good day too?'

'It was okay I suppose. I have to talk to Dad later about a field trip they're organising.'

Eagerly Akina questioned, 'Can I come too?'

'No! It's for boys, not soppy girls,' he sneered.

'Pack it in!' Mattie cautioned. 'I'm driving.'

Once the initial excitement subsided, the children chatted quietly during the rest of the journey home.

Over the coming weeks, Akina found her school-work no more challenging than that at her previous

87

school. It was also more convenient for Mattie and Mark, having Akina and Adam in the same school.

It was approaching the end of term, a Friday, and Mark's turn to pick up the children at four o'clock.

When Adam wandered down the steps, Akina still hadn't appeared and he paused at the kerb to talk to Becky who was in the same class as Akina.

'Akina's in the cloakroom talking to Davina,' she told him. 'I'll go and tell her to hurry up.' She raced up the steps and as she disappeared from view a car pulled up by the kerb.

A few seconds later Becky yelled, 'Adam, she's coming.'

As Becky was making her way back to the gate, the driver stepped from his car. 'Adam,' he called, 'Your dad's asked me to pick you up. I work at the hospital with him. He's stuck in theatre.'

'Oh right, thanks. I'll have to wait for my sister.'

'Sister?' the man said looking puzzled. 'He never mentioned…' He stopped mid-sentence and Adam became suspicious. Recalling his father's warning, never to talk to strangers, he took a step back.

The man lurched forward and grabbed him. '*Get in the car!*' he yelled brusquely, manhandling him into the passenger seat. He locked the door with the key and as he turned, came face to face with Becky who had witnessed his violent actions.

Swiftly he ran round the car, jumped in and drove away whilst Becky watched in horror and disbelief as Adam hammered frantically on the window.

As Akina approached she quickened her pace on hearing Becky's screams. 'Becky, what's wrong?'

The child could barely speak. 'It's…it's…Adam,' she stuttered, tears rolling down her cheeks. 'A man took him…a man took him away…in his car.'

The headmistress had heard the child scream and she hurried outside to determine the cause of all the commotion. By the time she reached the girls, both were hysterical.'

'Mrs. Jennings,' Akina yelled. 'Someone's taken Adam…a man in a car.'

At that moment, Mark pulled up by the kerb and seeing the two distressed girls, he jumped from the car and hurried towards them. Believing they might have been quarrelling he spoke calmly. 'It's alright. Do you want to tell me what's going on?'

It was Mrs. Jennings who gave him the shocking news. 'Mr. Wyndham, I believe your son Adam has been abducted. It happened just a moment ago.'

'*Help him!*' Akina screamed. '*Help him Dad!*'

Mark froze on the spot whilst trying to absorb the horrific disclosure. He too couldn't form his words. '*No…no!*' he shouted. 'No…er…tell me again what you mean. Where's my son? Where's Adam gone?'

Becky's mother, who had just arrived, ran to her daughter's assistance as other inquisitive bystanders gathered around the frightened children to ascertain the cause of the commotion.

'Let's take this inside,' Mrs. Jennings said, taking charge. 'I have to telephone the police immediately. Mr. Wyndham…*Mr. Wyndham,*' she called louder, 'Please…we have to go inside and call the police.'

'What's happened Becky?' her mother questioned anxiously and only when Becky stared ahead as if in a trance did Akina screech, '*Somebody's got my brother. A man drove him away in a car and Becky saw everything.*'

Mark too was in a trance as he took Akina's hand and accompanied Mrs. Jennings into the school.

One of the teachers was standing beside the door. 'What's wrong?' she asked Mrs. Jennings quietly.

'Mr. Wyndham's son Adam, has been taken away by a stranger in a car. Would you arrange for some tea to be brought in please? I'm calling the police.'

As soon as she'd called them, Mark called Mattie and mumbled, 'It's me.' He stared ahead until Mrs. Jennings took the receiver from his hand to explain what she believed had happened.

'Oh my God,' Mattie cried. 'I'm leaving now. I'll be there in ten minutes. Please don't let Mark drive his car. Keep him there with you.'

'Don't worry. I'll keep a watchful eye on him.'

'I can't get Becky to talk to me,' her mother wept.

'She's a little girl and she's had a terrible shock,' Mrs. Jennings said kindly. 'It's only to be expected. I believe she was standing next to Adam when that man bundled him in his car.'

'Did she say *anything*…anything else about who he was or what he said?' Mark asked frantically.

'No, just that some man took him away. As I was walking along the path to the gate, I saw a blue car drive off. That could have been him. Becky didn't say anything else. I'm really scared Dad.'

He held her in his arms. 'I'm sure the police will find him,' he told her calmly, though when uttering those words of comfort his heart was breaking.

The screech of police sirens could be heard in the distance, becoming louder as three cars hurtled into the school driveway.

Mrs. Jennings hurried outside and briefly outlined what had happened before leading two officers indoors where she introduced them to everyone.

Bending down, one of the policemen asked Becky if she had ever seen the man before but she merely stared ahead, seemingly unaware of his presence.

'This is Adam's sister and she saw a blue car near the gate. It could have belonged to a parent though. She didn't actually witness the abduction. The only one who saw him was Becky,' Mrs. Jennings said.

'I'd like to take her home now please,' her mother stated. 'My daughter's clearly traumatised by what she saw and she can't tell you a thing in her present state of mind.' After giving the police her name and address she left.

'This is very unusual Sir,' the more senior officer told Mark. 'A man turns up in broad daylight at the precise time your son comes out of school and then, using force, bundles him into his car. The only time that would usually take place is when an estranged father had certain issues with his wife. I take it you *are* the boy's father.'

'Of course I am you damn fool. I wouldn't have said I was had I not been.'

'Sorry Sir. We have to check and ask what might appear to be stupid questions in order to find a lead. There appears to be no motive for this abduction. I take it you have no idea as to who he could be?'

'If I had even the remotest idea, do you think I'd

be wasting time standing here talking to you? I'd be out there looking for him like you ought to be.'

The officer cleared his throat. 'I understand your distress; I really do Sir, but the only thing we have to go on is the possibility it was a blue car and that isn't very much. I'm satisfied however, having seen the state of the sole witness that it was an abduction and there are steps I can now take to find your son. Do you happen to have a photograph of Adam?'

He fumbled for his wallet. 'I have one here.'

He checked the time. 'With a bit of luck, we'll get this on the six o'clock news. Is this a recent photo?'

'It was taken just a few weeks ago. What are the chances of you finding him?'

'The sooner we start, the better the odds, Sir. We will do everything we can…rest assured. I just need a few details now; his date of birth; what clothes he was wearing and an approximate height and weight. Also, does he have any distinguishing features?'

'Such as?'

He shrugged. 'Anything you can think of that can help the public spot him, if for instance, he walked with a limp.'

'*Walks!*' he retorted heatedly. 'Let's keep this in the *present* tense. I want my son found *alive* and he doesn't have any distinguishing features.'

'Mark!' Mattie cried, running into the room. 'Oh God Mark, what's happened?' She threw her arms around him and wept. 'Did anyone see anything?'

Akina ran to her sobbing. 'It was horrible Mattie. Adam was forced into a car with a strange man.'

'It'll be fine darling. You'll see. Please don't cry.'

'We'd best be on our way,' the officer told Mark. 'I have all the information I need at the moment but I'll call you should there be anything else I require. I'm told that our forensic team has finished outside for the time being and the area's been cordoned off. If anybody contacts you, my number's on this card. Try to remain calm if you do hear from your son's abductor and inform us immediately.'

'Is that likely?'

'As there's no apparent motive it's a possibility; that's all I can say at this stage of our enquiry. I'm very sorry Sir but let's try to remain positive.'

Mark shook the officer's hand and on the verge of tears pleaded, '*Please*…find my son.'

'Like I said, we'll do everything we can and we'll keep you informed of any developments.'

'I'll fetch another pot of tea Mr. Wyndham,' Mrs. Jennings said. 'Please, sit down both of you. You're in no fit state to drive at the moment. Try to relax.'

'*Relax*? How the hell am I supposed to relax?'

'Mark, Mrs. Jennings is just trying to help. Leave it in the hands of the police. We can do nothing.'

He sighed heavily. 'Why would anyone do this? He's just a little boy. He'll be terrified.' He held his head in his hands. 'If I've told Adam once, I've told him a hundred times not to speak to strangers. If I'd got here sooner, this would never have happened.'

'Stop it Mark. Blokes like that are opportunists. It could have been anyone's child. He just happened to be in the wrong place at the wrong time.'

'Adam *didn't* talk to him Dad. That man *dragged* him into his car. It wasn't your fault.'

Mark stood up. 'I need to get out of here. I should be at home in case the police are trying to contact me. Why are we hanging on here for a cup of tea?'

'Five minutes Mark…sit down for five minutes, please. You're shaking like a leaf. You can't drive a car in your state. The police won't know anything yet. Why don't you find Mrs. Jennings Akina, and help her carry the tea?' As Akina disappeared from view she added, 'Try to think positive and allow the police to do their job. If they get Adam's photo on the early news, he could be home before long.'

Mrs. Jennings poured their tea. 'I've put plenty of sugar in as it's supposed to help,' she told them.

Akina sat down quietly beside Mattie with a glass of juice, sipping it slowly.

'Did your friend say what that man looked like?' Mark asked. 'Was he someone she knew?'

'She didn't say Dad. She just screamed that a man had taken him. I've already told you.'

'She was in shock Mr. Wyndham. After the initial outburst she didn't speak again. Perhaps when she gets home and feels safe she might be able to add to what she said earlier.'

'Has anything like this happened here before?'

'No, never and I'll ensure it doesn't happen again. I'll keep the children inside school in future till the parents come inside to collect them.'

Mark stood up once more. 'Thank you for the tea Mrs. Jennings. I'm fine now. It's not far to drive.'

She scribbled her telephone number on a sheet of paper and handed it to him. 'Please call me as soon as there's any news. I hope you don't have to wait long. I've every confidence Adam will turn up safe and well.'

'Thank you. I only wish I shared your optimism,' Mark sighed.

Mattie switched on the television for the six o'clock news and when the local news was broadcast fifteen minutes later, Adam's abduction was the headline story, complete with photograph.

Mattie had already contacted all family members and close friends with a brief account, promising to update them with any positive developments.

There were several calls from Mark's colleagues who had seen the news item, one of whom was Dr. McAndrew offering her support.

The senior police officer they had spoken to earlier called later that evening to say there had been no positive response from the news bulletin and he suggested that Mark should consider making a television appeal to the abductor for the safe return of his son and which Mark agreed to do the next day if Adam had not been found.

As each hour slowly ticked by, the reality of the situation became more meaningful and grave, with Mark barely able to control his emotions. By eleven o'clock he had disposed of half a bottle of whisky and had had nothing to eat.

Thankfully, Akina, exhausted by the trauma, had fallen asleep in Mattie's arms and when Mattie took her upstairs to bed, she fell asleep once more.

'I've made you a slice of toast Mark,' Mattie said.

He snapped, 'No thanks. I don't want anything.'

'Please Mark…just try to eat. I've made you a hot drink too. You'll be ill if you keep drinking whisky on an empty stomach. Are you coming up to bed?'

'No, I'll stay where I am in case the police call.'

Dismayed, she enquired, 'What…all night?'

'Look, you go up to bed. Don't bother about me. I'd not sleep if I came to bed.'

'Will you come on the sofa then? Try to get a few hours sleep darling.' She went upstairs and returned with two pillows and a blanket. 'Rest here Mark,' she pleaded, plumping up his pillows. She covered him with the blanket, kissed him goodnight and left him to his thoughts.

When she came down the next morning Mark was sleeping soundly, his toast and tea untouched on the table beside him.

The television appeal later that day was a gruelling ordeal for Mark. Reading from a prepared script, he strove to contain his composure whilst pleading for the safe return of his son and as he reached the end, he broke down and wept.

'You did fine,' Mattie told him. 'Come on Mark; let's go home.'

The police officer drove them home and accompanied them inside. Emily was waiting with Akina.

'I'll put the kettle on,' Mattie said. 'Do you prefer tea or coffee?' she asked the officer.

'A cup of coffee would be welcome. What's that you're drawing young lady? Is it your house?'

'Yes and afterwards I'm colouring it in for Adam for when he comes home. It's for his room.'

'I bet you like drawing pictures don't you?'

'Yes, she does,' Emily answered on her behalf.

Mark returned to the living room after hanging up his coat. 'Please, sit down,' he told the officer. 'Did you make any further contact with the family of the child...the witness?'

'Yes, and she still won't speak. Arrangements are underway for Becky to be assessed by a child psychologist early next week if there's still no change.'

Akina's ears pricked up. She tore a sheet of drawing paper from her book and picked up her coloured pencils, replacing them in the cardboard container. 'Just because she isn't speaking, that doesn't mean she isn't thinking,' she told the officer. 'We learned at school that kids can *express* themselves in different ways. Our teacher gave us an exercise to do but we hadn't to speak. She called a girl out to the front of the class and asked her to show us she was happy without making a sound, so she smiled and then she asked her to show she was sad, so she pulled a sad face. Then she asked what we'd do if we were lost in a foreign land where no one could speak English and we wanted to find the railway station. I put up my hand and said I would draw a train and that was the correct answer so will you take these to Becky's house and tell her that Akina, that's me, wants her to draw a picture of that man who took Adam. Tell her she can keep my pencils, I've got plenty.'

'Well...er...I don't think it'd help much. It's very hard to draw a person and I don't think her mummy would like her to do that, in fact I think she wants her to forget about what she saw.'

'Well she won't; not before Adam comes home. I'm a kid too. I know. So, will you ask her mummy please, from me?'

'It does no harm to ask I suppose but I wouldn't build up your hopes,' he replied.

Mark looked at him with desperation in his eyes. 'We're clutching at straws here. We don't know if he's old or young, black or white. That young girl holds the key. She's the only one who actually saw anything. Maybe she can draw the car too. It might confirm that it's blue…anything to help us.'

The officer nodded, emptied his cup and stood up to leave. 'If I make any progress…or rather *when* I make any progress, I'll call you at once.'

Mark's appeal, broadcast on the evening news, was heartbreaking and Mattie's eyes were riveted to the screen as her husband's body language stated more than any amount of words could convey. Her heart went out to him. She moved closer and took hold of his hand as he sobbed. 'It's been over twenty-four hours without a lead. Surely somebody somewhere has seen Adam. I'm going crazy here.'

She rested her head against him without speaking. There were no words to ease his pain.

Mark closed his eyes and was shortly slipping in and out of slumber. Every so often his body would jerk and awaken him.

Mattie was concerned. 'If I make a sandwich, will you try to eat it? You can't carry on without sustenance. You'll be ill. Why not try a ham sandwich? You've had nothing since yesterday.'

'I'll pass thanks.'

She sighed with frustration, not knowing what she could say or do to help him. He was exhausted and dark rings encircled his eyes.

'Why not have a shower?' she suggested. 'I think that might make you feel better.'

He grunted. 'Do you now? Well I happen to think it won't. Look, I'm sorry. I know you're trying to help but leave me alone, please Mattie.'

In the hope he'd have some later, she went in the kitchen and made a plate of sandwiches. When she returned he was staring into space with tears coursing freely from his eyes. She curled up beside him.

Akina came downstairs to ask if there'd been any news. Mattie smiled caringly. 'Not yet darling but I'll let you know the moment we hear anything.'

'Didn't that policeman come back?'

'No. Perhaps Becky didn't feel up to drawing or maybe she didn't get a good look at the man.'

Akina sighed. 'I'm tired. I think I'll go to bed. All the time I'm awake I'm thinking about Adam. I've finished his picture and left it on his bed.'

'That's nice darling. I'll come up shortly to tuck you in. Would you like a story?'

'No thank you. I just want to go to sleep Mattie. I hope they find Adam soon. I really miss him.'

It was just before nine when the door bell rang and Mattie opened the door to Detective Inspector Hurst who was leading the investigation.

Mark's heart missed a beat when he walked in the living room with a grave expression.

'I'm afraid nothing positive was gained from my visit to Becky Carr's. I just wanted you to know I'd tried my best. Her parents were reluctant to subject their child to further trauma when asked but when I explained the request was from your daughter, they relented. I tried speaking to the child myself. I told her that Akina, being a little girl herself, understood how difficult this was for her. I gave her the paper and coloured pencils for her to draw a picture of the man and the car, showing anything at all she could remember. At first she just stared into space and as I continued to talk to her parents, she tipped out the contents of the box and began to draw a picture. It's rather poor I'm afraid and tells us nothing. It's just a simple sketch of a face and could be anyone.'

Mark sighed. 'Thank you for trying. What about the car? Did she draw that?'

'Yes and it was a blue car.'

'Do you have the drawing?' Mattie asked.

The officer removed it from his pocket and gave it to her. 'Like I said, it tells us nothing.'

Mattie passed it to Mark who nodded in accord.

'Will you give these back to Akina please? I told Becky she could keep the pencils but I imagine she wanted no reminder of that event she'd witnessed.' He arose. 'I'm sorry my efforts proved fruitless.'

Their conversation had been overheard by Akina, who, having been aroused from sleep by the door-bell had crept downstairs hoping the visitor was the bearer of good news about Adam.

Carrying her huge Mickey Mouse, she wandered into the living room.

'You should be in bed. What are you doing down-stairs?' asked Mattie.

Rubbing her sleepy eyes she replied, 'I heard the doorbell.'

'I'm sorry. That was me,' the police officer said. 'My word…that's a big Mickey Mouse! Why, he's nearly as tall as you are!'

'I got him from Disney World in America. I take him to bed with me.'

With a smile he said, 'It must be a very big bed.'

'Will you show me Becky's picture please?'

'It doesn't help Akina. You should go back to bed now,' Mark told her.

'But I want to see the picture first. Where is it?'

Mark nodded at the officer who took it from his pocket and passed it to her saying, 'She's sent your coloured pencils back. I told her you said she could keep them but she pushed them towards me.'

She studied the picture. 'She was angry when she drew this. She broke my red pencil.'

'What makes you say that?' Mark asked.

'That's obvious…because she hasn't used it. She used brown instead. At school we're taught to *improvise*,' she emphasised, 'if we need something we haven't got. She's drawn a brown mouth and every kid knows a mouth is red.'

Mattie opened the box and removed the red pencil to find the point broken off to the wood. She held it up to show the officer and Mark.

'I'm impressed,' the officer said quietly to Mattie.

'Does the drawing tell you anything else?' Mark asked hopefully.

'It doesn't tell me who he is. I don't know him.'

'He appears to have dark brown hair with blonde streaks if you look closely,' the officer said.

'No he *doesn't*,' Akina contradicted. 'He has *red* hair.' Impatiently she continued, 'I've just told you; Becky didn't have a red pencil so she's coloured his hair brown and used yellow on top to make it look red. She's *improvised*. He definitely has red hair.'

'I'll consider myself told off,' he said as an aside to Mattie as Akina studied the picture more closely.

'There's something else. I wasn't sure at first but now I am. He's got what Jimmy Trevelyan had. He was in my class at school in Devon. I can't remember what it's called…you should know Dad, when you have something like a birthmark but it wasn't a birthmark…it was a…'

Mark sat up straight. 'A disfigurement?'

'No, I've never heard that word. He called it…er, a hare-lip…that's what he has, a hare-lip.'

Mark snatched the drawing from her hand. 'Christ Almighty…I know who's taken him,' he cried.

'Who?' the others called out in chorus.

'God, I can't remember his name. It'll be on the records at the hospital…in fact you have his details at the station. His son was crushed in an accident at work a few weeks ago. It was in all the papers and the HSE was involved too.'

'The fork-lift truck accident?' the officer asked.

'That's the one. I had to tell the boy's father he'd died. He was a red-head and had a hare-lip.'

Akina intervened, 'Was it Travis Hargreaves who died Dad?'

He looked surprised. 'Yes, that's the name. How do you know that?'

'Adam told me. Travis was in his class at school. It happened just before I started there.'

'He never said anything to me. I'll get my coat,' he said jumping up. 'Can you find out the address?'

DI Hurst placed a hand on Mark's shoulder. 'I'm sorry Mr. Wyndham. *You* won't be coming along.'

'Like hell I won't. That mental case has taken my son and if he denies it I'll knock it out of him.'

'Yes and that's why you won't be coming along. At this stage we don't know for certain and I don't want you being arrested at the scene for assault. It's a good lead that the police team will follow up.'

'It's the only bloody lead and a six-year-old child has done all the police work,' he yelled. 'What have *you* lot actually done apart from arranging the news bulletin followed by an appeal conducted by *me* for the *public's* help?'

'I'm seven actually!' Akina remarked, though her indignant retort couldn't be heard above the noise.

'I understand your concern Sir but we mustn't be hasty.'

'Hasty? You don't know the meaning of the word and you're wasting more time now when you could be calling the station for the address. *Do* something for God's sake!'

As the officer left the house, Mark sped after him and jumped in the passenger seat.

'You stay in the car otherwise I'll arrest you my-self and don't for one minute think I won't. This is a police matter,' he advised in a dour tone.

Mark was soon to retract his sardonic declaration about the officer's lack of haste when the latter flew through the town with blue light flashing and siren blaring in what could best be described as a white knuckle ride.

He had arranged for two other cars to be present and they were waiting at the end of the street when their car turned in. He parked behind the others, got out and spoke to the other officers and on foot, four of them approached the house. Two officers walked to the rear of the house as DI Hurst and a colleague knocked at the front door.

From where he was positioned, Mark was unable to see the blue Vauxhall parked in the driveway but its presence removed all doubt DI Hurst might have had earlier about the identity of Adam's abductor.

'Mr. Hargreaves?' he questioned as a man opened the door.

'That's right. I think I know why you're here but it isn't what you think. Please come in.'

The officers glanced at each other before stepping inside and were even more surprised when led into the lounge to find a young boy sitting cross-legged on the rug in front of the television, eagerly watching a cartoon programme.

'It appears you're going home a day earlier than planned Adam,' Mr. Hargreaves said.

Adam looked up at the two police officers.

'I'm Detective Inspector Hurst. Would it be right to assume you're Adam Wyndham?'

He nodded his head. 'That's right,' and standing up enquired, 'Is Dad with you?'

'He is Son. He's waiting in the car.'

'Can I go to him?'

'No, not yet…in a little while,' and turning to Mr. Hargreaves asked, 'What's going on Sir?'

'If you didn't know that already, you wouldn't be here. I kidnapped this young boy and brought him here. I wanted his father to know how it felt to lose a child…only for a couple of days though…not for-ever like my son. Oh yes, I know his father. He was the one who let my son die.'

DI Hurst cleared his throat and stepped forward. 'Joshua Ian Hargreaves, I am arresting you in con-nection with the abduction of Adam Wyndham on the fifteenth of July nineteen-seventy-seven.' After reading him his rights he added, 'Would you like to get your coat Sir? You're coming with us.'

'You'd better nip upstairs and collect your things Adam. Make sure you don't forget anything as I'm likely to be away for a long time.'

'Okay Josh. Please don't hurt him,' he said to the police officer. 'He's a kind man and he lost his son a few weeks ago. He was in my class at school.'

'Don't worry about it Adam. You collect all your stuff like he said and then you can talk to your dad.'

Mark checked his watch anxiously. With no sign of any police action he was growing increasingly more impatient and could sit quietly no longer. Why was it taking so long? What had they discovered when they went inside the house? Had they even got into Hargreaves' house? The questions were endless as he stepped from the car and walked up the street.

It was easy to find the right house. It was the only house not to have twitching curtains and inquisitive spectators at every window.

He waited in the shadows, mindful of DI Hurst's warning for what seemed an eternity until the door suddenly opened. Straining to see through the darkness as a figure appeared in view, he recognised the perpetrator who was being led down the path by an officer but there was no sign of Adam.

Mark leapt from the shadows as they approached and confronting him face to face screeched, '*What have you done with my son, you bloody moron?*'

'Stand back Sir,' the officer said, raising his hand. 'Adam's fine. Let us pass then go inside and see for yourself.'

'You sick perverted git! I hope you rot in hell. If you've harmed my son in any way, I'll bloody-well kill you myself and bugger the consequences.'

He ran up the path and into the house to find DI Hurst talking quietly with Adam. Unable to contain his emotion a moment longer, his eyes flooded with tears as he flung both arms around his son, hugging him as he sobbed. For several moments no dialogue was exchanged and it was Adam who finally broke the silence. 'I'm alright Dad. Josh didn't hurt me. It was scary when he shoved me in his car but when he said who he was, I wasn't scared anymore.'

'Has he touched you…done anything to you?'

'Dad…*listen*…you never listen. I have to listen to you but you don't listen to me. Josh is a good kind man who wouldn't hurt anybody. He's really ill and no one will help him…nobody listens to *him* either.

That's why he took me away because he said it was the only way he could make people listen. He was bringing me home tomorrow.'

'Yeah, right!' Mark snorted.

'You see what I mean Dad? You *still* won't listen. Forget it.'

Mark was furious. 'I've been half out of my mind with worry. You're just a young boy and you don't understand. He's a dangerous man who needs to be locked up where he can't get his hands on someone else's child. He had no right to take you away.'

'I know but he's sick Dad.'

'I'm glad we're in agreement about something.'

DI Hurst moved towards them. 'I suggest we get this place locked up and get you two home. I had a word or two with Hargreaves whilst your boy was packing his bag. It does seem he has psychological problems, not that I'm exonerating his actions mind you, but I don't believe there was any *molestation*,' he whispered, 'of your son. His version of the cause of his actions is the same as Adam's. He's lost both his wife and son recently and has received little or no support from his GP, he alleges. He wanted *you* to know how he felt. I think it was a cry for help.'

'Why me?'

'He believes you let his son die.'

Mark was dumbfounded. 'I did everything I could to save him. I'd *never* let a child die; I wouldn't let *anyone* die if there was any way to…'

'I know Sir but you asked and I'm repeating what Hargreaves said which clearly highlights his mental state…the way he's thinking.'

'It doesn't explain why he was so heavy-handed when bundling Adam in the car.'

Adam joined in the conversation at that point. 'I know why. Josh said he worked with you and that you were still at work. If Akina had been with me, we'd both have got in but as usual she was gassing with one of her mates. When I told him I'd have to wait for my sister, he started to say he didn't know I had a sister. That's when I backed away because I knew something was wrong. He grabbed me then. Ask Becky; she'll tell you what happened Dad; she was walking towards me and saw everything.'

Mark decided to defer any mention of Becky until they were home. 'Would you call my wife please?' he asked DI Hurst.

'I think she'll have been informed by now. One of my officers was going to call her from the car. I'll drop you off and I'll be round to see you tomorrow. I'm on duty at ten so it'll be after that. There's still a few odds and ends to tie up.'

As Akina and Mattie anxiously awaited Adam's return, a car pulled up outside. Akina dashed to the window and shrieked, 'They're here!'

Adam bounded inside, seemingly none the worse for wear following his ordeal.

'Adam…oh Adam,' Akina cried. 'I thought we'd never see you again.'

Mattie clung to the two of them before wrapping her arms around Mark.

'I'm okay Akina. Josh took good care of me.'

'*Josh?*' Mattie mouthed silently to Mark. '*Who's Josh?*'

'His abductor would you believe! Josh and Adam are on Christian name terms, *big* buddies!'

'Are you really alright darling?' she asked him. 'I can take Akina upstairs if there are things you want to discuss privately with your dad.'

'No, don't bother. He doesn't listen anyway.'

Mark was angry. 'Don't *dare* speak about me like that. I can't begin to describe my feelings since you disappeared. You don't know how I've suffered.'

'Yes I *do*! I know how Josh hurts so it's the same. He can't eat; he can't sleep and he cries all day and there's no one to help him. He loved Travis.'

'And can't you see I love *you* too? I don't understand you at times Adam. You didn't even mention Travis's name to me yet you told Akina everything about the accident. Why?'

He started to cry. 'Because I'd heard you talking to Mum about a child who'd died. You were really freaked out about him and when I went into school and found out it was Travis, I didn't want to upset you again; that's why I didn't tell you.'

'Come on, don't cry darling,' Mattie said, giving him a hug. 'I called Becky's mum earlier and asked her to tell Becky you were safe. She was *very* upset yesterday but I'm sure she'll feel much better now. Can you eat a sandwich?'

'No thanks; I had a big tea. Josh made steak and onions. He's a really good cook Mum. I wish there was something we could do to help him.'

'I know what *I'd* like to do to him,' Mark snorted.

'You could show the man a little compassion and advise the police you weren't pressing charges. The way I see it he needs help, not further punishment,' Mattie remarked sympathetically.

'Are you for real Mattie? After him sending me to hell and back, you want me to help him?'

She took hold of his hand. 'At least *you* got back from hell but he's still there. Whatever happened to the Hippocratic Oath? "First do no harm". All I ask is that you think about it, please. If Adam was able to forgive him, as the victim, can't you try?'

'Did you say you'd made some sandwiches? I'm starving,' he announced changing topic and glaring at Adam added, 'I've had nothing at all to eat since lunchtime yesterday nor have I slept. Do you know how that feels Son? Have you any idea?'

His response though simple was frank. 'Yes Dad; Josh told me.'

Mark looked deeply into his son's compassionate eyes and filled with emotion he held him close. 'In the morning we'll sit down and talk Adam. I have a few bridges to cross yet and it's time you were in bed.' He kissed the top of his head. 'I'm so happy you're home, Son.'

The next morning Mark suggested he and Adam should go for a walk. For most of the night he had been wide awake, soul-searching for the best course of action to take but had reached no firm decision. With numerous unanswered questions clouding his ability to reason, he needed time alone with his son.

Excitedly Akina cried, 'Can I come too?'

'Not this time darling. I just need time alone with Adam but we won't be too long.'

'Why don't *we* make a cake?' Mattie proposed.

Her obvious disappointment was instantly quelled as she asked, 'Can I put the cherries on top? It can be called a, "*happy you're home*" cake for Adam.'

'It can indeed,' she agreed winking at Mark, her eyes speaking her approval of his actions.

There was an uneasy silence at first as the two of them made their way to the park until Mark spoke. 'Tell me about Josh…Mr. Hargreaves.'

'What do want to know?'

'I want to know everything from the moment he took you.' He watched him take a deep breath.

'Well, it was scary at first because I didn't know who he was or what he wanted. I tried to get out of the car but he'd locked the door. I remember yelling at him to stop the car and let me out. Then he told me he was Travis's dad and that he wasn't going to hurt me. I believed him then because I remembered I'd seen him before waiting by the school gate.'

'Go on.'

'I think I asked what he was doing and he gave a funny laugh. He told me he was giving you a taste of your own medicine. Then he laughed louder and said that *was* funny…giving a doctor a taste of his own medicine. I didn't know what he meant and he didn't explain. Then he said he wanted to talk to me about Travis and that I hadn't to worry. I told him you'd be angry and he said that was alright and that he hoped you'd be angry enough to *do* something because you were a clever man.'

'Did he explain what he meant by that?'

'No, but I worked it out later when we'd spent a bit more time together. He wanted you to help him.'

'Didn't you try to run away when you got to his house?'

'No. I thought he'd take me back home after he'd talked about Travis.'

'So you didn't feel threatened in any way?'

'I don't know what that means Dad.'

'It means did you ever feel you were in danger?'

'No, I've already told you, he's really nice.'

'Nice men don't take other men's children away.' He paused. 'I want to ask a question now that you must answer truthfully. Did he touch you at...?

'You don't need to explain,' he butted in. 'I know what you mean and *no*, Josh didn't do anything to me. We just looked at photographs together.'

'Photographs? What kind of photographs?'

'Of Josh and Travis, like when they went fishing and camping together. They went somewhere most weekends. There were some of Travis's mum too. Josh said he missed her as much as Travis. When I told him my mum was dead, he was sorry. He said it must have been hard for you. Travis and his dad went cycling a lot too. They were always together. I could tell Josh was a really great dad. I miss Travis too. He was a good mate. We didn't hang out with other kids in our class because they were childish. I know we're all the same age but the others don't act their age.'

Mark laughed. 'I'm pretty sure they do. It's more likely that you and Travis were different. At times I find it hard to believe you're only seven, like I find it hard to believe Akina's only seven too. So carry on; what else did you talk about?'

112

'I'm nearly eight Dad. I can't think what else we talked about. Oh yes, I told him I had riding lessons so we talked about that for a bit. Josh bet you were the better rider and he laughed when I told him *you* wouldn't know the front from the back of a horse as you didn't ride with me. I wish you would Dad. It was fantastic on holiday when you came swimming with me and Akina. I like us doing things together. Before you married Mattie, I knew you were tired when you got home from work and you had to see to our tea, but it would have been great to sit down together after tea and do something. I'd like horse-riding much better if you came too but I expect it'll be different when Akina starts her lessons. I won't be by myself then. Did you ever go anywhere with *your* dad? Did *he* ever take *you* fishing and stuff?'

Mark didn't answer. He was preoccupied fighting back his tears and shaking his head in disbelief and dismay at his shortcomings.

'Dad?'

'I thought I was doing okay Son,' he sighed. 'I'm a crap dad aren't I?'

'I didn't mean that. I was just…'

'It's alright. You don't have to apologise Adam. I didn't do much with my dad but then I had a mum, unlike you. I'll make it up to you,' he said, ruffling his hair. 'God, I feel so bloody guilty now to think I fell asleep most nights and when I woke up, you'd gone to bed.'

'Mum and Akina are there now Dad. It was when they weren't there that I missed having you around. It's okay now because I've someone to talk to.'

113

'Don't make me feel worse than I already do Son. So, what are we going to do about Josh? Do we tell the police he needs medical help? I doubt they'll be too happy. Did you know your kidnap was on television on the news and that I went on too to make an appeal to your abductor to bring you home?'

'Wow! Did you really go on telly? I missed that. I was watching cartoons.'

Mark expelled a loud guttural laugh. 'You missed the best one then. I was crap at that too. Let's make our way home Son and see what we can do to help Josh.' Tucking his arm round Adam's shoulder he said, 'I doubt you've ever heard of Alexander Pope. He wisely said, "Good-nature and good sense must ever join; to err is human, to forgive, divine."'

The inference if not the words was clearly understood as Adam looked up at his father and smiled.

As they turned the corner into their avenue, Adam giggled when Mark proclaimed, 'Oops! PC Plod's already arrived. He'll be stomping up and down on his flat feet now because we're not there. I'd totally forgotten *he* was coming this morning!'

'You won't let them lock Josh up, will you Dad?'

'I'll do my very best Son; I promise.'

Following a long and detailed discussion, DI Hurst stood up to leave and Adam went upstairs.

'What do you suppose the chances are of getting the charges dropped in favour of an agreement from him to undergo psychiatric treatment?' Mark asked.

'Well, for a start, I didn't charge him last night. I wanted to give you the opportunity to rethink your options once you'd spoken to Adam. The first thing we need is psychiatric evaluation. Only then can we arrange to refer him for treatment but this is an unusual case. Hargreaves was known to you; his son was known to Adam and although Adam agrees he had ample opportunity to leave the house, he chose to stay. He made no attempt to call you either, yet there were at least a couple of telephones he could have used. To me, that doesn't sound like your son was being *detained* by Hargreaves against his will. As to the abduction, that's more complex. He was seen bundling Adam in his car; he doesn't deny that and has made a statement to that effect.'

'I know but he panicked when Adam backed off.'

'Be that as it may, prior to that he coerced Adam with a falsehood, that being that you'd sent him to collect Adam because you were stuck in theatre. I have to tell you, *that* is still abduction.'

'He's right Mark; it is,' Mattie joined in.

'Then he locked him in the car; he detained him. I don't want the pitiful guy to be sent down any more than you do. He's a victim of system failure and I'll write that in my report together with your plea for leniency.' With a twinkle in his eye he went on, 'I have to say I was a bit surprised by your change of heart Sir, my having overheard that you were yelling obscenities at him outside the house and threatening to kill him but I shrugged that off as having misheard my colleague since I'd made it perfectly clear that you must *not* leave the car, had I not? On second thoughts, it might be wise *not* to answer that question, Mr. Wyndham.'

'*Mark!*' Mattie cried looking shocked.

'When are you likely to know something?' Mark queried with a guilty expression.

'Soon, I hope. We're holding him in a cell at the moment but he seems happy enough. He has some-one to talk to and he was playing chess with one of the officers last night. Apparently, his son was very good at chess and regularly beat his father.'

That revelation was yet another knife in the heart for Mark…a further activity that Josh had regularly enjoyed with his son.

'I'll be in touch soon Mr. and Mrs. Wyndham and I'll do my utmost to obtain what's called an out-of-court disposal.

As Mattie closed the door behind him, she turned to Mark. 'How *could* you Mark?'

'I thought he'd harmed Adam,' he said contritely.

'This is why we have a judge and jury. It's called a Judicial System. It's there to protect people from the likes of you who'd take the law into their own hands and create anarchy.'

'Yes Ma'am! Come here and give me a kiss. You look so sexy when you're being officious.'

'If you want to do something useful, go and fetch the children please. Tell them lunch is ready.'

'What's for afters?' he smirked.

'Definitely not that! Seth and Steph will be round with the baby in about an hour.'

'Well Paul! Aren't you a smart young man? I love his outfit, Steph. They make such lovely clothes for babies nowadays.'

'Aye, and they cost plenty too Mattie,' Seth made known. 'It costs more for his gear than for mine and he's already growing out of stuff he's hardly worn.'

'Take no notice Mattie. Almost everything Paul's got has been bought for him by other people.'

Seth wouldn't be silenced and was determined to have his say. 'Exploitation, that's what it is Mark. Shops know how gullible women are. They hike up the prices every other week just to line their greedy pockets when instead they should be helping folk at such a difficult time.'

Mark felt he should nod in agreement and Mattie was furious with him. 'Don't encourage him Mark! Seth always talks rubbish and when I have *my* baby I'll want the best too.'

'See what I mean Mark? Gullible!'

Steph's ears pricked up. 'Er...is there something you're not telling us Mattie?'

'What? Oh no,' she laughed. 'I'm not pregnant. I was just thinking ahead, that's all.'

Mark breathed a sigh of relief at her response. 'As long as you're only *thinking*, that's fine. I can cope with *thinking*.'

Steph made a mental note of Mark's disagreeable comment. She'd speak to Mattie about it later if the opportunity arose. 'Where are the children?'

'Upstairs. They'll be down shortly,' Mark said.

'How's Adam now?'

'He seems fine. You know Adam; he takes everything in his stride.'

Steph grunted. 'Well, I for one will be glad when that evil bloke's behind bars for what he did. When

I was a baby, Mum used to leave me outside in the pram all day. I daren't leave Paul outside at all and if I take him out in the pram, I'm constantly looking over my shoulder in case someone's following us.'

Mattie gestured to Mark to say nothing. 'It was a one-off Steph so I wouldn't worry about that,' she told Steph reassuringly.

Akina's voice could be heard on the stairs. 'Here endeth the peace and quiet,' Mark chortled.

'Aw…isn't he gorgeous?' Akina cried, seeing the baby on Steph's lap. 'Look Adam; isn't he lovely?'

Disinterestedly he replied, 'He's alright!'

Steph couldn't hold her tongue. 'Like father like son,' she stated acrimoniously.

Mark howled with laughter. 'Don't expect us men to act maternal. That's the woman's role Steph. We just help make babies by providing the essential…'

'*The children are here!*' Mattie cut him short.

Aware he had overstepped the mark, he turned to Adam. 'Find your football and then Uncle Seth and I will take you to the park for a kick-about…okay?'

'Can I come too?' Akina asked eagerly.

'Certainly you can. Get your coat.'

'It'll give you time to get all your baby talk done. We'll not be too long,' said Seth. 'My word, that's a nice new football,' he added as Adam reappeared.

'It's not new. I've had it ages haven't I Dad?'

'Yes Son,' he replied guiltily as yet another knife pierced his heart. 'Come on; let's get it dirty.'

As the door banged closed, Steph questioned, 'Is everything okay between you and Mark? He's very cynical of late.'

'He's fine. He's still wound up about Adam.'

'He doesn't seem fine to me and what was all that about it being alright to *think* about babies? That to me sounds as if he doesn't *ever* want a baby. Have you discussed it?'

'I've hinted. We've not actually sat down and had any meaningful dialogue about it. He'll come round in time. We've only been married a few months.'

Changing topic Steph asked, 'Is Meredith all set for the wedding on Saturday?'

Mattie laughed. 'She's as crazy as I was the week before mine. She never talks about anything else at work and she's convinced nothing will go right.'

'I was an absolute wreck until I got to the church and then I remember telling myself, "To hell with it! What will be, will be," and I just got on with it.'

'I suppose all Brides are alike. It's a big day.'

'Did they finally decide on a honeymoon?'

'Yes. They're off to the Canadian Rockies.'

'Mmm...nice. I wish we'd had one, a honeymoon. Seth wouldn't spend that money at the time in case it wasn't ours and then later, when we'd established it *was* ours, he said it was better to save it.'

'It was a peculiar how-do-you-do for a stranger to give you all that. I wonder where he is now.'

'Bill? Heaven knows. He could be anywhere. By the way, you promised to tell me about an incident in your past when you got back from honeymoon. Do you remember?'

She paused reflectively. 'Yes, I remember Steph.'

'So? I'm waiting.'

'Do you want the long or short version?'

Steph pondered but a moment. 'Better make it the short version or the boys might be back before you get to the end.'

'Okay! When I was fourteen and placed in foster-care I was repeatedly raped by my foster-father and I killed him.'

Steph laughed. 'Don't muck about. Come on; tell me the truth. We haven't much...' She stopped mid-sentence when she looked into her tearful eyes. 'My God Mattie! You *are* speaking the truth.'

There was silence for a few moments until Mattie murmured, 'That's why I was terrified of men and I carried it through my teenage years without telling Seth and Jack. They only found out the night we all went out when that creature assaulted me. That was my foster-mother and she used to beat me black and blue. It was the foster-home from hell but they got their come-uppance in the end.'

'So that's what she meant when she shouted you should have got life. I never imagined anything like that. It crossed my mind that some guy might have tried to accost you because it was obvious you were scared of men. Now it makes sense why Seth kept deferring the wedding. He was afraid to leave you.'

'Yes and that's why I moved away or you'd never have got married. I couldn't ruin your two lives too. Meredith was Sam's friend at University and it was at her suggestion I went to Devon. For the record, I didn't murder the guy; I killed him accidentally. He stood in my path, leering and touching me as I tried to make my escape, so I cracked him twice with my tennis racquet and he dropped dead at my feet. I ran

120

off and got as far as the railway station where Sally was walking through with Sadie. Sadie recognised me from school and told her mother she believed I was running away because I had a bag on my back, so Sally made me go home with her where I poured out the whole sorry tale. When the authorities were informed, I had to go for a medical check and I was pregnant. Both Sally and Charles were unbelievably kind and I'll never be out of their debt,' she sighed.

'I'm so sorry. Did you have a termination?'

'Yes, a few days later. I had my whole life ahead of me and I already knew what work I wanted to do in later life, besides which, I couldn't bear to carry that monster's baby in my belly. A child myself, the decision was an easy one that I've never regretted.'

'Does Mark know everything?'

'Yes and he was very supportive. Not many know the full story and I want to keep it that way. It's still a very painful memory to this day. Sadie knew I'd run away, that's all. She was never told why so she knew nothing about the sexual abuse. Charles knew about that but not the pregnancy; Sally knew everything as did Meredith, who represented me, and the only others who knew were the authorities and then Jack and Seth after that night out when the hideous ex-foster-mother suddenly emerged from the mire.'

'That must have been terrifying to see her.'

'That's putting it mildly,' she snorted. 'Anyway, let's drop it. You got the long version after all.'

'As it's confession time, I've got a secret too that I've shared with our mutual confidante, Meredith.'

'So are you going to share it with me? Before you

121

answer, does Seth know? I don't want to be placed in an awkward situation. He's my brother.'

'Yes, he knows but no one else knows and I mean no one. You remember that wad of money we got at our wedding reception?'

'Two thousand pounds from Bill?'

'That's right...except that his name's not Bill; it's Steve. His name's Steve.'

'Is that it?' she asked sounding disappointed.

'If only...' She paused and took a deep breath but Mattie cut in before she could explain.

'You're not going to tell me he's a bank robber?'

'No Mattie; it's worse. I'm going to tell you he's my dad!' She burst into tears and Mattie jumped up to comfort her. 'Steph, don't be silly. Your dad was killed before you were born. Your mum's a widow. She told me everything, how he was bombed in the Korean War. She received a telegram from the War Office. She gets a War Widow's Pension. Where's all this nonsense coming from?'

'It's true Mattie. Meredith can confirm it's true. I have evidence; I showed it to her but the thing is, I can't tell Mum and it's a terrible secret to keep.'

'Are you absolutely certain he's your dad?'

'There's no doubt about it. He left a letter for me at the veteran's club in identical handwriting to that on a photo Mum used to have on the dresser.'

'And did he say he was your dad in the letter?'

'No, but he intimated as much. He wrote that he thought I'd work out who'd sent the money.'

'That's a terrible secret to have to keep Steph. Do you think you'll ever find him again?'

'I hope so but there's little chance of it. It hurts so much when I think of him waiting in a taxi outside the church to catch a glimpse of me, when instead he ought to have been by my side giving me away. Meredith believes, and so do I, that he changed his identity following the incident owing to his horrific injuries as he didn't want to be a burden on Mum.'

'If that's right, it was a self-sacrificing act to give up the ones he loved. He was obviously a kind and thoughtful man and was there for you on your wedding day with a generous gift. I'll make a pot of tea. I'm being very inhospitable today. I'm sorry.'

Paul had fallen asleep in Steph's arms. She placed him in his pram and followed Mattie through to the kitchen. 'It's a beautiful house this. I see something different every time I come round. Maybe someday Seth and I will have a bigger house. Did he tell you he might be up for promotion?'

'No, not a word. Perhaps he's waiting till he gets it. I hope he does. He's very conscientious.'

She laughed. 'He has a different speaking voice at work you know. He's so *posh*! He doesn't use bad grammar there like he does at home. Call him at the Library one day. Just crack on you're a customer.'

'I'll do that,' she smirked. 'Our Seth with a posh speaking voice! Jack would give him a right ribbing for that. Was that the door? I think they're back.'

Mark lumbered his way into the kitchen. Panting for breath he gasped, 'I'm gagging for a drink.'

'You want whisky, so early in the day?'

'No, a gallon of water. I'm bloody knackered.'

'Me too,' Akina piped up behind him.

Mattie cast a brief disapproving glance at Mark.

'Sorry Mattie and to you too Akina. I ought not to have said that. I didn't know you were there.'

'Was it naughty?'

'Very naughty, so try to forget it please.'

'Okay! I'll try.' She ran over to the kitchen door. '*Adam*, if you heard Dad say he was bloody knackered, you have to forget it because it's naughty.'

Steph was in stitches. 'I have all this to come!'

'Believe me; you don't know the half of it!' She carried the tea into the living room and placing the tray on the table asked, 'Who'd like a slice of cake? Akina and I baked this earlier.'

Winking at Mattie, Steph remarked, 'Wow! Look at the cherries, how nicely they're arranged on top. You're so clever Mattie.'

'*I* did those,' Akina cried proudly.

Mark sat down beside Adam. 'Did you enjoy that kick-about Son?'

'It was great Dad. Can we do it again sometime?'

He smiled. 'Yes, and we're going to start doing a lot of things together...like a proper family.'

Mrs. Jennings was waiting near the school door for Adam to arrive the next day. His Headmaster was there too as Mark escorted Akina and Adam inside.

'I was so happy when Mrs. Wyndham called me to say Adam was safe,' she told Mark. 'I can't even begin to imagine your relief and I couldn't believe it was Travis's father who'd committed that terrible deed. Mr. Hargreaves always came across as a kind and caring man.'

'He's obviously a desperate man but maybe now he'll get the help and support he needs. I must dash. I have a busy day today. Adam insisted on coming in today and outwardly he seems fine. You have my number if you need me for anything. Thanks again for your kind help on Friday and I'm sorry if I came across as rude or ungrateful.'

'You didn't...not at all. Come along children.'

'Wait inside for me after school,' Mark told them.

Meredith was eager to learn if Adam had recovered from his ordeal the moment Mattie appeared.

'He didn't regard it as an ordeal,' she told her and described what had transpired. 'It turned out to be a hell of a weekend. The phone never stopped ringing and people were turning up at the house every few minutes. I hope things are better next weekend.'

'Why? What's happening next weekend?'

'Nothing much! A close friend's getting married.'

Meredith screeched with laughter. 'Do you know, I'd completely forgotten about that!'

'Is everything finalised now?'

'Pretty well. Are you sure you'll be okay on your own here for two weeks when we go away?'

'To quote that very close friend of mine, no one's indispensable. I won't do any of your cases though as you didn't bother to do mine when I was away.'

'Huh! That's a joke! Nobody's allowed to touch any of your files, Miss Efficiency.'

She smiled. 'Ah yes, but I had a brilliant teacher, *you*, whereas you didn't. By the way, Steph told me all about her dad yesterday.'

'That does surprise me, not that I'm suggesting in any way that you'd repeat it to her mum.'

'Point proven M'Lud,' she remarked on a laugh.

'Why, what do you mean?'

'Client confidentiality Meredith. You've betrayed a trust. I just set a trap; you walked right into it! I'd never have done that. I'm far too smart.'

'For a start she wasn't a client and what's said in this office stays in this office,' she snarled irritably.

'It was still a secret though.'

'Shut up!' she laughed. 'You are smart though. I could never entrust this place to anyone else. We're a good team. I was speaking to our accountant early this morning who says we can pay ourselves a hefty bonus, which means you might not need the blood money after all for this year's school fees.'

'Nice one. Did he say how much?'

'At least a couple of grand each.'

'Mmm! That'll do nicely.'

It was Tuesday before Mark heard from DI Hurst. Arrangements had been made for Josh Hargreaves to undergo psychiatric evaluation, coincidentally by a colleague of Mark's, though as Mark explained to Mattie, he wouldn't be privy to any findings. That however didn't prevent him from talking to his colleague prior to the referral to acquaint him with particulars of the abduction, at the same time advising he believed the man was in need of urgent counsel before he turned to self harm or something worse.

There was no further police contact that week.

6

Saturday turned out to be a warm and pleasant day for Meredith and Andrew's wedding.

It was an intimate civil ceremony and afterwards the fifteen guests were taken to a small private hotel in the country for the wedding breakfast.

Sadly, Meredith's mother had passed away a few years earlier following a short illness and it was the first time Mattie had met her father, best described as a young-at-heart, sprightly, sixty-year-old with a wicked sense of humour and a new-found joie-de-vivre. Meredith was astounded to overhear him tell Andrew he wouldn't mind five minutes alone with their shapely and pretty young waitress whose skirt barely covered her knickers.

'*Dad!*' she cried, looking round to see if anyone else had overheard. 'Just behave!'

She was soon to regret her critical intervention as he looked her in the eye. 'Don't for a moment think Andrew's the only man here with lead in his pencil. There's life in the old dog yet.'

Everyone shrieked with laughter except Meredith whose face was crimson with embarrassment.

Mattie prodded her and smirked. 'You can choose your friends but you can't choose your relatives, as I discovered to my cost at *my* wedding.'

Their laughter subsided but not for long, for when the young waitress returned to clear away, Jim was the cause of further humiliation to Meredith when, with a sigh, he stated, 'You're a bonny lass. I wish I were cross-eyed so I'd have two of you to look at.'

The waitress giggled and hurried away.

Astounded, Meredith whispered, 'I can't believe I'm hearing this Mattie. Dad's usually so quiet and I can't begin to imagine what Andrew's boys must be thinking when a man of his age behaves in such a way. Dad's Alex and Ben's granddad now we're married.'

'I wouldn't worry. Look at them; I'd say they're quite enjoying it and waiting for his next quip.'

'Well, I for one am dreading Dad's speech. How much has he had to drink?'

She shook her head. 'I haven't a clue.'

Their dialogue was interrupted by Jim who arose and tapped on his glass. 'Your attention please.'

A cold shiver ran down Meredith's spine and she glanced at Andrew nervously.

'Ladies and gentlemen, boys and girls. My being here today is a great pleasure. I only wish Margaret, Meredith's mother could have been here too for she would have been proud to see our daughter looking so lovely and so happy...correction...she *was* happy until I stood up to speak but I won't embarrass you darling, so don't worry. I'd like to start by welcoming Andrew, Alex and Ben to our family. Marriage is like starting a new job. You find yourself in unfamiliar territory, unsure of what to do and it can be quite a lengthy learning process. You'll make mistakes along the way so learn from them. Never forget Andrew, you'll be under constant scrutiny, your every move closely monitored so beware and don't for one moment think that turning up with a bunch of flowers will be seen as a romantic gesture. That, my friend, will be seen as an admission of guilt, so save your money and confess. Meredith will get it out of you anyway. She's a woman; they always do, so being up-front at the outset is the easier option. Take it from one with experience who knows.'

There was a titter of accord from the females.

'Marriage is about sharing, sharing the bad times as well as the good and always being around to love and support each other. Always remember that and your life together will be as equally happy as mine has been. On a less serious note, I believe the father of the Bride is expected to make the odd humorous comment and there are a couple of things I'd like to mention, not just to Andrew and Meredith but also to any other married couples present today. To the ladies I say this; rather than nag your husband to do little jobs around the house, tell him you're getting someone in because you believe he's too old to do them. Believe me, it works every time. To the men I offer food for thought. Were it not for our wives, reminding us by act and deed, we men would blissfully sail through life believing we were perfect.'

Jim's dry remarks were answered by a shrill burst of laughter.

'Finally, I'd like you all to stand and join me in a toast to the Bride and Groom. May you enjoy true happiness and long life, Meredith and Andrew.'

'Meredith and Andrew,' they repeated.

'Thanks Dad,' Meredith said with a sigh of relief.

When it was time to leave, Mattie gave Meredith a hug, 'Everything's been lovely and it was great to meet your dad. He's such a character.'

'Yes, *I've* had an eye opener too!' she concurred.

Mattie and Mark settled down with a cup of coffee after the children had gone to bed. 'It was a brilliant wedding,' Mattie remarked. 'I love weddings but I suppose that's a girl thing. Andrew's such a warm-hearted guy. I wonder if they'll want a family.'

He looked surprised. 'A *baby* you mean?'

'Yes Mark...a baby. What else could I mean?'

'She's a bit long in the tooth for motherhood,' he snorted. 'She must be forty if she's a day.'

'Actually, she's still in her thirties like you and I don't consider *you* too old for fatherhood.'

'Well no, in the clinical sense I'm not but...'

'*But*,' she interrupted. 'There's always a *but* every time I raise the issue. What's wrong with you? Are you saying you don't want us to have children?'

'My God!' he hooted. 'We're in the *plural* now!'

'Well? Answer the question please.'

He inhaled deeply. 'No Mattie, I *don't* and I wish you'd drop the subject.'

What Mattie said next had not been pre-planned and she was as shocked as Mark as the words tumbled from her lips. 'Then I suppose I'd better phone Dr. McAndrew and arrange a termination because I'm pregnant Mark.'

She hadn't meant to give him the news in such a

callous manner. She had hoped a fitting opportunity would present itself for such a revelation when they were enjoying a quiet moment but it was too late to retract her retort now; the words had been spoken.

Mark had never looked at her that way before, nor had she seen him so angry. '*Do that!*' he bellowed. '*Do it whilst there's still time!*'

Without a further word he grabbed his jacket and car keys, rushed out and slammed the door behind him, leaving Mattie totally mystified by his actions.

'Mark! This is an unexpected pleasure,' Chris said as he opened the door. 'Are you on your own?'

'Yes, Mattie's at home with the kids.'

'Come on in. Give me your coat. Whisky is it?'

'Mmm, sounds like a good idea.' He collapsed on the settee, staring into space, his bizarre demeanour instantly recognisable by Chris who decided against pressing for an explanation.

'Didn't you go to a wedding today?'

'Yes, Mattie's partner, Meredith. There wasn't an evening reception so it ended an hour or so ago.'

'Right...' he murmured, not quite knowing what to talk about next. 'Was it nice?'

'What?'

'The wedding. Was it a good do?'

He nodded and said distantly, 'Yes, it was okay.'

'Good!' There was a further pregnant pause. 'For God's sake Mark, tell me what's going on. You're obviously not here for a social call. You look awful. Is it something you want to talk about?'

'No, not really.'

He took that as meaning it was, otherwise Mark wouldn't have turned up on his doorstep. 'Have you had a barney...you and Mattie?'

'You could put it like that. Mattie's gone and got herself pregnant hasn't she?'

With an inner smirk, though with a straight face he asked, 'Artificial insemination?'

Mark glared at him. 'No of course not.'

'Then it's *you* who got her pregnant. It takes two to tango Mark. So tell me, why is her having a baby such a bad thing? She's a young woman; it's only natural she'd want children. Surely you knew that when you married her? It's blatantly obvious *she's* pleased or we wouldn't be having this conversation. What's the problem?'

'*What's the problem*?' he repeated. 'The bloody problem is I don't want her to have it.'

Chris was stunned. 'But why? It can't be a financial issue. You're young enough so I don't see what all the fuss is about. Do I assume you didn't discuss this before you were married?'

'Not in so many words.'

Chris shook his head in disbelief. 'You either did or you didn't. It's not a trick question Mark.'

'Alright we didn't! I wrongly assumed as she had Akina and I had Adam she'd be satisfied with that.'

'Hang on. Akina's adopted and Adam is *your* son. It's reasonable she'd want one of her own with you. You were wrong not to have discussed it with her.'

He shrugged. 'Well, she's having a termination so that puts paid to it so let's talk about something that isn't as contentious.'

132

'No, let's *not* Mark. You have to live with your-self when you've killed an innocent child.'

Mark stood up. 'Thanks for the drink. I can see no point in wasting more of my time here. I'd hoped to find *you* a little more supportive.'

'You wanted my blessing?' Chris scoffed. 'I'm a Catholic so you've come to the wrong person. Give it careful thought. You could lose Mattie over this and I'm certain you wouldn't want that. I'm sorry I can't be of more help mate. No hard feelings?'

'None. I won't be changing my mind though and take it from me, I intend making that perfectly clear the minute I'm home.'

There was no sign of Mattie when Mark arrived home. The living-room lamps were turned off and when he poked his head round the kitchen door, the table had been set ready for breakfast. Seeing that, he deduced she had gone up to bed.

He sat for a while with his thoughts before lock-ing up and going upstairs where he was astonished to find an empty bed.

After checking on the children he opened the door to the spare room where, through the darkness, he made out a figure. Mattie sat up as he turned on the light. 'What's this Mattie? Why are you in here?'

Curtly she snarled, 'I'm trying to get some sleep.'

'I see. Is this how it's going to be from now on?'

'You tell me Mark. I've been thinking about what Meredith's dad said about marriage and sharing and I tried to make a list of what *we* actually share but having come up with zilch, it started me thinking. I work full-time in a challenging job; I drop off and

133

collect the children more than you do; I come home and make the tea; I do the washing, the ironing and clean the house and although I'm loath to mention it, I entertain Adam since you seem to have neither the time nor patience to do *anything* with him...'

'You listen to...'

'*I haven't finished yet!* You asked the question so permit me to answer, then you can say your piece. It struck me that instead of getting married, you'd have saved a fortune by employing a housekeeper. There are plenty of brothels around for your sexual gratification with a host of girls regularly tested for sexually transmitted diseases. For added protection, you could also take precautions rather than leaving the initiative to your partner. That appears to satisfy all your needs, so the question I ask myself is why must *I* be expected to fill those needs? Your mother never went out to work, whereas I do. I work very hard. *We* are a different generation, not that you've noticed. Adam mentioned how you drop him off at the stables when he goes for his lesson and show no interest in his progress; you don't even walk part of the course. Instead, you sit in the car reading medical journals until he returns. I'm not at all surprised he didn't attempt to escape from Josh Hargreaves. He was doubtless glad of all the attention. It's not enough just to pay for a first-class education Mark. You're his *dad* for heaven's sake.'

He was astounded by her outburst. 'You hate me, don't you?' he said quietly, searching her eyes.

Mattie shook her head. 'No, I love you. I love you very much but I feel used, deceived and very hurt.'

'I love you too. I know I'm a useless dad; in fact I admitted the same to Adam last week and promised I'd change. He told me about all the activities Josh Hargreaves used to enjoy with his son and I felt as guilty as hell. For the seven years following Sarah's death I was full of self-pity and anger, when instead I should have got off my idle arse and been a proper father to Adam. Sadly, I can't change the past but I want to make amends by being a good husband and father in the future. I am *so* sorry for my behaviour and for yelling at you and I don't want you to have a termination. If that's what you really want Mattie, our baby, then believe me, please; I want that too.'

'My criticism's not about our baby. It's about you omitting to mention you didn't like children. Don't forget I brought Akina into this marriage, a young innocent child. You should have told me. That was very wrong of you. You certainly had me fooled.'

'I don't understand where you're coming from. I adore kids. I love Adam, I love Akina and when our baby's born I'll love him or her all the more Mattie because that baby will be *ours*.'

'Then *I* don't understand *you* Mark. Why kick off about my pregnancy if you like children so much?'

'Because I'm *terrified*, *terrified* of losing you like I lost Sarah. Childbirth was the cause of her death. She suffered a depressive illness soon after Adam's birth and took her own life. You know that.'

'For God's sake Mark! The odds against the same thing happening to me must be at least a million to one. Be honest with me; is that the only reason why you didn't want us to have children?'

'Of course it is. I can't believe you didn't realise. I don't want to lose you too. Life wouldn't be worth living without you.' He held her in his arms. 'Come to bed with me, please. Don't stay here. I want you beside me because I need to hold you and from now on, I'll make a determined effort to do better. I *have* taken you for granted. I see that now but I won't do so again. You have my word.'

Mattie heard the sincerity in his voice and saw the tears glistening in his eyes. More than anything she wanted their marriage to work and was prepared to do everything in her power to help Mark adhere to his promises.

The next morning Mattie awoke to the rattling of crockery as Mark placed a tray by her bed. 'Breakfast in bed, Mattie Wyndham!' he said. 'I'm afraid I won't be able to do it during the week when I'm at work though.' He leaned towards her and kissed her tenderly.

'That's lovely Mark. Thank you...oh and you've picked me a rose too.'

'I got up early. How did you sleep?'

'Very well. Did you?'

'If I'm honest, not too well. I did a lot of thinking though. Now that the kids are on holiday, I thought we might have a break somewhere for a day or two. We had such an amazing time in Florida.'

'I don't want to fly Mark, not in the early stages of pregnancy but a few days away would be lovely when Meredith gets back. It'll still be August so we should get some decent weather. Nothing too active mind you.'

136

He cleared his throat. 'Don't laugh but I'm going horse riding with the kids this morning. Akina still hasn't had her first lesson and it's about time yours truly started acting like a father. If you like, you can tag along and watch if you've the time to spare.'

She laughed. 'I've loads of time to spare now you are sharing the chores.'

'Good, it's sorted then. After the lesson, we'll nip back, have a quick shower and get changed. We're going out for lunch. It's Sunday and from now on, that's our family day when I'm not on call. We're leaving here at ten-thirty so get your breakfast!'

Akina was very excited when Mark told her and Adam was equally thrilled to have a riding partner. Mark had made no mention that he was to ride too in case he changed his mind at the last minute and Mattie had been sworn to secrecy. From childhood he had been afraid of horses when one had broken loose in a circus ring. It had galloped into the crowd close to where they were sitting and several people had been taken to hospital. For a young child, that had been a terrifying experience.

Mark weighed up the horse from top to toe whilst Akina and Adam chuckled at his fearful expression. 'Is there one a bit smaller?' he asked optimistically.

'Aye, we've plenty smaller,' the stable-hand told him. 'Way too small for you though. Yer feet'd be draggin' on t'ground.'

That would have suited Mark just fine but to save face he nodded his head. 'I don't have a riding hat,' he made known, hoping that might be a get-out.

''ang on. I'll fetch one. 'aven't yer ridden afore?'

'No, this is my first attempt,' he said nervously.

He returned with a hat. 'Try that. I reckon that'll do yer. I'll give yer a leg up and don't go gallopin' off cos there'll be a lass wi' yer,' he told him on a guttural laugh. 'She'll learn yer what to do.'

Galloping off was the last thing on Mark's mind. He was praying his horse was too big to gallop. He was terrified and when his horse took one tiny step he yelled, '*Stop!*' much to the amusement of Akina and Adam.

Akina could hardly wait to move off.

'Do you fancy a race Dad?' Adam queried with a mischievous grin.

'No and keep right away from my horse. I don't want you encouraging it to start running.'

The young girl ran through the basics before they made a move and after Mark's horse had walked a yard or two he felt rather more at ease but found the whole experience disagreeable. He couldn't believe anyone could ride a horse for pleasure.

Akina enjoyed it thoroughly and rode at the front with Adam. For Mark it was the worst experience of his life and he heaved a sighed of relief when his lesson was over. After dismounting, every bone in his body ached and he could barely sit down in the car to drive home. 'It feels like someone's shoved a brick up my...'

'*Alright* Mark,' Mattie cut in and Akina giggled. 'Was that another naughty word you were going to say Dad? My bum hurts too but it was great. When are we coming again?'

'*Never* will be too soon for me Akina. I think, in

fact I'm sure I'll be giving lessons a miss in future. You can ride with Adam and I'll walk round. Why don't we all join a knitting club instead?'

'You're a wimp,' Adam scoffed. 'You'd get used to it in time.'

'I'll take your word for that, Son. I like both feet firmly on the ground. Look sharp as soon as we get home, by the way. We're all going out to lunch.'

'Great Dad,' Adam shrieked. 'Where to?'

'You'll have to wait and see but there *might* be a playground.'

The reasonably priced pub-restaurant on the edge of town catered for families, with a separate extensive children's menu and their recreational facilities were wide-ranging.

'We'll definitely come again,' Mark stated. 'I've enjoyed it today. I've been such a fool and because of that I've missed out on so much.'

'Life's a learning process Mark. We all get things wrong from time to time. The thing is you've put it right. By the way, how's the butt?' she laughed.

'Killing me,' he whispered. 'It was a horrendous ordeal but I found the mental torture worse. There's a medical condition called *hippophobia*. It means a fear of horses and I'm convinced I suffer from it. I was terrified when it was standing still but that was nothing compared to how I felt when it moved. I'll still take them riding and I'll walk round, keeping my distance but I'm definitely not riding again. I'm thinking of taking them swimming. They enjoyed it in Florida and so did I.'

'Good idea. I might come too before I get too big

and ugly. I used to swim quite a bit at University. It helped me unwind.'

He stroked the nape of her neck. 'You might gain a little weight but you'll still be my beautiful wife. Yes, do come with us. Gentle exercise is supposed to be good for pregnant women.'

Later they curled up together on the sofa when the children were in bed. 'Are you sure about the baby now Mark?' she asked as he stroked her hair gently.

He kissed the top of her head. 'Yes, I'm delighted and I can't stop thinking about it. We're going to be alright aren't we?'

'Yes, I'm sure we are. I'm sorry for the things I said yesterday. I was angry but that doesn't excuse my behaviour. I said some hateful things.'

'Nothing I didn't deserve. I said my share of hateful things too. When I stormed out of here I went to see Chris.' When she raised her eyebrows he added, 'Well, I had to talk to someone!'

'I see. The Old Boys' Club.'

He grinned. 'That's what *I* thought but I left with my tail between my legs. He took your side so I left after a few minutes.'

'You didn't have an argument did you?'

'Don't worry. We simply agreed to disagree. So, I was wondering...how do you fancy an early night?'

'Why, what did you have in mind?'

He smiled. 'I wouldn't say *no* to a bit of that sexual gratification you politely mentioned last night.'

She laughed. 'Er...hang on. Aren't you forgetting something...your painful butt?'

'You just let me worry about that.'

140

The following day Mark made enquiries with their usual Travel Agency about short-break holidays in England. There wasn't an exceptional choice at that late stage but the ones remaining had been significantly reduced. Mattie was happy to go along with Mark's preference and was thrilled when he called to say he'd made the reservation for a five-day stay in Devon at a hotel overlooking the sea, within only a few miles of where she had lived with Sam.

'That sounds amazing,' she said when he read out the details. 'I know *someone* who'll be very pleased about that. I never even thought about Devon when we discussed it. Great choice Mark.'

'I get some things right then?' he questioned.

'Occasionally,' she replied whimsically.

He laughed. 'So how's work going on your own?'

'Huh! Don't even ask. I'll kill Meredith when she gets back. I'm sure she told everyone to ring today. All I've done is answer the phone.'

'Are you in court this week?'

'Yes, tomorrow and Thursday.'

'How about I collect the kids from Emily's then? I'll start on the tea and you can get an extra hour or so in whilst it's quiet.'

'You're an angel! Have I ever told you?'

'Er...no. That wasn't quite the way you put it. I'm pretty sure *devil* might have been on the tip of your tongue in the not too distant past but I take consolation from the fact many a wife would have thrown her husband out for less.'

'It crossed my mind but then I remembered it was *your* house so I had to reconsider my options.'

141

'I don't know what I did to deserve you darling. I love you so much. Whilst we're in Devon, I'd like to take you back to that nice restaurant. You know the one I mean...The Thatched House. That was the first night we ever spent together. Remember?'

Softly she murmured, 'Of course I remember. I'll never forget our first time. It was amazing.'

'Devon? We're going to *Devon?'* Akina screeched, her cheeks aglow with elation. 'Can we go back to see our house Dad?'

'We'll probably drive by and take a peek. Don't forget, other people are living there now. We can't encroach on their privacy.'

'Now that I know how to swim, we can go in the sea, Adam. Mummy would never let me before.'

'You might prefer the hotel pool when you see it. I'll certainly be trying that out and so will Mattie.'

'Will we have our own room again Dad?'

'I don't know yet. Hopefully,' he said, glancing at Mattie and winking.

'You winked at Mattie. Is it another honeymoon?'

'Mmm, I'm hoping so,' he told her, taking hold of Mattie's hand.

She moved her hand away speedily before further questions could be asked. 'You're worse than those pertinacious double-glazing salesmen Akina. Every answer gives rise to another question. We won't be going for another two weeks so please, try to quell your exuberance in the interim.'

Mark howled with laughter at her reply. 'I didn't understand a word of that. Did that mean *shut up?*'

She joined in the laughter. 'Something like that.'

Indignantly she stormed upstairs. 'I'll go and tell my puppet all about it then. He'll listen to me. Are you coming up Adam?'

'In a minute. I want a word with Dad first.'

'What's on your mind Son? Come on, spit it out,' he coaxed, conscious of Adam's reticence.

'I wondered if you'd heard any more about Josh.'

'Not since Monday of last week Son. I assume the assessment is still ongoing. It takes time but I don't think there's anything to be worried about. The last I heard, he was going to a clinic. The police haven't brought any charges as far as I'm aware but I'll tell you if or when I hear anything more.'

'Thanks Dad.' He went upstairs to join Akina.

'Are you pleased we're having a break Mattie?'

'Yes and will I be ready for it when Meredith gets back. By the way, will you stop all that innuendo in front of the children? I'm already dreading Akina's probing questions once she knows we're having a baby. She prattles on relentlessly and I don't doubt Adam will be ear-wigging when she asks.'

'It's simple enough to explain to a seven-year-old girl. Just tell her the baby grows from an egg like a chicken. Just don't mention the cock,' he guffawed.

'Why don't *you* tell *both* of them!' she snapped. 'You're supposed to be the medical man. I bet you haven't told Adam yet and he's a year older.'

'No, I haven't. Why don't we tell them together?'

'Get lost! No way am I saying *anything* with you there; I'd be too self-conscious and tongue-tied.'

'That'd be a first,' he howled.

The modern hotel exceeded all their expectations. Built on the edge of a cliff, it boasted uninterrupted sea views as far as the eye could see.

'It's fabulous Mark,' Mattie commented, wandering around the spacious reception area with the two children close at heel.

'Can we see our rooms now?' Akina asked impatiently. 'I hope we have enormous beds again, like the ones we had in Florida.'

'I think you'll find they're smaller here, like those we have at home but I'm sure it'll be a nice room.'

They went to the children's room first, a delightful room with matching three-quarter beds.

'Bags it; the one under the window!' Akina cried, throwing herself on the bed.

'You can have it as it'll be cold over there,' Adam snarled. 'I don't want it!'

'Pack it in, both of you,' Mark told them sternly. 'You two always find something to squabble about. Heaven only knows what it'll be like when we have three, Mattie.'

Akina's ears pricked up instantly. 'Three? Three what? What do you mean Dad?'

'Nice one Mark!' Mattie snorted. 'If you have the key handy, I'll just slip next door. As the question was addressed to you, I'll leave you to answer it, as well as all the others that will undoubtedly arise.'

It was a sheepish Mark who appeared in the room some fifteen minutes later. 'Am I in the dog-house again?'

'Not at all. Actually, you did me a huge favour so thanks. Did they buy your chicken story?'

There was a guttural chuckle. 'Alright, there's no need to rub it in. It was simply a slip of the tongue.'

'Seemingly it's a bad habit of yours. Your mother told me you weren't fit to know anything. So, how did it go?' she questioned light-heartedly.

'Er, okay.'

'Liar,' she laughed.

'Alright...I made a complete hash of it. I thought I was doing okay until Akina began firing questions at me but I think I might have redeemed myself in your eyes by telling them it was a secret for now.'

'Like *I* told *you* and how long did that last? Truly, it doesn't matter. At least now it gives them time to get used to it. I was merely deferring the inevitable out of cowardice. By the way, I love the room. I've never seen a four-poster bed before except in glossy magazines. Thank you for that Mark. It's fantastic.'

'Nothing's too good for my wife. I wanted everything to be perfect for our new start. Pity about my big mouth. Not the best of starts.'

'It's forgotten.' She clasped her arms around his neck. 'It feels nice to be back in Devon. I have such fond memories of Sam.'

'Me too,' he murmured.

In the adjoining room, the children were involved in deep discussion about the new baby when Mattie went in to check on them. She was taken aback to hear Akina say, '*You* can't have babies cos you're a boy. Dad said you don't have things girls have.'

'Well, I have a thing *you* don't have,' Adam told her to which she replied, 'Go on then; show me!'

Mattie's heart missed a beat as Adam jumped up

and moved towards her. 'Look at that! That's called Adam's apple,' he boasted haughtily. 'It's there on my neck, and *you* haven't got one of *them*.'

Unimpressed she said, 'So what? I've got Akina's eggs!'

Mattie stifled a giggle. 'Come on you two. We're going out for something to eat.'

Mark laughed heartily at the revelation later that evening. 'Parenting is such a challenge,' he sighed. 'You never know what kids will say next.'

'Husbands too!' she reminded him.

The short break in Devon proved most enjoyable and the weather was kind too. The last full day was spent in Torquay where Mark took the children to the beach whilst Mattie wandered round the shops to find a present for Adam's birthday in three days' time. Mark was keen for Mattie to check out fishing tackle, knowing that would be a welcome gift and there was no better place to enquire.

Taking advice from the proprietor, an avid angler, she chose two sets, paid for them and told him her husband would return later to collect them.

'Don't forget Dad; you promised you'd drive past our house,' Akina told him. 'I want to see if it looks any different.'

It was less than a fifteen minute drive and when Mark slowed down by the gate, Akina's eyes filled with tears as poignant memories were recalled.

'Can we go in, please Mattie?' she begged.

'No darling; other people live there now.'

Persistent as ever she cried out, 'Look! That's the little girl, Annabelle, who came with her mummy to

146

look at the house.' Before Mattie could stop her she opened the door and ran to her, calling her name.

Mattie jumped out and followed her as the child's mother appeared in view.

'I'm so sorry,' Mattie said. 'You probably won't remember but we lived here before you moved in. I'm afraid Akina became rather emotional to see the house she grew up in.'

'It's Mrs. Peters, isn't it? I'm Anne Saunders.'

'That was Akina's surname and her grandparents' too. My name's Mattie Wyndham and my husband Mark and I adopted Akina recently. We came down from the north where we live now for a few days' break and Akina wanted to drive past the house.'

'That's understandable Akina,' she said, smiling sympathetically. 'Actually, I'm delighted to see you because we were making room in the garage loft a few weeks ago and came across a box of papers in a corner. It's probably rubbish but we didn't want to throw it out in case you came back for it. We didn't spot it at first and it was and still is covered in cobwebs as if it's been there for ages. I'll ask Ben, my husband to get it down for you. There was no way of contacting you. Our solicitor had no forwarding address for Mrs. Peters.'

'I don't want to put you to any trouble.'

'It's no trouble whatsoever. Why not come inside and have a cup of tea whilst you're waiting. It looks as if the girls have already gone in. You fetch your husband in and I'll put the kettle on.'

'Thank you. I'll ask Mark to give your husband a hand in the garage.'

Whilst the men were dusting off the cobwebs and removing the dead spiders from the box, the women chatted about the changes made to the house.

'You've done a lovely job Mrs. Saunders,' Mattie told her. 'I hardly recognise the place anymore.'

'The name's Anne. Thank you. We love it here. I especially like the sea air having been brought up in the city. Have a look upstairs. We've made quite a few interesting changes since we bought one of the apartments that came on the market soon after you left. This is Dominic's bedroom. He's eleven and in common with most boys of his age, he likes his independence. He also makes a lot of noise,' she told her with grimace. 'He plays loud music.'

'It's great,' Mattie said, wandering through what could best be described as a self-contained flat. 'He certainly is a lucky boy to have a pad like this.'

Akina and Annabelle were playing a game when they entered Annabelle's room.

'Don't say we're leaving already,' Akina moaned. 'We're only half way through this game.'

'Five more minutes and then we are. We're going out for a meal later and I have to pack yet.'

'Annabelle's got a brother Mattie,' Akina said.

'I know. Have you just two?' Mattie asked Anne.

Mark, Ben and Adam appeared in time to hear the tale end of their conversation.

'Yes, just the two,' she sighed. 'We'd have liked another but it hasn't happened yet.'

'We're having another baby soon aren't we Dad?' Akina piped up in earshot of everyone. Realising by the black look on Mark's face that she'd spoken out of turn, she bowed her head. 'Sorry! You told me it was a secret. Didn't you know Mattie?'

Mattie and Anne exchanged smiling glances. 'Of course I knew Akina and so will everyone else very soon, thanks to you.'

'Well, I'm really excited so it's very hard to keep a secret if you're excited,' she stated in her defence. 'Dad told me and Adam all about it, how it grows from an egg like a chicken and when it's ready, you lay it like a chicken lays an egg and...'

Anne and Ben were hysterical.

'I don't think I said that Akina,' Mark interjected with a red-faced sideways glance at Mattie.

'No, the teacher at school told us that bit. She said when Mary had Jesus, she laid *him* in a manger.'

The adults' loud laughter reverberated around the house. 'How about we have that cup of tea?' Anne chuckled. 'You can always rely on your children to embarrass you when least expected. I think that was very brave of you Mark, taking on such a task. Ben would never volunteer to do so with our two. I even had to tell Dominic. Annabelle's only five so she's too young to understand yet.'

'Believe me, I didn't volunteer Anne,' Mark said. 'I was brow-beaten into it for opening my mouth!'

'I'm so pleased you called in today and if you're ever here again you must call and see us. So where are you going for your meal?'

'The Thatched House,' Mark told her. 'It's about six miles down the main road, on the right.'

'I know the place,' Ben said. 'I've passed it many a time. Is it alright?'

'Yes, it's lovely,' Mattie said. 'Mark and I went there on our very first date. That's why we thought we'd go back. You're welcome to join us, that's if your evening's free. We're eating at seven-thirty as we'd like a reasonably early night. Mark has a long drive home tomorrow.'

Anne looked at Ben for his approval. 'Why not?' he said. 'Dominic should be home shortly. Yes, I'd like that. I've often wondered what it was like. How about we see you there around seven-fifteen?'

'Suits me fine.' Mark said. 'I'll nip in and change the reservation from four to eight. I take it you'll be bringing the children?'

'If that's alright,' Anne remarked. 'You can meet Dominic. You'll get on well together Adam, though he's rather a chatterbox, unlike you.'

They laughed when he rejoined, 'I am too when it isn't all baby talk.'

'Right we're off,' Mark stated jumping up. 'Look forward to seeing you later. We'll be in the bar.'

'What a lovely family,' Mattie remarked as they made their way back to the hotel. 'I'm looking forward to tonight and it'll be nice for the children too. By the way,' she said quietly, 'don't forget to pick up the fishing tackle and hide it in the boot. It'll be interesting to see if you can keep schtum about that for the next couple of days.'

'Point taken Mattie. I can but try!'

'I don't mind Mark, honestly. I was telling Anne earlier where we met and how intimidated I felt by your immaculate appearance and position then, but as you were keen to tell me, deep down you're just a normal guy with the same concerns, emotions and weaknesses as any other guy and that's what I love about you. Besides I'm happy that Akina's excited. I'd hate her to feel her nose was being pushed out.'

'So I'm forgiven then?'

'There's nothing to forgive.'

As Mark turned into the restaurant car park, Anne was getting out of their car with the children.

Akina and Adam ran across to meet Dominic and by the time they'd taken their seats at the table, the four children were chattering happily together.

'I'm impressed,' said Anne. 'If the food's as good as the décor we'll have a great evening. I'm having lobster. What do you fancy Mattie?'

'I had the braised lamb last time and it was lovely so I'll try that again.'

'Can I have that please?' Adam asked.

'Certainly darling. Choose whatever you like. I'm sure you'd like the chicken Akina.'

'Okay, I'll have that then.'

'I've no doubt Mark will want steak,' Mattie said.

Anne smiled. 'Ben too. I think that's a *man* thing. They've no imagination when it comes to food.'

'I heard that!' Ben said.

'So what are you having then?'

'Er...steak,' he responded guiltily.

'I rest my case,' Anne chuckled.

'So tell me Anne, do you have a job or are you a busy housewife?'

'Both. I'm a free-lance interior designer but most of my work is for an exclusive property developer.

I design and furnish their show-homes. I do a lot for hotels too. It involves a bit of travelling but it pays well and I pick stuff up at discounted prices for my own use, bits and pieces I'd never pay such prices for in retail shops. It's one of the perks of the job.'

'You've certainly put your expertise to good use in your home. It's lovely, everywhere. I'm hopeless at anything like that. I'm not in the least creative or artistic although I did change a few pairs of curtains when I moved into Mark's house earlier in the year when we got married.'

'That explains a lot,' she commented. 'I've never before seen a man so attentive to his wife. He never takes his eyes off you. He seems a really nice guy and Adam's the absolute image of his father. He'll break more than a few hearts. Have you both been married before?'

'Mark has. Sadly, his first wife died not long after Adam was born. He's a hospital Consultant. That's how we met when he was treating my brother.' She laughed. 'I didn't even like him at first, or if I did, I didn't know it. He scared the hell out of me. He did nothing to hide his feelings but all I could see was a serious and well-dressed professional with whom I had nothing whatsoever in common. Thankfully, he was very persistent and as a result, here we are now happily married.'

'I met Ben on a building site...not very romantic. He's an engineer and was involved in the construction work. He invited me to lunch a couple of times on the pretext of discussing the project work, which we never did and eventually confessed that it was a

152

scam because he fancied me. I tried to act coy but secretly I was delighted because I felt the same way about him. Ben's been married before too but was divorced at the time we met. His first wife strayed because he was always at work, trying to build up his business. Still, that's her loss and my gain. Had she been a little more patient she would have had a good and caring husband. So, are you excited about your first baby?'

'Very. I can hardly wait but it's early days yet.'

'Do you have a job Mattie?'

'Yes, I'm a solicitor.'

'Oh my God...an academic! I was a numbskull at school. It was my own fault though. I'd sit doodling throughout all my lessons. I was always in trouble and couldn't wait to leave. I've done alright though. I enjoy my work and it helps pay the bills. Ben and I are fortunate as we both enjoy our work. Returning to something you said earlier, last year I hosted a television series, just a regional one, not national. I did a dozen episodes on home make-overs, simple tips and advice and nothing the average handy-man couldn't achieve. Is Mark a DIY enthusiast?'

'I wouldn't say enthusiast. He'll do things under sufferance but he's quite good, yes.'

'Then give me your address and I'll copy the four tapes and send them on. Each of the tapes has three programmes. Besides, I'd like us to keep in touch.'

'Me too. I've enjoyed our time together and your kind hospitality earlier. What's your opinion of the restaurant?'

'Brilliant. We'll definitely be coming again.'

It was quite emotional when they said goodbye as if they had been friends for years.

Mark shook Ben's hand vigorously. 'I've enjoyed our discussion. It's been a pleasure to meet you.'

'The pleasure's all mine,' he responded. 'I believe I heard the women making arrangements to keep in touch so who knows, we might meet again. I hope we do. Have a safe journey home.'

The four children said goodbye to each other and waved as they hurried to their respective cars.

Mattie sighed as they approached their hotel. 'It's our final night. These five days have slipped by far too quickly but I've enjoyed them so much. Tonight especially was an unexpected bonus. They're a nice couple and their two children are so well behaved.'

Turning to their children she smiled affectionately to see them curled up together and fast asleep. 'It's been great for the children too. It's nice to do things as a family isn't it?'

Mark smiled thoughtfully. 'Yes it is. I just hope I haven't left it too late to make amends.'

'You haven't,' she reassured him.

'I'll attend to the children tonight,' he said. 'You can go straight up and get ready for bed because it takes you ages.'

'Why, what's the rush?'

As he parked the car he leaned across and kissed her gently. 'That, Mrs. Wyndham is for me to know and you to find out,' and with an evocative wink of the eye murmured, 'I'll not be long.'

7

'Am I relieved to have you back!' Meredith said. 'I was praying you wouldn't decide to stay longer. It's been chaotic here and we've a load of new clients.' She threw her bag on her desk. 'What time did you come in today?'

'Seven o'clock! I felt a bit guilty leaving you with all the work when you'd just returned from honeymoon. Besides, I can shift a heap of stuff before the phone starts ringing.'

'How was the break?'

'Amazing, but we'll chat over lunch if you don't mind. I want to hear about the Rockies. I'm coming in tomorrow morning for an hour or so too.'

'*Saturday?*'

'I don't want to face this lot on Monday. Mark's on duty so the children can go to Emily's. She'll be glad to see them and I'll pick them up around ten-thirty. Incidentally, before Akina has chance to tell anyone else, I'm pregnant.'

'*Pregnant?*' she screeched with excitement. 'How did that happen?'

'What...you want a detailed résumé?' she smiled.

'*No!* I don't know what I meant. I'm *thrilled*.'

'Me too. Right, the rest you'll hear at lunchtime.'

'When's it due? Just tell me that.'

'No, I said lunchtime. Shut up now. I'm busy.'

Mark called her later to ask if she'd told Meredith their good news.

'Yes, first thing. She's delighted. She particularly enjoyed your chicken and egg anecdote.'

He laughed. 'I'll never live that down will I?'

'Not if I've anything to do with it.'

'You still love me though?'

'More than ever, just as I adore your entertaining idiosyncrasies.

'I had a word with Helen about my concerns and she told me not to worry. I feel reassured now. She was delighted for us too.'

'I'm sure she was. Have you talked to Chris yet?'

'I haven't seen him but I'll find him. I think he's keeping out of my way but I need to thank him for making me see sense.'

'We'd better tell the relatives tonight Mark. I've no doubt Emily will know already.'

He laughed apologetically. 'She overheard me tell Akina not to mention the new baby, so she does.'

She shook her head. 'You really are the limit.'

It was Adam's eighth birthday on the Sunday. As a special treat, Mark and Mattie arranged a party with a few of his school friends at the family restaurant they had visited a few times since Akina had joined him for horse riding lessons. He was pleased with his fishing tackle and more so to learn Mark would take him fishing mid-week after school. It was to be a father and son activity and Adam eagerly looked forward to his first experience.

The promised tapes from Anne arrived a few days later and Mattie could hardly wait to watch her new friend on television.

The makeovers were impressive for low financial outlay and Mattie was particularly enamoured by a stunning nursery. Mark, equally enthusiastic stated, 'I could do that with no trouble. It's just a question of having the right ideas. Anne's definitely good at what she does. She's so creative and imaginative.'

'Does that mean you *will,* in the spare room?'

'Of course it does, darling. I'll enjoy doing it for our baby.'

She threw both arms around him. 'I want everything to be perfect for our new baby. Thank you so much Mark. I'll help too.'

She hurried away to call Anne who was pleased the tapes were being put to good use.

'I might be doing a further series. Seemingly the first series was well-received,' she told Mattie.

'I'm not surprised. What I've seen so far is great. I've loads of ideas now for this place but we'll have to see how the nursery looks and more importantly how Mark's stamina holds up.'

'How is Mark?'

'He's fine in fact we all are. I've had no repetition of morning sickness with this one...' Although she paused mid-sentence, Anne picked up straight away on her inadvertent disclosure. 'I might as well come straight out with it. As a young teenager in care, my foster-father raped me and got me pregnant so I had a termination. It's not a subject I like to discuss, or even think about. Please don't tell Ben. Few people know about it and I prefer to keep it that way.'

Anne was horrified. 'I'm so sorry Mattie. I won't breathe a word to anyone. I take it Mark knows?'

'Yes, we don't have secrets. At the time we met I was twenty-four. He was caring and thoughtful and he taught me all men weren't alike. I'd never had a boyfriend previously because I was scared of men. I owe Mark such a lot. He brought me back from the brink of insanity and helped restore my confidence. He's one in a million and I'd do anything for him.'

'I don't know what to say Mattie. *Sorry* sounds so inadequate. I can't believe how such a terrible thing could happen to a child in care.'

'It still happens, occasionally, not so much in care nowadays but when vulnerable young children are left in the company of others. You'd be surprised to hear some of the things I hear in my line of work.'

'But you're okay now?'

'I'm better than okay. I'm fine. I watch Akina and Adam like a hawk though. That'll never change.'

'Yes and I'll be keeping an eye on my two from now on. By the way, there's a possibility I could be in Manchester in a couple of months so perhaps we could get together if it comes off. It's a city-centre development...apartments. I'll keep you posted. I'll be at a hotel in the city centre for a couple of days so a girly shopping day would be great if you're up to it. I'll know soon so I'll call you when I do.'

'Will Ben be coming too?'

'No, I'll be on my own. Besides, I don't want Ben to know how much I'm spending. Get real Mattie!'

She howled with laughter at Anne's wry humour.

'I'll keep my fingers crossed that I can still waddle about by then. Meanwhile, take care and be sure to convey our best wishes to Ben and the children.'

It was Saturday the twenty-second of October and Mattie's twenty-sixth birthday.

Mark, unknown to Mattie, had arranged a surprise birthday party at a local restaurant and had invited their closest friends and relatives. Akina and Adam had been told the four of them were going out for a family meal. Mark was determined this was a secret Akina would not reveal.

For the past three weeks, Mark had been working hard on the nursery, hoping it would be completed in time for Mattie's birthday and she was bursting with curiosity when he banned her from the room.

Earlier that day he had brought the box of papers down that had been sitting in the spare room since their trip to Devon. Searching through the variety of folders, Mattie found they were simply old records relating to the guest house that went back as far as the sixties.

She arranged the documents in two piles; the ones for destruction and the ones she should keep in case the Inland Revenue were to raise enquiries arising from the sale of the business. It was then she had a thought. What if there was some information in the earlier documents relating to the identity of Akina's father? Sam had mentioned that the young Japanese man had been a guest for a few weeks and they had become close friends. She smiled to re-call her glib quip to Sam, '*Exceptionally close.*'

Sadly, the visitor had returned to Japan, unaware of Sam's pregnancy and according to Sam's version of events, no arrangements had been made to keep in contact, for living at opposite ends of the globe, there was little point in prolonging the relationship.

Calculating back from Akina's date of birth, conception had to have taken place in July sixty-nine, Mattie deduced. That fell in the sixty-nine/seventy tax year. It took only moments to find the appropriate folder, sitting on top of the stack for destruction and Mattie swiftly retrieved it.

Fingering meticulously through scores of invoices she spotted one with what appeared to be the name *Yukio*. That certainly sounded like a Japanese name. Unfortunately there was no additional information other than the duration of the visit from the first to the thirtieth of July and the invoice was for twenty-nine nights' accommodation.

After making a complete search throughout June, July and August, she found nothing else. Although there were a couple of German names and three or four French names, there were no further Japanese names; the rest were English so Yukio had to be the one. Yukio had to be Akina's father...but what use was that knowledge in isolation? Was that his forename or surname and where in Japan did he live?

There were no answers to Mattie's questions. She folded the invoice and placed it in a drawer to show Mark later. After returning the recent documents to the box, she tied it up with string and placed it in an empty cupboard in the study, leaving Mark to burn the obsolete documents later.

Mark appeared later that afternoon, dripping with perspiration and worn out. He forced a weak smile. 'That's done I'm glad to say and don't dare say you don't like it. I'm knackered and I need a shower.'

'What were you banging?'

'I've just re-laid the carpet and it was really hard work. It's a big room. *That* was more stressful than a full day in theatre.'

She stood up and kissed him. 'I appreciate all the hard work. How long will it be before I can see it?'

'Everything's finished. You can see it now.'

'Really?' she screeched with excitement. 'You've finished *everything?*'

'Everything. It might need dusting but that's all.'

'Does it look nice?'

'Er...what do you mean...nice? It looks absolutely brilliant even though I say so myself. Come upstairs and I'll show you. I think you've been patient quite long enough.'

'I can't wait to furnish it now. It's just a pity that the cot we liked, the Spanish one, was so expensive but I'm sure there'll be others we'll like.'

'I expect so,' he said, gesturing with his hand for her to open the door. 'Happy Birthday darling.'

Nothing could have prepared her for the sight she beheld and for some time she remained speechless before bursting into tears. 'Oh Mark, it's beautiful; it is, it's absolutely beautiful.' There was too much to take in at first glance but the one thing that stood out was the cot. 'Mark, you got the Spanish cot!'

'And the bedding too. Nothing's too good for you or our baby, Mattie. How about the curtains then?'

'They're lovely and they match the wallpaper.'

'The wallpaper came with co-ordinating fabric so I had a quiet word with Emily. She's pretty nifty on a sewing machine. The hard part was getting everything here without you seeing it. I chose yellow and white because it's perfect for a boy or a girl.'

'This is much nicer than the one on Anne's tape. I love everything about it Mark. You're so clever.'

'Don't forget, Anne had to work to a tight budget. I can't take credit for everything though; I received a little help from the shop assistant as I didn't have a clue about which wallpaper to buy.'

Mattie wandered across the room to take a closer look at the unusual table lamp. 'You've thought of everything, haven't you? Had I been left to furnish the nursery, I'd have ended up with a hotchpotch of things that didn't match at all. I'm clueless at anything like this. I can't believe how fantastic it looks. Have the children seen how it's been progressing?'

'No but they'll be back from Emily's soon.'

'Thank you Mark. You've worked so hard. I love it. I'll enjoy spending time here with the baby.'

'Right, I'm having my shower. I must stink rotten after wrestling with that carpet! Don't forget, we're eating at seven-thirty.'

Mattie stayed behind in the nursery as Mark left, totally mesmerised by the transformation. It'd been the dreariest room in the house prior to his intervention and now it was the most beautiful. Stroking her visible bump, she spoke quietly to her baby. 'We're over half way there now. I love you very much and I'll make sure you have all the things I never had.'

There was a further birthday surprise when Mattie entered the restaurant to find her friends and family waiting to greet her but an even bigger surprise was the presence of Anne, Ben and their two children.

'I don't believe it,' she screeched, hurrying to hug them. 'When was all this planned?'

'Two or three weeks ago,' Anne laughed. 'Ben's driving back tomorrow with the children but I'll be here another three days. I got the Manchester job so I'm meeting them on Monday. That leaves Tuesday free for shopping. I've already spoken to Meredith who tells me there's nothing pressing for Tuesday. In fact she'd like to join us.'

'I'll have to rearrange two appointments I've got booked in for Tuesday,' Mattie said.

'Done! Mark called me when he knew Anne was coming so I've moved them to Thursday,' Meredith told her. 'It'll do no harm to close the office for one day. When we're in court nobody's there and if it's urgent, they'll leave a message.'

'You're a devious lot aren't you? You've let me down Akina. I thought you'd have let slip what was going on like you normally do.'

'I probably would if I'd known. Dad didn't say.'

Mark smirked. 'I wonder why?'

Mattie kissed him. 'Thank you darling. It's such a lovely surprise.' She wandered around the guests to welcome them and stopped to talk to Annabelle and Dominic who were pleased to see Akina and Adam again so soon after their previous meeting.

During the course of the evening it transpired that Ben had booked a two-bedded room for the night.

163

'If you wanted them to, Annabelle and Dominic could stay over tonight. Our two have twin rooms in case friends stay over. Then, you can call tomorrow before Ben leaves and see what I have to show you,' Mattie said. 'I'm not saying what.'

'Oh yes...the nursery,' Akina piped up.

'*Akina!*'

'Oops! Sorry! I've done it again haven't I?'

'Just promise me something Akina. When you're grown up, please don't ever consider employment in British Intelligence. *That* would be catastrophic.'

Everyone laughed at the child's response. 'It's not likely as I don't know what the heck you're talking about.'

'You'd do a brilliant job as a Town Crier, Akina,' Mark chuckled.

'I don't know what *that* is either. Do you want to stay over Annabelle? Please say *yes*,' she pleaded, purposely ignoring the adults' mirth at her expense.

Mattie tried to calm her exuberance. 'That's up to Annabelle's parents who might have other plans.'

'No, not at all,' Ben said. 'It's a fine idea but they have no pyjamas with them.'

'We've plenty *and* spare toothbrushes. Just think about it. You don't have to decide right away.'

Once they'd eaten, Mattie opened all her presents and thanked everyone.

'There's another here from me,' Mark told her.

'You shouldn't have Mark. You've done enough. This is the best birthday I've ever had.' She tore off the paper to find a cute baby outfit she had admired when they were out shopping some weeks ago. 'Oh

Mark, you remembered I liked this one. I'd hoped the shop would still stock this when I got around to buying it,' and addressing the others as she passed it over to them added, 'I was afraid to tempt fate by buying baby clothes too early.'

'Let me give you a money-saving tip Mattie. All your friends will buy clothes for your baby as soon as he or she is born so don't buy any more. You'll get loads. I know I did,' Steph told her.

'That's sound advice Mattie,' Rachel chipped in. 'It's true and the same is true for teddies and other cuddly toys. Just try to resist the temptation, unless you intend having another baby after this, in which case you can hand them down.'

As Mark coughed, choked and spluttered over his drink, Mattie chortled, 'No Rachel...not right away, but maybe later.' She winked at Mark.

When the evening was drawing to a close, Mattie thanked her guests once more for their attendance.

'We *will* take you up on your offer,' Anne stated. 'My two will never forgive me if I refuse.'

'Great. Pick them up after ten. I'll see they've had their breakfast by then. I've thoroughly enjoyed my party. I'd no idea Mark was planning this.'

'Yes, well, it's all part and parcel of the *new leaf*,' he whispered.

Ben stood up. 'We'll say goodnight then. Thanks for a superb evening and behave you two,' he told the children. 'We'll see you in the morning.'

'I'll go in Emily's taxi,' Mattie told Mark. 'You'll not get six people in your car. The driver will drop me at the door and I have my own key.'

Mattie arrived home first and sorted out the night-wear for Dominic and Annabelle and as she walked downstairs, Mark and the children arrived.

'Come on, I'll show you my room,' Akina cried excitedly. 'It's a really comfy bed Annabelle.'

Annabelle ran upstairs with her as Dominic went into the kitchen with Adam. 'Do you want to look at my stamp collection? I've tons,' Adam advised. 'They were Dad's but he gave them to me.'

'Yes I would. I collect stamps too. I bet you don't have a penny black.'

'You're right. Why, have you?'

'Huh, I wish! Mine belonged to my granddad. He said in those days, you could buy foreign stamps all over the place. Not many places sell them anymore. I see them sometimes when we're on holiday. Let's have a look what you've got.'

They charged upstairs to Adam's bedroom.

Mark flopped down on the sofa, exhaling noisily. 'I can't remember the last time I felt as tired as this. I think I've overdone things today but it's been very rewarding. Did you enjoy the party darling?'

'Yes, thank you Mark, I did...very much. I'd like a word about something though.' She poured him a drink and handed it to him. 'You don't have to keep buying me things. I know we've had words and one or two minor differences but all couples do. You're making me feel very guilty about those things I said in anger. I can't retract them and I apologised at the time. We were both at fault. It wasn't just you and I think you feel you have to keep proving something to me. Well you don't Mark. I love you very much

166

and that will never change. If or when I start to feel neglected, I'll tell you. I'm happy with our life together and appreciative of all the hard work you've done in the nursery. I'm also glad you arranged the party for me. It was thoughtful of you and I had a fantastic time.'

'So what's the problem then?'

'To put it in simple terms, you're walking on eggshells, afraid to step out of line. I want the old Mark back...the Mark who gets a telling off for forgetting to put the toilet seat down; the Mark who forgets to wipe his muddy feet at times when I've mopped the kitchen floor and most of all the Mark who doesn't need to tell me every hour how much he loves me.'

'I'm sorry.'

'And that's another thing. Stop apologising all the time. Just get annoyed for heaven's sake and bang the occasional door. I do! Well...say something!'

He laughed. 'What do I say? I can't say I'm sorry can I? I refuse to stop repeating I love you because I do and the last time I tramped through the kitchen with muddy feet, you made me clean it up so I can't win. I really envy guys who claim they understand women. I'm damned if *I* do. If we do nothing, that's neglect and if we do something nice, that's guilt.'

She laughed with him. 'I guess you're right.'

'There's no *guessing* about it. I *am* right.'

Suddenly remembering the invoice in the drawer she went to get it. 'This was in that box of papers.'

With a quizzical expression his eyes scoured the front, then flipping it over he looked on the reverse that was blank. 'What? What am I looking for?'

'The *name* at the top...*Yukio*. Look at the dates he stayed...July, nineteen-sixty-nine. No? You haven't a clue what it is, have you?'

'Yes, an invoice for some guy named Yukio.' All at once the penny dropped. '*Akina's father?*'

'He has to be Mark. The dates fit and there aren't any others with Japanese names and all other guests at that time were short stay. All invoices, numbered consecutively, were there. I also checked all June's and August's invoices to be absolutely certain.'

'Have you told Akina?'

'No, of course not. What would be the point? It's the only information I have. I know nothing about the guy other than what Sam told me. I don't know whether Yukio's his first or last name. In any case, Sam said she'd never have contacted him if she *had* known his whereabouts.'

'Then I suggest you destroy that. You know what Akina's like at ferreting around. It's no use anyway as it tells you nothing. Right, I'm ready for bed. I'll check on the boys if you'll attend to the girls.'

When Mattie climbed into bed, Mark was asleep and snoring. Laughing, she prodded him in the ribs and when he awoke with a jolt, commented, 'It's so good to have the old Mark back.'

Bewildered he looked at her questioningly.

'You were snoring like a choking warthog.'

Without a word in response, he turned on his side and fell asleep again instantly.

By the time Anne and Ben arrived the following day, the children were washed and dressed and had enjoyed a hearty breakfast.

Annabelle ran towards them. 'I liked staying here Daddy. Akina told me a story before I fell asleep.'

'That's nice. What about you Dominic? Have you enjoyed your sleep-over?'

'Not half! I sifted through Adam's foreign stamp collection before we went to bed. He has hundreds. He's given me some duplicates I didn't have.'

'How was the hotel?' Mark asked.

'So-so,' Ben said. 'Being in the city, it was noisy. This is a nice area. How long have you lived here?'

'Since I married my first wife; I'd say ten years or so. I intended moving from here when Mattie and I were getting married but she liked both the location and the house so I redecorated and we stayed.'

'It's a beautiful property,' Anne declared, casting her eyes around the living room. 'It has a great deal of potential, not that I'm criticising,' she was quick to add with an apologetic smile. 'I see things differently in my line of work, stripping everything back to the bare bricks with my eyes like a blank canvas and then I let my imagination run riot. It's a way of life. I do it everywhere I go; I can't help it. You're a very neat decorator Mark I have to say.'

'Thanks. I have a steady hand so that helps.'

'Come on, I'll show you round and you can take a look at Mark's *pièce de résistance*,' Mattie said.

Ben stepped forward. 'Can I come too?'

'We'll all four go and I can no doubt learn a little from Anne's evaluation of my labours,' Mark said.

She laughed. 'I promise not to say a word.'

'Oh but you must Anne,' Mark insisted. 'Healthy criticism is vital. I'm more than happy to learn from

169

my mistakes for I'm sure Mattie's already working on my next project.' When he shot a glance in her direction, although she looked at him blankly, she smiled secretly at his sixth sense. Mattie was indeed giving thought to Mark's next assignment and Anne was just the person to advise her.

They ended their tour of the house at the nursery.

'Let's see if this looks familiar,' Mattie remarked, opening the door.

Anne stepped inside and looked around critically. 'Wow! I imagine this is some transformation from what was originally a spare room. Am I right?'

'You are. So...professionally speaking, what's the verdict?' Mark asked.

'Simple. It's perfect. I can't fault anything.'

'Much as you'd like to?' he grinned.

'On the contrary, I prefer to provide constructive criticism. Negativity is so demoralising when someone's tried hard to do a good job. This is better than the makeover on the tape but it obviously cost more than my meagre budget allows. It's splendid Mark.'

'Thanks. You provided the inspiration though.'

Mattie sighed. 'It's the nicest room in the house.'

Anne nodded in accord. 'It's soothing and I really like your choice of colour and harmony and you've done it at the right time. Many people leave it until the last minute and then bring their new baby into a home smelling of paint. Not very bright!'

'Why not take Ben out to see the garden?' Mattie suggested.

'That sounds ominous,' Mark commented. 'What are you scheming now Mattie?'

With an air of innocence she replied, 'Who, me?'

Anne quizzed her the moment they disappeared. 'What's on your mind Mattie?'

'Something that's been of concern for some time. I neither want to give up my independence nor lose my legal skills. As you're aware, I'm in partnership with Meredith and I don't want that to end but with a baby due in four months, changes will have to be made if I'm to carry on working as I can't be in two places at once. I definitely wouldn't want to put my baby in a stranger's care. Meredith hasn't raised the issue yet but it's only a question of time before she does and so I was hoping you could come up with a suggestion about how to create an office here, so I could work from home. It doesn't have to be a large office; just enough space for a desk, chair and filing cabinet would suffice.'

'Have you a spare bedroom?'

'No, they're all in use and they aren't big enough to split. The children have lots of stuff and they like to spend time in their rooms. It'd have to be some-where downstairs. An extension would be ideal but there isn't time and it would be far too expensive.'

'Let's wander round again and weigh it up. There might be an easy solution. I assume you don't want to alter your lounge?'

'Mark would never agree to that. I was wondering if the dining room might be an option. It's spacious so we could still manage were it a little smaller.'

It took only moments for her to modify the dining room in her mind. Turning the table sideways and moving it towards the large bay window at the front of the room created a huge amount of space and the sideboard would fit perfectly in a recess beside the fireplace. The smaller window in the second recess would provide sufficient light for the office and the filing cabinet would fit in that recess nicely.

'Basically, all you need is a wall across here and a separate doorway into the office. It's quite a simple task and if Mark's not up to joinery work, a tradesman could have it up in a day, ready for plastering. A filing cabinet would easily fit in that recess and you'd have plenty of room for a chair at the front of your desk too if clients were to call here.'

'You make it sound so easy.'

'It is. Do you know any joiners?'

She shook her head. 'I can't say that I do. Besides I'd have to discuss it with Mark first. He might not want me to work from home. He might not want me to work at all but I can't give everything up after all my hard work.'

Mattie heard the men making their way back and she and Anne returned to the kitchen. Nothing more was said about the matter and after a quick coffee, Ben wanted to leave so they'd be home before dark.

Mark went upstairs to call the children.

'Let me know how Mark reacts,' Anne remarked quietly. 'If he's keen on the idea, I'll send a couple of sketches to show him what we've discussed.'

The children thanked Mattie and Mark and Akina and Adam accompanied them to the car.

'I'll phone you tomorrow about the arrangements for Tuesday,' Anne said. 'We might as well make it a full day if you're up to it.'

'Don't worry; I'll be fine. I can't even remember the last time I had a shopping day with the girls.'

As Adam and Akina bounded back upstairs, Mark sat down to read the Sunday Times.

Mattie decided to capitalise on their free time together. 'I've been thinking Mark...'

Peering over the top of his newspaper he stated, 'I don't like the sound of that. When a woman thinks, it means trouble, hard work or both.'

She poked him in the ribs and he laughed. 'Don't be so sexist Mark or I won't tell you.'

Mark laughed again. 'I bet you do! Come on; put me out of my misery and tell me what you've been scheming with Anne. I knew something was brewing when you sent us out of earshot.'

'I wasn't scheming at all,' she said touchily. 'I'm trying to plan for our future, for our future financial needs. I've been giving thought to what will happen when the baby's born.'

He shrugged. 'What's to think about? We'll have to draw the reins in. You'll be needed here at home with the baby.'

'Oh I see! *You've* already decided.'

'Correction. *You* decided when you got pregnant,' he told her disagreeably. 'It was nothing to do with me. *I* didn't tell you to stop taking the pill.'

'Forget it Mark. You're obviously in one of your argumentative moods. You read your paper because I refuse to discuss anything with you when you're being awkward and for your information, I did *not* stop taking the pill; I've *never* taken it!'

As Mark's mouth fell open in disbelief, she strode

from the room and went into the kitchen to prepare lunch, half expecting he would follow but he didn't.

Mark ate his lunch in silence and as soon as he'd finished he spoke quietly to Adam. 'Would you like an hour or so fishing this afternoon?'

'Great! Are we going now?'

'As soon as you're ready. Find something warm to put on. It's a bit nippy today. I'll get the tackle.'

Without a word to Mattie, he and Adam went out.

'What's up with Dad? He was cross when I spoke to him. Did I do something wrong?' Akina asked.

Mattie smiled. 'No darling. Dad and I just had a difference of opinion about something that's all.'

'Does that mean an argument?'

'Yes...kind of. How about we bake a cake?'

'A yummy chocolate cake?'

'If you like.'

Mark was furious at Mattie's disclosure. How could she have been so deceitful? She had allowed him to believe she had been taking precautions when from the outset, she had been determined to get pregnant and had she uttered a single word to him? Had she ever raised the matter of their having children? The answer to both questions was a categorical *no*! She certainly hadn't heard the last of it, he snorted and their discussion would resume once...

'Are you listening Dad?' Adam said impatiently.

'Sorry! I was miles away. What?'

'I asked if we're going to the same place we went last time. I liked it there.'

'Yes, we are Son.'

Throughout the afternoon Mark remained morose, offering nothing more than monosyllabic replies to Adam's questions and when the wind turned colder, Adam was pleased by Mark's suggestion that it was time to head home. Neither had caught a fish; their dialogue had been almost non-existent and Adam's feet felt like solid blocks of ice.

On their way back to the car park, Mark remained in deep thought, rehearsing his speech in readiness for his arrival home until his attention was diverted when Adam called out, '*Josh!*'

Mark turned as Adam ran across the car park towards a familiar blue Vauxhall car. Breathlessly he cried, 'I thought it was you. Do you feel better?'

'Hello Adam. It's good to see you again and yes, I do feel better. It's been a long uphill struggle but I think I'm finally making some progress. Have you been fishing?'

'Sort of. I didn't catch anything though.'

'Well, Adam, it's like all activities. It's not about winning; it's the taking part that matters. I often go home having caught nothing too, in fact Travis did better than me most times. I remember one day...'

He halted mid-sentence and stepped back as Mark approached and recognising the look of alarm in his eyes, Mark held out his hand as a gesture of friendship. 'Mr. Hargreaves. I trust you're a little better.'

Josh shook his hand. 'Thank you Mr. Wyndham. I do believe I've finally turned the corner, thanks to your intervention. I sure as hell didn't deserve your help following the distress I caused your family but I was desperate. I wasn't in control of my actions or emotions so I'm relieved to have been afforded this opportunity to apologise. I really am very sorry.'

'It's forgotten. I've often thought of how I might have reacted, given your circumstances but I can't begin to imagine your grief. On reflection, I wasn't proud of the way *I* behaved. I'm glad you received the treatment you needed. Is it still ongoing?'

'Yes, I have to visit the shrink...sorry, psychiatrist every couple of weeks. I look forward to my visits. It feels good to talk quietly about things of concern. When did wars ever solve anything? Diplomacy is always the better option. That's what I should have done instead of blaming other people. I should have listened to my GP instead of insisting I'd be okay. I blamed him when I was the one not listening. Then I became angry and frustrated when things began to get on top of me.'

Mark nodded. 'I understand but thankfully you're on the mend now.'

'Yes, thank God. I met a young lady at the clinic. She too was going through a bad patch after losing her mother a few months ago. We provided comfort for each other. She found me easy to talk to as I did her and we've been seeing each other occasionally. It's nothing serious; it's merely a diversion but it's good to have found a friend who understands grief. It's such a lonely existence I lead now, so the odd night out gives me something to look forward to.'

'I'm sure it does. Do you have a job to return to?'

'Yes but I haven't been able to face that yet. I'm unable to set foot in the place where Travis died. It holds too many painful memories and...'

'Then why not sell it?' Adam interrupted.

'Believe me Adam; I've thought of nothing else these past few months.'

Mark was taken aback. 'I didn't realise that Alpha Distribution was your company. I wrongly assumed you were an employee.'

'I bought an empty warehouse and brick by brick I built it up with sweat and toil to provide financial security for my family in case anything happened to me. What a joke! My family's gone now and I have no interest whatsoever in the place anymore. What use is wealth with no one to share it? I'd rather be destitute living from hand to mouth with my family. Nothing in the world is more important than one's wife and kids...*nothing*.'

Following a few reflective moments Mark agreed. 'I hope you continue to make good progress. Don't make any hasty decisions. It's been good to see you again, to clear the air, so to speak.'

Josh held out his hand. 'Thanks for your support Mr. Wyndham. It's greatly appreciated. Don't lose interest in angling Adam. You'll find it to be a good father and son time.'

Mark was quiet and meditative during the journey home. Once again, Josh Hargreaves had given him food for thought. Mattie had indeed raised the issue of their having children and he had merely brushed aside her needs and wishes without giving them due consideration. That had been very wrong of him.

'Thanks for being nice to Josh,' Adam said. 'He's a good man. I like him.'

Mark nodded. 'You're right Son. He's had more

than his fair share of tough luck. When you talk to a man like Mr. Hargreaves, it makes you grateful for everything you have.' He turned to face Adam. 'I'll always be here for you Son. Don't ever forget that.'

'Look!' Akina called as Mark entered the kitchen. 'I've made a cake and it's really yummy.' She was decorating the top with lots of chocolate buttons as he glanced over her shoulder.

'Mmm! It looks delicious. I think I'll have a slice of that now.'

'And *I* think you'll wait for your tea,' Mattie told him demonstratively. 'It'll be ready shortly.'

'What are we having? I'm starving.'

'Fillet steak and mushrooms.'

'Can't be bad. Listen, can you spare me a minute? I want a quick word about something, upstairs.'

She followed him to the bedroom. 'It'll have to be quick. What's on your mind?'

Softly he said, 'You are.' He took her in his arms. 'I'm sorry darling. I was a widower for seven years and it turned me into a cynical, self-centred boor. I saw Josh Hargreaves whilst I was out with Adam.'

'You didn't have a run-in with him did you?'

'On the contrary. We had quite an agreeable chat. He brought me up to speed about his treatment and he's feeling much better now I'm pleased to report.'

'So what's this about?'

He grimaced. 'My utter stupidity in not appreciating what I have here with you. I've made so many stupid mistakes in the past few months we've been together. I'm grateful you're adult enough to ignore my childish shortcomings. I want to reiterate what I said before, that I'm delighted we're having a baby. I'm pleased you ignored me and took the initiative because, left to me, it would never have happened, I'm ashamed to admit.'

'Listen, I'm used to standing my corner. Give me your hand...right hold it just there. Do you feel anything?'

He laughed aloud. 'Wow! Is it kicking?'

Mattie nodded and smiled lovingly. 'Do you have any preference?'

'No. As long as you're both alright, that's all that matters.' He kissed her meaningfully. 'I love you.'

'I know and I love you just as much, irritating as you are. Come on, I'm ravenous and I'm eating for two remember.'

8

It was mid-December and almost seven months into her pregnancy, Mattie was now starting to find her daily routine demanding.

'I could have done without Christmas this year,' she told Meredith on a sigh. 'Just thinking about all the shopping wears me out.'

'Can't Mark help?'

'He does. He's been absolutely brilliant. He never stops. He's made a great job of the office and don't forget he had to redecorate the dining room too. It's hard work after a long day at the hospital. Adam's been a great help too. He enjoys working with his dad and it's been an invaluable confidence boost. In many ways he's not like a little boy. He missed out on all the kisses and cuddles a mother would have showered on him. He's independent and less affectionate than your average eight-year-old. Akina, on the other hand, is very affectionate but they do have one interesting characteristic in common; both are old way beyond their years.'

'And so were you when you were only fourteen, I recall. You carried the weight of the world on your shoulders though I imagine that's normal in a single parent household, where so much is expected of the children.'

'You can say that again. As the eldest, I filled the role of the missing adult. Mum worked really hard.' She sighed reflectively. 'Having said that, we were always happy. It was only when taken in foster care that I discovered the true meaning of misery.'

Changing topic Meredith asked, 'Is Jack home for Christmas?'

On hearing his name, Mattie beamed with delight. 'Yes and I can't wait. I haven't seen him since our wedding and I spent so little time with him then.'

'Is he staying at your place?'

'No he'll be at Seth's. I don't have a spare room.'

'Couldn't you have put the children together?'

'No Meredith, definitely not. I've done that twice on holiday through absolute necessity. The last time was when we went to Devon. There was a thunderstorm one night and when I crept in to check on the children, I found Akina asleep in Adam's bed.'

'So what's your point? Most children are afraid of thunder and lightening.'

'For an intelligent woman, you can be pretty dim at times. They're not related Meredith! They aren't brother and sister. I can't allow them to sleep in the same bed, whatever the reason. It's morally wrong. I know they're only young children now but every day they grow older so I'm nipping it in the bud.'

Their conversation was interrupted by Mark who called to enquire if Mattie could take a longer than usual lunch break. 'What's turned you on?' she said on a laugh. 'I take it this is another date?'

'Not at all. I've had a couple of cancellations for my morning surgery and since you have such a pile of shopping to do, I'm offering my help. There's no ulterior motive.'

'Come when convenient then. Thanks Mark.'

'Mark must have been listening to our earlier conversation,' Meredith said. 'He's very considerate.'

'He's amazing. Our evening meal will be ready to serve by the time I get home. Does Andrew cook?'

'*Andrew?*' she squealed with laughter. 'You have to be joking. I don't know how he coped with two boys when his first wife left. I bet everything they ate came from a can or cardboard carton. He's good at cleaning up and ironing though so that helps. I do everything else mind you.'

'I've been meaning to ask for some time...do *you* want children?'

She replied without hesitation. 'No! I'm a career girl. I've no patience so I'm glad Sam didn't ask me to take on Akina as I'd have had to refuse. We have Alex and Ben and now they're older, we enjoy our freedom. We'd hate to be lumbered with a baby.'

'*Lumbered?* That's a bit over the top. I can't wait to have mine.'

She sneered. 'See if you say that in another fourteen years when you're my age. I'll be forty next.'

Mark wandered up to the office a short time later to collect Mattie.

'Mmm! Trendy suit,' Meredith remarked, eyeing him from head to toe. 'What's your secret Mark?'

He looked puzzled. 'Secret?'

'The secret of your eternal youth. Have you been having the odd nip and tuck on the quiet?'

He grinned boyishly. 'It's obviously married life that agrees with me. Remember Meredith, I have a beautiful young wife to pander to my every need.'

Mattie slapped his arm playfully. 'Just behave!'

Meredith laughed. 'Well, whatever you're getting Mark, it suits you. Keep it up!'

'I fully intend to,' he guffawed in response.

'The shops are lovely,' Mattie sighed, sitting down at her desk. 'I love Christmas decorations. We used to make ours when we were young. I still remember the lengths of paper chains we made. In spite of our limited means, Mum always bought us a small pine tree. They smelled so fresh. Once, a neighbour gave us an old battered tin and when we got the rusty lid off, it was full of glass baubles. Jack was mesmerised as they glistened in the light. Happy days!'

'Did you get all your shopping done today?'

'Pretty well and we also had time to slip home.'

She chortled. 'For a quick one?'

'No! To hide the Christmas presents in the office. Fortunately it has a lockable door that keeps Adam and Akina's prying eyes away from everything. It'll be handy when I get round to wrapping them, that's if I ever find the time.'

'Do they still believe in Father Christmas?'

'I don't know. When they're together they're a bit *deep* if you know what I mean. We openly discuss Father Christmas but I'm not sure if they're merely playing along for my benefit. Very little escapes the two of them.' She laughed. 'I well remember Jack. He was about nine or ten before he knew. Seth had known for years but he didn't tell Jack. One day he ran all the way home from school heartbroken after some boys had shattered his dream and when Seth confirmed it was true, the two of them finished up fighting. Jack was devastated...his whole world had fallen apart.'

She smiled. 'He was the baby though wasn't he?'

'Yes and Seth and I tried to protect his innocence. Jack doesn't remember Dad and was only ten when Mum died. At least I was a teenager when we went into care and old for my years as you pointed out...'

Their discussion was cut short by the telephone. It was Mark and he grunted, 'You won't believe this. A letter has just been delivered by hand from Josh Hargreaves. He'd like Adam to have his son's bike. Can you believe it? The nerve of the guy! I've a...'

Mattie cut him short. 'Calm down Mark. What's your problem with that?'

He grunted again. 'I knew you'd take *his* side.'

'I'm not taking *anyone's* side. I just asked you a simple question. Presumably you want my opinion or you wouldn't have phoned me.'

He sighed with exasperation. 'Have you forgotten he abducted my son?'

'Technically he did but he didn't harm Adam. It's water under the bridge Mark. You made your peace and that should be an end to it. I assume it's simply a kindly gesture. Read the letter to me.'

He paused momentarily. 'You can read it later.'

'No, read it out now. I don't want you pacing up and down all afternoon. Has he made any reference to the abduction?'

'No, not a word. He says it's a good bike, that he knows Adam doesn't have a bike and his son would have been happy for Adam to have it.'

'And that's it?'

'Yes, more or less. It's just a short note. I won't allow it though. If Adam wants one, I'll buy one.'

'Right! I take it you'll reply and thank him.'

He paused. 'Well...er...I was wondering if you'd like to send a typed letter from the office?'

'What, with an official letterhead? You have to be joking! Besides, it's nothing to do with me. As you pointed out, he offered it to *your* son not mine.'

He ignored her cutting remark. 'Correct me if I'm wrong but I understood you were obliged to follow your client's instructions?'

'Not when the instructions are ridiculous. Besides you're not a client. I couldn't act for you if I wanted to which I don't and if you want Meredith to act for you, then you'll pay her fee like any other client or find another solicitor.'

There was a pause. 'Are you annoyed with me?'

'Yes, you could say that! You don't think things through properly. I agree it'd have been better had Mr. Hargreaves not made the offer but since he has, it'd be awkward and embarrassing to refuse. At the end of the day, he's got his son's bike to dispose of and Adam was a friend. There's no ulterior motive Mark. Why not ask Adam if he wants it?'

'Now who's being absurd? It's obvious he will.'

'So take it and move forward. He's a decent guy who means no harm and if it makes you feel better, make a donation to Cancer Research.'

Further silence followed as he digested her words. 'I'll think about it. We'll discuss it later.'

By the time he arrived home Mark had reached a decision and not wishing to appear petty-minded he would accept Josh Hargreaves' offer politely for to refuse would be hypocritical after shaking his hand as a gesture that his actions had been forgiven and forgotten. Their meeting had also served as a harsh wake-up call for Mark who had learned significant lessons about fatherhood and for which he owed the man a huge debt of gratitude.

The dreaded encounter went better than expected. Akina, who had insisted on tagging along, anxious to meet the man who had snatched Adam, adhered to her promise to utter nothing contentious.

For once, to Mark's surprise, she remained true to her word, doubtless because Mr. Hargreaves, recalling Adam had a sister, had boxed up an assortment of games for her to take home.

There was no mistaking her sheer delight. 'I *love* games,' she told him excitedly, rummaging through the box. 'Thank you very much.'

'My pleasure,' he murmured thoughtfully. 'Travis loved board games. He was very competitive.'

Mindful of a sudden change of tone to one of sadness, Mark commented, 'Akina's very competitive too. She keeps us on our toes when we play games.'

'Then I'm pleased they'll be put to good use. So, what do you think about your new bike now you've had a good look at it Adam? I've taken it apart and cleaned and oiled it thoroughly.'

For a moment he was tongue-tied. 'It's...it's great

186

Josh. I...I've never seen one like this before. Thank you and I'll take really good care of it.'

'Can I ride it too Adam?' Akina piped up.

'No, you can't! It's *mine*!' he snapped.

Mark laughed. 'I think that's a cue to leave before the fight starts. By the way, I'm making a charitable donation to cancer research.'

'That's very thoughtful. Thank you. Come on, I'll give you a hand to the car with everything.'

As they stepped outside, the first snowflakes were beginning to fall.

'Wow! It's snowing,' Akina cried. 'I love snow.'

'I hope it snows on Christmas Day,' Adam said, 'I'm very happy to have Travis's bike. Thank you.'

Josh stepped forward and shook his hand warmly. 'You're very welcome, young man. It's what he'd have wanted. Take care and have a nice Christmas.'

'You too,' Adam replied.

As tears welled in his eyes, Mark shook his hand. 'It'll get better with time. I know...I've been there.'

Akina hadn't failed to notice the tears in his eyes and she scampered back to Josh, throwing her arms around his neck. 'You're so kind, Mr. Hargreaves. Thank you very much for the games.'

The children waved until the car was out of sight and the lasting memory was of Josh standing under the street lamp that illuminated the ever increasing flutter of pure white snowflakes. It was going to be a white Christmas.

Mattie grinned like the proverbial 'Cheshire Cat' as Jack walked into their house. Hurrying towards him she hugged him. 'I'm so happy you're home. I hate it when you have to go away.'

He took a step back, eyeing her up and down. 'I'd heard from Seth you'd got a big lump. Are you sure that baby's not due until late February?'

She's not as big as Steph were,' Seth cut in. 'She were absolutely enormous.'

'It's great to be home again Mattie. You've got a grand place here. I'd like to look round if it's okay.'

'There'll be plenty of time for that later Jack. I've made us all afternoon tea. I'll just put the kettle on.'

Jack laughed audibly. 'Hark at her...afternoon tea! Are we having little sandwiches Mattie?'

'But of course, tiny cucumber sandwiches like the three of us used to have with Mum on Sundays *and* home-made currant cake as well.'

As Akina and Adam rifled through Jack's bag to see what he'd brought them, Jack sat down beside Seth and Mark. 'Keeping busy Mark?'

'It never eases. Are you still as enthusiastic about the Navy?'

'Absolutely! I can't imagine ever doing anything else. Don't mention it to Mattie but I might sign on for longer. The longer the term, the better the pay.'

'I'll pretend I didn't hear that. She misses you.'

'I know but I get shore leave. I'm not the settling down type like you lot. I enjoy the smell of the sea, the camaraderie and...'

'And the smell of engine oil,' Seth butted in on a laugh.

He nodded and grinned. 'Aye, that too Seth.'

'So tell me, have you made Admiral yet?'

'Not quite...but I'm working on it,' Jack smirked with a sideways glance at his brother. 'I'm hoping to make Petty Officer soon so that'd be another step up the ladder.

Mattie yelled from the kitchen. 'Jack, come and talk to me and tell me all about Singapore.'

He picked up a neatly wrapped parcel and made his way to the kitchen where Mattie was arranging the food on a plate. 'Here...something for the baby. I'll get it something else when I know what it is.'

Her eyes lit up and eagerly she tore at the paper. 'Oh Jack! How beautiful...a Christening Robe.'

'I couldn't resist it. I got it in Singapore. If I can't make it to the Christening, you'll know I'm there in spirit. It's pure silk and it'll do for a boy or a girl.'

She threw her arms around his neck. 'You can't imagine how much I miss having you around Jack.'

'Aye I can Mattie. I miss you lot just as much but be happy that I'm doing what I've always wanted to do. It won't be forever.'

She quickly dried a tear from her cheek. 'Is it still snowing hard?' she asked, changing topic.

'Aye it is. The roads will be blocked soon at this rate. D'you remember when we were kids how we used to sledge down Morgan's Hill on three planks Seth had nailed together? We must have been mad.'

'Yes, happy memories Jack. I remember all kinds of enjoyable incidents from our childhood days. We had some great times,' she reflected with nostalgia.

'Reminiscing again?' Mark interrupted.

Mattie smiled. 'You know us Mark...always harking back to something. Look what Jack's bought us

189

for our baby.' She held up the Christening Gown.

'That's beautiful Jack and very thoughtful. Thank you. I just came to see if you needed a hand.'

'Thanks. Take in that tray please. Jack and I will fetch the rest. I'm so looking forward to Christmas Day with all of us together. Steph and I have finally sorted the arrangements. We're to have Christmas Day here but Steph will help with the food.'

Jack looked concerned. 'Don't be doing too much Mattie. You're in no fit state with a baby due soon.'

'I'm alright Jack...trust me. I'm more concerned about you and pray the Falkland Islands' affair gets resolved soon. I don't want to see you placed in any danger should there be a war.'

He winked at her. 'Stop fretting Mattie. Haven't I told you? I'm Jack the Invincible.'

'Please...don't say such things. Don't tempt fate.'

'Then stop worrying. It'll take a damn sight more than that to bring *me* down. How about those tasty cucumber sandwiches now? I'm ravenous!'

In spite of Jack's reassurances, Mattie remained concerned. Diplomacy didn't appear to be resolving the areas of conflict and many people believed war was inevitable to defend British Sovereignty of the Falklands.

When Jack returned to sea early January nineteen-seventy-eight, Mattie was distraught. 'Promise me you'll take good care of yourself,' she pleaded with tears rolling down her cheeks. She flung both arms around his neck and hugged him. 'You're still my little brother Jack. You always will be.'

190

Mark led her indoors as the taxi disappeared from sight. 'Jack's in no imminent danger, Mattie. I feel sure it'll be resolved satisfactorily.'

'I wish I could share your optimism,' she sighed. 'Why did he have to join the Navy?'

'Because that's all Jack ever wanted. It's *his* life. You must accept that. You chose *your* career. Shall we go out later for a bite to eat?'

'No thanks. There's stuff in the fridge to eat up. I just need to rest for a while.'

Mark took the children across to the park, leaving Mattie to her thoughts.

During their absence she shed further tears. Deep within her were sickening thoughts she couldn't put into words. She had a vision of a burning ship and Jack was calling out her name...but soon, calm descended as she fell into a deep and welcome sleep.

It was Mattie's final day at the office. With just two weeks remaining before the due date, she had at last succumbed to pressure from Mark. Meredith gave her a prettily adorned Moses Basket containing an assortment of baby clothes.

'They're lovely; everything's lovely,' Mattie said smiling happily. 'Thank you Meredith. I'll miss you so much but I'll be back soon...promise.'

'You take whatever time you need. We'll keep in touch by phone on a daily basis and when you're up to it, I'll send you cases you can handle at home.'

It was in the early hours that Mattie aroused Mark. 'I'm sorry to disturb you but would you make me a cup of tea please? I'm restless and can't seem to get to sleep.'

'Is it the baby? Do you think it's coming?'

She snorted. 'I think this baby's staying put. I'm already three days overdue. I feel so uncomfortable but I've probably just eaten too much.'

He wasn't convinced but didn't wish to alarm her. He went downstairs and returned with a hot steaming mug of tea. 'Try and sit up Mattie.' He plumped up her pillows. 'How do you feel now?'

'Like I said, restless.' She sipped her tea until her eyelids began to droop. 'I feel I can sleep now. I'm sorry I disturbed you; I won't bother you again.'

'Listen! If you need anything, anything at all, you wake me again – right? It's not a problem.'

She yawned. 'If you say so.' She closed her eyes and Mark remained alert until her breathing became shallow, as in sleep. There was no further activity during the night and Mattie was sound asleep when he next awoke. He slid out of bed quietly and made the children's breakfast prior to taking his shower. Mattie was wide awake when he returned. 'How are you feeling now?' he enquired.

'A bit tired but otherwise alright. I think I'll clean the windows today.'

That was the confirmation Mark needed, that the baby was on its way. He had learned about women acting strangely and cleaning the whole house prior to the birth of a child. 'There's nothing wrong with the windows Mattie. The urge for household chores is common before giving birth. I guess it's hormone related.'

'Don't be ridiculous Mark. They're filthy.'

Softly he said, 'Nothing's filthy in this house. It's the baby; it's on its way; trust me.'

She threw back the covers and got out of bed but as her feet touched the floor she yelled and gripped her stomach. 'Ouch, that hurt.' Her knees gave way beneath her as another sudden and stronger rush of pain presented. 'Something's wrong,' she cried.

Mark smiled. 'No Mattie. Everything's fine. The baby's coming.'

'How would you know?' she snapped, as beads of perspiration gathered on her forehead. 'When have *you* ever given birth?'

Ignoring her outburst he asked, 'Can you manage some breakfast? It'll pass time. You've quite a long way to go yet.'

Mattie stared at him in disbelief. 'Breakfast? Did you say *breakfast?* Is that the best you can do?'

'What do you expect me to do Mattie? I can tell it to get a move on but I doubt it'll take much notice.' He patted her brow with his handkerchief. 'Has the pain eased off a bit now?'

'Yes, maybe it was a false alarm.'

He cupped her face in his hands. 'It's alright to be scared. You'll be fine darling, trust me. Shall I help you back into bed?'

She nodded.

'When the pain comes again we'll time the intervals. Just remember your breathing exercises. That should help you. Once you feel settled I'll drive the children to school. It'll not take me long.'

'Aren't you going to work today?'

'What? And miss the floor show? Not likely. I'll be by your side all the time now.'

That brought some relief. 'Thanks. I don't want to be alone.'

He smiled. 'I never had any intentions of leaving you alone. Had I been at work, I'd have come home right away. You know that. Try to rest now.'

The children were standing by the door when he went down. 'We'll be late now,' Akina complained. 'We'll be in trouble if we're late for registration.'

'Just get in the car,' Mark said impatiently. 'You won't be late at all. You're like an old woman!'

Adam glowered at her censoriously and elbowed her through the door.

Within fifteen minutes Mark was back home and he hurried upstairs to find Mattie panting heavily.

'I've just had another. That was a lot stronger but it's easing off a bit now. It came at five to nine.'

For the next three hours there was no change and then the contractions gradually became stronger and more frequent. At ten minute intervals Mark called the hospital and was told to take her in.

Within an hour of admission she had reached the final stage of labour; she had sworn *never* to have another baby; she had yelled at Mark how much she hated him...and then her anger changed to tears of joy and laughter on hearing her new baby cry.

'Well done Mark!' the midwife said. 'I bet you're exhausted.'

'*Well done Mark?*' Mattie repeated quizzically. 'I don't believe that! What's *Mark* done?'

'It's very stressful for the father,' she said, with a

wink of the eye in Mark's direction. She passed the baby to Mattie adding, 'And well done to you too. You have a beautiful daughter, perfect in every way and she weighs seven pounds ten ounces.'

Mattie sobbed tears of happiness. 'Just look at her Mark and tell me; isn't she the most gorgeous baby you've ever seen? Look at her tiny hands and feet. I can't believe she's finally here.'

He wrapped his arms around her and peered at the baby's face. 'She's the absolute image of you. Just stay like that and I'll take a photo.'

'Allow me,' the midwife insisted. 'This photo is definitely for the hospital notice-board. Everyone's waiting on tenterhooks. They all know you're here.'

'Is Chris around?' Mark asked. 'If so, I'd like him to be the first to see her.'

'I'll just check. Give me a minute.'

When Chris ambled in, Mark was overcome with guilt, his eyes glistening with tears. 'Stop worrying mate,' Chris said kind-heartedly, shaking his hand. 'We can all make irrational comments from time to time.' He kissed Mattie and whispered, 'Well done! She definitely looks content.' He winked. 'I'm glad she looks like you, not Mark. The two of you have something very special. Sadly, I'll never know this kind of emotion as I've left it too late. I should have kept my eye out for a wonderful girl like you. I've missed the boat now.'

In an attempt to lighten the mood Mark rejoined, 'Absolute baloney Chris! There's always Lucille to fall back on if you're desperate. I'll lay odds *she's* still available.'

His reply was obliterated by the ensuing laughter.

When Chris left, Mattie called Seth to tell him the exciting news, advising she was Mrs. Winterton as the receptionist tried to connect her. Mark looked at her quizzically.

'I'll explain later,' she said on a giggle. 'I've been dying to do this for ages.'

Seth's ultra-polite sophisticated voice was totally unrecognisable when he answered. 'Good afternoon Mrs. Winterton. You're speaking to Seth Henshaw. How may I help you today?'

Finding it impossible to control her laughter she screeched, 'Seth Henshaw. I can't believe my ears.'

There was a moment's silence before he stuttered, 'Oh...er...it's you Mattie. Sorry, she got your name wrong. I thought it were a member of the public.'

'I *am* a member of the public and therefore insist on being afforded the same courtesy as any other.'

There was a further awkward pause. 'I...er...only meant...'

'Shut up Seth! I'm winding you up. I *did* give the wrong name, deliberately. I wanted to hear the cut-glass voice I'd heard so much about. *Very* posh!'

Irritably he asked, 'Is that why you called me?'

'Not entirely. There's another small matter I just wanted to mention in passing. You're an uncle!'

'Who to?'

'Really Seth! Such dreadful grammar...and you a Librarian. *To whom* you should be asking.'

The penny finally dropped. 'Mattie, is this true?'

'Yes. She was born about twenty minutes ago and we're fine. Mark's a bit rough round the edges,' she added with irony and he laughed. 'It happened very quickly so I couldn't let you know.'

'You sound great. I'm so thrilled for you. I can't wait to write to our Jack. He'll be over the moon. I imagine Steph will be at work shortly and she'll be surprised when she hears. What does she weigh?'

'Seven pounds ten ounces and her name's Mair.'

'I like that. You rest now and we'll come and see you as soon as we can. I'm so proud of you Mattie.'

As she hung up there was a knock at the door and Steph walked in. 'Dark horse,' she remarked. 'That was quick. I didn't even know you were in labour.'

'It was easy, no trouble at all,' she made known.

'Huh!' Mark butted in. 'Half an hour ago she was leaving me. She hated me.'

Steph laughed. 'That's quite normal during labour Mark. I'm sure I said some nasty things too.'

'I didn't mean it,' Mattie said contritely. 'It'll be much easier next time. I'll know what to expect.'

'*What?*' Mark screeched.

Steph cooed over the baby as she slept in Mattie's arms. 'I'd like a girl next time,' she murmured.

'Since everyone's ignoring me I'll take the phone back,' Mark declared.

During the rest of the day, Mattie received many visitors and when Mark returned that evening with both children, Akina's joy was beyond description. Adam however, true to form, eventually obliged by flashing a brief dispassionate smile.

Emitting an audible sigh, Mattie flopped down into an armchair. 'It feels great to be home. I hate being away from my family. Here, pass her to me Mark.'

Gently, he handed the sleeping baby to her.

'Look, this is your new home,' she said softly. 'I hope you like your nursery too. Your daddy worked hard to make it pretty for you. Wait till you see it.'

Mair opened her eyes, yawned and promptly fell asleep again.

It was time for Akina to make her contribution. 'I hope you know Mair hasn't a clue what you're talking about. She doesn't understand words yet. Look how long it took me to learn to talk and I still don't know *every* word and *I'm* nearly eight.'

With a dry smile Mark quipped, 'Well, I must say you had me fooled Akina. I wouldn't have thought there were any words you didn't have on the tip of your loquacious little tongue.'

She grunted. 'Well, there's *one* for a start.'

Mattie tittered. 'Dad's teasing darling. I'm trying to familiarise Mair with my voice so she'll remember me because she can't see anyone yet. That word means *make known*. You should talk to her too and then she'll learn to remember your voice as well.'

'Right. Shall I read her a story then?'

She nodded. 'I reckon that's a good way to start.'

Over the next few weeks, Akina's help was invaluable. She enjoyed being around Mair whenever she could and Mattie actively encouraged her involvement so she wouldn't feel neglected.

'I'm going to have lots of babies when I grow up. I think Mair's really cute,' she told Mattie one day.

'Then you'd better work harder at school. Babies

cost lots of money to feed and clothe so you'll need a well-paid job.'

'I always work hard!' she protested. 'I know lots of things other girls in my class don't know.'

Mattie couldn't argue with that as Akina's school reports were outstanding, Adam's too. Thankfully, each of them appeared to have an insatiable appetite for knowledge and their preferred leisure activities were reading books and playing competitive chess.

By the time Mair was two months old, Mattie was spending a few hours each day in the office, whilst Mair slept contentedly in her Moses basket.

Every phase of Mair's development over the next four years brought great joy to the whole family. A sweet-natured and happy child, she was the apple of Mark's eye. He absolutely adored her.

Conversely, Akina and Adam were becoming the cause of concern as their school work was reported to be showing a marked deterioration.

Mark held Akina wholly responsible, maintaining she had too much influence over Adam and Mattie was inclined to agree, having observed how moody she had become of late. 'It's puberty,' he told her. 'You must talk to her Mattie; make her see sense or she'll wreck her own and Adam's chance of success if she carries on like this. I don't want Mair picking up bad habits either. At this age she's impressionable. She's already started mimicking Akina's rude behaviour and it has to stop.'

'I think it might be better were we both to talk to them. That way they'll know we're both concerned. I have to point out however that Adam doesn't *have* to follow Akina's lead; approaching age thirteen he should know right from wrong and should make his own decisions,' she stated defensively.

He acted hastily to suppress an argument that was brewing. 'Mattie, they're *our* children, they're not yours and mine. I'm concerned about both children and you're right; we *will* talk to them together. My role in this is equally as important as yours, so let's make it this evening, okay?'

She nodded. The matter had to be addressed; she accepted that, but in her mind there was no doubt at all that she'd been preoccupied with another matter of late, thus permitting the children's behaviour to spiral out of control. Someone else was the cause of much graver concern, loss of appetite and sleepless nights and that was her brother Jack who occupied her thoughts every moment of every day. The headline news featured details of the Falklands' crisis on a daily basis. Yesterday's newspapers, in particular, had sent shock-waves through her system. On that day the twenty-sixth of March nineteen-eighty-two, the Argentine military junta had decided to invade the islands, according to British Intelligence. That meant war was inevitable and what part would Jack play in that? Would he be detailed to the Falklands?

She had last spoken to Jack over a week ago and he had merely laughed off her concerns, stating the issues would be determined without bloodshed. On reflection, she had been naïve to believe that. Jack's aim had been to pacify her. He had most likely been aware for some time that he would be drafted to the South Atlantic in that eventuality and *that* no doubt had given rise to his brief and unexpected telephone call. She was distraught, and mindful of her earlier terrifying vision, she prayed to God that Jack would return home safely. She prayed for all other British personnel caught up in the conflict too.

'I hope this is important,' Akina snarled, directing her remark at Mattie as she sat down beside Adam.

Mark was incensed. 'You listen to me young lady unless you relish the thought of being grounded for a month! I won't tolerate your disagreeable attitude any longer. Is that understood?' He paused to await a reply. '*Well? Answer me!*'

She glanced up briefly and looked away. 'Okay, I understand, right? Is that it? Can I go now?'

'That's *exactly* what I mean. There's going to be some major changes here, starting from now and as for you Adam, I'm terribly disappointed with your behaviour. You've become obstinate, lazy and rude; your school work has deteriorated considerably and your teachers are now at the end of their tether with the pair of you. If you don't show any improvement over the next week or so, we'll move you to another school and don't for a moment think we won't. We refuse to continue paying exorbitant school fees for time-wasters. Most children would be cock-a-hoop with a mere fraction of the opportunities afforded to you two, so you'd better take heed.'

Mattie felt she should make a token contribution and offer the children the opportunity to talk about anything of concern that might have contributed to the recent changes in behaviour. 'Are either of you having any problems at school?'

201

Though Akina remained stony-faced, Adam said, 'The work's a lot harder now and we get too much homework. If we did it all we'd have no free time.'

'So, tell me what you've been doing today.'

'Nothing much. I watched TV in my room.'

'Did you finish your homework?' Mark asked.

'We haven't got any,' Akina jumped in, elbowing Adam in the ribs but it didn't escape Mark's notice.

He glared threateningly at Adam. 'You know I'll call the school if I have to, so how much homework did you get this weekend and have you done it?'

Avoiding eye contact he replied, 'I got maths and physics...I think.'

'You *think?* I guess that means you haven't even started it yet!' his father argued impatiently.

'I was going to do it later honestly, but you called me downstairs.'

'Oh *right!* It's *my* fault. Okay, I'll make amends. I promise not to disturb you any further. Make a start now and you can finish it tomorrow.'

'What, after horse-riding? Aren't we going out to lunch?'

'No, not tomorrow Son and you won't be horse-riding either, so you'll have all day to do it and then I'll check it and if it's not right, you'll do it again,' he said calmly. 'All privileges are withdrawn now until you learn not to lie to me. The same applies to you Akina. Go to your room; keep right away from Adam until you've finished all your homework too, then Mattie or I will check yours.'

As she opened her mouth to speak he interrupted, 'It might not be a bad idea to keep it zipped Akina, particularly with Easter holidays fast approaching. I have rather a mean streak when I'm provoked.'

Without a further word they disappeared upstairs, Mark's warning clearly understood.

All daily newspapers continued to carry headline news relating to the Falkland Islands and none of it good. Reports that the Argentine Navy had landed on the islands with thousands of troops only served to intensify Mattie's pre-existing anxieties. Following the troops' seizure of South Georgia and South Sandwich on the third of April, the United Nations Security Council passed a resolution calling for the withdrawal of those troops. The Argentine response was to send more troops, a move popular in Buenos Aires if not throughout the rest of the world.

Despite the threat of sanctions and more attempts at mediation, the troops remained in situ.

It was a few days to Easter when Mark suggested a short family break to Mattie. 'It might take your mind off it for a few days,' he remarked sensitively. 'Worrying achieves nothing. Jack might not be involved in the conflict if it comes to that, so wait and see. All will be revealed in the fullness of time.'

'I know you mean well Mark but I'd rather stay at home. Can you imagine how guilty I'd feel if somebody was trying to contact me and I wasn't here? I have to stay here. You could take Akina and Adam. They've earned it. They've behaved very well since we talked to them. Mair could stay here with me.'

He held her in his arms. 'I'll have to think about that. You know I hate being separated from you.'

'Yes, but you need a break. It'll also demonstrate

to the children that good behaviour is rewarded.'

During the short camping trip to the Lake District, Mattie remained at home within arm's length of the telephone and kept abreast of all news bulletins.

Mair, taking full advantage of Mattie's undivided attention for a few days, pleaded for stories at every opportunity and, sitting cross-legged on the rug, she listened wide-eyed for hours to the antics of Noddy and Big Ears in Toyland.

Mattie enjoyed those special moments when Mair would climb on her lap and give her a huge hug and she in turn would look deeply into the clear smiling blue eyes of her dearly-loved daughter, whose skin glowed like fine porcelain. She was a truly adorable child and Mattie felt blessed to be her mother. Were it not for the unease brought about by the likelihood of war, her life would be perfect in every way.

Mark telephoned regularly during his absence for updates and thankfully there was no bad news.

On the twenty-fifth of May HMS Coventry was hit by three bombs dropped by Argentine Skyhawks. It made headline news as there were many deaths and casualties. It was closely followed by another bulletin, the demise of the MV Atlantic Conveyor hit by an Exocet missile and resulting in more deaths and casualties. Mattie was frantic, having no knowledge of Jack's whereabouts but instinct told her he must be caught up in this ferocious war.

Mark held her close as she sobbed for the victims and their families. Although he fully understood her pain and anxiety there was little he could do to ease her suffering but offer words of comfort and hope.

The children were playing together upstairs when the telephone rang and as was the norm over recent weeks Mark and Mattie exchanged anxious glances. 'I'll get it,' Mark said, jumping up.

For several moments he didn't speak and Mattie listened with bated breath. 'Try not to worry. I'll be there in two minutes,' she heard Mark state calmly. 'I'll fetch my bag. You'd better call an ambulance.'

She leapt to her feet as he replaced the receiver. 'What's wrong Mark? Who needs an ambulance?' she questioned fearfully.

'Norman. That was Emily. He went upstairs for a nap a while ago and she can't wake him. I think we must accept that no more can be done for him. He's been living on borrowed time for a while now.'

'Poor Emily. Norman's her soul-mate.'

He nodded. 'Poor Akina too. She thinks the world of her granddad. She'll be heartbroken. She hasn't any blood-relatives left apart from Emily when her granddad's gone. Would you have a word with her? I don't want her to see him in his present state.'

She nodded sensitively. 'Yes, I'll talk to her. Just call me when you can.'

Following Mark's call, Mattie drove the children to the hospital to say goodbye. Akina had borne the news better than expected and as she leaned across the bed to kiss her granddad she whispered, 'You'll see Mummy again very soon and she'll take care of you. I'll always love you and will you tell Mummy I love her too?'

'I'm sure he will,' Mattie said reassuringly.

By the time they left, Norman was close to death with Mark anxious to have all three children off the ward before that happened.

'I'll stay with Emily,' Mattie told him. 'I'll drive her home later.'

Norman never regained consciousness and passed away shortly afterwards with Emily still holding on to his hand.

Mattie fought back her tears as Emily sobbed, 'I have to say I've expected this for a while. I've seen a marked deterioration in his condition over recent months. I'm going to miss him so much Mattie.'

Mattie held her in a compassionate embrace. 'Try to be positive. He's at peace now and we're here for you. You can visit us whenever you want and we'll help you with all the arrangements.'

It was eleven o'clock by the time Mattie arrived home and she was disturbed by the presence of an unfamiliar car parked on their drive. With pounding heart she hurried indoors and was surprised to find Lucille sitting across from Mark.

With a feeble smile, Lucille looked up at her.

Mattie couldn't help but notice how different she looked minus the usual plastered make-up. She was dressed well too in a fair-isle jumper and calf length camel skirt with long black boots.

'Hi Lucille; this is a pleasant surprise. To what do we owe the pleasure?' she enquired.

It was Mark who replied. 'Lucille has something to tell you. I think you'd better sit down Mattie.'

Mattie was confused. What could Lucille possibly

have to say of interest to her? She had hardly seen her in the past few years. Her mind was racing.

'Would you like *me* to explain?' Mark offered but she shook her head, clearing her throat nervously.

'I had a visitor this evening Mattie but before I go into detail I need to make it clear there's nothing to worry about, really there isn't; I've been assured.'

Mattie was becoming concerned. 'Is it Seth? Has he been admitted to hospital again? We've been out all night. Norman, Akina's granddad, passed away earlier,' she gabbled incomprehensibly. 'Do tell me Lucille. Tell me Seth's going to be alright.'

'He's fine Mattie. This isn't about Seth. It's...'

'*Tell me then,*' she cut in anxiously. 'For heaven's sake Lucille tell me what's wrong. Get to the point. You've never been reticent in the past when imparting bad news.

Mark walked towards her and perched on the arm of her chair. 'Take it easy darling. Just give Lucille a chance to explain. This isn't easy for her.'

Lucille looked up with tearful eyes. 'It's Jack not Seth. Jack's been injured in the Falklands...but he's going to be alright, honestly. The man said so.'

For what seemed an eternity Mattie didn't speak. This wasn't real. How could Lucille know anything about Jack? There must be some mistake unless she was up to her old tricks again, scaremongering. The two of them hardly knew each other. They'd met a couple of times that's all, once at a party and then at their wedding and why would anyone have told *her* had it been true?

'Is this another of your sick jokes Lucille?'

Lucille burst into tears and Mark intervened. 'Just hear her out Mattie. She's speaking the truth. Jack will recover fully, given time and proper care. He's in no danger He's been air-lifted to a hospital ship. He's suffered a fractured femur and burns.'

The reality began to dawn and Mattie recalled the repetitive nightmare of Jack on a burning ship. She burst into tears and Lucille comforted her. 'They'll fly him home as soon as he's fit to travel. The man told me that.'

'What man? How do you come to be involved in all this? Why did this so-called man not call here to tell me? Did you find out through the hospital? I'm Jack's next-of-kin. They should have informed *me*, not *you*.'

Lucille glanced at Mark who nodded his head. 'I think you should tell Mattie everything,' he said.

'What do you mean? Mark? What else is there to explain? Don't tell me there's more bad news.'

At that Lucille's lips broke into a coy smile. 'That depends on how you look at it. Don't blame me for keeping this from you. It wasn't my idea and I was dead against it so don't shoot the messenger. It was Jack who insisted you mustn't be told as he didn't want you to know he'd be involved in the Falklands war. You're not next-of-kin Mattie. I am. Jack and I were married five months ago.'

Whatever she was expecting to hear, it certainly wasn't that and her mouth fell open in disbelief and before she could stop herself she laughed out loud. 'Is this some kind of joke?' Instantly she regretted her offensive reaction to the news. 'I'm really sorry

Lucille. I'm stressed out and I didn't mean that at all. Of course I'm delighted for you...for you both. I was just shocked to hear that Jack had got married. He always said he'd wait until he'd finished in the Navy. I didn't know you were seeing each other.'

'We've been seeing each other since we first met at your New Year's Eve party ages ago. We met up again at Steph's wedding. Jack wanted me to write to him when he went back to sea but it was my idea not to tell you we were seeing each other as I knew you'd never held me in high regard. I admit I was a flibbertigibbet back then and I knew you wouldn't approve of our relationship but I love him Mattie. I love him very much and when he comes home, I'll make him better. I might have my faults but I'm a damn good nurse.'

Mattie threw her arms around her. 'We used to be friends Lucille. We even shared a room in London. I was different from you though. I couldn't relax in a man's presence whereas you were gregarious and flirtatious, but I was the one who wasn't normal. I really envied your audacity. Still friends?'

'Of course,' she laughed.

'So is Jack really going to be okay?'

'According to that guy, his injuries aren't too bad. He has a few burns on his legs. A burning beam fell across his thigh as he was trying to help a mate.'

'The fractured femur shouldn't cause a problem,' Mark interrupted to ease her concerns. 'He's young and he's alive so we must thank God for that.'

Mattie nodded in agreement. 'Why not start again from the beginning Lucille and tell me everything.'

Mark stood up. 'I'll stick the kettle on and make a cup of coffee. Besides, I've heard it all once.'

'So who was the man who came round?'

'He's what they call a Casualty Notifying Officer. He was really nice. As you can imagine, I was very upset and he said he'd stay as long as I wanted him there. He explained that once Jack has been brought back to the UK, a casualty support team will take us to see him. I reckon Jack was fortunate for it could have been much worse as the vessel had been hit by an Exocet missile. A lot of men died.'

'Jack could have been killed too,' Mattie sighed. 'So, I think you'd better tell me all about this secret wedding of yours...five months ago you say.'

'Yes. We were married in a civil ceremony a few days after Christmas. We travelled to Portsmouth. It had been arranged for quite a while.' She laughed. 'Jack said he wanted to make an honest woman of me as we'd been ducking and diving every time he was home on leave. I'm sorry you couldn't be at the wedding but that's the way he wanted it. Don't be too hard on him when you see him.'

'Listen, if that's what you and Jack wanted then I'm happy for you both. All I ever prayed for was a joyful, fulfilling life for my brothers.' She grinned. 'Our Jack...married. I can hardly believe it. I take it Seth doesn't know?'

'Nobody knows Mattie. I was sworn to secrecy.'

She roared with laughter at that. 'Knowing you as I do, I bet you found that a hard task.'

She joined in the laughter. 'You're right. I was so happy I wanted to shout it from the rooftops.'

'Getting back to Jack, will the Casualty Notifying Officer keep in touch with updates?'

'Yes, he said I'd be kept informed. He left some paperwork with me but I haven't had time to read it as my priority was to get over here to tell you.'

Mattie smiled. 'Thank you Lucille and I'm sorry I was so rude to you earlier. I was in shock.'

'It's fine. I'd probably have reacted the same way in your shoes. When will you tell Seth and Steph?'

'First thing tomorrow so please, try and keep it to yourself till I've spoken to them. By the way, I like the new look...very becoming.'

'Well, I'm a respectable married woman now. I'll show you our wedding photos next time I see you. I didn't dare bring them tonight in case you tore them up, *sister-in-law*,' she chuckled.

Mattie reflected on what had been an eventful and shocking few hours, touching the lives of so many. Tears had been shed and more would undoubtedly follow but in time, Emily and Akina would learn to live with their tragic loss and Jack would hopefully make a total recovery with everyone's help. In the meantime, the family members would continue to draw strength from each other and life would go on as before.

9

'Jack's coming back this week,' Lucille screeched down the telephone excitedly. 'I've just had word. I don't know which hospital it'll be yet but they'll let me know and then they'll take us to see him. Won't that be great Mattie?'

'It's the best news ever! He mentioned in his last letter that he might be returning soon. He's still on traction but Mark says that's normal.'

'He'll need plenty of physio once he's discharged but I'll keep him at it. I can be very persuasive. I've had years of practice in my job. It'll help his mental state too once he's home and mobile again.'

'Try to make it a weekend visit if you can so that I can send the children to one of their grandparents. No doubt Steph will want to do the same with Paul. Besides, there's likely to be more than a few pitiful sights on the ward so it's hardly a place for children to be charging about.'

'You're right. I'll let you know when I next hear.'

As Mattie replaced the receiver, Meredith looked up. 'Lucille?'

'Yes. Jack will be back soon. She's just heard.'

Meredith sighed. 'That's great news. I'm so glad.'

'Me too. I just hope and pray he doesn't go back in the Navy. If he makes a complete recovery he'll be expected to but it'll be terrible for Lucille, much harder than for the rest of us.'

'Are you happy about her being Jack's wife now you've got know her better?'

She nodded. 'She's a completely different person now. I never *dis*liked her. She was a bit of a chump but her heart was always in the right place. She got the blame for a few misunderstandings that weren't entirely her fault and there was never any malicious intent. She just had a loose tongue.'

'Didn't she use to fancy Mark?'

Mattie giggled. 'Yes, but then she fancied *anyone* in pants in those days. She had the hots for Chris as well who sang at our wedding but he gave her short shrift too. What matters is, she loves Jack and she'll take proper care of him. She'll be a good wife in all respects. I like her much more the way she is now and she never fails to bring a smile to my face.'

'Quite an inspirational summation Ma'am!'

'True though, and you know what they say, *better the devil you know*. Jack could have turned up with one of those *ladies of the night* he'd encountered on his travels. He's no angel and I believe Lucille will have a stabling influence. What he needs is a strong minded woman with lots of personality and she fits the bill perfectly. I think they're well-matched.'

It was a journey of mixed feelings, jubilation to be seeing Jack again but apprehension about his state of mind. Lucille had been informed he could suffer mood swings. Post traumatic stress was common in war victims and many experienced flash-backs.

Armed with that knowledge, they walked into the ward with foreboding. Jack was sleeping when they approached, traction strings supporting his left leg.

Lucille leaned over timidly and stroked his hand.

He opened his eyes, smiling warmly. 'Hi Podgy! Long time no see. Give us a kiss.'

As she held him he sobbed, his body shaking with emotion. 'It's alright Jack. You're going to be fine. The war's over now. You're safe.'

'I lost my best mate Lou. I couldn't save him. I'd almost reached him when a beam fell over my leg. I couldn't move but I tried; I tried hard. I were close; very close yet unable to help and I had to watch the poor bugger die. There were flames everywhere and he were screaming. That's all I remember.'

She stroked his hair. 'It wasn't your fault Jack. It wasn't anyone's fault. Bad things happen to people all the time. You can't blame yourself.'

She wiped the tears from his cheeks. 'Look who's here to see you Jack...Mattie and Seth. You have to put on a good show for your brother and sister.'

As he turned to face them, his bottom lip began to quiver again.

Mark moved forward. 'How's the leg mate? Have they had you playing football yet?'

His mood changed instantly and on a shrill burst of laughter rejoined, 'You've got to be joking. This leg's a bloody liability. I can't even get out of bed for a pee. Have you ever tried peeing in bed Mark?'

Seth smirked. 'You didn't have any trouble when you were a kid. As I recall you were still peeing in bed when you were five. I should know. I slept with you and woke up soaked every morning.'

'*You lying bugger!* Tell them it's not true Mattie. I'll get out of this bed and give you a bloody thump if you spread malicious lies about me, you cretin.'

Jack's protestations could barely be heard above the laughter.

'Come here Mattie and give us a hug. I've missed you.' As she leaned over him he whispered guiltily, 'Sorry about the wedding, that you missed it.'

'Me too but you made a great choice. Lucille will take care of you when you're home.' She kissed his cheek lovingly. 'Try to be strong now Jack. Look to the future with your wife.'

'Aye Mattie. I know you're right but life's a bitch at times.'

She nodded. 'Don't I know it? And what did you say when you found out about me? You told me to put it all behind me and in time I did. You will too.'

'Don't I get a hug too?' Steph piped up. 'I'm the only one who's missed out.'

'Er...and me too,' Mark cut in. 'Can I have one?'

'No, you bloody can't!' Jack quipped with a loud guttural laugh. 'You're not my type.'

Lucille turned to Mark. 'Thanks for that Mark. It means a lot to me to see Jack laugh again. It's right what everybody says about you at work. You really are brilliant. Twice you've managed to raise a laugh out of him. Do you honestly think he'll be okay?'

'I do, given time. Jack's had a double trauma. He lost his mate too and is riddled with guilt about that but he'll come to terms with it in due course.'

After the brief initial emotion, Jack settled down

to enjoy the conversation with his visitors, catching up on all the news and the benefit gained from their visit was apparent to his doctor who ambled in for a few minutes. Mark seized the opportunity to speak with him aside regarding Jack's injuries and learned that most of the burns had healed satisfactorily with few remaining scars. Whilst there was still a way to go with the fractured femur, recent x-rays displayed promising results, he informed Mark.

'We'll all be back again this evening,' Mattie told Jack as they prepared to leave. 'We'll be here overnight so we'll see you again tomorrow too.'

With a grunt he replied, 'Leave Seth at the hotel. I don't want him here destroying my reputation any further,' and with a raucous guffaw beckoned Seth to his side. 'Thanks for coming mate. I know now what you meant when you once said it were a very long day, stuck in a hospital bed. I've been looking forward to this day for weeks. It's been great to see you. Glad you could make it.' He held out his hand and as Seth edged nearer he grabbed out and pulled him close for a brotherly hug. 'Take care of Mattie. I know she worries, and for the record I were six.'

'Six?' he queried.

'When I stopped peeing in bed but if you repeat that to anyone, I'll kill you when I get out of here.'

Seth laughed and their eyes met for a split-second though long enough for both men to acknowledge the brotherly love that bonded them. 'It'll get better Jack and we can't wait to have you home.'

'Aye, the feeling's mutual Seth. See you later.'

Lucille joined the others in reception after spending some time alone with Jack and when the visits came to an end the next day, they all returned home in high spirits knowing Jack would soon be joining his family unlike many other unfortunate victims on Jack's ward who, with horrendous injuries, would undoubtedly be hospitalised for months to come.

He finally arrived home on the thirty-first of July, reliant on crutches and in need of physiotherapy but to be back in his home environment was a colossal boost to his mental state, although there remained a way to go to full recovery.

'Are you sure that's everything Emily? Did you go through all Norman's drawers too?'

'I think so but you can check if you like. He only had those four over there.'

Mattie walked over to the tall-boy and opened the top drawer. Apart from a couple of shirt buttons it was empty. She removed the drawer and banged it over the waste bin before wiping it out with a damp cloth. After following suit with the other three she replaced them.

'I'm going to stick my jumpers in the top two. It's pointless leaving them empty.' She sighed heavily. 'I always liked Norman in this brown striped shirt. It reminds me of the very first time we met. He was wearing a similar shirt then with a cream tie and he looked so handsome. We were at a wedding. I was nobbut a lass then,' she laughed. 'Happy days!'

'Then why not hang on to it? Lots of people keep a memento of a loved one. Put it in your wardrobe and he'll always be here with you Emily.'

'I should, shouldn't I? Yes you're right; I will.'

Mattie moved the bags of clothes to the landing. 'If you give me your jumpers I'll fold them for you and put them away and then I'd better be off. Mark will have our tea ready and we're seeing Jack later.'

'Yes, that unfortunate boy. How's he doing?'

Mattie shrugged. 'He's giving Lucille a very hard time. She's been at home with him this week. It'll be worse for him next week when she's gone back to work. He finds physio so stressful and she has to badger him to do his exercises. We're all trying to offer support but he's loath to help himself.'

'You never know, it might be better when he's on his own. If he wants anything he'll have to get off his backside and get it.'

'Akina's offered to go round but I can't make my mind up whether to let her or not. She's only twelve and it's a big responsibility.'

'What's the alternative? She's a good cook so she could at least make him something to eat and reach and fetch for him. If there's a problem she can contact you. She can be a little madam you know and she'll make him fend for himself. She used to do it with Norman when he wanted something. He didn't half tell her off but she wouldn't budge. She's very headstrong like Sam was...chip off the old block.'

'Well it's that or nothing. There's nobody else *but* Akina. I doubt Adam would want to go.'

Emily smiled. 'Stop worrying Mattie. Akina will cope with Jack just fine and Adam will be here with me. Besides, I enjoy Adam's company. He's such a polite lad and enjoys doing the garden for me. Mair

218

will have my undivided attention so she'll be happy too and if it transpires that Akina dislikes caring for Jack, she's welcome here as well. I'll cope for four weeks or so until they're back at school.'

Mattie had finished folding the jumpers. 'I'll give it some thought. I think that's the lot now. I've put your jumpers in the top two drawers. There's some papers you might want to sort out in your drawer.'

'Throw them in one of the bags. It'll be rubbish.'

As Mattie gathered them all together she paused, for lying face up at the very back of the drawer was a business card bearing the name Yukio Hashimoto. For a moment she was dumbstruck, the question at the forefront of her mind being *why? Why* had she hidden it at the back of a drawer where Sam would never find it? But then why keep it at all? Why not simply destroy it? The realisation suddenly dawned. She had been afraid Sam, her only daughter, might leave her...leave her to search for the father of her child. It had been a calculated decision, some might say selfish, but not totally so, for hadn't she hidden the card where it would be found after her death?

'Is everything alright?' Emily asked, interrupting her thoughts.

Stuffing the remaining items into the rubbish bag she stuttered, 'Er...yes, I've done now. I really must get home. I'll just nip these bags down to the car.' Without a further word she hurried from the room.

Emily followed her to the door. 'Don't go without your handbag,' she called after her.

Rushing back Mattie faked a smile. 'I'd forget my head if it were loose. See you soon. Must dash!'

During the short journey home, her mind was in a whirl. She almost wished she hadn't found the card, because now she had, an important decision had to be made. With a busy evening ahead she needed to eradicate it from her thoughts until she could confer with Mark but that need proved impossible. Whatever Mark might say, she knew what she must do. That man was Akina's father. He had to be found.

'You're playing with fire Mattie,' Mark cautioned. 'No good can come of this after so long. It'll all end in tears and imagine the long-term effect on Akina if her father were to reject her. Emily had the good sense to realise that and you should too.'

'Emily's motives were egocentric, otherwise why keep his business card? She didn't want to lose Sam and her grandchild. Japan's the opposite side of the world from here. If Sam had gone looking for him she might never have returned but even Emily had moral principals. She couldn't destroy the evidence of Akina's paternity. Tell me I'm wrong.'

He snorted. 'It doesn't matter what I say, does it? Akina was placed in *your* care, not mine. You'll do what you have to do, with or without my blessing. I just hope it doesn't backfire on you and if you intend going ahead with this hair-brained plan, might I suggest you don't mention it to Akina until it's a *fait accompli*. I don't want to see her heart broken even if you do.'

Mattie jumped up. 'I'm off to bed. You can be so obtuse at times. You have the audacity to denigrate *me* for doing the right thing after *you* wanted to see

Josh Hargreaves locked up when he was a mentally ill man. I should have known better than to discuss it with you Mark.'

He threw back his head and roared with laughter as she stomped furiously from the room. Never in a million years would he understand women.

Akina pandered to Jack's every need for a couple of hours like the proverbial mother hen, clearly deriving pleasure from her role as his carer and Jack, in turn, enjoyed the attention lavished on him but little did he know how calculating she could be.

After washing the breakfast pots, she removed a game of Monopoly from her bag and set it up.

'I haven't played Monopoly for years,' he said. 'I used to like that. What else have you brought?'

'Chess. Can you play?'

'Can I play?' he hooted. 'I was the junior school champion. You're in for a hard time young lady.'

He was playing right into her hands. 'I like doing deals Uncle Jack, so, if I win, promise you'll walk to the end of the street and back with me. Deal?'

He smirked. 'Beat *me* at chess and I'll walk to the end of the earth. Deal!'

She smiled smugly. 'It's okay. I'm happy to settle for the end of the street.'

They played Monopoly for a couple of hours until it was time to prepare lunch. Jack wanted a cheese and ham omelette with crusty bread after Akina had checked the contents of the fridge. It smelled delicious when she carried in his plate to show him.

'Follow me,' she said, walking into the kitchen.

221

'But I eat my meals in here Akina. Fetch it back.'

'You *eat* at the *table*,' she stated demonstratively.

Left with no option but to comply, he raised himself up carefully and headed to the kitchen, puffing and panting.

She set his mug of tea beside him. 'You're such a drama queen. I'll have you fit for the London Marathon by the end of August. You see if I don't.'

'Less of the lip or I'll box your ears,' he snarled.

She laughed. 'You'll have to catch me first.'

Jack fixed his eyes on the tall slender girl whose beauty knew no bounds, and not only that, she was wise beyond her years. Earlier he had wanted to cry out and run for cover to obliterate the horror of that fateful day in May, yet in the space of a few hours a young girl, little more than a child, had uplifted him and given him a new perspective on life. 'You'll be here tomorrow won't you?' he asked humbly.

'That depends on whether you keep your promise to walk to the end of the street.'

He smiled. 'That were hypothetical, dependent on you beating me at chess. It ain't going to happen.'

'But if it does?'

He nodded. 'Then I will. You have my word.'

After lunch she cleared away the plates and set up the board. Jack rubbed his hands together zealously and planned his opening strategic move but Akina's counter moves proved well conceived and rapid in response, a worthy opponent he quickly deduced.

At the end of the game she grinned. 'Right Uncle Jack. Walkies! I forgot to mention; *I'm* pretty good at chess too. I'll get your jacket.'

It was strange, Jack thought, how satisfying it felt to have the sun on his face and once he'd walked a few yards the discomfort eased and his pace quickened, though he walked with a pronounced limp. 'I think you might be right about that Marathon, lass. We'll have to do this again tomorrow. It feels good to be outside for a change. Lucille will be surprised, especially when she learns I didn't use my crutches, all thanks to you. What spurs you on Akina?'

'What? You mean the challenge?' and he nodded. 'I guess it fuels my resolve to succeed. It's the same when I play games. I only ever play to win. I made a promise to my mother that I'd always do my best and I've kept that promise...well most of the time. I allowed my schoolwork to slide a bit but Dad found out and went mad, with Adam too.'

'It must be difficult, living up to someone else's expectations.'

'Not really. I just try to do my best. Take physics for instance; I'm useless at that but I still try to keep up with the others. Adam helps me. He's brilliant.'

Jack frowned. 'I were a thick-head at school who never listened to nowt the teacher said. I were forever in trouble for summat.'

She giggled. 'You certainly paid little attention to English grammar but I like how you talk. It's nothing like the way Uncle Seth and Mattie talk.'

'Aye, well, Seth were always reading. I weren't a scholar but we're all different and our Mattie threw herself into her studies after the trouble she'd had.'

At that Akina's ears pricked up. 'What trouble?'

'See what I mean about being a thick-head? I run

off at the tongue. I open my gob without getting my brain in gear first. It were a long time ago when we were in care and Mattie were knocked about by her foster-parents,' he prevaricated. 'Promise you'll not tell her I let it slip...promise?'

'Okay, although I don't see what all the secrecy's about. I don't suppose for a minute it was her fault.'

'Well that's the way she wants it...no reminders.'

Though unconvinced by his explanation, she nodded in compliance. 'It's physio tomorrow morning. I'll come too, then I'll know what you have to do.'

'So you can put me through more misery?'

'Misery?' she laughed. 'Speak the truth and admit you're enjoying all the attention.'

He slipped his arm through hers. 'Aye, I am lass. You're like a breath of fresh air. You've done me a power of good today...apart from when you beat me at chess, that is.' Tears but a blink away sparkled in his eyes. He had turned the corner. He was back on the road to recovery, made possible by the help of a twelve-year-old girl to whom he owed an enormous debt of gratitude.

10

'Come on, move yourself Akina,' Mattie called up-stairs as the eight o'clock news broke. 'You don't want to be late for school on your first day back.'

She threw a napkin on Akina's plate and poured a glass of orange juice as she heard her run across the landing. 'Cereal okay?' she asked as Akina took her place at the table.

'Whatever,' she murmured impassively, taking a small sip of her juice. 'By the way, I'll be late home tonight.'

'Oh? Why is that?'

'I'm going to Olivia's for tea. Her dad's picking us up after school.'

'So what about your homework young lady?'

She emitted an exasperated grunt. 'Just give me a break! Besides, we're unlikely to get homework the first day back and I *do* have a life outside school.'

'Pardon me! You've just had six weeks' holiday so don't make out you're hard done by. You know schoolwork takes priority. How will you get home? Do you want Dad to pick you up?'

She shrugged. 'I'll call you if I do.'

Mattie glanced up as Mark appeared. 'I've made you ham sandwiches for lunch and there's a pot of fresh coffee there if you've time for a drink.'

He glanced at his watch. 'It'll have to be a quick one. I've a busy schedule today.'

Adam, who hadn't spoken one word, continued to butter his slice of toast meticulously, spreading it to the very edges until none of the bread was visible.

'If you intend eating that Son, I suggest you stop mauling it and make a start or you'll be walking to school. I'm leaving in two minutes,' Mark told him.

Adam looked up with sleepy eyes and proceeded to eat his toast in silence.

Suddenly Akina piped up, 'Why is everybody so bad tempered this morning?'

Mark smiled. 'No one's bad tempered. You know we have to make an early start to avoid the traffic.'

Adam's chair legs grated noisily on the tiled floor as he rose. 'I'll just nip up for my bag. I'll meet you at the car in a couple of minutes Dad.'

Akina hurried up after him. 'I bet you're glad to be going back to school.'

He nodded. 'I am. Six weeks is far too long for a holiday. I'll be glad to get back to my studies.'

She laughed. 'Always the little book-worm, aren't you? The only thing I'll be glad about is being back with all my mates and getting out of this place for a bit of peace. This has been the third summer without a proper family holiday. I know they're saving up for Japan next year but they earn pots of money. Heaven alone knows what they spend it all on.'

He flashed a derisive glance. 'For starters they're forking out for three lots of school fees though why they bother for you beats me. The first summer you spent with Uncle Jack; we went back to Devon last summer and at Easter we went to Paris. You can be so inconsiderate at times. Mum and Dad work very hard and you rarely lift a finger to help. You never used to be so obnoxious. Why do teenage girls have to make everyone's life a misery?'

She laughed scornfully. 'My word, who's rattled *your* cage? Come on, spill the beans. Has your girl-friend given you the elbow?'

'Just shut it. I don't have one,' he snapped back.

At that she cackled mockingly. 'Seems I was spot on then. You've obviously been dumped!'

The brief conversation was interrupted by Mattie who called, 'Final warning! Your dad's waiting.'

Grabbing his bag, Adam ran downstairs and Mair was waiting by the door. 'See you later Mum,' he said, kissing her on her cheek. 'Have a good day.'

'You too Adam. Bye darling.'

As he shot through the door, Mattie smiled. Adam was so well-mannered and affectionate, just like his father. Whilst clearing the remaining pots from the table, Akina appeared wearing mascara and lipstick, her tie loose over her partly unbuttoned blouse, her skirt turned over at the waist, shortening the length.

Sighing, Mattie glared at her. 'Don't start Akina; I don't have the time. I'm in Court later and I've a lot to do first. Straighten your uniform and wash all that make-up off. Your dad can go without you and I'll drop you off but you're not going in like that.'

Arrogantly she snapped. 'Says who?'

'Says *me*...now *do* it!' Mattie told her crossly.

'You can't dictate to me what I can and can't do. You're not my mother!' she yelled.

227

Irately she contradicted, 'As a matter of fact I am! I adopted you in case you've conveniently forgotten and prior to that I was your guardian. That gives me legal rights and responsibilities, so don't *ever* speak to me like that again, do you hear?'

The quarrel ended there as Akina knew she would have to comply, otherwise her pre-arranged outing to Olivia's could be in jeopardy and she didn't want to miss the opportunity of spending time in Luke's company. Luke, Olivia's brother was seventeen. He was full of fun, good looking *and* had his own car.

As Mattie awaited her return, her thoughts were cast back to nineteen-seventy-six….eight years ago. She sighed heavily. What an eventful year that had been, the year she had met Sam, and it had been a major turning point in her life. Sam was terminally ill then and desperately seeking a suitable guardian for Akina and from the first moment she set eyes on the child, Mattie knew she would take on the role. Akina, an enchanting five-year-old, was fully aware of her mother's terminal illness yet she displayed a stoicism seldom seen in such a young person. They had bonded instantly and Sam had been allowed to enjoy the rest of her days in the knowledge that her daughter would be loved and cared for by Mattie. It had been a distressing few months, watching Sam slowly ebb away but Sam, a young woman of great courage, had maintained her dignity until the end.

When events had earlier conspired to keep Mattie and Mark apart, Sam had also been instrumental in getting them together and for that fact alone Mattie would be eternally indebted to her.

Mattie turned round when Akina reappeared and smiled. 'That's so much better and believe me, you don't need make-up on those large expressive eyes, or your flawless skin. You're a beautiful girl. Many a girl would give her right arm to look like you.'

Akina's air of displeasure quickly changed to one of amusement. 'That really is a daft turn of phrase. Imagine sacrificing an arm to have a prettier face. I can see lads fighting over a girl with only one arm.'

'It's simply an idiom and not meant literally. So, that's what all this is about...boys?' Mattie asked, her lips curling into a wry smile.

With a red face she blustered, 'Er...no...I didn't mean that. I only meant...'

'It's okay. I suppose you're no different from any other teenager but it's better to keep boys guessing. Be thankful for your natural beauty. So, who is he?'

'I don't know what you mean,' she replied curtly. 'Are we ready? I don't want to be late for school.'

As she dashed out ahead with the sunlight shining on her jet black hair, Mattie knew this was just the tip of the iceberg. Although only fourteen, she was already stunning, having Sam's tall willowy figure and her birth father's oriental facial features, undisputedly a dynamic combination of genes. She was also intelligent and strong-willed and Mattie knew she would be quite a handful in the years to come.

'Sorry I'm late Meredith,' Mattie remarked, sitting down hurriedly at her desk. 'I know we've a lot on today. I intended being here sooner but Akina was playing up.'

Meredith laughed. 'It's called the joys of mother-hood. I'm thankful Andrew's two are boys or rather young men. What's she been up to now?'

'Oh, nothing much but I had to make a stand. If I give her an inch she'll take a mile. She waltzed into the kitchen wearing make-up for school, so we had words when I asked her to wash it off.'

Meredith chuckled. 'Teenage girls! I remember it well. I used to spend forever getting ready to go out and then my mother would yell, "You can get back upstairs and get all that muck washed off your face or you're going nowhere." So, what did Mark say?'

'He'd already left but I doubt he'd have said any-thing. You know Mark, anything for the easy life. Besides, she has him eating out of her hand. What worries me is, she's only fourteen but she'd pass as sixteen easily. She's as tall as Adam now.'

'Yes, she's certainly blossoming. By the way, you know what day it is tomorrow don't you?'

'Yes, that's why I didn't say much. It'll be eight years tomorrow since Sam died. Maybe that's why she's been so edgy these past few days.'

'Does she talk about Sam much?'

'No, not really. I wish she would talk to me about her memories. I'd be a willing listener but it has to be her decision.'

'And Sam's ashes? Does she still have them?'

She sighed. 'Yes, the casket's still on her dressing table, where it's always been since we moved in. I never raised it again after the first time. She told me then that she felt her mother was close and that was where she wanted her to remain. I don't think she's ever accepted me as her mother. I'm just the person who takes care of her.'

'That's absolute rubbish Mattie. Akina thinks the world of you. Don't be envious of somebody she's lost. She had her such a short time and for the most part Sam was ill. Perhaps she's afraid she'll forget her if she parts with the one tangible thing she has left. Do you ever show her photographs of Sam?'

'I don't have any. Emily probably has though. I'll ask when I next see her. I don't want Akina thinking I'm trying to shut Sam out.'

'It might be an idea to have a nice picture of Sam framed for Akina to have in her room. You can get copies made even without a negative. Does she ever mention her father?'

'I can't recall she has, other than when referring to her mixed race but then she never knew him. It's odd isn't it how things emerge as part of life's rich pattern?'

'How do you mean?'

'I mean Akina…an unexpected consequence of a whirlwind liaison between Sam and a Japanese guy. It was nothing more than a fling and as they made no arrangements to keep in touch when he returned home, he doesn't even know of Akina's existence.'

Meredith nodded. 'There must be millions of kids like that worldwide, conceived as a consequence of a drunken night out, a holiday romance or...'

'Or rape!' she intervened bitingly. 'Do you think we could drop the subject now please?'

Meredith had unintentionally touched a nerve and was sorry but Mattie was thankful since she hadn't disclosed she had found Yukio Hashimoto's details. She had made her decision; it would be disclosed to no one and she alone would take full responsibility for the consequences of her actions.

Mark arrived home later than usual that night. He looked tired as he flopped down in an armchair and kicked off his shoes.

Mattie walked over and put her arms around him. 'Bad day?' she asked, brushing her lips against his forehead affectionately.

'No, it was just a long list and a few took longer than normal so I was late doing my ward round. By the way, I saw Helen McAndrew at lunchtime and she was asking about you. She'd like you to pop in one lunchtime for a chat.'

'What about?'

'Just a chat, nothing in particular. She only works there Mondays and Thursdays now though.'

'I'm surprised she's still there at all. She must be sixty if she's a day.'

He threw back his head and roared with laughter. 'She wouldn't speak to you again if she heard that. She's barely over fifty.'

'That can't be right. I was fourteen the first time I saw her and she looked fifty then. You're wrong.'

Convincingly he said, 'No, I'm not. When you're a kid everyone seems old. I'm forty-three and she's probably nine years older than me, no more.'

Jokily she commented, 'Yes, I'd say you looked a year or two younger than Helen McAndrew.'

'Come here,' he said grabbing her and pulling her onto his lap. He kissed her amorously. 'I've missed you today. You've been on my mind all the time. I don't suppose the kids are out?'

'I thought you were tired?'

'Never too tired for you. So are the kids out?'

'Akina's gone for tea to Olivia's; Adam's upstairs doing his homework and Mair's watching TV.'

'Huh! Foiled again. Kids! Who'd have them?'

She sighed. 'I'd have liked another. It would have been nice to have another of *ours*, a brother or sister for Mair but it didn't happen. I'm not complaining though. I love our others so much.'

'You're only thirty-three so it could still happen. Why not take Helen up on her offer of lunch? Talk to her Mattie. She's an excellent gynaecologist and there might be a simple explanation.'

'Yes! We both know what *that* would be. We've already had this conversation. I've no desire to reap up the past. It took long enough to obliterate it from my mind and I nearly lost you owing to what happened. Besides, it's far too late now. Mair's six so drop it please.'

He changed topic. Any reference to her childhood in the foster-home evoked distressing memories. 'It appears you're saying you're happy the way things turned out between us?'

She smiled lovingly. 'You know I am. It was the best thing that ever happened to me, marrying you, and you were there for me when Sam was ill at that stressful time in my life. I'm pleased I have Akina, despite her efforts to wind me up from time to time. We had words again this morning.'

'What about this time?'

At the end of her revelations he laughed. 'She's a teenager. What were you like at fourteen?'

When she gave him a cutting look he apologised. 'Sorry...I didn't think. I meant girls are much more challenging in their early teens than boys. I'm sure Adam will start to kick off before too long.'

'I doubt that. He has his head screwed on. Do you reckon he'll follow you into medicine?'

'It's what he wants to do if he gets good grades. He's good at science subjects but English Grammar lets him down badly, so that'll have to improve for him to get a place in Medical School.'

'Why? I thought medical terminology was written in Latin,' she quipped.

'Yes, like most of your legal jargon but you don't write to clients in Latin or speak it in Court do you? I'm serious; he really needs to improve his English. He's a *terrible* writer.'

'I've yet to meet a doctor who isn't. I thought that was a prerequisite. Maybe I can help. He probably just needs a confidence boost. When I was at school girls always did better than boys in English but they were pretty useless at science subjects.'

'I agree Mattie but that's because girls clack more and don't have logical minds,' he scoffed. 'What's for dinner?'

She allowed his remark to pass without comment. Besides, he was probably right. 'I've made chicken and mushroom pie. It'll be ready now so I'll go and call the children.'

After dinner, Adam went to his room whilst Mark put Mair to bed, then he and Mattie settled down to watch the television. It was turned nine-thirty when Mattie next checked her watch. 'Akina's late Mark. She knows to be home by nine-thirty when she has school the next day.'

'Relax. She'll be here before long. You worry too much. She can't come to any harm at a friend's.'

Adam was crossing the upstairs landing when he heard a car. He peered through the window as two figures emerged. One was Akina and the other was the driver, a youth unknown to Adam. He watched the youth walk round the car and was aghast to see him take Akina in his arms. She made no attempt to stop him when he kissed her and as Adam continued to watch in disbelief, Akina wrapped her arms around him in response.

He ran downstairs to the door and flinging it open yelled, 'Get your filthy hands off my sister!'

Mattie and Mark ran to the door to investigate the cause of the commotion as Adam repeated angrily, 'Get your filthy hands off her!'

'And what if I don't?' the youth was heard to say, followed by a cackling laugh.

'I won't tell you again,' Adam yelled, making his way down the drive, closely followed by Mark and Mattie. Adam was about to strike him as Mark interceded and addressing the youth asked, 'Who are you and what are you doing here?'

'I'm Luke...Olivia's brother and I've just brought Akina home that's all and this cretin came hurtling towards me bawling obscenities.'

'Go inside please,' Mattie told Akina.

'But I...'

'*Now* please,' Mattie repeated in raised voice. 'I think you'd better leave er….Luke.'

Luke snorted. 'Typical! That's the thanks you get for driving a girl home to make sure she's safe.'

'*No girl would be safe with you*,' Adam shouted. 'You're disgusting. She's only fourteen. Find a girl your own age to maul and keep right away from my sister in future or you'll be facing much more than a bawling cretin.'

With a scathing sneer, Luke eyed him from head to toe. 'In your dreams, little boy…in your dreams. You'd better get inside now. I'm sure it's way past your bedtime.'

'Just leave it Son,' Mark said as Adam took a step forward and turning to Luke added, 'I suggest you keep away from Akina in future if you know what's good for you,' and without further comment, Mark ushered Mattie and Adam indoors.

Akina had scampered up to her room and was in tears when Mattie opened her bedroom door. 'I hate Adam, showing me up like that!' she yelled. 'Who does he think he is? I wasn't doing anything wrong. Luke had driven me home and was just giving me a goodnight kiss, that's all. Adam's outburst was so humiliating Mattie. Now he'll tell Olivia and she's a right gob on her so tomorrow it'll be all over the school. I'll be the laughing stock.'

'Come downstairs and we'll talk calmly.'

'I will *not!* I refuse to be in the same room as that moron,' Akina retorted tearfully.

'It's not open to discussion,' she said forcefully. 'I want to know exactly what happened.'

Blowing her nose noisily she accompanied Mattie downstairs where Mark looked up and saw her tear-stained face.

'It's okay Akina. We're not angry,' he said softly. 'Sit beside me and explain what happened.'

'There's nothing to explain,' she said defensively. 'Luke kissed me goodnight, that's all. It was only a peck on the cheek. Why *Adam* had to stick his ugly, fat, interfering nose in I'll never know.'

'He was merely looking out for you. You can't be too careful these days. How old is that boy?'

'Er….sixteen I think. He could be seventeen. I'm not sure,' she prevaricated.

At that point Mattie intervened. 'He was driving a car so he's at least seventeen. I think Luke's too old for you. He should be dating girls his own age.'

'Like Dad did? He's *ten* years older than you.'

'That's different. I was in my twenties when I met Dad. You're only fourteen. You should be having a good time, meeting lots of boys of your own age. I don't want you to see Luke again.'

Akina was mortified and burst into tears. 'That is *so* unfair. You'll do *anything* to spoil my pleasure. As for you, you snitch, you've caused all this with your lies. I hate you Adam!'

'I wasn't lying. That moron was pawing you and you were letting him.'

'Right, I think that's enough,' Mark said sternly. 'There's no harm done so there's no need for name-calling. Adam was just showing concern, Akina.'

She offered no response to Mark but instead gave Adam a black look. 'I'll get my own back. You see if I don't,' she snarled through clenched teeth and at that, went back upstairs to her room.

Akina was subdued the next morning at breakfast, worrying about the likely reaction of her classmates should Olivia choose to broadcast details of the previous evening's contretemps. In addition, today was the eighth anniversary of her mother's death, a day that never failed to evoke poignant memories.

Akina continued to stir her cereal around the bowl but made no attempt to eat it.

'Shall I make you some toast to take to school?' Mattie asked quietly. 'You might feel hungry later.'

She shrugged. 'It's up to you. I wish I didn't have to go today. Thanks to Adam's big gob, I'll be the butt of everybody's jokes once Olivia's done broadcasting it round the school about last night.'

'I thought Olivia was a friend? Besides, in Luke's shoes, I'd be too ashamed to mention it to *anyone*, least of all my younger sister and I'm quite sure he wouldn't want his parents knowing he came on to a fourteen year old girl.'

Argumentatively she replied, 'I'll be *fifteen* soon.'

'Not for another seven months Akina and by then Luke will be *eighteen*, wanting to go drinking like all eighteen year old boys and he can't do that with an under-age girl, so please let it drop.'

Unwilling to let Mattie have the final word Akina snarled, 'He already goes in pubs. He easily passes for eighteen.'

'Does he now? If that's the case, then he's *totally* unsuitable for a fourteen-year-old and I don't want him driving you home anymore. Understood?'

She muttered something in reply but Mattie didn't catch it and then added, 'I'll wait for you by the car. The sooner I get through today, the better.'

For the first five minutes of their journey, not one word was exchanged. Akina turned on the radio and stared out of the window.

Mattie decided to end the uncomfortable silence. 'How about we buy a tree, something like a flowering cherry that we could put in the garden for your mum? We could put it where you'd see it from your bedroom window. She loved flowers and trees. We could choose it together and Dad would attend to it. What do you think? I miss her too darling and I've never tried to take her place. I just want what's best for you. I promised I'd always keep you from harm and that's all I'm trying to do. So, would you like a tree, or is there something else you'd prefer?'

She thought for a few moments before answering. 'Yes, I think she'd like that. What if we ever moved house though? We'd have to leave it behind then.'

'Not necessarily. That's the reason I suggested a flowering cherry. It could easily be transplanted if the need ever arose.'

'Great. Can we get one today?' she asked eagerly.

'I don't see why not. Come to the office after you finish school. I'll call Dad to meet us there.'

'Thanks Mattie and I'm really sorry about earlier, the way I spoke to you. I'm a bit crusty today. You know what day it is, don't you?'

'I'd never forget that darling. I loved Sam too. It was cruel, the way she was taken away but dreadful things happen in life and we must move on. I know she wouldn't want you to be miserable. By the way you might have a surprise in a few days. I'm working on something I'm pretty sure you'll like.'

'What's that?'

'Well now, it wouldn't be a surprise if I told you.'

'Just tell me if it's something nice.'

'Of course it is and I'm saying nothing more.'

As Akina stepped from the car, she leaned across and kissed Mattie on the cheek. 'I love you heaps,' she said with a beaming smile and Mattie drove off with a sense of warm radiance throughout her body.

The Garden Centre had an abundance of flowering trees and shrubs that Akina closely scrutinised.

Mark, who joined them minutes after their arrival, offered constructive suggestions until Akina finally selected a pink flowering cherry. It was growing in a large pot, too big to fit in either car, but one of the greenhouse boys offered to deliver it later as he had a trailer and lived close by. 'You'll be able to shove it in the ground in a couple of months,' he informed Mark. 'Meanwhile, leave it in the pot. It'll be fine.'

'It's for my mum,' Akina told him. 'She's dead.'

He looked shocked. 'I'm er…sorry about that.'

'It's alright. It was a long time ago. These are my adoptive parents,' she said with a beaming smile.

'What about your real Dad? Where's he?'

'Japan I expect. I never knew him. He was never married to my mum and didn't hang around to face the consequences. I guess they only did it the once and she got caught. It happens doesn't it?' she said with an air of authority.

'*Akina!*' Mattie cried as Mark howled with laughter. She tugged Akina's arm and dragged her away. 'Don't you *ever* speak about your mother like that! That's disgraceful!'

She was mystified. 'Why? What did I say wrong? That's what happened isn't it?'

'No! It wasn't like that at all. He was at the guest house for a few weeks and he and your mum spent time together but when he left, they didn't arrange to keep in touch. There seemed no point when they lived at opposite ends of the earth. When your mum later discovered she was er…having you…'

'Pregnant,' she butted in. 'The word's *pregnant*.'

'Right well…er…when she found out, she had no way of getting in touch with him. I'm quite sure if she had he would have been there for you.'

'So he didn't just use her and abandon her then?'

'Of course not! Whatever gave you that idea?'

'I don't know. She never discussed it with me.'

'I should hope not at your age. You were only six when she died.'

She looked ahead pensively. 'I wonder what he's like. I've often thought about that…whether I might have Japanese brothers and sisters. I'll never know though will I?'

Mattie cast a sideways glance in Mark's direction and gave her a hug. 'No darling, sadly you won't.'

Akina's next revelation sent shock waves through her body. 'There are two girls in our class at school that are pregnant. Imagine in this day and age that they were stupid enough to have unprotected sex.'

'What I find hard to believe is that fourteen-year-

241

old girls are *having* sex – unprotected or otherwise.'

'Loads in our class have but I don't fancy the lads *they've* been with so I'll wait for someone better.'

As Mattie recovered from the shocking disclosure Mark returned from the cash point. 'The young man will be along with the tree in thirty minutes. I need to make room on the path to get past with the tree.'

Mattie's thoughts ran riot throughout the journey home, remembering her anguish at the foster-home, when, after being separated from her two brothers, she had been repeatedly subjected to sexual abuse. It beggared belief that Akina at the same tender age could talk about her school pals' experiences as if it were acceptable these days. Mattie couldn't believe it. She would have to discuss it with Mark once the children were asleep. Children...that's just how she regarded them, not as young adults. Both their older children were in need of a sober tutorial about the facts of life and in need of it now, although Mattie wasn't looking forward to her session with Akina.

'That lad's here with the tree,' Akina called.

'Dad's out there so he'll give him a hand,' Mattie replied. 'I'm going to Nana's for Mair now.'

Akina bolted downstairs two at a time and rushed outside as the youth appeared carrying the tree with the help of a younger boy.

'Do you need a hand?' asked Mark.

'No, we're okay thanks. I called home first to ask my brother to help me lift it off the trailer.'

Akina smiled at the younger lad who looked to be about fifteen and he returned her smile.

Though one would not describe him as handsome, there was a friendly, affable aura about him.

'If you've got a spade handy, I'll dig the pot in to stop it blowing over,' the older one told Mark.

'Cheers. I'll fetch it,' Mark said, hurrying away to the garden shed.

Addressing Akina the younger one asked, 'Don't you go to that posh Grange school?'

She nodded. 'Yes I do. How did you know that?'

'I've seen you there a few times.'

'I doubt that,' she giggled. 'It's a girls' school.'

His brother guffawed. 'What did I tell you? I said you'd get caught out wearing a girl's uniform. Your cover's well and truly blown now.'

'Shut up you clown!' he spat. 'A few weeks ago I was working there as an apprentice electrician and there was a problem with the heating that turned out to be electrical. I hope it's working alright now.'

'It's fine. You obviously did a good job.'

'I didn't do much at all,' he confessed. 'I was just the gopher then, "*gopher* this," and "*gopher* that," all day long, week in week out.'

'How old are you?'

'Seventeen in a fortnight. How about you?'

At that opportune moment Mark returned with the spade and his brother whisked him away.

She watched him make light work of the digging, whilst eyeing him from head to toe. He had a kind smile and seemed nice...*very* nice in fact.

As they heeled in the pot, Adam came outside and wandered over. Recognising Martin, he greeted him warmly. 'Hi. I thought it was you when I saw you

243

through the window. I didn't know you did gardening work.'

'I don't. I'm just helping my brother. Will you be training on Saturday?'

'All being well. Will you?'

'I'm hoping to. Listen, I'm having a party a week on Saturday. It's my birthday and a few mates will be there. There'll be a few girls there too. It's not a rave-up but you're more than welcome if you want to come. Bring your sister too. What's her name?'

'She's called Akina.'

'Nice name. I've seen her at Grange.'

He pondered. 'I'll let you know on Saturday.'

As they were leaving, Martin gave Akina a beaming smile. 'It was nice talking to you. I didn't know Adam was your brother. We play footie together on Saturdays. Maybe I'll see you around.'

'Maybe,' she answered bashfully.

'Here, get yourselves a drink,' Mark interrupted, pressing a couple of pounds in the older lad's hand. 'I appreciate your help. Thanks a lot.'

Over the next few days Akina busied herself around the house, helping at every opportunity.

Mistakenly, Mattie assumed the sudden attraction to household chores had arisen due to the promised surprise a day or two earlier but nothing could have been further from the truth.

Determined not to blot her copy book as Martin's birthday party approached, Akina knew she must be on her best behaviour. Whilst Mark was happy for Adam to go, Mattie had reservations about Akina's safety at a party of teenagers of varied age range.

'You can't keep her tied to your apron strings for ever Mattie,' Mark warned. 'If you don't give her a little trust and freedom, she'll do things behind your back. Adam will be there to keep an eye on her. He seemed a decent young lad I thought, rather quiet.'

'Yes and you know what they say about the quiet ones. I'm not happy but I suppose I'll have to agree to it or I'll be an ogre. You made your feelings clear enough in front of her. *You'd* let her do anything!'

There was a splutter of cynical laughter at that. 'I, unlike you, wouldn't build up her hopes regarding her biological father. I deliberately haven't brought up the subject with you since you found his details, but I've no doubt you've tried to make contact with him and *that* is a damn sight more detrimental than anything that's likely to happen at a birthday party.'

'Is that so? Well, for your information, I have *not* tried to contact him at all.'

He breathed a sigh of relief. 'I'm glad you finally came round to my way of thinking. Believe me, it's for the best.'

Though Mattie was livid she bit her tongue. She'd let him believe what he wanted to for now. Her plan was already formulated and at the right time, she'd implement it.

'Those are amazing!' Mattie remarked to the sales assistant in *Photosnap*. 'I can't believe how they've turned out, considering there were no negatives.'

'Technology's improving every day,' he advised. 'You'd be surprised what else we can do. Take this leaflet. It might give you a few ideas for Christmas presents. Less than a hundred shopping days to go!'

She thanked him and hurried back to the office to show Meredith who was equally impressed. 'Akina will be over the moon. They're beautiful. Will you give them to her this evening?'

'I might distract her for a while to give Mark time to hang that big one. I'd rather she was alone when she saw them. She'll be very emotional I'm sure.'

'I agree. Have you decided about the party yet?'

Heaving a sigh Mattie nodded. 'Against my better judgement I'm letting her go. Maybe if I show trust in her she'll honour that trust by being sensible. She told me recently that two fourteen-year-olds at her school were pregnant and shocked me more by adding that she couldn't believe they'd had unprotected sex...as if it was the *norm* to be having sex at their age. I don't know what this world's coming to. I'll be relieved when she's married. Raising a teenage girl's an absolute nightmare.'

'Do you think *she* has...had sex?'

'She says not. She says she doesn't fancy the lads at school, so she's hanging on till she finds one she likes, her words, not mine. It's such a worry.'

Meredith nodded. 'Rather you than me.'

'We're going to see Uncle Jack tonight. He hasn't seen you for ages and they have some holiday snaps they want to show us.'

'Are we all going?' Akina asked.

Mattie shook her head. 'No, just the two of us.'

'I hate photos. They're so boring. Must I go too?'

246

'Yes, if you want to go to that party on Saturday.'

Her face lit up. 'Does that mean I can go then?'

'It means I'm still thinking about it. We'll have to see how you behave between now and then.'

She flung both arms around Mattie's neck. 'I love you so much! You won't regret it...honestly.'

'Dad will take you and collect you at eleven.'

'*Eleven o'clock?*' she screeched. 'It'll hardly have got going by then. Make it twelve o'clock, please.'

'Don't push your luck or I might change my mind again.'

'Okay...*okay*, I'll do you a deal Mattie. I'll wash up for a week if you make it twelve...*pleeease*?'

'Eleven-thirty. That's final, and you wash up for a fortnight.'

She beamed with delight. '*Yes!* Thanks Mattie.'

Mattie laughed as Akina rushed upstairs, yelping excitedly. She could do deals too and they had each made a conquest. Akina had wheedled an extra half hour out of her but Mattie would have allowed her to stay until twelve if pressed further. Additionally, she had no dishes to wash for two weeks. That was the way to do deals she mused smugly.

'How's my favourite slave-driver?' Jack chuckled, hugging Akina warmly. 'Great to see you again.'

'I'm doing okay thanks. How about you?'

'Oh, you know, can't grumble.'

She laughed. 'That makes a pleasant change.'

'*Akina,*' Mattie cried. 'Don't be so *rude*.'

Jack leaped to her defence. 'Leave her be Mattie. I'm not bothered what she says. We had some right

247

humdinger battles when she were looking after me. I must admit though, she were right every time and I were wrong. Look how she got me walking proper again. She's a belter and so is her brother too. I've a lot to thank Adam for, getting me that job when no other bugger would gimmie the time o'day. Salt o' the earth, that Josh Hargreaves.'

'Do you still miss life in the Navy?' Mattie asked.

He paused to think. 'I do and I don't if you know what I mean. I missed it like hell at first but it's got better. Besides, I'm used to being at home now with my pretty wife.' He looked at Lucille and smiled. 'I wouldn't go back now. I've everything I want here and soon we'll have some happy news for you. I'm not allowed to tell you yet, Lucille says.'

Mattie and Lucille exchanged glances. No words were spoken. The smile on Lucille's face said it all.

'He has such a gob on him,' she laughed. 'I made him promise not to tell you yet. It's early days.'

'Did I tell you? *Did I?*' he protested. '*She* gave it away Mattie. *Tell* her!'

Mattie gave her a hug. 'I'm really thrilled for you both. As for you Jack, leave me out of your family squabbles. I have quite enough of my own, thanks.'

'I'll tell you what Mattie,' Jack said. 'I never for a minute thought I'd get wed and have a kid before I were thirty. Just shows how wrong you can be. It's a damn good job Josh Hargreaves had that vacancy. I remember Seth telling me how expensive it were, feeding and clothing a baby.'

That was the second reference to Josh Hargreaves but Mattie made no response. No one outside their

248

immediate family had been told the identity of the person guilty of Adam's abduction and when Mark discovered Adam had approached him to enquire if he could find any work for his uncle, a war veteran, Adam had been severely chastised by his father and grounded for a month for making him feel beholden to a man who had committed such a heinous crime against a member of his immediate family.

Akina thought the ensuing baby-talk would never end but she had to grin and bear it. There followed a drawn-out holiday snap conference during which each was analysed and described in fine detail. She was relieved when it was time to go home, standing up promptly and waiting by the door for Mattie.

As they drove away Mattie gave a satisfying sigh. 'Wasn't that nice? I've had such a lovely evening.'

Akina's nod in accord disguised her true feelings, that she'd have preferred sitting naked in Antarctica in the middle of winter, sticking pins in her eyes.

Mair was already asleep when they arrived home. True to form, Akina hurried upstairs. Mattie caught Mark's eye and he nodded to advise that the picture of Sam had been hung. They awaited her return but half an hour later she still hadn't reappeared.

'I'd better check on her.' Mattie said. 'Maybe she hasn't noticed it yet.'

'Mattie, she couldn't miss it! It's right facing her as she walks in the bedroom. She's probably upset.'

Gingerly Mattie tapped on her door and heard the tearful response, 'Come in.'

Akina was face down on the bed sobbing bitterly. Mattie perched on the bed beside her, stroking her

249

hair. 'I miss her very much too darling. I'm sorry. I should have done this sooner.'

'I'd almost forgotten what she looked like,' Akina sobbed. She turned to Mattie, revealing red swollen eyes. 'Thank you so much. It's the best picture I've ever seen of Mum. Where did it come from?'

'From Grandma. She helped me choose the nicest one. She has a lot more photos of your mum so you should ask to see them next time you visit her.'

'Mum was lovely wasn't she?'

Mattie smiled thoughtfully. 'Yes she was, in both body and mind. She was also very courageous. All she cared about was your happiness. I often wonder what she'd think of you now.' Choosing her words carefully she asked, 'Are you happy? We don't see eye to eye always but that happens in most families. Parents of all species try to protect their young.'

She dried the tears from her face. 'I know that and yes, I am happy here. I knew from the first moment I saw you that you'd take good care of me. Adam's my best friend and I love Mair too...you and Dad as well,' she added on a splutter of tearful laughter.

'So you like the photographs?'

'They're great Mattie, all of them. Thank you.'

11

It was Saturday, party-day and the expression, *cat on a hot tin roof,* could not have applied to a more worthy recipient, for Akina had been twitchy since dawn.

Adam grunted as she barged into his room, half a dozen outfits over her arm. 'Which of these should I wear tonight?'

'How would I know?' he snapped irritably. 'You should knock before you come in here. I could have been undressed.'

'So? What have you got that nobody else has?'

She laid out the clothes on his bed. 'Help me pick something Adam. You've more idea than me. What do girls wear to parties?'

'Anything they want. It's not a film premiere. It's just a few teenagers having a laugh, that's all. Wear a frock or trousers. It doesn't matter.'

She gathered up her clothes indignantly. 'You're a fat lot of use so don't bother. I'll ask Mattie.'

With a sarcastic lilt in his voice, he yelled, 'Close the door on the way out.'

Over the course of the day she changed her mind several times about what to wear and Mattie's input had at best been vague. She decided to call a school friend who regularly went to parties. That proved a total waste of time too. In the end she opted to wear a calf length black skirt, a white top and boots.

They had been told to arrive around eight o'clock and at ten past Mark was still pacing up and down the hall impatiently. 'Go and find out what's wrong Adam,' he said, annoyance ringing in his voice. 'I can't believe it takes all blasted day to get ready for a house party! She's been up since six o'clock!'

As he reached the stairs, Akina's footsteps could be heard, hurrying along the landing.

Mark made no attempt to conceal his displeasure. 'This is *our* Saturday night too Akina. You're very inconsiderate. I have to go to work smartly dressed every day and it takes *me* less than half an hour.'

Mattie intervened to suppress any back-chat from Akina. 'You look really nice darling. Have a lovely time and make sure you behave yourself.'

'*You look really nice darling,*' Adam mimicked in a high-pitched voice, pushing her through the door.

'You shut your trap! You obviously didn't spend much time getting ready,' she snarled in response.

'Huh! Chance would have been a fine thing since you've been in the bathroom all flaming day.'

'*That's enough!*' Mark bellowed. 'You're like a couple of kids.'

The rest of the journey continued in silence until Mark said, 'Eleven-thirty. Not a minute later!'

'Yes Dad,' they answered in chorus.

'And behave,' he called after them.

Martin greeted them warmly. 'I'd almost given up on you. I thought you weren't coming. Squeeze in and get yourselves a drink.'

'Happy Birthday Martin,' Akina said, giving him his present. 'It's from us both. We hope you like it.'

'Great!' he said, opening the envelope. 'A music voucher...I'm really into music. Thanks. You'll find food in the kitchen. Just help yourselves.'

Adam wandered off to talk to some of his football mates, leaving Akina alone though not for long.

'May I pour you a drinky poo, sweetie?' asked an odd looking chap wearing multi-coloured beads of varying length. 'What's your poison?'

When she appeared baffled, he quickly rephrased his question, 'What do you drink, petal?'

'Er...orange juice please.'

He was surprised. '*Orange juice?* That's hardly a party drink. How about a teensy splash of gin in it?'

Forcing a smile she said, 'No thanks, I might try one later.'

'Suit yourself. So tell me, where are you from?'

'We live near the garden centre, a couple of miles down the road.'

He laughed. 'I didn't mean that. I meant where do you *come* from? Where were you born?'

'Devon.'

'Devon? Well, you're obviously not English.'

He was beginning to irritate her. 'I'm as English as you are,' she snapped.

He nodded. 'You're probably right there. I come from Wales. My dad's Welsh, my mum's English so that makes me half and half. I gather you're half and half too? I'm not trying to be offensive. You're very pretty but with an oriental look....yes?'

'Yes, you're right. I'm half Japanese.'

'I thought so. You have beautiful skin and lovely clear expressive eyes. How old are you?'

She smiled. 'That's not an appropriate question to ask a young lady. How old do you think I am?'

'Seventeen?'

She giggled and decided to play along. 'How did you know that? I'm impressed.'

'Easy! I'm a fashion photographer, glossy magazine stuff. I shoot models all the time. I spotted you the moment you walked in. You'd be a great model. You have everything, height, style, beauty and most of all mystery...the perfect combination. A new teen fashion house has just opened. It's called *Youth* and they're after a suitable model to carry the label. I've already submitted shots of two potential candidates. If you're interested, I could take some of you. It'd be quite an accolade being selected as the new *Face of Youth* and think of the money you'd earn. It'd do my reputation a lot of good too.'

She was becoming scared. 'Er...I don't think so. I don't get much free time. I'm a student so I'm very busy but thanks for asking.'

'It'd all be above-board; I promise. My dad and I are reputable photographers on the High Street. I'll tell you what; take my card and think about it. Talk to your boyfriend about it. He's on his way over.'

Akina turned to see Adam approaching. 'Adam's not my boyfriend,' she laughed. 'He's my brother.'

At that his face lit up. 'Mmm! Introduce me then please. My name's Evan. He's *gorgeous!*'

After the initial shock, she giggled. 'You'd be out of luck with Adam. He's definitely into girls.'

254

'Huh! Story of my life!' he sighed.

Akina didn't see Evan again until much later. She had gone outside for a breath of air as it was stifling indoors. Martin joined her as he wanted a cigarette.

'Want one of these?' he asked.

Why not, she thought, taking one from the packet. 'Thanks.'

He moved closer to light it. 'You look really nice tonight Akina. I'm glad you came.'

'Me too. It's been great and the food was terrific.'

'I'll tell Mum; she made everything; she's a good cook. Can I see you again? I'd really like to.'

'I suppose,' she mumbled. Never having been on a date she felt a little tongue-tied.

'I'll call you then if that's okay and we'll arrange something. What time's your dad coming for you?'

She checked her watch. 'In about ten minutes. He said eleven-thirty.'

'I'd best get your coat then.'

She was about to put out her cigarette when Evan wandered outside. 'My card, in case you decide to get in touch with me but don't leave it too long. It'd be a shame to miss out on such an opportunity.'

She took it and slipped it in her bag.

It was hard to see clearly through the darkness but Mark studying them intently, had seen the cigarette in her hand. When he honked the horn, she turned, and recognising his car, she quickly stamped on the cigarette. 'I'll find Adam,' she called.

Barely a word passed Akina's lips on the journey home. Mark remained stony-faced and silent whilst Adam gabbled incessantly about the party. Surely if

Dad had seen her smoking he'd have mentioned it she kept telling herself. He'd have said *something*.

Mattie was keen to hear about the party but Akina kept her comments brief, having glanced at her dad a couple of times. Anxious to make a quick exit she said she was tired and went up to bed.

'I'll be up shortly,' Mark said when Mattie made known she was tired too.

'You're quiet. Is anything wrong?' she asked.

Mark was preoccupied with his thoughts. 'What? No, not at all. I just need to look for something.'

Mark waited until the household was quiet before going up to bed. He listened outside Akina's room. There wasn't a sound. He opened her bedroom door quietly and crept to the bottom of her bed. She was fast asleep. After leaving the graphically illustrated macabre details of a smoker's lungs on her bedside table together with a note he left the room. It simply said, '*Forewarned is forearmed and when you have studied this, I'd like you to return it to me, together with your comments about the dangers of smoking.*'

Akina awoke early the next day, thoughts of Martin filling her mind. She wished it had been possible to spend more time with him, to learn more about him and she hoped he would call her as promised. It had been a terrific party, and meeting Evan had been an eye-opener as well. Following her initial unease she had warmed to him and given his proposition some thought. It'd certainly do no harm to visit his shop on the High Street and ask to see some of his work.

She sat up in bed and stretched and as she turned

to look at her watch, she spotted the documents left by Mark.

She read his note first. A swift blast of adrenaline shot through her body. He knew; he had seen her.

She studied the grisly picture, read the descriptive narrative and burst into tears, concerned about what would follow. She felt ashamed. They had put their trust in her and she had abused that trust.

Carrying the documents, she took her place next to Adam at the table where Mark proceeded to eat his breakfast in silence. As soon as he'd finished he asked, 'Are those for me Akina?'

'Yes Dad,' she said in a barely audible whisper as she handed them to him.

'Funny, I can't seem to find your written answers to my question,' he stated coldly.

'Sorry, I didn't know you wanted it writing down. I was going to tell you later, after breakfast.'

He turned in his chair to face her, his eyes staring deeply into hers. 'How about we do it now? I think your brother and sister might be interested to know what you have to say.'

She looked at Mattie and back at Mark. 'I'd rather Mair wasn't here for this.'

'Oh, but I insist,' he remarked and addressing the others he explained, 'It's a kind of quiz. I get to ask the questions and Akina, no one else, gets to answer them, so let me start by asking what my job title is.'

'You're a doctor,' she mumbled.

'Speak up girl then everyone can hear.'

Sensing something was wrong, Mattie intervened. 'What's going on Mark?'

With a brief insincere smile he replied, 'All will be revealed in due course. Did you say *doctor*?'

She nodded. 'Yes in a hospital. I think you're the Consultant.'

'*Senior* Consultant actually. I was promoted again last year after a great deal of hard work as I had to earn more to help pay for my children to attend an expensive private school. I mistakenly believed that they'd appreciate a higher standard of education but apparently, *one* of my two daughters is hell-bent on self-destruction. So, Akina, what kind of Consultant am I? In which field do I specialise?'

She lowered her head. 'I don't know Dad.'

'I'll enlighten you then. Cardiothoracic surgery is my field of expertise. Do you know what it means?'

'I think cardio is to do with the heart.'

'*Good girl!* We're finally making progress. What vital organs can be found in the chest cavity?'

'Er...heart for one....'

'And...?' he prompted.

'Lungs too?'

'*Correct again...*that's cardiothoracics, so are you aware of the major cause of disease to such organs, often resulting in death? You may hazard a guess.'

Without hesitation she answered, 'Smoking.'

'*Right...*so what advice might you offer someone, say a young girl like you, if you saw her smoking?'

'I'd tell her to stop because it's very dangerous.'

'Good, and would you also tell her it didn't make her look older or more sophisticated...just stupid?'

Tears coursed down her cheeks. 'Yes Dad. I'll not do it again, ever...I promise.'

'*Akina,*' Mattie cried. 'Whatever were you thinking about? How long has this been going on?'

'You've got it wrong. It was only one,' she wept. 'Someone offered me a cigarette and I didn't like to refuse. I've never done it before.'

'Were you drinking alcohol too?' Mark asked.

She shook her head. 'No Dad. I had orange juice, that's all. Adam knows. Tell him Adam.'

'I only saw her with orange juice. We didn't stay together all the time though so I can't be certain.'

She glared furiously at her brother. 'I can always rely on you to drop me in it can't I? I did *not* drink any alcohol. Did you though? Tell Dad the truth.'

His cheeks reddened. 'I had a glass or two of beer but nothing stronger.'

Mark was livid. 'You're under age and shouldn't be drinking alcohol at all!'

'I know but a lot of my mates were there and they were drinking beer and stuff. I'd have looked a big sissy drinking fruit juice wouldn't I?'

Akina wrapped her arms round Mark's neck. 'I'm really sorry. It'll never happen again. I know you're angry and you've every right to be angry.'

'No Akina, I'm not angry. I'm just bitterly disappointed. I put my neck on the line when persuading Mattie to allow you to go to that party and you let me down. I knew parenthood wouldn't be easy but I never bargained for sheer stupidity. What kind of example does that set for Mair? I'm disappointed in you too Adam and we won't be going horse-riding today. You can both stay in your rooms for the rest of the day. It'll give you time to reflect.'

Without a further word they left the room.

'I can't believe this,' Mattie sighed. 'You actually saw her smoking a cigarette?'

'Listen. It's not a big deal, one cigarette. I had to make a stand though and hopefully it won't happen again.' He chuckled. 'I remember my dad catching me having a crafty fag at the end of the garden. The first thing I knew he was grabbing me by the scruff of the neck. He yanked me indoors and took his belt to me. I never did it again. It's part of growing up, experimenting with things. I'd had a beer or two at Adam's age as well. I was a bit of a rebel. Dad was rarely around; I was the man of the house and very old for my years. Don't ever tell Akina and Adam though. So...do you have any guilty secrets?'

'No, I don't think I have. I didn't have the money or lifestyle to experiment. Had things been different who knows what I'd have done? I didn't even have a boyfriend before you.'

'I know. Any regrets about marrying me?'

'Stop fishing for compliments Mark. Perhaps I'd have done better had I not been in such a big hurry to marry my first boyfriend,' she smirked.

Seeing the playful glint in her eye, he pulled her towards him. 'I certainly couldn't have done better. You're the best thing that ever happened to me but I'm pretty sure I've said that a hundred times.'

Suddenly feeling a tug on his sleeve, Mark looked down. 'Must *I* stay in my room all day *too* Daddy?' Mair asked wide-eyed.

'No my precious, of course not. I was just thinking maybe you'd like to go to the park.'

'Oh yes please. Can I go on the swings?'

'I don't see why not. Are you coming Mattie?'

She declined. 'I've two meals to rustle up now we aren't going out.'

Fascinated by the jangling cow-bell hanging above the shop door, Akina moved to the counter where a middle-aged man was sifting through a huge pile of photographs. He looked up and smiled.

'Does Evan work here?' she enquired.

'He certainly does and don't tell me...you must be er...Akina?'

Her lips broke into a beaming smile. 'How do you know that? I didn't say I was calling today.'

'Let's just say, *a little bird told me.*' His amiable smile put her at ease. 'He's with a client, though he shouldn't be long. I heard it was a good party.'

'It was, yes. I take it you're Evan's father. He said you worked together.'

'I am and he told me all about you...very excited he was...describing in great detail how perfect you were for *Face of Youth*. He even called the agency.'

'Agency?'

'Yes, all models work with an agency. They send new recruits to us to create a portfolio and then they send the photos of suitable models to companies for their consideration. The girl who's with Evan right now has been a mail catalogue model for years but she's nine now and needs her portfolio up-dating.'

'So little children work as models too?'

'Of course. Old people are needed as well.'

'I never thought of that. Does it pay well?'

'I believe so. One child got a hundred pounds for a twenty-minute session, his mother told us. We're only involved at the portfolio stage. We hardly ever see them after that unless they need fresh photos.'

At that point they heard voices and a girl ran into the shop ahead of her parents, closely followed by Evan who was obviously delighted to see Akina.

'Won't be a mo,' he said, handing a boiled sweet to the young girl. 'You did really well today Cindy. I'm sure your new photos will be lovely. I'll be in touch when they're ready,' he advised her parents.

Akina giggled to hear the cow-bell clang again as the family left the shop. 'I like that bell,' she said.

Evan flicked back his hair and grinned. 'This *is* a pleasant surprise. I'd all but given up on you. Does this mean you're going ahead?'

'Not exactly. I'd like more information first.'

Pulling forward a chair for her he raised his eyebrows. 'Coffee? Can I get you a coffee?'

'No thanks. Actually, I don't have long.'

'Fire away then. What's on your mind?'

She cleared her throat. 'Er...well...it's the photos. I wanted to make it clear that I won't er...'

'Ducky,' he cut in; 'you don't do *anything* you're unhappy about. Let me explain. I take photos of all kinds of people from babies to pensioners who are fully clothed. Many girls though want to be photographic as opposed to fashion models. They're the ones who are skimpily clad or bare all. I'm trying to find a teenage girl with the requisite qualities to sell fashion to young people. She must be no older than nineteen as she must represent the younger generation. I'd only need head and shoulder close-up shots of you and a couple of full length shots to show you have the correct shape, stature and figure to pull off the job. It's that simple and when you're signed up with your agent you'll already have discussed what you will and won't do and you'll have a Contract.'

'That's right,' Evan's father intervened. 'There's nothing to worry about. We're reputable photographers who only deal with reputable agencies.'

Somewhat relieved Akina stood up. 'If I decide to go ahead what happens next?'

'First I need a consent form signed by one of your parents as you're under eighteen and then I'd take a few photos to send to the agency. If they were interested, as I'm sure they would be, you'd have to see them to proceed from there.'

'Where would that be, the agency?'

'Local. They're in Manchester. If you can get the consent form signed quickly I could do your photos in the morning. I have somebody coming in at nine-thirty so I could do yours at ten-thirty.'

Akina's head was spinning. Though she'd like to go ahead, she would never get written consent from Mattie or Dad. In addition Sunday was horse-riding day, which meant there was little likelihood of her seeing Evan. 'I'm not sure I can make it tomorrow but if I can, I'll be here by ten fifteen,' she told him.

They left it at that and Akina went home feeling disheartened.

That night there was a heavy thunderstorm. News reports covered the severe damage caused to overhead cables and roads and there was also a serious coach crash where some passengers had still to be cut from the wreckage. Moreover, reports of further road traffic accidents continued to emerge.

'It's likely I'll be called out tonight,' Mark said. 'I imagine there'll be some chest injuries and they aren't as well staffed at the weekend.'

Barely had he uttered the words when his bleeper rang. He called in and was advised that A & E was swarming with casualties, mainly walking wounded but there were several serious cases too.

'Be careful how you drive. It's absolutely treacherous outside,' Mattie cautioned. 'It's very windy.'

He brushed his lips against her cheek. 'I'll be fine and I'll call you when I'm coming home.'

It was absolute mayhem at the hospital. 'What do we have?' Mark asked, removing his coat.

The junior doctor looked troubled. 'I moved the worst over here but more keep arriving. We've instructed the ambulance crew not to bring any more casualties here. We can't cope with what we've got. There's a couple for you to look at but I doubt anything can be done for them and there are a lot with fractured ribs. I think it's going to be a long night.'

Mark studied the notes for the two patients. 'Call theatre and prep Mr. Jackson on the left. Make the other comfortable and get his relatives in. He'll not make it but I'm in with a chance with this one.'

The next time Mark checked the time it was three in the morning.

'Right, that's me finished for the night. Don't call me again before midday tomorrow. Contact Doctor Akhtar with any problems you can't handle.'

Mattie was still awake when Mark arrived home. 'I was worried as you didn't call me. Was it awful?'

Matter-of-factly he remarked, 'It was just like any other day but more of it. It's never a picnic Mattie. I was able to save one guy who was hanging on by a thread. It never ceases to amaze me how some folk still drive like maniacs in bad weather conditions. A young chap overtook me on my way home doing at least seventy. When will they ever learn?'

'Have you had a hot drink?'

'No and I don't want one. It'll keep me awake. If possible, keep the noise down in the morning.'

Mattie arose early and woke the children. 'Dad's still fast asleep and mustn't be disturbed. He was at work until the early hours so try to be very quiet.'

'We're not going horse-riding then,' Akina stated, feigning discontent, her mind working overtime.

'No, it isn't fit. It'd be a quagmire on those lanes. We'll go and see Nana to check if she's okay.'

'I might go round to a mate's,' Adam chipped in.

'I might too,' Akina said. 'I'll call Becky later.'

'Suit yourselves. I'll just take Mair then.'

Akina busied herself in her room until the others had left. By a quirk of fate she had been granted an opportunity to see Evan; all that remained now was a means to provide a signature on the consent form. Creeping downstairs she entered Mark's study and looked on his desk but there was no document to be found bearing a signature. Frustration took over as she rummaged through his drawers. There *had* to be *something*, she snorted to herself and with only one drawer remaining she was frantic. The final drawer contained stationery equipment, paper clips, pencils and the like but no paperwork. As she was about to close it she noticed a plastic card that on closer inspection was the answer to her prayers.

With quivering fingers she tried to copy his signature, sadly without success, and after more bungled attempts she stuffed the card in her pocket and left.

It was over an hour later before she had perfected it. By that time, she had put into practice what she had learned from a friend who frequently forged her mother's signature on school reports at Grange. She was annoyed for not having tried that sooner since it was easy to turn it upside down and copy it. That way you didn't stray into your own style of writing, since you merely replicated the meaningless scrolls and lines. Once done and turned the right way up, it was near perfect.

She checked the time and it was almost ten so she had to hurry and after destroying all evidence of her deed, she returned the card to its rightful place, shot from the house and ran all the way to the shop.

On her way home she called at Becky's but there was no one home. She scribbled a note to say she'd called and pushed it through the letter-box. Akina's mission was accomplished, her earlier whereabouts accounted for by her perfect alibi.

It was Wednesday when Evan called her about the photographs that were ready for collection. She had been on tenterhooks all day at school, believing he would call that evening and each time the telephone rang she grabbed it before anyone else could.

As Akina hung up Mark winked mischievously at Mattie. 'New boyfriend?' he said with a dry smile.

'That's for me to know and you to find out,' she snapped in reply, 'and *you* can wipe that silly smirk off your face Adam or I'll crack you one.'

He guffawed. 'I'd like to see you try!'

'Okay that's enough you two. We're just having a bit of fun, that's all.'

'At my expense as usual,' she grunted touchily.

Akina ran upstairs the minute she arrived home the next day. She threw her school uniform on the bed, got changed and hurried downstairs. 'I won't be too long, Mattie. I'm nipping to Becky's to borrow her maths book. I've forgotten mine.'

'Be quick. Your tea will be ready in half an hour.'

Barely able to contain her excitement, Akina ran all the way and burst into the shop breathlessly.

Evan beamed. 'I can't wait to show you these,' he said. 'They're brilliant even though I say so myself. You're very photogenic.' He passed her the photographs one by one and she was equally enthusiastic.

'They're fantastic Evan. Do you think the agency will like them?'

'They already do. I called round with a set earlier and they want to see you as soon as possible to sign a Contract and pay the enrolment fee. Then they'll get the ball rolling, so to speak. I'm very optimistic Akina but you must be prepared for disappointment if another model is chosen. There'll be hundreds if not thousands in the running for this and if you're not chosen this time, there'll be other opportunities.

Mail order firms are always looking for models for their catalogues. This is your set so take it with you so you can show the photos to your family.'

'Thanks. How much do I owe you?'

'I'll invoice the agency and they'll sort it out with you later. Just get in touch with them soon.'

'Thank you for all you've done,' she gushed, her face radiating with pleasure. 'I'll keep you posted.'

The portfolio included three enlargements as well as twenty small photographs and was too large to fit in her bag. She had expected a smaller packet, like the ones with holiday photographs, so that created a problem. With no other option Akina would have to confide in Emily and leave it there until she could take it home. Also she needed to borrow money for the agency fee since she had none to pay it.

Although surprised, Emily was pleased to see her. 'Have you come on your own in the dark?'

'Yes, I've something to show you and it's a secret so you have to promise not to tell anyone.'

She laughed. 'Oh well, if it's a secret you'd better come in quickly before anyone sees you.'

They sat down on the sofa and Akina opened the portfolio and showed her the photographs.

Emily was impressed. 'My word, they're lovely.'

'I had them done on the High Street. They're nice aren't they? They're for a competition I'm entering. A new teen fashion house is opening and it makes all kinds of stuff, clothes, make-up and things like that. When they launch something brand new, they want someone to appear on their posters. It's part of their advertising campaign, so they ask teenagers to send in photos and they choose the person they like best. Do you understand?'

'I think so darling. You're going to send them one and you want me to say which I like best.'

'No Nana. My agent does that but I've got to sign up with one first and I don't have the money to pay their fee so I was wondering if you'd pay it and I'll pay you back as soon as I can.'

Emily had deep reservations and without a clearer understanding of what Akina was getting involved in, she felt unable to help. 'Does Mattie or your dad know you're here?'

'*No* Nana! I've told you, it's a secret.'

She pondered for a while. 'I'm sorry darling but I don't think it wise to help you with something your parents know nothing about. I'm quite sure they'd be happy to support you in this but I…'

'Then help me, *please.* Dad and Mattie don't have much money and can't afford to pay the agency fee, so you're my only hope. I can't go any further without your help and you've lots of money.'

'It isn't about money Akina. It's about my interference in a family matter. Can't you see that? Your dad would be furious if I were complicit in an issue he disapproved of and even more so to discover I'd settled the agency fee because he couldn't afford to. He's a very proud man and it would hurt his pride immensely so *never* tell him what you just told me.'

'Right, I have to go,' she sighed heavily. 'My tea will be ready. Can I leave these photos here?'

'I'd rather you didn't Akina. Mattie often pops in, and don't look at me like that. You haven't thought it through properly. I have no wish to stand in your way but I feel very strongly that this is a matter you have to discuss with your parents and if they agree, I'll happily give you the money…call it an advance of your wages as you're always doing little jobs for me around the house.'

Emily found her a plain bag and dropped a couple of magazines inside for Mattie. 'If anyone asks, you can say I've sent her some light reading. It's a half-truth I know but much better than a lie. All the best with your venture. I hope it works out for you.'

'Sorry I'm late! I went to Nana's on the way home. I'll just take my things upstairs and she's sent you some magazines Mattie.'

'I'm just dishing up so look sharp,' Mattie called.

Akina rammed the bag under her bed and hurried back down. 'Anything I can do to help?'

'Just call your dad. Tell him tea's on the table.'

'No need,' he said sitting down. 'I'm here. I heard all the commotion. What are we having?'

'Steak and onions,' Mattie said, handing him his plate. '*Man food,* as you call it.'

Mair stirred hers round the plate with her fork and pouted. 'I don't want any now I know what it is.'

'That's one of your favourites,' Mattie coaxed but she was unyielding. 'I don't eat men! I *won't!*'

Adam, the only one at the table to understand her concern, burst out laughing. 'You dummy Mair. It's called *man food* because *men* like it. It's beef from a bull and you like that. It's not from a *person.*'

She looked to Mark for confirmation, knowing he

270

would never lie to her. 'That's true Mair; now come on, eat your meal before it gets cold. It's delicious.'

With all the jocularity around the table, the others failed to notice Akina's sombre mood. All her plans and all her efforts had been for nothing. There was simply no way out of this predicament. Without the fee she couldn't call the agency; without the agency to promote her, her dreams were shattered. 'I'll skip dessert if that's okay. The steak was lovely but I'm full. If no one's using the bathroom, I'd like to have a shower and my hair needs washing too.'

After taking her shower, she made a half-hearted attempt to do her homework but found her concentration drifting away from *As you like it,* to the *Face of Youth.* The soliloquy she was supposed to learn by heart, *All the world's a stage,* just wouldn't sink in, no matter how hard she tried. Finally, frustration took over and she jumped into bed, burst into tears and cried herself to sleep.

'*Akina!*' Mrs. Jennings called as she passed by her door. 'Your mother's just phoned. She can't collect you till later. She'd like the three of you to stay in school until she gets here. She said you and Adam should start your homework.'

Akina smiled sweetly. 'Thank you. I'll tell Adam. Moron,' she cussed as she went on her way. Mattie was *not* or ever would be her mother. If her mother had been alive *she'd* have supported her dream.

'What's with the long face?' Adam asked, blowing his painful nose as she approached.

'What's with the red nose, Rudolph?' she jibed.

271

'I've a rasping cough and I'm full of a cold. I feel lousy. I just want to go home and get to bed.'

'Tough! Mattie won't be here for a while. She left a message with Mrs. Jennings. She expects us to do our homework while we're waiting.'

His eyelids drooped heavily. 'You suit yourself. I'll not be doing any. I feel absolutely knackered.'

'Yes, you look knackered. Why didn't you go and lie down in the sick bay this afternoon?'

He blew his nose again. 'Cos we had physics.'

'So? I don't follow,' she remarked quizzically.

'I can't afford to miss a lesson. I'm all behind.'

She peered around the back of him and chuckled. 'Yes, your bum does look a bit on the big side.'

He wasn't amused. 'Bugger off! I'm in no mood for your childish remarks. Grow up!'

'Adam Wyndham! I'll tell Dad you swore at me.'

'You'll be telling him a bloody sight more if you don't clear off. Go and find Mair.'

Mattie had arranged to meet Mark at *The Top Shot* photographers at four o'clock, following her shock discovery the previous evening when she had gone upstairs to get the magazines Emily had sent. Akina was in the bathroom at the time, so Mattie looked in all obvious places to find them. As she was about to abandon her search she spotted the partly concealed bag under Akina's bed.

Curiosity got the better of her when she removed the magazines and on further inspection of the portfolio, was horrified to find Akina's photographs.

It had not been her intention to pry for she always

272

afforded the children their privacy but remembering how she had been abused and exploited at the same age caused grave concern.

After making a mental note of the photographer's details, she returned the bag and entire contents to its original location and left the room hurriedly.

Akina didn't come downstairs again that evening and Adam had gone to bed early after complaining he had a headache so once Mair was asleep, Mattie informed Mark of her discovery. He was astounded too. 'What are you saying...that they're sleazy?'

'Oh no, quite the opposite Mark. They're elegant beautiful photographs but that's not to say he hasn't taken others. The point is, she's never mentioned it so it's clear she's hiding something, otherwise why the secrecy? Why hide them under her bed? Akina doesn't have enough money to pay for professional photos like those. They aren't passport type snaps.'

'What are they then?'

She scratched her head. 'It's hard to explain. Take a look in this magazine...at the models...they're just like that, professional poses. For my own peace of mind I need to get to the bottom of this. I'm going to see the photographer tomorrow. I know the shop. It's next door to Woolworths.'

That provided some relief for Mark. 'It's unlikely to be a sleazy joint, bang in the middle of the High Street wouldn't you say?'

'You're so naïve Mark. They're hardly likely to draw attention to their shady activities in a grubby back street with an illuminated porn sign above the door. They display an aura of respectability and that way no one suspects anything like no one suspected the Parkes who'd been vetted for fostering and look what they were like...monsters.'

Mark took her in his arms. 'Times have changed since then Mattie. You'd no one to turn to for help but it's different now. Kids are more confident and Akina's got her head screwed on. I'm sure there's a simple explanation. She's wilful and headstrong but she's certainly not stupid. I'll come with you.'

Mattie arrived a little after four to find Mark waiting outside the shop. 'Let me do the talking Mark. I've been thinking; if anything improper is going on they're bound to be on the defensive when I talk to them and I'll pick up on that right away.'

'As you wish,' he agreed.

She approached the counter and with a civil smile directed at the middle-aged male arranging photograph frames, asked, 'Are you the owner?'

He returned a welcoming smile. 'I am indeed and how may I help you today?'

'I'm Mrs. Wyndham. This is my husband and...'

He cut her short. 'You must be Akina's parents, a truly delightful girl, though I have to say you hardly look old enough to be her mother.'

Far from taking that as a compliment, she turned to Mark with an expression conveying her previous concerns that *that* was how young vulnerable girls were exploited by older men...smooth talk.

Mattie instantly disliked the man but because she was there on a mission she had to continue. 'We've seen the photos you took of our daughter and...'

He interrupted again, infuriating her. 'Correction! I can't take credit for that. It was my son who took those photographs, in fact I hear him coming now. I do very little nowadays. I'm just the errand boy.'

Evan flounced towards the counter followed by a girl of about ten. 'What did I promise you for being a good girl?' he asked, ruffling her hair. Removing the lid from the sweet jar he pulled out a handful to give to her.

Mattie was horrified beyond belief. She couldn't speak and the ensuing silence continued till Evan's father introduced them to his son.

'I am *thrilled* to make your acquaintance at last,' he jabbered with enthusiasm. 'Dad, take Jane to the kitchen and make my guests some coffee please.'

Evan extended his hand that Mark felt obliged to shake but Mattie declined to reciprocate. 'Did you hear how we met...at Martin's party? The moment I saw her I knew I couldn't let her go... the girl of my dreams. Only once in a lifetime does one ever find the perfect girl and she was that.' He flicked back his hair and sighed heavily. 'Those eyes, those clear expressive eyes that overflowed with joy and mystery, her skin, her stature, her figure, in fact everything about her was so faultless but believe me she wasn't easy to persuade. I had to do a little coaxing but I finally won her over and I'm very appreciative of your support.'

Mark was mortified. Mattie had got everything so wrong but there was no way to stop her now as she retorted, 'Our support? What do you mean by that?'

Before Evan could answer Mark intervened, eyeing the skinny-rib jumper and multi-coloured scarf wrapped twice around his neck. He elbowed Mattie. 'I suppose you have an eye for such things in your profession er...Evan isn't it?'

'Yes, we live in hope that someone really special will walk through that door. We get so many hopefuls and I really hate to disappoint them. It's a cruel game. It's not just a pretty face that matters; it's the whole package and Akina's got everything. I think she stands an excellent chance of being selected.'

Though nodding in accord Mark couldn't imagine what Evan meant by the word *selected*.

Mattie, still on another wave-length asked, 'How do you get around the law when your, shall we call them *candidates,* are under age?'

Evan's father returned with their coffee in time to hear her question. 'We never flout the law if that's what you're asking. We always get written parental consent before taking photos as we did with Akina.'

'Really? Did Akina get a copy of hers? I only ask because it's better to have the requisite paperwork in case someone should ask to see it.'

'Not a problem my dear lady,' Evan muttered as he scooted past her. 'I'll just copy it for you. As it's addressed to us, we don't normally make copies but in your case I'll make an exception. There you go,' he added, handing her the copy. 'It's just as clear as the original...signed M. Wyndham.'

'That's me then,' Mattie said, closely scrutinising the document. 'No, I can't say that's *my* signature.'

'Could be mine,' Mark jumped in, taking it from her. The young bugger, he said to himself. Wait till

I get home. 'Yes, it's mine alright. Excellent copier you have here Evan and better than mine by far.'

'Mum's here,' Jane shrieked running to the door.

She burst through the door full of apologies. 'I'm so sorry Evan. Please forgive me. The traffic's diabolical. I hope you haven't been any trouble Jane.'

Evan chuckled. 'No more than usual though I had to coax her with sweets to do the final few shots.'

'Say thank you to Evan,' her mother told her.

She ran to Evan and hugged him. 'Love you loads Evan and I'll see you again soon.'

'Take care sweetheart, you too Mrs. Hammond.'

As the door closed behind them Evan remarked, 'Jane's ten and one of the most sought after models for mail catalogues. She's a natural like Akina. Has Akina contacted the agency yet? There's only a day or two before the closing date.'

Mattie, utterly confused stared ahead blankly and Mark answered for the two of them. 'We're sorting everything out this evening. We just needed to see you first.'

'Understood lovey,' he chortled, shaking Mark's hand once more. 'Is there anything else?'

'No, that's everything now thanks,' Mattie said, swallowing the remains of her coffee hurriedly and heading for the door.

Mark nodded amiably and followed her outside.

She glared at him furiously. 'Never in my entire life have I felt as embarrassed or uncomfortable as I did in that shop, and that guy Evan, is he queer?'

He threw both arms in the air. 'Thank you Lord! Finally she twigs! Didn't you feel me elbowing you

277

in the ribs? I was more embarrassed than you were. You should listen to yourself. You stood there po-faced intimating they were child molesters. They're photographers Mattie, plain and simple; respectable guys just earning a living. I admit I had my doubts at first but you refused to see what was staring you in the face and by the way, the word's *gay* now, not *queer*, so try to remember. *Queer* is offensive.'

'Oh, I will *lovey*,' she sneered, 'like I'll remember who signed Akina's consent form too. I don't know who's in more trouble once we're home Mark, you or Akina, stitching me up like that.'

He laughed. 'You still don't get it do you? I only admitted to that to get you out of the place. I'm not washing my dirty linen in public. I signed *nothing*. The young bugger forged my signature; damn good it was too. Almost had *me* fooled.'

Mattie shook her head in disbelief. 'I'd better get over to the school and mark my words, as soon as we're home, Akina's got plenty to answer for.'

Nothing more was said until Mattie had cleared the table after their evening meal when Mark took Mair upstairs to read her a bedtime story. He left a snack by Adam's bed as he'd gone straight upstairs when he got home from school.

After tucking Mair up in bed, Mark called Akina downstairs.

'What's up? Am I in trouble?' she asked glibly as she followed him into the lounge.

'You tell me,' he replied, sitting across from her on the sofa next to Mattie.

She shrugged and stared at them inquisitively. 'I don't know what you mean.'

It was Mattie who dropped the bombshell. 'I was late collecting you from school today as your Dad and I went to see Evan.'

For some time Akina remained silent, the colour draining from her cheeks as she caught Mark's deep penetrating gaze. They knew everything.

'We're waiting,' Mark said.

Tears gushed from her eyes. 'You've blown it for me haven't you? I knew you wouldn't support me. I should never have shown those photos to Nana but I needed money for the agent. I should have known she'd tell you.'

Mark smiled inwardly, remembering a customary saying of his father's, *give a man enough rope and he'll hang himself.* How many more shocking revelations were to come he wondered. A little prompting was required. 'Start with Martin's party and tell us everything,' he said sternly.

Akina exhaled noisily and began with her initial encounter with Evan soon after she arrived and how she had warmed to him later following earlier concerns. 'I never told him I was seventeen Dad. When he asked how old I was I asked him to guess and *he* said that. I didn't lie to him.'

For the first time Mattie contributed. 'So did you correct him? If not that's lying by omission.'

'No I didn't, not that it mattered. As long as I was between thirteen and nineteen it was alright. Evan wasn't *after* me if you know what I mean, well not that way. In case you didn't work it out, he's gay.'

'I worked it out,' Mark said with a straight face.

She went on to explain in detail about the fashion house, that she'd have to register with the agency as soon as possible, sign a Contract and pay the fees.

'So let me get this right,' Mattie interrupted. 'You went to Nana for money intent on handing it over to the agent and signing a Contract without a word to either of us?' and when Akina nodded she went on, 'Do you have any idea how difficult it is to read a Contract? You can't just sign anything they throw at you, you silly girl. In any case, you're under age to sign a Contract. Were you *ever* going to tell us or did you believe the first we'd know was when your photo flashed by us on a passing bus? How on earth did you think you'd get away for the photo shoots? You've thought nothing through, and whilst we're on the subject, did Evan not ask for written parental consent prior to taking you in his studio? He's in a great deal of trouble if he didn't, lady.'

Mark's ears pricked up as Akina stammered and stuttered over her words. 'Er...well...yes...he did.'

'So where is it? *I* haven't signed anything.'

'I did it. I signed as Dad,' she answered in barely a whisper. 'I'm sorry. It was a dream. I wanted it so much. I reckoned you might let me carry on if I was accepted. I also thought you might be proud of me for once as I always seem to be in trouble for something or other. It's rotten at times being fourteen. I wanted to give you some money back for taking me in when I was six and I could have earned a lot with that. Years ago I heard you both arguing about my school fees, about who should pay, and I didn't like that, so now I'm older I wanted to help out because I wanted to be loved as much as Mair's loved.'

Mattie gasped, her hands covering her face. She looked at Akina through her tears and Mark was too startled to speak. 'Darling, we love *all* our children the same. We used to cuddle you all the time when you were little like we cuddle Mair now. Can't you see we're upset at what you've done? We love you very much. We're just trying to protect you from a dangerous world and we didn't *take you in*, as you put it, likening yourself to a stray dog. We wanted you as a daughter. We loved you then; we love you now and always will and I can't imagine why you'd think such a thing.'

'Then explain why you were yelling about who'd pay my school fees. *Why* Dad?'

He held his head in his hands and sighed. 'I'm so sorry Mattie. I never meant for this to happen. She must be told now. She's old enough to understand.'

'*No* Mark!'

'*Yes* Mattie! You can't keep hiding from the past. It's the only way Akina will believe us, if we speak the truth so do you tell her or do I?'

She inhaled heavily. 'I'll tell her then. Would you make us all a coffee please? I'd rather do it alone.'

As Mark left the room, Akina looked concerned. 'You're scaring me Mattie. What's there to tell? Is it something about Mum?'

'No, it's something about me.' She hesitated. 'My mother died when I was fourteen and the three of us had to go into foster-care. You probably know that but you don't know that mine was the foster-home

281

from hell. My foster-mother beat me black and blue on a regular if not daily basis and my foster-father, well he er...' She paused again. 'I can't do this.'

Akina went to sit beside her and took hold of her hand. 'Yes you can Mattie. Nothing you say can be worse than I'm imagining.'

Mattie nodded, tears flooding her eyes and with a tremor in her voice revealed, 'He persistently raped me for six months. Finally, when I could bear it no longer, I planned my escape but he tried to stop me and I accidentally killed him.'

Akina was visibly shocked. 'What happened? Did you tell anyone?'

'Not right away. I ran away. I was going to catch a train to London but Aunt Sadie had just got off a train and she saw me and told her mother. It was a stupid idea of mine, so you see we can all do stupid things when we're young. She persuaded me to go home with them and she alerted the authorities who went to the house and found him. Things were a lot different then. I had no one to turn to whilst I was being abused. I could never have discussed such a topic with my teacher and besides, he'd already told me that were I to tell anyone, I'd be locked up. Kids weren't street wise then like they are now. Anyway, there was a big hullaballoo about it. Social Services were to blame and ended up paying me compensation but I always thought of it as blood money and could never bring myself to touch it, that was until I wanted to send you to Grange. As Dad was paying Adam's fees, I said I'd pay yours, and *that* was the cause of the argument as it reaped up the past. Dad always got angry to think of that vile man and what he did to me. It was nothing to do with you darling or your school fees, that's the truth.'

Akina clung to her and wept. 'I'm sorry Mattie. I can't begin to imagine what you suffered. You must have been really terrified of men after that. Is that why you never had a boyfriend before Dad?'

A soft smile illuminated her face. 'Yes, Dad was very persistent though. I recall an incident at Uncle Seth's wedding when we came out of church. Dad was hanging around by the door, hoping to have a few words with me and during the ensuing conversation you asked him if he was married. When he said he wasn't, you remarked, "That's good, neither is Mattie." I could have died. I shot away and gave you a right telling off once we were out of earshot.'

She giggled. 'And what did Dad say?'

'He thought it hilarious. He roared with laughter, which only made matters worse.'

'It worked out right in the end though, didn't it? Maybe I did you a good turn.'

She smiled reflectively. 'I'm sure you did.'

'You really love Dad don't you?'

'Yes I do, like I love all my family, *you* as much as Mair and Adam,' she stressed. 'My concern was and always has been for your safety. I don't want to see you put at risk, after the horror and violence I'd had to contend with at your age.'

'I know and I'm sorry. What I did was deceitful. I should have asked you; Nana told me that. I'll get over my disappointment in time. At least I have the photos. What did you think of them?'

'They're lovely. I have to say, Evan's good at his job, credit where credit's due.'

'Earlier, when you were ranting on about the risks I didn't get the chance to say I'd already told Evan I wouldn't take my clothes off. I'd made it clear *that* stipulation had to be written in my Contract, so I'm not completely stupid.'

'No one's suggesting you are, in fact Dad told me you nearly had *him* fooled with that skilfully forged signature. I'll have to keep a more watchful eye on you in future and for the record I do *not* rant, ever! I discuss concerns in a firm but civil manner.'

Akina laughed. 'If you say so. I imagine Evan's disappointed in me for forging Dad's signature and lying about my age.'

'He probably will be if or when he finds out. Dad covered for you about the signature issue, saying it was his and your age never cropped up.'

'That's a relief. Thank you Mattie. Listen, I don't want a drink. I'd like to go to bed. Say goodnight to Dad from me and tell him again how sorry I am.'

En route to her room, she looked in on Adam. He was sleeping, the snack by his bed untouched. She pulled up his covers, turned out his light and crept out quietly. From there she went into Mair's room, kissed her goodnight and sighed, feeling blessed to have such a warm loving family who cared.

12

'So, what have you decided?' Mark asked.

'It's not up me. This has to be a joint decision.'

'I'm happy with what feels right to you, Mattie.'

'Typical bloke...always sitting on the fence. To be honest I can't decide; I need more information first. I won't allow anything to interfere with her school-work. She's losing a day today, looking after Adam but there's no other option. I couldn't expect Emily to nurse an infectious boy at her age. If *she* caught his cold it could kill her.'

'You'll make the right decision as you always do and it'll be fine by me. Right Mair, come on now or I'm going to be late for work.'

As Mark left, Akina appeared with Adam's tray. 'He's eaten his breakfast. He looks better but wants to stay in bed. You can go now. We'll be okay.'

'Have you any homework to do?'

She was about to say she hadn't as Mattie glared at her. 'I've some Shakespeare to learn so I can do that. I'll make some sandwiches for lunch, so *go*.'

'You look flushed,' Meredith commented as Mattie rushed into the office. 'Don't tell me; let me guess; you've had problems with Akina again!'

'Life's one *huge* problem at the moment. Adam's

285

off school with a cold and yes, we've had another barney with Akina. You'll never believe what she's been up to this time.'

Meredith listened open-mouthed. 'The young imp and you had no idea anything was going on?'

'None whatsoever! Like I said, I couldn't believe my eyes when I saw the photos. I had visions of all kinds of abuse and porn. *She's* the same age I was when it happened to me, so I suppose I overreacted. I saw it as history repeating itself. I was absolutely frantic when I left here yesterday.'

Meredith handed her a mug of coffee. 'I could tell something was wrong yesterday but I didn't want to stick my oar in and my suspicions were confirmed when you left early but you can't blame yourself. It must be very difficult raising a teenage daughter as wilful as Akina. You can't watch her all the time. I suppose she's acting like the injured party now.'

'No, she was fine after we had our discussion but later I felt guilty. She had a dream and I shattered it. Mark and I discussed it after she'd gone to bed and we couldn't reach a decision. Do we support her in this and let her go ahead or never mention it again?'

'That depends on your reasons. Parenting isn't a popularity poll. It's about raising children to adulthood with acceptable standards of behaviour. I believe they should earn privileges, not demand them. That's how I was raised. It's a tough question but at the end of the day, what harm could it do were she to continue? There must be hundreds of contenders so the likelihood of success would be minimal. At least that way there'd be no winners or losers.'

'Says the person who's just told me parenthood's not a popularity poll! I don't want to appear weak by giving in, neither do I want to appear dictatorial by refusing. I've asked myself what I'd have done had she come to me in the first place.'

'And...?'

'I don't know. That's the truth. I need to speak to the agent and then I can make an informed decision. If I can arrange a meeting today I'll finish at noon.'

'You missed all the action last night when you went to bed. I was in big trouble with Mattie and Dad.'

'So? That's nothing new,' Adam said rubbing his eyes and yawning. 'What have you done this time?'

She removed the photographs from the bag. 'Take a look at these first, then I'll tell you.'

He studied them closely. 'Hey, these are amazing! I didn't know you'd had these taken.'

She laughed. 'Neither did Mattie and Dad.'

'So you're saying they kicked off about these?'

'Not exactly. I'll start at the beginning.'

He listened without interruption until she reached the end of her colourful account. 'You forged Dad's signature? No wonder he went berserk.'

'Actually he didn't. Mattie was much worse. She kept firing questions at me and Dad never took his eyes off me. You've seen his deep penetrating stare when he's angry, but he didn't say much. I met the photographer at Martin's party, that gay bloke.' She chuckled. 'He really fancied you.'

'Get lost!'

'I kid you not. He thought you were my boyfriend

287

and when I put him right that you were my brother, he said you were gorgeous and wanted an introduction. I should have set you up, saying *you* were gay *too*, considering what you're always doing to me.'

'You'd have been bloody sorry if you had.'

She giggled. 'Not half as sorry as you.'

'So I take it Mum and Dad weren't impressed.'

'That's the understatement of the decade. Put paid to any aspirations I had of being a top model.'

He took hold of her hand. 'Knowing you, you'll get over it. I'm really sorry cos you're a damn sight better looking than some of the models I've seen in magazines. All my mates think you're amazing.'

'Well, Martin obviously doesn't. He promised to phone me but hasn't done.'

Adam felt guilty and turned away but she picked up on his brief uncomfortable expression.

'What? *What?*' she screeched. 'Tell me; have you been shoving your interfering nose in again?'

'*Alright!* Yes I have! I saw him offering you a fag and I was livid. I didn't want to make a scene at the party, so when he asked for your number, I wrote it down wrong.'

She dragged the pillow from beneath his head and walloped him. 'You're obnoxious Adam! Why are you always spying on me?'

'I'm looking out for you, that's all. Any guy who offers a fourteen-year-old a fag isn't fit to associate with a sister of mine and look at all the trouble you were in when Dad caught you smoking it.'

'It wasn't his fault. He thinks I'm seventeen and I could easily have refused had I wanted.'

'No Akina, you told Dad you didn't *like* to refuse, so if he'd wanted to get into your pants, I suppose you'd have found *that* hard to refuse too.'

'*No* I would *not* and you're not my keeper so butt out! I'm sick of folk telling me what to do.'

She gathered up her photographs and headed for the door. 'There's food in the kitchen for lunch so if you want it, get up and get it. I've done waiting on you and when I see Martin, and trust me I *will*, I'll tell him what you've done and I hope he gives you a good thump next time you're at football.'

He laughed scornfully. 'He'll be lucky! I don't go anymore. I haven't been for ages so...'

Realising he'd made a faux pas, he hesitated. 'I'll get my sandwich,' he said hurriedly, trying to cover his tracks but Akina was quick off the mark.

'Hang on a minute; you leave here every Saturday with your gear, so if you aren't off to football, then where are you going?'

'It's none of your business so keep it out.'

She cackled indignantly. 'None of my business? I like that, considering *you* can't keep your nose out of *mine*. Tell me!'

'It's nothing, honestly...alright, I have a part-time job. Dad's way behind the time with pocket money and I know they're stretched, so I don't like asking for more. A bloke I know wanted someone to do his books so I do that on a Saturday. It's just four hours and he offered me a tenner so I couldn't refuse.'

'A tenner? Does he want anyone else?'

Avoiding eye contact he said, 'You're in enough trouble without sneaking off doing a job as well.'

She was pretty sure Adam was hiding something and had her suspicions. His body language fuelled her determination to dig deeper. 'This bloke you're working for...who is he?'

'Er...just some bloke I know,' he said shiftily.

'It's Josh Hargreaves isn't it?' When Adam didn't answer, her face stretched into a broad grin. 'Oh my God!' she screeched with laughter. '*Every dog has its day*, as the old familiar saying goes. I can't *wait* to tell Dad. He'll go absolutely apeshit!'

Adam felt well enough to join the others for dinner and took his place at the table. 'I'll be fit for school tomorrow,' he told Mark. 'I don't want to miss anything vital with my 'O' levels coming up soon.'

'I'm glad to hear you're knuckling down Son. I'm proud of you and I hope you'll do the same Akina.'

She smiled sweetly. 'Don't worry about me Dad. I've learned lots of things today, haven't I Adam?'

'Yes,' he croaked.

'Enlighten me then,' Mark stated with interest.

She cast a glance in Adam's direction to find him studying his fingernails as if they were a new addition to his hands. 'I have a test coming up so I spent the morning on a soliloquy from, *As you like it.* It's by William Shakespeare and goes; *"All the world's a stage and all the men and women merely players. They have their exits and their entrances, and one man in his time plays many parts."* It's true though when you think about that isn't it Dad...I mean, take Adam for example; he's constantly in and out doing football and stuff isn't he?'

Adam was squirming in his seat and was grateful for Mattie's intervention. 'It doesn't actually mean on a day to day basis Akina. It talks about the seven stages or acts of men or women from infancy to old age. You should read it again with that in mind and you'll see what I mean.'

'Oh right, thanks. I must have misunderstood.'

'Literature was never my strongest point,' Mark admitted. 'I was more of a maths man myself.'

'Adam must take after you then Dad. You're not too bad at maths are you Adam? I bet you'd make a good accountant, bookkeeping and the like.'

Adam stood up. 'Can I be excused please Mum? I have a headache and I want an early night.'

'Can I too?' Akina asked. 'I'd like to spend more time on my soliloquy now you've explained it.'

She followed Adam upstairs to his room. 'Right, I'll do a deal with you. I want half your earnings for my silence, starting from next week.'

'You can get bloody lost! I'm not working all day and paying travelling expenses to earn a fiver.'

'You work four hours and you go on your bike. If I tell Dad who you're working for you'll be earning nowt *and* you'll get a load of earache, so suit yourself. It'll teach you to keep your trap shut in future when I've got a date.'

'I'll give you three quid and not a penny more.'

'I said half. That's the deal or I'll snitch. I'd have told him at the table but I've got Christmas presents to buy. You want a present don't you?'

He sneered. 'Not if I'm paying for it with my own money cos then I'll have to buy you one, so that's two I'm paying for and it's not fair. If you weren't crap at maths you'd see that.'

She winked. 'I'm only crap at maths when I want to be. Life isn't fair so get used to it. My heart was set on being a fashion model but I can't; I wanted to go out with Martin but you had to stick your oar in just as you did with Luke, so learn like I've had to learn to live with life's disappointments. I'll leave you with another Shakespearian quote, *"Goodnight, goodnight, parting is such sweet sorrow that I shall say goodnight till it be morrow,"* and *that's* when I want your answer.'

'You're early,' Meredith said to find Mattie busy at her desk at eight o'clock when she arrived.

'I wanted to catch up on yesterday's work before the mail arrived. I'm nearly done. Mark's taking the children to school this morning.'

'How did it go with the agent or would you prefer to change the subject?'

She swung round in her chair. 'It went okay, yes. I still hadn't made a decision when I arrived. After I'd spoken to Evan again things were a little clearer but I had to make sure that nothing would interfere with Akina's studies and the agent put my mind at rest on that score. I finally decided to go ahead and sign the Contract, not because I was pandering to a whim. I felt her school work might deteriorate were I to be heavy-handed, so it's blackmail if you like. I was assured she'd be chosen for some work, if not the role she really wants and I can easily put a stop to it if she fails to pull her weight at school.'

'Cute! I like that, so what did she say?'

'I haven't told her. She's on her best behaviour at the moment so that's my trump card when she starts playing up again. I doubt I'll have long to wait.'

Meredith laughed. 'I told Andrew last night and he confessed that his childhood dream was to be an engine driver, whereas I wanted to be an air hostess and marry a pilot. Did you have a dream?'

'A ludicrous one, yes. When I was little, I would hide under the bedclothes, yearning for a handsome prince to climb through my window and whisk me away to his castle in the sky.'

She smiled. 'Yours came true then didn't it?'

'I was just thinking the same,' she sighed.

Everything happened very quickly over the following few days. On Friday morning, Mattie received a call from the agency. *Youth* had scheduled a photo shoot for a dozen girls the following Tuesday and Akina had been one of those selected to attend. She was stunned as she jotted down the details.

The following week was half-term and presented no problem as Mattie was taking leave to be home with the children.

Akina's excitement was beyond description when Mattie delivered the news. She couldn't eat her evening meal and was awake for most of the night.

'Turn up looking like that and they'll not let you through the door,' Mark teased the next morning.

'I think you're pretty,' Mair said. 'I think you'll win, so take no notice of Daddy. I might be a model when I grow up cos I like dressing up in Mummy's clothes. I put her lipstick on too *and* her beads.'

'Do you now?' Mattie stated sternly. 'I wondered who'd broken my new lipstick.'

Mair turned a deaf ear to that. 'Did you put *your* mummy's lipstick on when you were six like me?'

Mattie reflected and doubted her mother ever possessed a lipstick. The clothes she wore beneath her pinafore were old and drab in fact the only time she recalled her mother in anything decent was the last Christmas they'd all spent together. She had looked lovely that day, wearing a bright red dress, no doubt acquired from a church jumble sale and remodelled to fit. 'I don't remember Mair,' she prevaricated. 'It was a long time ago.'

'In the olden days,' she sighed. 'Our teacher told us how people didn't have cars and televisions then. Whatever did you find to do?'

'Excuse me!' she cried above the others' laughter. 'I'm not *that* old.'

'She is,' Mark whispered audibly in Mair's ear.

Changing topic, Akina looked at the kitchen clock and remarked, 'You're going to be late for football, Adam.'

'Is that the time?' he shrieked. 'See you later.'

Mattie stayed behind to dry the breakfast pots. 'I don't know what to wear on Tuesday. What do you think Mattie?'

'Just wear something you feel comfortable with. I imagine they'll provide clothes for the photo shoot. They have your portfolio and know what you look like. This will be more about how you perform. Try to be confident but not argumentative. Be on your

294

best behaviour and remember to smile. You're very attractive when you smile.'

'I'm worried about what I'll be up against. I bet a lot of the others have done this before.'

She tried to allay her fears. 'I'm sure photo shoots are all different. Just pay attention to what they tell you and you'll be fine.'

Akina paced the bedroom floor. They were leaving in an hour and she was beginning to panic; so much rested on her performance. Evan had been delighted when told she had reached the final twelve and had wished her luck.

Mattie called her downstairs. 'Time to go Akina,' and for the umpteenth time that morning Akina shot to the toilet.

'It's not the end of the world if you aren't chosen. I doubt you'll even be told today. I know how competitive you are but think how much further you've got than hundreds of others. Don't have me wishing I hadn't signed up for you. The last thing I want is for you to make yourself ill. Come on, chin up.'

There were only two girls in reception when they arrived, sitting at opposite sides. One stared ahead vacantly while the other smiled weakly at Akina.

By eleven o'clock another seven had arrived making a total of ten. Half were with parents or friends and the remaining five had come alone.

'*They've* obviously done this before,' Akina said, referring to the unaccompanied ones. 'I'm glad you came with me.'

One girl strutted up and down, eyeing the competition. 'Is this your first time?' she asked Akina.

'Yes,' she murmured with a nod.

She laughed mockingly. 'A rookie! I never imagined they'd consider a rookie for this job. I've been doing this for years, since I was three. I notice two haven't turned up.' She plonked down on the chair next to Akina. 'They're probably on holiday, being as it's half-term. I should have been in Spain now with my mates, so I'll be ripping if I don't get this job. They've no right arranging photo shoots during school holidays. I left in July. I'd had enough of it.'

Mattie leaned forward. 'I understood it was open to girls from age thirteen so that's why it's arranged now so it doesn't interfere with schoolwork.'

'Your sister's a bit of a know-it-all isn't she?' she whispered, nudging Akina and grinning but Mattie had overheard. 'Actually I'm her mother, so thanks for the compliment.'

'I'm right though aren't I? Why bother studying if you can earn good money modelling clothes?'

Akina smirked as Mattie replied irritably, 'I find your reasoning rather shallow. Education's the fundamental instrument of life. Bear in mind you'll not profit from your looks ad infinitum. There'll come a time when prettier girls than you are selected and so I ask myself what you'll do then, as you appear to have such low regard for education.'

For some moments she remained tongue-tied, her embarrassment evident. She turned her attention to Akina. 'I'm Laurel. What's your name?'

'Akina.'

'Nice name. Is that your proper name?'

296

'Yes, why? Isn't yours?'

'Oh no! I changed it to Laurel as it's classier than mine. My mum called me Edna after an old aunt of hers. Horrible isn't it?'

Akina giggled. 'I agree. You look nothing like an *Edna*. Have you done a lot of modelling work?'

'Yes, I've been all over the world.'

'Sounds amazing,' Akina said wide-eyed.

'Believe me, it's not. It's boring at times, sitting about waiting to be called. You miss all your mates too while you're away. It's not half as glamorous as it's cracked up to be but it pays well.'

'Does your mum go too when you go abroad?'

'No, she works. They provide a chaperone when you're under age who watches you like a hawk.'

Akina looked round. 'Two girls have disappeared from over there. Maybe they've gone to the toilet.'

'No, they've just gone in. A woman came out for them. We shouldn't be long now. I'm starving. I've hardly eaten anything for a week. I'd gained a few pounds and I had to get it off. I'm having a massive breakfast as soon as I get out of here.'

One of the missing girls walked back through the room and Akina tried to read her body language but she gave nothing away as she left with her mother.

A smartly dressed woman approached. 'Are you Akina? Would you come with me please?'

'Good luck,' Laurel said. 'Show em what you're made of kid.'

Mattie smiled. 'Remember what I said. Chin up.'

Portraying a confident air she arose and followed her from the room, yet within, her pounding heart was screaming out that it was make or break time.

'She'll be fine,' Laurel told Mattie. 'They're used to dealing with children of all ages. I was scared the first time I came Mum told me, but they were really great. We might know the result tomorrow.'

'So soon?'

'Listen, they'll probably have made their decision already. They'll be making sure they've got it right. According to my agent, they'll pick three to represent three age groups between thirteen and nineteen and one of those, the lucky one, will be the *Face*.'

Mattie had to admit the girl was well informed. 'I imagine you have a few disappointments when lots of young people are competing, like today.'

Laurel shrugged. 'You win some, you lose some. That's the way it goes but I can't grumble. I get my share. I don't lose sleep over it if I'm not selected.'

As Akina returned Laurel was called in. 'I've left my number with your mum,' she told her. 'Give me a call when you hear anything. Don't forget.'

'I won't and good luck,' Akina called after her.

'How did it go?' Mattie enquired.

'Okay but I'll tell you everything once we're out of here. Can we get a drink please? I'm gagging!'

Over a cool drink, Akina related how scared she'd felt initially. 'Everyone seemed to be staring at me when I walked in and no one spoke until Grant, the photographer, asked how old I was. He's very witty and had everyone in stitches so I felt okay then. He took lots of photographs of me in different outfits in front of various backdrops and said I was a natural. The others were making notes and then one woman asked about my likes and dislikes at school. When I said I enjoyed lessons but that school dinners were putrid they howled with laughter and said theirs had been repulsive too. They liked my hair. There was a hairdresser in the room who kept changing the style for different shots by twisting it around her fingers and using a pointed wooden stick to hold it in place. Her favourite expression was *fabulous* and she was really clever Mattie. It took only seconds each time and it looked *fabulous*,' she giggled. 'I wish I knew how to do it like that. So yes, I'd say it went pretty well. I wouldn't be scared next time. Shall we skip lunch and go home? I want to tell Mair and Adam everything that's gone on. I bet it's on Dad's mind too. I might call Laurel later to see how she got on.'

It was the main topic of conversation throughout the rest of the day and at her second attempt, Akina succeeded in speaking to Laurel who felt her photo shoot had gone equally well.

The next day when Mattie answered a call, Akina was on tenterhooks but as the discussion continued, it appeared Meredith was the caller. A few minutes later, she summoned Akina. 'Someone would like a word and you might as well hear it in person,' she said, her expressionless face giving nothing away.

'Aunt Meredith?'

'Answer it and find out,' was her sharp response.

Akina felt downhearted. It wasn't Aunt Meredith. It was obviously Laurel calling with her news. She felt close to tears. 'Hi, it's Akina. Who's that?'

'Hello Akina. It's great to talk to you at last. This is Bernie from the Ferris Model Agency and I have great news. You may not be aware that *Youth* were seeking three models to represent three age groups between thirteen and nineteen and I'm delighted to say you've been selected as their representative for the middle group, age fifteen to sixteen.'

There was silence as she took in the information.

'Would you like me to tell you again? Bernie said on a ripple of laughter.

'Er...no, I understood. It's just that I can't believe it. Wow! That's nice...I mean, that's fantastic. It's better than fantastic.' She giggled. 'I can't think of anything to say but thank you. Thank you so much.'

'Don't thank me. You did all the work. They like everything about you, particularly your personality. They believe you'll be an excellent ambassador for their fashion and beauty products and so, with that in mind, you've been chosen as the *Face of Youth*.'

Again there was silence. This wasn't true she told herself. Any minute now she would wake up to find it was all a dream. 'I'm in shock. *I can't believe it!*' she shrieked. 'Thank you. I'm lost for words.'

Bernie laughed. 'I need to speak to your mother again meanwhile I suggest you sit down, relax and take it all in. I'm delighted Akina, especially as this was your first photo shoot. Well done.'

She beckoned Mattie. 'Bernie wants you again.'

'I knew you'd win,' Mair hollered excitedly. 'So will you be on telly now Akina?'

'I might be, on adverts. I really don't know Mair.'

Adam took her in his arms. 'Good on you! There was never any contest. I'm really pleased because I won't have to give you half my earnings now.'

300

'Cheeky monkey! I still can't believe it though. I feel numb. I have to call Laurel and let her know.'

Mattie consulted her list of notes. 'Right, we have to see the agent this afternoon about your Contract. That must be agreed and signed and then first thing tomorrow morning you're going to New York for a photo shoot. You'll fly back on Saturday and arrive home Sunday morning.'

'New York USA?' she queried.

'There's no other New York dummy,' Adam said.

'You'll be coming too won't you Mattie?'

She shook her head. 'No darling. I've a family to see to here but there'll be a chaperone to take care of you so you'll be quite safe.'

As she was about to protest Mattie said, 'Are you saying you don't want to go? If so I'll call the agent back. She believes the other two girls will be going as well and one will be younger than you. I'd never have passed over such an opportunity at your age.'

'No, no, I'll be okay. It's just that I've never been on a plane with strangers. I'm not keen on flying. I want to call Laurel now if that's everything and can I call Dad after that?'

'Yes but hurry up. We have to pack a bag for the trip. It's a good job you have a passport.'

Buzzing with excitement Laurel answered the call and screeched, 'I was hoping it'd be you. Have you heard anything yet?'

'Yes and it sounds like you have too, so come on, tell me what you got.'

'The seventeen to nineteen job. How about you?'

'I got fifteen to sixteen...and the *Face*.'

'Brilliant! Can't say I'm surprised though. No one else stood a chance against you.'

'I can't believe it. I only heard a few minutes ago so it's still sinking in yet. Are you off to New York tomorrow?'

'Yes, I think all three of us are but I don't know who got the youngest age group. I doubt it was that one with the humongous legs though.'

Akina laughed. 'You are awful but I have to say I noticed them too. It's a shame as she was gorgeous but for her legs. She had lovely blue eyes.'

'We'll have to try and sit together on the plane.'

'Yes, I'd like that. I can't wait to see New York. I have to call Dad now so I'll see you tomorrow. I'm glad you were picked too.'

Manchester Airport's check-in area was swarming with people and Akina, who had been given a blue recognition badge, looked around apprehensively to find other members of the group. There was no sign of Laurel but catching sight of another girl who was present at the shoot, she wandered over. 'Hello, I'm Akina. I take it you're on the New York flight?'

She nodded and smiled. 'Yes, I'm Katie.'

'Are you the chaperone?' her mother questioned, looking somewhat perturbed.

Akina laughed. 'No, I'm a model like Katie so I'll have one too but I haven't spotted anyone else yet.'

Mattie joined in the conversation. 'I was assured the chaperone will take good care of the children. I was rather anxious when told she was going abroad but they'll all hang out together I'm sure.'

'There's Laurel,' Akina said, waving her arms to attract her attention.

Adam turned to behold a stunner as Laurel waved and hurried towards them.

'Mum's just dropped me off. The traffic's awful,' she said breathlessly.

'This is Katie,' Akina told her.

'Hi Katie. I remember seeing you on Tuesday.'

Adam moved in closer and in the absence of any introduction by Akina said, 'Hi Laurel. I'm Akina's brother, Adam. I've heard a lot about you.'

Smiling, she eyed him from head to toe. 'I expect it's too much to hope that you're our chaperone?'

'I wish,' he replied, his eyes smiling back at hers.

Reluctant to be ignored Mair chirped, 'I'm Mair. I'm Adam and Akina's little sister. I've never met a real model before. Do you get lots of money?'

Mark stepped forward. 'It's not polite to ask such questions darling.' Smiling apologetically he added, 'She's overwhelmed. I'm sorry.'

'Not nearly as much as I'd like to earn,' she told Mair. 'Are you going to be a model too?'

She giggled. 'I don't know yet but I like dressing up in my mummy's pretty clothes.'

At that point two women approached wearing the same badges and introduced themselves as Kim and Betty. Betty, the older one was their chaperone. 'If you'd like to say goodbye to your parents now we'd better join the queue,' she said, taking charge.

'We'll be off then,' Mark stated, kissing Akina on the cheek. 'Good luck. Hope it goes well for you.'

Mattie hugged her as tears filled her eyes.

303

Adam smiled warmly at Laurel. 'Hope you have a great time.'

En route to the hotel Akina was mesmerised by the sights, Katie too and all three girls were delighted on their arrival to be sharing the same room.

'I'll be in the room next door,' Betty informed the girls. 'You don't leave the room under *any* circumstances without me, is that clear? There's a phone on the desk. Any problems, you call me. If I'm not there, leave a message and wait in the room. Is that clear too?'

'Yes Betty,' they answered in unison.

'Good. I can see we'll get along very well. Here's my number. Empty your bags now and then we can go for our lunch...say fifteen minutes.'

As she left, Laurel jumped up and mimicking her gruff voice mumbled, *'Any problems you call me. If I don't answer you wait in the room. Is that clear?'*

Akina and Katie laughed heartily. It was going to be a great weekend.

'I wonder what Akina's doing. I can't stop worrying. It's the first time we've ever been separated.'

'No it isn't,' Mark contradicted her. 'The children often spend a weekend with their grandparents.'

'You know what I mean. She's alone in a strange country. It's different altogether staying with grandparents. What if she's lonely and scared?'

Mark laughed. 'Akina lonely and scared? Get real Mattie. She's never been a shrinking violet. Take it from me, she'll be having an absolute ball and making the most of her time away from your eagle eye and that's what we should be doing. How often do we get any time to ourselves in the evening? Adam won't be home until eleven and Mair's fast asleep.' He slipped an arm round her, twisting the curls that fell about her shoulders. 'I like your new hairstyle. It's softer and makes you look ten years younger.'

'I *am* ten years younger,' she taunted.

'Alright, no need to rub it in. I asked for that. We do okay though don't we?' he said, gently brushing his lips against her cheek.

She smiled. 'I wouldn't change a solitary thing.'

She fidgeted anxiously at the meeting point, whilst waiting for Akina to appear. It seemed to be taking forever for passengers from the New York flight to pass through, and then suddenly, Mattie spotted the three girls with the chaperone.

When Katie's parents, waiting beside Mark called out to their daughter, all three dashed towards them, gabbling with excitement.

In an aside to Katie's father, Mark commented, 'It appears they've had a good time.'

'I was just thinking the same. We were more than a little concerned to learn she'd have to go abroad. This is all new to us and she's only thirteen.'

'Same here. Akina's fourteen but still a child.'

'I think we're making tracks now,' Mattie cut in. 'The girls have all exchanged numbers so I imagine our phones will be red hot for a while. It was nice to meet you,' she told Katie's parents.

During the journey home Akina rarely stopped to

draw breath as she gabbled excitedly about all her experiences. 'New York's fabulous,' she told them. 'They took us all over the place to do shoots and on Saturday I had to leave the others for four hours to go to a studio where there was a make-up artist. She spent ages on my face and my skin felt lovely when she'd finished doing my make-up but then, when I looked in a mirror, although I didn't seem to have much on, I looked a lot better.'

'That's the secret of make-up,' Mattie explained. 'Lots of women think plastering it on makes them look nicer but it doesn't. This is the message they'll be trying to get over to the young girls they're hoping will buy it. Did they take photos of you then?'

'Did they! They took loads! Earlier the three of us had been to Brooklyn Bridge for a shoot. They took dozens with the Statue of Liberty in the background as well and we went to the top of the Empire State Building. That was really exciting but Katie was a bit scared. We shared a room at the hotel and had a good laugh. Laurel was brilliant at mimicking our chaperone, Betty. She was alright though once you got to know her properly. She had to be strict when she was looking after three nutty teenage girls.'

'I won't argue with the nutty bit,' Mark quipped.

'So why didn't Adam and Mair come with you?'

'Adam's revising for his mocks and Mair went to Nana's to show her the puppet you gave her.'

'I wonder if the three of us will ever be together on other jobs. We got on really well in New York.'

'Not unless *Youth* calls you in for something else. The others might meet up but you're contracted to

Youth for a year so you can't work for anybody else during that time. That's clearly stipulated. They'll no doubt need you for additional promotional work, considering the fee they're paying. It's an obscene amount of money for a teenage girl to earn.'

'How much is it?'

'Much more than Dad and I earn added together for years of hard work. That's your nest egg for the future Akina and I hope you realise how lucky you are to have landed such a job at your tender age.'

She shook her head. 'No Mattie. I've already told you, I want you and Dad to have that money, to pay you back for the school fees and to put towards our holiday to Japan in the summer. We wouldn't even be going to Japan if it wasn't for me.'

Mark pulled into a lay-by and turned to face her. 'Akina, we've had this conversation already and we won't be touching one penny of that money. Is that clear? How can you even *imagine* we'd allow you to pay your own fees? You're our daughter just like Adam and Mair are our children, so let me make a deal with you as you're so keen on making deals. If or when I'm in need of money, you'll be the first to know, alright? Meanwhile, it'll be invested for your future needs so don't mention it again, please.'

Recognising a tone of annoyance she dropped the subject and sighed. She'd never understand adults.

It was Mattie's birthday the next day and Akina had bought her gift at the Duty Free shop in New York. It was her favourite perfume and she couldn't wait to give it to her. As expected, Mattie was delighted.

307

'When you've got a minute, I'd like a word about something,' Akina said.

'Is something wrong?' she asked with concern.

'No, nothing like that. I just want to talk to you in private.'

'Will it keep until after school? We're running a bit late this morning.'

Recognising a desperate plea in her eyes she told Adam and Mair to get their lunch boxes and wait in the car. As Adam closed the door, Mattie sat down beside Akina. 'Okay, you have my undivided attention now. What's on your mind?'

'I want to say something I should have said a long time ago. It'd have been a lot easier then. I know I can be a bit stroppy at times but I don't mean it and I'm always sorry afterwards. I talked to Laurel a lot when I was in New York. She has no dad as he left when she was a few months old. Her mum's had to struggle to make ends meet so she's always had to fend for herself while her mum was out at work. It got me thinking about how lucky I was, having you and Dad for parents. You're always here for all of us. You've even made time now to listen when you should be on your way to work. What I'm trying to say is that Laurel loves her mum even though she's rarely around, because she's sensible enough to see that her mum does her best.' Her bottom lip started to tremble as she continued, 'I had my mum for six years that's all, and for those six years, despite poor health for half of them, she put me first, right until the end when she made provision for my future care with you. You see, she knew your care would be as

308

good as hers and it has been Mattie. No child could have wished for better but I was angry I suppose at losing Mum and I wouldn't let you get close to me. I cringe now to think back to when Dad suggested I call you Mum, at the way I reacted and how upset you were. The only excuse is that I was a little girl who didn't understand your feelings and then, as I grew older, I couldn't bring myself to talk about it, until now that is. I hope I haven't left it too late and I'd like you to open your card now.'

Akina's eyes welled with tears as Mattie removed the card from its envelope.

Overwhelmed, Mattie didn't speak and with tears but a blink away, smiled fondly to read the words, *'To Mum, all my love, Akina xxx.'* Finally she murmured, 'This is the best birthday I've ever had.'

During the next few weeks Akina's weekends were crammed with *Youth* engagements and with Christmas fast approaching there wasn't a moment to lose on promotional work for the vast array of products.

On several occasions she met up with Laurel and Katie at catwalk events, one of which was in Paris, and where, at the end, each was given a huge box of goodies containing clothes, accessories and beauty products, together with photographs of their shoots.

'That's all my Christmas shopping taken care of,' said Laurel on a laugh. 'It's been hectic but great.'

Akina and Katie both nodded in accord and after saying their fond farewells, they went their separate ways to enjoy a richly-deserved Christmas break.

13

'What do I buy the girl who has everything? This is so difficult,' Mattie said as they scoured the shops. 'You've got more clothes than anybody I know and it's the same with cosmetics. I can't buy chocolates because you're so careful about your weight. What about a new school bag?'

She laughed. 'Gee thanks Mum. That'd be great, I don't think! Besides, they don't bother what kind of bag you use at our age. I have loads of *Youth* bags I could use. Let's cross over to the other side and see if anything takes my fancy there. Look, there goes another bus with my mug-shot all over it.'

Mattie grimaced. '*Akina*, I wish you wouldn't use that awful expression. You sound like a gangster.'

She giggled. 'Lighten up. You should be used to it by now. There's an idea,' she said, stopping by a Travel Agency. 'You and Dad could buy me some Japanese yen for my birthday. I can get something I want in Japan then. I hate asking for money every time I want something.'

'Maybe, but it doesn't stop you,' Mattie smirked. 'Actually, that's a good idea because my poor feet are dropping off. I'll call the bank tomorrow.'

She linked Mattie. 'It's terrific to have a day out together. I hardly ever see the family these days.'

'Make the most of the time left. There's only six months to go and it'll be over. You've enjoyed the experience haven't you?'

'I wouldn't have missed it for the world and Katie and Laurel are amazing friends. I'm glad they'll be at my party on Sunday.'

Mattie chuckled. 'That'll be two more bottles of *Face eau de parfum* to add to your collection.'

'They wouldn't dare,' she laughed.

'My little Akina, fifteen years old in a few days. How time flies,' she sighed.

'Er...I'm almost as tall as you now so not so much of the 'little'.

Mattie lumbered into the house on Friday evening laden with shopping bags and exhaled noisily.

Mark jumped up. 'I could have helped with those. What on earth have you bought?'

'I don't have time for the weekly shop tomorrow so I've got that as well as Akina's party food.'

'I'll help Dad shift everything,' Adam said. 'You sit down Mum and take it easy.'

Akina was already ferreting through the shopping bags to see what was there. 'I'll help with the food preparation tomorrow Mum,' she told her.

Mid-morning the following day Mattie received a telephone call from Mark's mother to say his father had been rushed to hospital following a fall. It was likely he had broken his ankle but of much greater concern he had complained of severe chest pains to the paramedics.

She summoned Mark immediately and explained.

'She was very vague and obviously in shock. She'd like us to go as soon as we can but try not to worry Mark. He's in good hands.'

'Right, leave what you're doing and let's go. Put what you can in the fridge Akina and then call Nana Peters to ask if she can have Mair for an hour or so. We'll collect Adam en route. It shouldn't take long for him to get out of his kit and get dressed.'

Akina froze on the spot. 'Can't we er...go without Adam? You know how long he takes getting ready for school. He has a key if he's home before us.'

Mark was incensed. 'He's Adam's grandfather so don't talk so stupid Akina. How would you feel if it were Nana Peters and we all went without you? Just hurry up and then we can be on our way.'

There was nothing else for it. Dad would have to know the truth but at least she would spare Mair the brawling outrage when he learned Adam was working for Josh Hargreaves.

She waited until Emily took Mair inside the house and inhaled deeply. 'Dad, you won't find Adam at football. He has a Saturday job now. He's saving up to buy Christmas presents,' she added to her disclosure in the hope it would soften the blow.

'Saturday job? Saving for Christmas presents in bloody April? *Truth Akina!* What's going on as I'm the only one who doesn't appear to know what my son's doing when he leaves home with his kit?'

'This is the first I knew,' Mattie cut in. 'Come on Akina. You can't keep secrets from your parents.'

'It's the truth Mum. He works for four hours on a Saturday that's all, to boost his pocket money. All his friends get more than him and he could never go anywhere with them. He didn't want to ask you for more as you'd have to do the same for all of us then and it'd cost too much when you're short.'

Mark was livid. '*Short; short?*' he yelled. 'When have you lot ever gone *short?* Anyone listening to you would think we're on the bloody breadline. He should have come to me if there was a problem and whilst we're on the subject, what sort of employer offers work to a fifteen year old lad apart from one seeking slave labour? I think it's illegal at his age to work for an employer. What's he doing anyway?'

'Bookkeeping Dad, that's all. It's not dangerous.'

Mark wanted to know more. 'What does he earn for four hours? Peanuts I shouldn't wonder. Exploitation, that's what it is, so come on...I've seen you with your heads together scheming and whispering. You're as thick as thieves. How much is this rogue paying Adam for four hours work?'

'Ten pounds Dad. He pays him ten pounds.'

At that revelation Mattie's mouth fell open while Mark was visibly shocked. A deafening silence ensued before Mark spoke again. 'More money than sense if you ask me to pay a young lad ten quid for four hours work. Where's Adam working? Does the unscrupulous moron have him fiddling his books on some dodgy car lot? Is that why he wouldn't tell me what he was doing?' He paused to await a response. 'Well? Where to? I need to be on my way.'

When Akina turned to him, her eyes revealed all and Mark's lips stretched into a wide sardonic grin. 'Dear oh dear oh dear! Don't tell me. Let me guess.

313

It's the iniquitous Josh Hargreaves, the blight of my bloody life who's given him a job.'

Mark held his head between his hands. 'First *you* forge my signature and then *Adam* goes to work for Josh Hargreaves. Where the hell did I go wrong?'

'Mark, leave it for now, please. We need to be on our way to see your dad,' Mattie said soothingly.

He started the engine and completed the journey without a further word. When he turned into the car park Akina mumbled, 'I'll nip in and fetch him.'

'Good idea,' Mark grunted with a cutting stare.

Adam looked up in surprise when Josh led her to the office at the far end of the factory floor. 'What are you doing here? What's up?'

'I'm really sorry Adam. The cat's out of the bag. Dad knows. I had to tell him because he needed to find you. Your granddad's in hospital. He had a bad fall and we're off to see him now. I did my best to persuade him to go without you but he wouldn't.'

With no regard to what his father might say or do he asked, 'How *is* Granddad?'

'I don't know. Grandma told Mum he might have broken his ankle but it seems he has chest pains as well. That's as much as I know.'

'Don't worry about telling Dad. Leave him to me. I'm sick of him treating us like kids. I'll be sixteen soon and old enough to leave home. I'm glad he's found out what I'm doing as I won't have to sneak about anymore now.'

'He'll not let you carry on here. He was ripping.'

'Huh! Let him try and stop me. I'll have a quick word with Josh to say I'll come back Monday after

314

school to finish off and I'll be out in a minute.'

Akina waited by the gate and they climbed in the back of the car together. Not one word was uttered before they arrived at George's bedside.

'What have you been up to?' Mark asked humorously, unhooking the chart from the end of the bed.

'Throwing my weight about, silly fool that I am,' he stated curtly. 'Never thought I'd end up in here.'

'Tell me what you remember,' he said, checking George's pulse.

'What I remember?' he repeated. 'I'm not senile. I remember it all. I fell over with a hell of a bang.'

Mark nodded. 'What about these chest pains you have? Describe them to me.'

'My ribs hurt when I breathe in and out.'

'You probably banged them in the fall. Have you been for an x-ray?'

'Aye and I'm still waiting to hear the results. The doctor was supposed to be here half an hour ago.'

'Someone's coming now,' Akina informed them.

The young doctor walked to the side of the bed. 'I hope you're feeling a little better now George,' he said with a genial smile. 'The pain relief should be starting to take effect soon and you'll be pleased to know I have the result of your x-rays.'

'The only thing I'll be pleased about is when I'm getting out of here, and less of the familiarity if you don't mind. It's Mr. Wyndham to you.'

Colour flushed the doctor's cheeks and he swiftly continued, 'Your x-rays show a transverse fracture of the tibial malleolus. To put that in layman terms it means...'

315

Mark cringed whilst awaiting the predictable outburst from his father.

'I know what that means,' he interrupted nastily. '*I've* forgotten more than *you*'ll ever know. Prior to my retirement I was Senior Orthopaedic Consultant for over twenty years so don't talk down to me like I'm the village idiot. Who's in charge here?'

'Mr. Jones,' he said clearing his throat. 'He's not in today though but Mr. Stillwood's in if you'd like to speak to him.'

'Ben? I haven't seen Ben for donkey's years. Yes ask him to come and see me.'

Celia smoothed her hand across the bedclothes as the doctor hurried away.

'*Stop fussing woman!*' he grumbled. 'You always have to be meddling with something.'

As Mark and Mattie shuffled uneasily neither one could have envisaged what would happen next.

'*Granddad!*' Akina declared intolerantly, much to their surprise. 'Don't be so obnoxious when people are trying to help you. You're the one who fell and caused the injury so it's no use trying to lay blame elsewhere. You weren't the high and mighty Senior Consultant at that doctor's age and he did nothing to warrant such rudeness. It's the trend nowadays to address people by Christian name so they feel more at ease. While you're here, you're just a patient like everyone else, no better and no worse. The way you spoke to Grandma was totally unacceptable too and as you're going to need constant help once you get home, you'd do well to remember that.'

His eyes remained fixed on hers until the end of

her delivery during which Mattie was too shocked to speak. Adam crept behind his father whilst Mark smiled, admiring her bold intervention for if anyone could bring the best out of George, it was Akina.

For a moment or two he was silent, analysing her words and then he threw back his head and laughed uncontrollably. 'You cheeky young pup! Come and give your granddad a big hug. I've not seen you for ages with all your gallivanting.'

'Do you promise to behave?'

'Aye I do lass. I'll give it a try.'

She gave him a hug and a kiss. 'I'm sorry you fell Granddad but it'll mend. Looks like the doctor's on his way back with someone else.'

'Ben Stillwood!' George cried. 'Isn't it time you were retiring and making room for up and coming young doctors like this lad to move up the ladder?'

He shook George's hand. 'Long time no see. I'll be going at the end of the year. We're going living in Portugal, spending our final days in the sun. So, tell me how you've managed to break your ankle.'

'It's all here in the notes,' the young doctor said. 'Mr. Wyndham had a fall.'

'No need for formality. The name's George,' he said, winking at him. 'I've a lot of pain in my chest too but I reckon I banged my ribs in the fall.'

'On my patch I diagnose and you listen,' Ben told him. 'But you're right. Your heart's much healthier than mine.' Recognising Mark he grinned. 'Mark. How many years has it been? You were just out of Med School last time I saw you. I heard you made Senior Consultant. Are these your children?'

317

'Yes, Adam and Akina. We have another younger girl at home and this is my wife Mattie.'

'Pleased to meet you Mattie. Mark always had an eye for a good looking girl and he certainly picked a stunner when he picked you.'

'Thank you,' she replied modestly. 'Adam's hoping to follow in the family footsteps into medicine. We don't know yet what Akina will do.'

'She's modelling presently,' George said proudly. 'Got herself a plum job at a new fashion house and they send her all over the world.'

'Oh, you've finished school then?'

'No, I'm only fifteen.'

'Fifteen?' I'd have guessed seventeen or eighteen. You'll be about eighteen won't you Adam?'

'No, I'm fifteen too but nearly sixteen.'

He shook his head in disbelief. 'Children grow up so quickly these days. They're young adults now at fourteen.'

'Tell me about it,' Mark said glancing in Adam's direction. 'I take it you have no children?'

'No, sadly it never happened.'

Mark laughed. 'Would you like my two eldest? I have to say they're a handful. You don't know from one day to the next what they're up to.'

'I'll pass then thanks. Nice to have seen you again Mark and you too George. We'll be sorting out that ankle of yours shortly so don't go anywhere.'

'I'm so sorry Granddad,' Adam said. 'If you need anything doing in the garden, I'll come over.'

Celia stroked Adam's hair. 'I've been saying for some time that we ought to have a gardener so I'll

318

get my way now. Don't any of you worry about me. I'll be fine with George. I can handle him.'

'I'd like to see you in the study Adam,' Mark said the minute they walked in the house.

Akina sneaked a look at her brother and raised her eyebrows. 'Good luck,' she mouthed.

Mark walked to the rear of his desk and sat down, gesturing to Adam to sit on the only available chair at the front of the desk.

Adam decided to start as he meant to go on. 'Job interview?' he asked with a snigger, slouching back in his chair.

'Show some respect Son.'

'Earn it then, don't demand it,' he answered icily.

Mark sighed. 'What's got into you of late Adam? You appear hell-bent on winding me up.'

'If you say so. After all you're always right aren't you? No one but you is entitled to have an opinion or make a decision. If this is about Josh, I didn't tell you because I knew how you'd react, so thanks for proving me right. Did it ever occur to you to think, maybe my son's showing a little initiative...after all he *is* a young man now in need of cash to splash? I don't need an answer because you obviously didn't. I approached Josh about a job because I can talk to him. *He's* prepared to listen and...'

'That's enough Adam. You've made your point.'

'No I haven't. You lack compassion. I know Josh once made a huge error of judgement when he was mentally ill but you aren't perfect considering how you neglected me when your first wife died.'

'Your *mother*!' he cut in furiously. 'I dispute that I neglected you. I had to raise you single-handedly. I gave you everything.'

'Mattie's the only mother I've ever known and as for you giving me everything, you failed to give me any love or affection. That's not a criticism though. As a single parent with a very demanding job, such a delicate balancing act couldn't have been easy for you. I've never held it against you but it's true. You bought me books yet I'd nobody to read the stories to me; you bought me a football but I'd nobody to kick it with me. I needed my dad but you were still grieving and bitter about your devastating loss. My point is that Josh had *two* tragedies in quick succession and I'd expect you of all people to understand how that felt. He's *not* a bad guy; I like him and if you can't or won't deal with that Dad, then you're the one with the problem. I'm not giving up my job because you don't like him. It doesn't interfere with my studies and lots of young people have part-time jobs, Akina for example.'

'Yes and she went behind my back too.'

Adam stood up to leave. 'Then ask yourself why Dad. I don't think it'll take long to find the answer. Stop dictating to us as if we're children because we aren't anymore. Show *us* a little respect too if that's what you want. If you haven't taught us right from wrong already, it's too late to start now.'

He walked from the room without another word.

It was all hands on deck the next day, preparing for Akina's fifteenth birthday party. With the exception

320

of Celia and George, her grandparents were coming as were all aunts and uncles, assuming there was no last minute cancellation by Lucille whose baby was due any day soon.

'What time's Laurel coming?' Adam asked.

Akina sniggered. 'Why, do you fancy her?'

Adam's red face and categorical denial confirmed her suspicions and with a throaty chuckle she jibed, '*The lady doth protest too much methinks,* to quote the words of William Shakespeare. You've got the hots for her.'

'I have *not*,' he insisted. 'Don't *dare* tell her that.'

'Why? You ruin my hopes of romance with every guy I fancy, so why should I not reciprocate?'

'Because I'm asking you nicely. Besides, I have a surprise for you. I've invited Martin to your party.'

She beamed with delight. 'Is he coming?'

'He said he was. He tried to call you and assumed he'd got your number written down wrong. I didn't make him any the wiser.'

She kissed his cheek. 'Thanks Adam. I owe you.'

'Remember that when Laurel turns up. No funny stuff, promise?'

There was a familiar knock at the door. 'That has to be Nana. I'll get it,' she called to Mattie. 'Right, I promise,' she told Adam who prodded her.

As she opened the door several cars were arriving and within a few minutes everyone except Jack and Lucille had arrived.

Paul, now aged eight, was overwhelmed by all the visitors and sat down quietly next to his mother.

Mattie smiled contemplatively. He was the image

of Seth at that age and had inherited most of Seth's characteristics too. Steph had told her that he was at his happiest with his head in a book and there was no shortage of books available, Seth now being the Chief Librarian at the Central Library.

When Jack and Lucille arrived a short while later, Steph jumped up to offer Lucille her seat. 'How's it going? Anything happening yet?' she asked.

Lucille exhaled noisily. 'I'm six days overdue and going mad! Every day when I wake up I think, "It'll be today," but there's no sign yet. You were lucky; Paul came early. Jack calls me at least three times a day. He can't wait to be a daddy. I've told him *he's* having the next one though if he wants any more.'

Mattie joined in. 'We're having party games later so perhaps a few belly-laughs might do the trick.'

'I'll cross my fingers then,' she sighed.

The teenagers had gone upstairs with Akina to see her presents. 'I've got a job next weekend. Are you working?' she asked the other two girls.

'No, what are you doing?' Laurel queried.

'Don't know. If you aren't coming it'll probably be in a department store. It's on Saturday morning.'

'Have you any photos I can see?' Martin asked.

She opened a drawer that was packed with photographs. 'At the top of the drawer there's some I had taken in Paris. Laurel and Katie are on some too.'

Adam stood up. 'I've seen them all. Do you want to go down now Laurel?'

She nodded, 'Yes, whatever. Come on Katie. You mustn't stand in the way of true love.'

Akina gave her a threatening stare whilst Martin

pretended not to have heard. 'Do you fancy going out somewhere next Saturday night?' he asked.

Caught off guard she stuttered, 'Er...yes...er...I'd like that. I'm not allowed in pubs though.'

'We could go to the pictures. Have a think and let me know. Here's my number. I don't have yours so will you write it down for me? I take it it's okay for me to call you?'

'Course it is, anytime.'

'These photos are terrific. I'm glad you met Evan and got that job. I'm always seeing you on buses, a photo I mean. Is that the end of it after a year?'

She shrugged. 'I dunno. They can keep me on for another year if they want but I have to think about my 'O' levels next year. I'll see what happens.'

'Had we better go back down Akina? I don't want to blot my copy book.'

'I suppose so. I'm glad you came today Martin.'

Though that wasn't an invitation Martin read it as one and cupping her face in his hands he kissed her gently on the lips. 'I've been dying to do that since I met you. I really like you Akina.'

It was her first real kiss and she felt awkward and shy but with a warm glow. 'I like you too,' she told him softly and hand in hand they went downstairs.

'Food's up,' Mattie announced when Akina had opened her remaining gifts and the young ones shot into the dining room instantly.

Mark had spoken but a few words to Adam since their contretemps but he had given much thought to Adam's criticism. He had to agree Josh Hargreaves might appear to others as an amiable decent guy yet much as *he* tried to warm to him, he couldn't. Mark had been awake for hours, going over everything in his mind until it finally became clear. It wasn't the abduction he held against him; it was the easy relationship Josh had with Adam, a relationship that *he* had never enjoyed with his son. At best he had been distant during Adam's formative years and at worst neglectful as Adam had pointed out and he had only himself to blame. Furthermore he didn't know how to put matters right.

Mark's concerns remained at the forefront of his mind until Mattie prodded him. '*Mark!* I'm talking to you. Go and get something to eat. What's wrong with you? You've been like this all day.'

'Sorry darling. I was miles away,' he mumbled.

'I overheard Martin discussing your photos Akina and I'd like to see them please when we've eaten,' Rachel said. 'We're so proud of your achievement.'

'I've finished so I'll go and find you a few.'

Adam was walking round topping up everyone's tea-cup. 'More tea Dad?'

'Yes, thanks Adam.'

'I was thinking of asking Laurel out on Saturday. I take it you don't have a problem with that before I make a fool of myself?'

'Er...no, not at all. She seems a nice girl.'

The conversation ended there but at least it was a move in the right direction.

With the exception of Lucille, the women cleared the table and arranged seating for the party games as Akina took charge. 'We're all playing Charades first,' she informed everyone.

'Oh no!' Bob cried. 'I'm useless at that. I always make a hash of it.'

'Tough Granddad, and since you obviously need more practice, you can go first.'

Rachel tittered. 'That'll teach him to keep quiet.'

'Can I go next?' Mair asked.

'Only if you win, so concentrate. Right Granddad, read the card and act it out without speaking. I can reveal it's a children's story.' She started the timer and Bob stood like a statue, staring ahead.

'*Goldilocks and the three bears*,' Mair bellowed and everyone laughed.

'Come on Granddad. Tell us how many words.'

'Four,' he said.

'You mustn't speak. Just stick up four fingers.'

He raised four fingers and continued to stand still.

'*Jack and the beanstalk*,' Mark contributed with a short burst of laughter

'*Cin-der-ell-a*,' Adam cried.

'Time's up!' Akina proclaimed.

Bob was delighted. 'That's the first time I've ever won,' he stated proudly. 'Not one of you guessed it was *Little red riding hood*.'

The scene was set for humour and Mark's former sullenness had for the time being been dispelled.

After two turns each Akina handed out paper and pens and stopped abruptly at Lucille who looked to be in some pain. 'Mum,' she said in a loud whisper. 'Be quick; I think something's wrong.'

Mattie hurried across and summoned Jack. 'What is it Lucille,' she asked anxiously.

'It's them flaming belly-laugh games. I think I'm

325

starting in labour. I've just had a really strong pain.'

Mark stepped up. 'Take it easy. Nothing's going to happen in a hurry. Akina, take your friends up to your room and find something to do. Take Mair and Paul too. Pass me my bag please Mattie.'

The men stood up and grouped in a corner whilst Mark checked her over. He smiled and removed his stethoscope, handing it to Lucille. 'There, listen to your baby's heartbeat. Everything's fine.'

'Am I in labour?'

'I'd like to say yes but it's too soon to tell. Let's see how you go on.'

Jack had already broken out in a cold sweat. 'Do we need to send for an ambulance?' he panted.

'Not yet for a while,' Mark stated calmly. 'Babies have the habit of taking their time and I very much doubt yours will be the exception to the rule. How about a cup of tea Lucille?'

'Sounds nice, yes please.'

'Is this your first?' Rachel asked.

She wriggled in her seat. 'Yes, so I'm a bit edgy.'

With a reassuring smile she counselled, 'When it gets to this stage we're all apprehensive. I used to tell myself that some women had a dozen children and that helped settle me. You'll be fine my dear.'

Mattie returned with Lucille's tea but as she was about to take a sip, another pain surged through her body and this time she yelled.

'It seems this little blighter's determined to prove me wrong,' Mark said.

'Looking ahead you should go home for Lucille's bag. You can't drive her home in this state Jack.'

'Tell me where it is and I'll go,' Steph offered.

She puffed and panted till the pain finally passed. 'It's in the hall, behind the door; it's tartan.'

Lucille poked Jack and laughed. 'It's happening; it's really happening. Our baby's coming.'

'I'll not be long,' Steph said, making for the door.

'Hurry up,' Jack shrieked in a tone of utter panic.

As Steph returned, an ambulance stopped behind her car and they all hurried inside.

'Good luck Lucille. Just keep telling yourself it's all worth it,' Mattie said as the crew helped her into the ambulance. 'You won't be long now and we'll come and see you tomorrow. Here's your bag.'

Mair had slipped out of the room and crept downstairs to see what was happening. 'Has Aunt Lucille gone to get her baby now?' she asked Mark.

He gathered her up in his arms. 'Yes darling.'

'Can she choose a boy or a girl or do they tell her at the hospital which she can have?'

'Kind of. Aunt Lucille won't know until she gets the baby so that'll be a nice surprise won't it?'

'If she doesn't like it, can she give it back?'

Emily laughed. 'She'll love her baby, Mair. Every mummy loves her baby.'

'Okay if you say so. I'm going back upstairs now. We're playing games.'

'Who wants a drink?' Mark asked, to which there was a general consensus of accord.

When everyone had been served, Mark raised his glass. 'I'd like to propose a toast to Lucille and Jack in anticipation of the safe arrival of their new baby.'

Mark's sentiments were echoed by everyone.

It was just after nine o'clock when the good news arrived. In a broken tearful voice, Jack told Mattie they had a beautiful baby boy.

'It's a boy,' she cried excitedly to the others. 'It's wonderful news Jack. Are they alright?'

'They're terrific, both of them. He has lots of hair and chubby cheeks. I still can't believe it. He'll be called John Henshaw, like me. Lucille's adamant he must be christened John. He weighs seven pounds two ounces and he has a right pair of lungs on him.'

'You're in for a lot of sleepless nights then. Give Lucille our love and tell her we're happy. My little brother Jack, a daddy. It's hard to take in. Hang on, Seth wants a quick word.'

'Well done Jack. A quick word of advice though. Get him potty trained soon so he won't be peeing in bed till he's six like you were.'

'You shut your rip or I'll give you a fat lip,' Jack guffawed. 'He's perfect Seth. I can't believe it yet.'

'You will when you're up all night, changing and feeding him. Make the most of your restful nights before Lucille gets home as there'll be no more for some time. He'll be worth it though. We'll be over to see the baby tomorrow.'

'I'm Aunt Mattie,' she murmured over the sleeping child. 'He's adorable Lucille, absolutely adorable. I could take him home.'

'Hands off,' said Jack, smiling lovingly at Lucille who looked content and happy. 'By the way Adam, you did me a favour in more ways than one, getting me that job. When I went round earlier today to tell the lads our good news, Josh gave me fifty-quid as well as the week's leave on full pay he'd given me.'

Adam's swift glance in Mark's direction detected his displeasure and quick as a flash Adam told Jack that he gave fifty pounds to all new fathers but only for the first child to help with their initial expense.

Jack however wouldn't be silenced. 'He's a good boss. Everybody likes him. According to one of the drivers, Josh's son had a fatal accident at the works. How tragic is that? Is Josh a mate of yours Mark?'

'No,' Adam interjected before Mark could reply. 'I knew his son. We were at school together.'

Anxious to change topic Mattie asked, 'Have they said when you can go home yet Lucille?'

'In a day or so but I'm in no hurry. It's a pleasant change for me to be a patient instead of a nurse and I get loads of visitors because everyone knows me.'

'How long do you wait for a baby?' Mair asked.

'A long time,' Mattie cut in, winking at Lucille. 'I think we'd better be off now because it's way past your bedtime Mair. It's been lovely to see you.'

Mark followed Adam upstairs when they arrived home. 'After seeing that faraway look in your eyes when Laurel left yesterday, was I correct to assume you'll be seeing her on Saturday?'

'Yes,' he answered without any elaboration.

'Good. I'm pleased for you. Keep your wits about you Son. Mistakes can be costly.' He tossed a small package on Adam's bed. 'Just in case,' he said with a twinkle in his eye and left the room.

The moment he left Akina shot in. 'Has Dad been having another go at you?'

Hiding the package under his pillow he said, 'He asked if I was seeing Laurel on Saturday, that's all.'

'So what did he say when you told him?'

'Nothing really, just that he was pleased for me.'

'I haven't told him I'm seeing Martin and I'm not going to so you'd better keep it zipped.'

'You be careful. Martin's seventeen and he's had a few girlfriends.'

'Well you can rest assured he won't be *having* me if that's what's bothering you. Nobody's having me till *I* say. Laurel's had lots of boyfriends but she's a virgin too so don't get any ideas unless you want a smack in the chops. It doesn't mean she's easy because she's from a broken home.'

'The thought never crossed my mind,' he told her with a feeling of disappointment.

Over the following weeks Adam studied diligently for his 'O' levels and rarely left the house except on Saturdays to do Josh's books. When he told Laurel his studies were of greater importance, she stormed off in a huff, bringing their short-lived relationship to an abrupt end but Adam wasn't perturbed as his sights were set elsewhere. That however had to be kept under wraps for the foreseeable future because once it became common knowledge, there'd be hell to pay at home.

Akina's interest in Martin waned even sooner as they had little in common and she found him rather shallow, though they parted on friendly terms.

'Why can't lads be like you Adam? Akina asked one evening. 'The ones I meet are so boring.'

'Search me!' he stated with a shrug. 'I bet you'd have liked Travis Hargreaves. He was an interesting lad and had a brilliant sense of humour.'

'Do you want me to test you on anything?'

'You can help with my English. I must pass that. I'm useless with pronouns and stuff. I'm okay with nouns and verbs but not prepositions and adverbs.'

She got a book and pointed to a sentence. 'Show me the nouns, then the verbs and look what's left.' When that presented no problem, she asked him to find an adverb. 'Think of an adjective that describes a noun like *blue* sky; an adverb describes a verb or adds to it as the name suggests. I'll give you a clue. They often end in "*ly*".'

'Dreamily...He smiled dreamily; is that one?'

'Yep! Easy isn't it? How did he *smile – verb –* he smiled *dreamily – adverb.* Shove up a bit.'

She climbed on the bed beside him and continued to explain other parts of grammar in simple terms.

The first thing Mattie noticed when she walked in was Akina sprawled across the bed, her arm around Adam's neck. 'What's going on?' she asked.

'English grammar. We're revising or rather Adam is and I'm helping him.'

'Well it's turned ten; you've got school tomorrow so it's time you packed up now.' She waited by the door until Akina returned to her room and hurried downstairs to report the details of her disconcerting findings to Mark.

'Slow down a bit,' Mark said. 'Tell me precisely what you saw, what they were doing.'

'Akina said they were revising.'

331

'What did you actually see or hear?'

'Akina was on the bed, leaning across Adam with an arm around his neck and he was looking down at a book. Then she mumbled something I didn't catch and he said, 'Oh right, I see now.'

'Sounds to me like they were revising then.'

'It's not right. It's too...er...familiar.'

He laughed. 'Familiar? They've been living under the same roof since they were six. Mair clambers all over him. Is that too familiar? They've always been together, thick as thieves like I've said before.'

'I didn't like it Mark and you'd have been upset too had you witnessed what I saw.'

'So what do you want me to do? At the end of the day they're not blood related. Akina has boyfriends and Adam has girlfriends.'

She grunted. 'Now you're being ridiculous. This must stop and stop now. I don't want them going in each other's room anymore. If Akina wants to help with his revision, they can use one of the studies.'

'What if they want to go to Grandma's together? Do we say they can't? Let's just keep our eyes and ears open. In a couple of years Adam will be going to University, Akina too a year later. I'm sorry but I won't damage this family more than I already have, based on a whim that might prove to be nothing.'

14

'Can I have another look at the itinerary Mum?'

'For heaven's sake Akina, you should know it off by heart, the number of times you've read it.'

She giggled. 'I'm excited! It's different for me. I told Mrs. Jennings about our trip and she said it was an amazing place, Tokyo. Adam's looking forward to a ride on the bullet train. I'm looking forward to everything and to think I could rub shoulders with my father somewhere and not know is such a weird feeling. He might not even live in Tokyo though; in fact he could live anywhere in the world. He could even be dead for all I know. Life's strange isn't it?'

'How do you mean?'

'Well, if Mum had kept in contact with him, they might have got married and lived in Japan. It makes you think doesn't it how people's lives can change course in an instant? I'd never have met you or Dad and I wouldn't have had Adam and Mair as brother and sister. Each of our lives might have turned out differently had my father given Mum his address.'

She sighed. 'Your logic is just like mine. I've said many times that if my mother had crossed that road earlier or later, she'd be alive today and I wouldn't have been put in that terrible foster-home. Still, I've a lot to be thankful for, the way things worked out.'

'I never told Adam what you told me.'

Mattie nodded. 'It's better that way. Right young lady, this is *not* getting the packing done so find the rest of your stuff, tell Adam and fetch it all in here.'

'Hold my hand Adam until we get up in the air. I'm really scared of this bit, taking off.'

He took Akina's hand in his and stroked it gently as the plane taxied along the runway. It seemed to take an eternity before it was airborne. 'Did you put a book in your carry-on? That passes time and helps take your mind off it. Look at Mair; she isn't in the least concerned.'

'Neither am I now we're up in the sky. I brought Scrabble for us to play. With your pathetic infantile knowledge of English I'll wallop you.'

'Don't be so sure following my crash course with you. I took onboard what you said about my writing and I think I did good papers in both Language and Literature. Time will tell. All the others were easy.'

'What are you taking at 'A' level?'

'They'll all be science subjects but to be honest, I'm sick to death of science. So what do you reckon you'll do when you leave school?'

With a shrug she laughed, 'Probably get married and have a load of kids right away to wind Dad up. Seriously, I haven't a clue. Are we having a game?'

'No cheating,' he told her as she set up the game.

She snorted superciliously. 'Why would I need to cheat against you? We'll play the best of three.'

Akina, true to form, won the first game but in the second, by a stroke of good fortune, Adam spotted his opportunity. With a triple word score exposed in two directions he attacked, changing kit into *kite* in one direction and adding *squared* in the other. 'Two triple word scores,' he boasted. 'And I got my "Q" on a double letter score too.' Quickly totting up his score he declared, 'One hundred and fifty-five!'

'Huh! You wish!' she scorned.

'Add it up yourself, smarty-pants and don't forget to add the extra fifty for using all my letters.'

Sceptically she calculated his score and conceded defeat. 'I'm fed up now so I'll give you this game. I'm tired and it's a long flight so don't wake me up until they bring a meal round.' She reclined her seat and closed her eyes as Adam grinned pompously at his having defeated the invincible Akina.

Fifteen hours later they arrived at their hotel.

'This looks very impressive,' Mattie said, casting her eyes around the spacious reception area as they waited in line to check in.

'Yes, it's a pity about the sleeping arrangements though,' Mark replied.

'Drop it Mark! Akina and Adam are *not* sharing a room and that's final.'

'I know; you're right. I was only making a point. Adam and I will be fine. It'll be beneficial for both of us to have time together.' Raising a controversial issue he continued, 'Did you bring that address with you?' and when Mattie nodded he exhaled heavily. 'I hope you aren't making a big mistake. If you find her father and he rejects her it'll break her heart.'

'Like I'm going to tell her if that happens! Really Mark, the things you say at times.'

He was puzzled. 'I thought you'd take her along.'

'That's *exactly* what I *mean*. For a gifted man you say and do some pretty dumb things. I know what's scaring you. It's like the obsessive Josh Hargreaves complex you have. You can't allow yourself to like the guy because you think he's trying to steal your son and that's the reason you don't want Akina to find her father, in case it happens again. If anyone's driving Adam away it's *you* by your actions Mark, not Josh Hargreaves. Akina thinks the world of you and that'll never change unless *you* make it happen and I won't deprive her of the opportunity to meet her birth father simply because you can't cope. Try to remember *you're* the adult.'

Frostily he cut in, 'Move up. I think we're next.'

'I'm shattered Mark and I probably said too much so I'm sorry. I'm only thinking of you. Spend your time wisely with Adam to rebuild your relationship. I'm constantly having minor skirmishes with Akina but they're soon over. It happens in all families.'

Akina wandered between the adjoining rooms. 'I'm having the middle bed. Adam and Mair can fight it out over the other two.'

'Adam's sharing with me,' Mark stated. 'It's girls in this room and boys in the other.'

'You're joking,' Akina complained. 'Why?'

'Because I said so!' he retorted demonstratively, thus preventing further debate. 'I want a word with your mum now if you don't mind so Akina, would you empty Mair's bag and your own and put everything away please. We'll be back in a minute.'

He closed the adjoining door and took Mattie in his arms. 'I'm so sorry about earlier; you're right, I *am* paranoid about Josh Hargreaves. The truth is, he was an excellent father and Adam knows that. Josh was everything I'm not. He put his family first. I do try to be a good father, I really do but I should have started sooner. I just worry I've left it too late.'

'Listen to me. Josh is a good man and also a very wealthy man. He has no one to splash his money on now so he gives people a hand when they're needy, like finding a job for Jack and allowing him a week off to be with his wife and new baby, in addition to the fifty pounds he doles out to new fathers to help with the expense. He's not trying to better you. He does it because it gives him pleasure to help people. Remind yourself what you did to help him when he needed it. No amount of money could buy the kind of help *you* provided. Adam knows you dislike Josh so it's obvious why he didn't mention he was working there. He knew exactly how you'd react and he was right.'

She kissed his lips fondly and sighed. 'You're so predictable. Try to see the best in people instead of the worst. Remember how you prejudged me before we were married, and every time you were wrong. You have eleven days to square things with Adam. Talk to him about Josh, about his business. Let him see you recognize his loneliness and maybe suggest that if he's alone at Christmas, he'd be welcome at our house for Christmas dinner.'

'Hang about Mattie,' he laughed. 'I'm not sharing my turkey with him!'

'Then share your heart with him Mark. It was all such a long time ago. Forgive him, not for my sake but because you know it's the right thing to do.'

He hugged her tight. 'I love you,' he murmured. 'Nobody could ever accuse you of seeing the worst in people. I'm really going to miss you. These next two weeks will be the longest of my life.'

'And mine too, but I'm sure we can play catch-up once we get home,' she giggled.

He gave her a squeeze. 'You can bet on it!'

The next day they boarded a coach for a sightseeing tour, exploring some of Tokyo's contrasting ancient and modern attractions, stopping first at the Tokyo Tower. Mark took several spectacular photographs from the observation platform and from there they went to the ancient Meiji Shrine, a notable example of Japanese architecture. Following a leisurely walk around the East Garden of the Imperial Palace, they were escorted to the Ginza shopping district before relaxing in a shaded spot to enjoy a long cool drink with their traditional Japanese lunch.

'Everything's different here,' Akina commented. 'Apart from that shopping centre, it's like living in another age, like time has stood still.'

'Trust me, it hasn't,' Mark made known. 'They're very intuitive in Japan, in most of the East I should say and way beyond the West in technology. You'll see that this afternoon when we visit the Ueno and Akihabarar shopping districts. They have electronic stuff on general sale that we've hardly seen in UK.'

'Don't we have a short cruise too?' Mattie asked.

'Yes, on the River Sumida. You'll enjoy being on a boat won't you Mair?'

She frowned. 'Yes, if I don't fall in the water.'

Mark scrutinized his guide. 'They're taking us to see a different temple this afternoon, I note. It's the Asakusa Kannon temple. Should be interesting.'

Akina and Adam poked each other and sniggered. Mattie flashed a critical glance and after she turned away, Akina burst into hysterical laughter as Adam whispered, 'Boring old fart,' in her ear.

Mattie wandered away to talk to the driver. Pointing to the address shown on the business card, she enquired how to get there from the hotel. With only two more days left prior to their embarkation for a seven day cruise around the islands, time was of the essence and there wasn't a moment to lose.'

He scratched his head and pondered for a while. 'We'll be stopping in that area later this afternoon. This address is in the Akihabarar shopping district. We'll be staying about an hour so you'll have time to find it. To get there by public transport from your hotel would be difficult so I'd recommend taking a taxi that would get you there in forty minutes.'

She thanked him and returned to the others.

'What was all that about?' Akina asked.

'Oh, nothing really. We were just discussing the shopping centre we're visiting later,' she answered with a half-truth. 'Your dad was right. It's primarily electrical stuff.'

'*Brilliant!*' Adam gushed, feigning enthusiasm, at the same time poking Akina who exploded into uncontrollable laughter again.

Mattie's thoughts were on another matter. Maybe she could organise a meeting with Mr. Hashimoto for the next day if anyone was around, she mused.

At the end of the enjoyable and informative river cruise they stepped ashore. 'I'll roam around on my own once we get to the shops,' Mattie said. 'I'll see you back at the coach.'

She spoke to the driver once more who gave her detailed directions and she hurried away to find the address. This was a bustling area with lively music bursting through every doorway and no shortage of shopkeepers aiming to lure her into their establishments with promises of quality items on sale at unbelievable knockdown prices.

Turning left at the next street took her away from the chaos into a more civilised area where elegant modern buildings contrasted sharply with the antiquated jumble of retail shops in the adjacent street. Checking the address again, Mattie searched for the number, aware she was close and feeling somewhat apprehensive she shuddered. Had Mark been right? Was this a terrible mistake to reap up the past? She hesitated to collect her thoughts whilst telling herself she had come this far and must go through with it. She took a few more faltering steps and suddenly she was there, reading the plaque by the open door.

A flight of steps led to the reception area and she walked confidently towards the desk where a young woman addressed her in English. 'May I help you?'

She had given no thought to how she would begin and smiled nervously, presenting the card. 'I would like to see Mr. Yukio Hashimoto please.'

'Do you have an appointment?'

'I'm afraid not. I'm just here until tomorrow and then I'm moving on. It *is* rather urgent though.'

'May I have your name please and would you tell me the nature of your business?'

'My name's Mrs. Wyndham and it's of a personal nature not business. He and I have a mutual friend in England.' She had given little away but hoped it was sufficient to whet the man's appetite for more.

She nodded. 'I see. Would you wait for a moment please while I see if I can arrange a meeting?'

She left by a rear door and returned only minutes later. 'Mr. Hashimoto will see you now but he has another appointment in twenty minutes.'

'That's perfect. Thank you,' Mattie said, following the receptionist down a corridor to a door at the end that opened into a luxurious office.

'Mrs. Wyndham,' she stated and left the room.

He arose, extending a hand to shake hers and gestured courteously to offer her a seat. 'I'm delighted to make your acquaintance Mrs. Wyndham. I don't believe we've met before but I'm informed we have a mutual friend in England, correct?'

He seemed a pleasant man though it was difficult to assess his age and was a far cry from what Mattie had envisaged. She had pictured him to be tall and slim whereas he was short and stocky, nothing like the man she'd have imagined being Sam's type.

'Yes,' she answered. 'It was some time ago, back in nineteen-sixty-nine. You stayed at a guest-house in Devon for a few weeks.'

341

He laughed. 'Yes, almost a lifetime ago but I still remember it well, particularly the hospitality. It was second to none.'

Mattie smiled. She couldn't argue with that.

'How is Sam?' he went on. 'I've never met anyone quite like her. I found her enchanting.'

'She was unique. Sadly, she died nine years ago.'

He was genuinely shocked. 'I am so sorry. I don't know what else to say.'

'I understand. The subject I wish to discuss with you is somewhat delicate. My presence here is not for monetary gain; there is no ulterior motive whatsoever. Let me make that clear. It is simply to make you aware of certain facts. What you choose to do about the information I impart is entirely up to you but I felt it right to tell you. I only found out myself recently when I came across your business card, as it was a secret Sam took to her grave.'

He sat bolt upright in his chair. 'Please go on.'

'I have a fifteen-year-old daughter who I adopted nine years ago. She's Sam's daughter and was born nine months after you left. She's called Akina. Sam told me that she'd asked for no further contact from the man with whom she'd had the relationship and who, Sam later discovered, had fathered her child. Since she had no idea where he lived, there was no means of getting in touch with him. She never gave me his name; she said he was a Japanese guest who had stayed there for several weeks. She asked me to promise that when Akina was old enough to appreciate it, I would bring her to Japan to see the culture and learn of her Japanese heritage, so in a nutshell that's why we're here. Akina knows nothing about this meeting or indeed that I found your card. This is her photo,' she added, taking it from her bag.

He took it from her in silence. 'She's delightful,' he said and paused for some time as she continued to stare at him. 'I see your motives are honourable when seeking to unite father and daughter but alas I am *not* Akina's father. If I were, I would welcome her with open arms Mrs. Wyndham. Yes, Sam was charming but we never had a physical relationship. I realise it's not what you want to hear but it's true. Please believe I would never reject my child under any circumstances.'

Though there was sincerity in his voice she found his response hard to believe and her eyes filled with tears. She felt humiliated and embarrassed.

With concern he asked, 'Where are you staying?'

'The Imperial,' she answered distantly.

'Since we have no further business to discuss, let me call a taxi to take you to your hotel. It's the least I can do. I'm very sorry for your distress.'

'No, no it's fine. I'll be alright thank you. There's a coach taking us to the hotel. It's just a five minute walk. My husband and children are waiting for me.'

'You have other children then?'

'I have a son who's sixteen and a seven-year-old daughter. They think I'm shopping. I was so afraid something like this might happen. That's the reason I didn't discuss it with Akina. She would have been devastated to learn her father had rejected her had it turned out that way. I'm sorry if I've offended you. That wasn't my intent. I came across your business card and so I checked copy invoices and found one in your name. Everything appeared to fit perfectly.'

'I would have deduced the same so no apology is required. I'm sorry you've had a wasted journey.'

She stood up. 'I have no other avenues to pursue so I guess Akina will never know the identity of her father. Goodbye and thank you for your time.'

'My pleasure,' he responded politely. 'I hope you enjoy the rest of your holiday.'

As Mattie was hurrying down the corridor in tears Yukio was drumming his fingers on the desk while waiting for the receptionist to answer the telephone. 'Yes, cancel *all* my appointments. I'm going out...I don't care who's here! I'm leaving right away,' he told her and sighing heavily he hung up.

Mattie checked the time and quickened her pace, arriving red-faced and flustered. 'We thought you'd got lost. Everyone else is on the coach but two have only just arrived. So how did it go?' asked Mark.

'Absolutely terrible but I'll tell you later.'

She clambered aboard and found a double seat at the rear of the coach out of earshot of the children. 'I can honestly say *that* was the worst experience of my life. He was there and he was very pleasant and listened patiently. I showed him her photograph and then he dropped the bombshell and said he wasn't her father as he never had a relationship with Sam.'

Mark was shocked. 'Did you believe him?'

'Surprisingly, I did. He came across as truthful.'

'So that's it then. Whether he's speaking the truth or not, there's nowhere else to go from here.'

Her eyes filled with tears. 'I wanted this so much

344

for Akina. I really thought I'd found him. I feel so demoralised now.'

He slipped an arm around her and brushed his lips against her cheek. 'Up to now, this holiday's been a total disaster. The kids are bored rigid, your efforts have failed and we're in separate rooms. Let's start over and try to make the best of it. We'll find somewhere nice for dinner tonight and put all this behind us. What do you say?'

Mattie smiled through her tears. 'Good idea. Did you buy anything at the shops?'

'No and that caused more aggravation. Adam and Akina both wanted to buy portable cassette players and I wouldn't let them so they stomped off ahead.'

She laughed at that. 'It can only get better Mark.'

It was almost nine o'clock when they returned from their evening meal. 'It's bed for you my precious,' Mattie told Mair. 'It's way past your bedtime.'

'I'll attend to her,' Akina said taking her into the room just as the telephone rang. 'It's for you Mum.'

When Mattie answered, the receptionist reported there was a gentleman named Hashimoto asking to speak to her in reception.

'Yes, thank you,' she replied cautiously, being in earshot of Akina.

'Are you okay Mum? You're as white as a sheet.'

'I'm just tired after the long journey and the busy day today,' she lied. 'I'll sit with Dad for a bit and then I'll I turn in.' She hurried to Mark's room and as luck would have it, Adam was taking a shower.

Mark was equally shocked. 'Shall I come too?'

'No, I'll be fine. I need to hear what he has to say this time. He might be less talkative with you there as well. If anyone notices I'm missing, I'm collecting tourist information from someone.'

Mattie wandered into the reception area but seeing no one she recognised she approached the desk. 'I was told someone was here to see me.'

'Yes Mrs. Wyndham. It's that gentleman there.'

He rose and smiled as she advanced towards him. 'Good evening. My name's Akio Hashimoto. Shall we sit down? May I get you a drink or a coffee?'

'No thank you,' she answered coolly.

'In that case I'd better get to the point. When you visited my brother Yukio earlier today, you left this behind, a photo of your daughter Akina. He told me about your conversation, that Akina's mother died a few years ago and then you took over her care.'

'My husband and I *adopted* her,' she emphasised strongly. 'We are her legal parents now.'

'Yes I understand that and I also understand your sole purpose in visiting my brother was to discover if he was Akina's father. Would that be right?'

'That is correct but he assured me he wasn't.'

He nodded. 'Let me talk to you about Yukio for a moment. He'd have felt awkward explaining this to you. Yukio was in love with Sam from the moment he saw her. It might sound ridiculous but it's true. She was vivacious, fun-loving and easy to love and although she enjoyed his company, she was unable to return his feelings because she had fallen in love with another man and entered into a passionate relationship with him. Yukio didn't know that and...'

'That's preposterous,' she cut in. 'You're blackening a woman's character because your brother is too cowardly to face up to his responsibilities and to think I believed him earlier. He was so plausible. You only have to look at this photo to see she's half Japanese. I wanted nothing from your brother and I made that clear. If however he had wanted contact with her, that would have made me happy for her. It was a selfless act on my part to try to unite her with her father, her heritage. If he had admitted his part, even if unwilling to be involved in any way I would have been just as happy to walk away, having done what I set out to do, and if you'd listen to yourself Mr. Hashimoto, you'd hear how feeble it sounds for *you* to inform me your brother knew nothing about this so-called other man, unless of course that man was...' she paused. 'Oh God, it *was* you,' she cried as she blinked away tears clouding her eyes.

'Well, Yukio knows now but don't worry. It was such a long time ago and he's forgiven me and I'm delighted to declare I'm Akina's father, in fact I'm very proud to be her father.' He laughed. 'Are you a solicitor by any chance?'

'Is it that obvious? I'm very sorry for my outburst and I *did* believe your brother earlier.'

'You helped me out. I was finding it very difficult to get the words out. It's not every day you find out you're a father and I have only known a few hours since Yukio stormed round to tell me face to face.'

'Were you shocked?'

'I was shocked to hear Sam died so young. Had I had my way, we'd have kept in touch but Sam was adamant that it was over. We lived at opposite ends of the globe, she argued and I was told not to write or call her. I didn't know Yukio had left his card.'

'And neither did Sam. You remember Emily, her mother? She hid it away in a drawer where it would only be found after her death. I think she was afraid Sam might follow you to Japan. I stumbled across it when Norman, her husband died. I was clearing out the drawers.'

'I'm glad you were,' he said with deep sincerity. 'How about that drink I offered you earlier? I feel we've a lot to talk about and I could manage one.'

'Thank you. I'd like a gin and tonic.'

She watched him walk away. He was a smart man with silvery patches at his temples, much taller than Yukio but both enjoyed the same pleasant manner. She hoped he could excuse her earlier rudeness. It had been a day of embarrassments.

He returned with her drink and took his seat. 'Tell me about Akina please. Is she happy?'

'Generally so though she has her moments of disquiet like all teenagers. She's doing well at school and a few months ago she entered herself for *Face of Youth,* a fashion house, and was selected, so now her photos appear all over the world, at least in the countries that sell their products. She's tall for her age and has plenty of lip if you understand that turn of phrase.'

'Cheeky,' he laughed. 'Obviously very pretty too as I can see from this photograph. I understand you have two other children, a boy of sixteen and a girl of seven. I hope you don't think it presumptuous of

348

me but I've brought a few gifts for them. I work in electronic equipment, games and the like but most Japanese do as you'll know. I'd be very grateful if you'd give them to the children. The small gifts are for your youngest but it'll be obvious when you see them. Our teenagers go crazy for personal cassette players so there's one each for Akina and your son, together with a selection of modern cassettes.'

'That's very kind of you. Thank you.'

'May I enquire whether you intend telling Akina about me?'

Surprised by his question she nodded saying, 'Of course if that's what you want. That was the reason I tried to find you, so I'd like to ask you a question. 'Would you like to see your daughter?'

Her question caught him off guard. He turned his head away and in a broken voice replied, 'Nothing in the world would give me greater pleasure. These last few hours I've thought of nothing else.'

'Right, there's no time like the present so I'll go upstairs and explain. Akina isn't aware I found your brother's business card. She knows you're Japanese but that's all she knows, so it'll take a little time to tell her everything if you can wait.'

As she arose, she caught her breath to see Akina walking towards her carrying a bottle of Cola. 'Dad told me you were down here seeing someone about various trips tomorrow. I hope it's not another day of temples. If I never see another temple again, it'll be too soon.'

Akio heard every word and laughed. 'They do get rather boring I agree. They aren't everyone's cup of tea as you say in England but we have lots of other interesting things like a cable car ride to see Mount Fuji and also many short river and lake trips. There is also our famous bullet train. That's a must.'

'Yes, my brother Adam's hoping we can ride on that. Could you arrange that for us please?'

'Akio Hashimoto at your service. I'm delighted to meet you and I can arrange anything for you.'

Recalling one of the phrases Mrs. Jennings taught her she replied, 'Amarini mo o ai dekite ureshii.'

'Excellent! You speak perfect Japanese.'

Akina giggled. 'My headmistress taught me that. It's the first chance I've had to practise on someone so I'm pleased you understood. I don't really know anything else but I wanted to try. I'm half-Japanese you see. You speak English very well but I suppose you have to in your job.'

'Most people do here. Would you like a drink?'

'Oh yes please. That's why I came down. My big greedy brother emptied the Cola bottle so Dad sent me down for another.'

'Cola with ice and lemon?'

'Yes please.'

'He's nice,' Akina said as Akio walked away. 'He has nice friendly eyes. I always notice the eyes.'

Mattie was choking back tears, tears of joy. Akina liked her father. That was a good start but how was she going to tell her everything now? He would be back soon. They had emphasised at University that once you had the court's attention you must get to the point at once before the window of opportunity was lost forever.

Mattie took a deep breath. 'I haven't been totally honest with you since we arrived here. When I left you at the shopping centre, I went to see somebody. Following on from that discussion, Akio Hashimoto turned up unexpectedly tonight. That was the phone call I received. He's your father Akina.'

For some moments she froze then her face turned scarlet and tears coursed down her cheeks. 'Is this true Mum?' she sobbed emotionally. 'You wouldn't lie to me about something like that would you?'

'Of course I wouldn't. I was about to come up to tell you when I saw you walking towards me.'

'But how do you know it's really him?'

'Because we've talked about your mum, how they fell in love but had to part. Trust me please Akina, he *is* your father. I was intent on finding him when I booked the holiday. I held information suggesting he might live here but I kept it from you as I didn't want to disappoint you if my efforts proved futile.'

Akio returned with the drinks and placed them on the table. Seeing the look in her eyes he knew she'd been acquainted with at least some of the facts and he smiled reassuringly. 'No one is making demands on anyone else Akina. I only found out a few hours ago too. If you want to ask me anything, anything at all, I'll do my best to answer you.'

'Anything at all?' she repeated and Akio nodded. 'Okay! Why did you get my mother pregnant when you knew you'd be leaving her?'

'*Akina!*' Mattie cried. 'You can't ask him that!'

Ignoring Mattie's intervention he turned to Akina. 'You have the right to know so I'll tell you. Your

351

mother and I loved each other deeply. My brother Yukio, who travelled to England with me, loved her too but your mother chose me. That meant we must keep our involvement secret. The three of us often went out together but when Yukio went off somewhere alone, we would arrange a clandestine meeting. It was an amazing, passionate liaison. We were in love but we were careful, that was until our final evening together when, in the heat of the moment, we acted foolishly. Seeing you now, I don't regret it for I know, having spoken to Mrs. Wyndham, that you brought great joy to your mother as you have to Emily and Norman and your adoptive parents. My only regret is that I didn't know about you sooner.'

'And if you had?'

'Naturally, I'd have wanted to be part of your life. I haven't come here simply to shake your hand and say, "Nice to have met you," and walk away. Whatever part I'm able to play from this day on will be my greatest pleasure so please don't dismiss me out of hand without giving my words serious thought.'

'Do I have brothers or sisters?'

'Sadly not. You are my only child.'

Those words rang in her ears like a beautiful symphony and brought tears to her eyes once more and her words likewise to his when she responded, 'I'm so pleased we've found each other. I've often wondered what you'd be like. What do I call you?'

He smiled affectionately. 'Since you already have a wonderful father, why not call me Akio?'

She extended her hand. 'I'm pleased to meet you at last Akio.'

On a short burst of laughter he replied, 'Amarini mo o ai dekite ureshii,' and she laughed too.

'What *does* that mean?' Mattie asked.

'I'm pleased to meet you too,' Akina told her.

'I've brought you and your siblings a few gifts,' he said, handing her a huge bag. 'For you and your brother there's a Sony Walkman cassette deck, the very latest model you probably won't have in UK yet. It records too.'

She screeched with delight. 'That's what I wanted to buy earlier Mum but Dad wouldn't let me. Adam wanted one too but Dad said we'd to wait until you were there. You'd gone off shopping, or that's what you told me then but you'd actually gone to see that man about Akio.'

'*That man* as you call him was Yukio, your uncle. I mistakenly believed he was your father.'

'So you dropped a clanger telling him about me?'

She glanced apologetically at Akio. 'I did!'

'He's forgiven me so no harm done, only good.'

'Thank you for your present Akio. I really wanted one of those.'

He smiled. 'It's a good job your dad put his foot down then or you'd have had two each.' He looked at his watch and stood up. 'Have you seen the time? I apologise for keeping you so long.'

'Will I see you again before we leave?'

'Wild horses wouldn't keep me away as you say, assuming your parents have no objection.'

'None whatsoever,' Mattie said on behalf of both of them. 'And in future, please call me Mattie.'

'Oh, just another quick question,' Akina piped up.

'Do I have Japanese grandparents and if so would I be able to meet them?'

'Yes, my mother's alive and she'll be delighted to meet you when I tell her about you.'

Akina beamed with happiness. 'I'll look forward to that. You'll call me then?'

'Of course! Goodnight er...Mattie. It's been such a pleasure.'

'For Akina and I too,' she sighed. 'Goodnight.'

Mark and Adam were asleep when Mattie knocked on their bedroom door.

'I thought you'd gone to bed ages ago,' Mark said rubbing his eyes.

'What, without saying goodnight? We were both downstairs. I thought you'd stay with Mair until we got back. Has anyone bothered to check on her?'

'I'll check now,' Akina said. 'She never wakes up though once she's asleep.'

'What took so long?' Mark asked. 'I can't think why he bothered to come back.'

'He didn't. That was his brother. He's the one and that's why he came to see me, to tell me.'

Adam looked perplexed. 'Can the two of you stop talking in riddles and tell me what's going on?'

Akina returned. 'Mair's fast asleep.'

'Good, so maybe you'd like to tell Dad and Adam who you've been talking to all this time.'

Her face lit up. 'My father! Mum's found him and he's really nice isn't he Mum?'

'Yes, he's a charming man.'

Adam looked shocked. 'I don't understand. How

354

on earth did you find him? I thought no one knew anything about him.'

'It's a long story. I had a lead and I followed it up but I was completely wrong. My error however led somewhere else and now we've found him. Akina will no doubt fill you in on the minutiae tomorrow. Suffice to say *mission accomplished.*'

'The *what*-tiae? What kind of word's that?'

'*Finer points.* 'If you read decent literature rather than comics you'd speak better English,' Mark said.

It was time for a wind up and Akina nudged him. '*You'll* be dead chuffed!' she stated, clambering on Adam's bed. 'Look at all this gear he's brought us. Some of it's for Mair but *we* got them super-duper cassette players that Dad wouldn't let us have today and these record so they're better than them others.'

'No! Wow! Shift yourself and let's have a shufti.'

'Hang about he's *my* father. You'll go nabbing all the best cassettes. I'm having a gander first.'

Mark was close to boiling point. 'Does that flaming school teach you *anything?*' he shouted angrily.

Mattie laughed. 'Calm down Mark. They're doing it on purpose to wind you up. What's got into you?'

'Come to my room Adam and we'll tip it all out. Dad's obviously got a strop on about something.'

Adam followed her and closed the door.

Mattie climbed in bed beside him, wrapping her arms round him. 'She's excited Mark. Let her have her hour of glory. She's just met her birth father for the first time. Imagine how you'd feel were it you.'

'I said they couldn't have those cassette players. He's just undermined my authority.'

'Don't be so silly. He didn't know about that. He sells that kind of thing. The man turns up to meet a daughter he didn't know he had up to a few hours ago and brings her a gift. What's wrong with that?'

'Is she seeing him again?'

'I would imagine so. He's her father Mark. We've had this discussion once. He won't pose any threat once we're home if that's what's bothering you so give me a goodnight kiss now.'

He sighed. 'I wish you could stay here with me.'

'You know I can't. Try to be happy for her.'

The next day's attractions promised to be more interesting as they headed off towards the spectacular Mount Fuji, travelling to an altitude of eight thousand feet. It was a clear sunny day and the view of the Pacific Ocean was breathtaking. After a spot of lunch, they were on their way again, this time to the Hakone National Park and by cable car they experienced stunning views and took many photographs of the volcanic Hakone Mountains.

When they thought the day couldn't get any better there followed a cruise on the serene Lake Ashi and Adam in particular was thrilled to return to Tokyo Station afterwards on Japan's renowned bullet train. It had been a wonderful day that everyone enjoyed thoroughly.

There was a message for them from Akio back at the hotel inviting them all to dinner as his guests.

'I might turn in early,' Mark told Mattie. 'You go if you like. I'm a bit tired.'

She was furious. 'Listen to me Mark Wyndham!

Stop being so petty! What's wrong with you? Don't tell me you're afraid of the competition. We're all invited and we're all going.'

'I wasn't invited last night when the three of you were enjoying your comfortable tête-à-tête. Oh no, you managed without me very nicely then.'

'It wasn't like that at all. I didn't know I was seeing *him* when I went to reception and was surprised to find a stranger. By the time I'd established who he was, you'd sent Akina down for a bottle of Cola and she barged in on our conversation. I was livid about that *and* you left Mair alone. I was just about to come up to tell you both when Akina turned up.'

'*Excuse me!* I didn't even *know* Akina had been down for a bottle of Cola. I wrongly assumed you'd taken her down without bothering to ask me if I'd like to meet him too.'

She snorted. 'Then you should have mentioned it, shouldn't you? Did you think I'd do something like that when I know how paranoid you are?'

Mark threw back his head and laughed. 'Yes I am aren't I? Sorry darling. I'll make it up to you.'

'Yes you will. You'll get showered and changed and you'll come to dinner where you'll be gracious and civil. Right?'

'Yes Mattie. Whatever you say. Are you coming in the shower with me?' he quipped optimistically.

'No! I'm calling Akio to accept his invitation.'

Akio was already waiting in reception when they went down and Mark felt anxious as he approached with outstretched hand. 'It's a pleasure to meet you. I'm Mark Wyndham. Please call me Mark.'

Akio bowed his head slightly and shook Mark's hand. 'Akio Hashimoto. It's rather a mouthful I'm afraid so call me Akio and I'm happy to make your acquaintance too.'

'I see you're wearing a tie. I wasn't sure whether to or not so I slipped one in my pocket just in case.'

'I prefer to remove mine if it's alright with you.' He laughed. 'Now had we been women, we'd have called each other first to discuss what to wear.'

'True,' Mark agreed, feeling more at ease. 'May I introduce the rest of our family, Adam and Mair.'

He nodded in acknowledgement as Adam stepped forward and thanked him for the gifts. 'I'm pleased you like them. They're the latest craze in Japan.'

'They're fantastic Akio,' Akina joined in. 'All my favourite music's on those tapes, Adam's too.'

'I earn my living, knowing what teenagers enjoy.'

'You're in sales I understand,' Mark said.

'Kind of. We export world-wide.'

Mark was impressed. 'A big business then?'

'Mega, with family links in manufacturing too.'

En route to the car park Akio asked, 'What line of work are you in Mark?'

'Medicine. I'm a Cardiothoracic Consultant.'

'Admirable. I have great respect for someone who can save lives. I expect Adam will follow suit?'

'Hopefully but time will tell. Young people today have different ideas to those in my day.'

They were whisked by seven-seater taxi to an impressive restaurant in an outlying district of the city.

'I was thinking of the children when I booked this place,' Akio told Mattie. 'It caters to all tastes. Here

358

in Japan, we're very big fish-eaters. I know it's not the norm in the West, so you'll find multi-national cuisine here including large American steaks if that happens to be your preference.'

At the end of the meal, Mark sighed heavily. 'I'm absolutely stuffed! That was one of the best meals I've ever had. I've thoroughly enjoyed the food and the interesting conversation.'

'My fish was yummy,' Mair piped up. 'I liked the chocolate pudding as well. Mr. Akio, may I ask you something? How come you're Akina's daddy when she already has a daddy?'

Akio didn't know what to say. 'Oh dear! Help me out please Mark. I'm out of my depth here.'

'I'll talk to you about that later,' Mattie promised.

'I believe you're doing a cruise of the islands for a few days,' Akio remarked.

Mark nodded. 'Yes, that's the more relaxing part of the holiday. I have to say though, today's sightseeing was amazing.'

'And I heard you got your ride on the bullet train Adam. How was it?' Akio asked.

'Fantastic. Everything was today. Fatigue was the problem yesterday. We'd travelled a long way from England the day before and it was hot yesterday.'

Akio excused himself to settle the bill and on his return spoke quietly to Mark. 'If you'd permit me, I would like to take Akina to see my mother. I understand you have one more day in Tokyo at the end of your cruise. My mother's very old and it may be the only opportunity she'll ever have to see her granddaughter. I know it's a lot to ask of you but would you think about it please? Adam and Mair would be welcome too, if you prefer it that way.'

'I'm sure we can arrange something. I'll speak to Mattie and let you know.'

'Are you ready to make tracks, as you say?'

Mark laughed. 'You're an excellent linguist Akio. I've noticed how you know all our expressions.'

'I visit UK two or three times a year and read lots of English books. I find English easy to learn.'

'Strange! I never did; it was my worst subject at school, Adam's too.'

Mattie cut in, 'Sorry to break up the party but we have to pack Mark. I think we ought to get back.'

Akio stood up instantly. 'The taxi's outside. I told him to return at nine-thirty. I'll ride with you to the hotel and then the driver will take me home.'

Mark jumped out first at the hotel. 'Thank you for a memorable evening. I'll call you later.' Everyone else thanked him and waved as the taxi drove away.

'What a nice man,' Mattie sighed, flopping down on Mark's bed. 'I'm glad you made the effort.'

Mark lay down beside her. 'It was no effort at all, he is and as long as he keeps his distance there's no problem. He wants to take Akina to see his mother when we get back. What do you think? Adam and Mair can go too he said.'

'There'll be fire and brimstone if we say no. He's a genuine guy and Akina might never get to see her grandmother otherwise. She must be quite old.'

'Do I call him and say it's okay for them to go?'

'Yes, it'll give us time to pack up in peace.'

He stared at her with raised eyebrows. 'We get an

hour or so to ourselves and you'd waste it packing? I think not. I know a better way of filling our time.'

'Do men *ever* think of anything else?' she asked.

Mark shrugged. 'I can't speak for everybody but *I* don't,' he guffawed, anticipating a slap that landed instantaneously. 'You look really sexy tonight.'

'Thanks but Sexy has to pack for tomorrow Mark. How are things going with Adam now?'

'Great. We talk a lot more so it's a start. I'd better call Akio. He should be home now.'

The six day cruise proved exhilarating. The waters were calm, the food was excellent and all the places they visited were interesting. Mair, who'd recently learned to swim, enjoyed the children's pool whilst Akina and Adam made the most of the larger pools before spending their evenings in the disco.

It was a sad day when they disembarked with the prospect of a lengthy flight to England the next day.

Mark had asked Akio to call at two and he arrived promptly, beaming with pleasure to see Akina and her siblings.

'What time shall I bring them back?' Akio asked.

Mark pondered. 'Six o'clock? Is that alright?'

'Perfect. See you later then. Right, let's see what Grandma's up to. She's been baking all morning so I hope you're hungry.'

'*I'm* hungry,' Adam announced and Mair nodded in agreement.

'Did they get off okay?' Mattie asked when Mark returned.

'Yes and they won't be back till six.'

'Good. That gives us plenty of time to pack.' She lifted a pile of clothes from the wardrobe and Mark promptly hung them back up again. He took her in his arms. 'As you said, we've lots of time to pack.'

True to his word Akio called from reception at six o'clock and Mattie and Mark went down together.

Akina was bursting with excitement. 'We've had *such* a good time and Grandma is really sweet isn't she Mair? She doesn't speak English but she taught us a game nonetheless and she let us fetch it home.'

'I had a game of chess with Akio but he beat me,' Adam said dolefully. 'He'll be in England soon on business so we're going to meet up. I'll trounce you the next time we play Akio, mark my words.'

He howled with laughter. 'You *wish* young man! We've all had a great time Mattie. It's such a shame you're not here longer. Mother says to tell you that you have three delightful children with impeccable manners. She's sent some cake. It's in that bag with some more cassettes so at least the children will be occupied during your long flight. It just remains for me to say it's been both a pleasure and an honour to meet you and I'll be eternally grateful to you Mattie for your efforts to find me.'

Mattie shook his hand. 'You'll keep in touch?'

'Without a doubt! Mark, what can I say? You've filled my role perfectly. No father could have asked for more. I thank you from the bottom of my heart.' He shook Mark's hand vigorously. 'Mair, you're a delightful little girl and I'm proud to know you and as for you Adam, get some practice in at chess.'

Everyone laughed but the tone quickly changed to one of melancholy when he turned to face Akina. 'I could never put into words how it feels to have met you. Never in my life have I known such emotion. It's a great privilege to be your father and I hope we can remain good friends. Be happy Akina,' he said in a tearful voice. 'I'd better be off before I make a complete fool of myself. Goodbye.'

He turned to walk away but before he had taken a dozen steps Akina called out his name and ran after him. Akio stopped and turned and she threw herself into his arms, sobbing uncontrollably. He closed his eyes savouring those divine moments as he held his child for the very first time. Memories of Sam came flooding back as if it were only yesterday. 'I loved Sam so much Akina,' he wept.

'I know and I can see why Mum fell in love with you. Please don't cry. I don't like to see you cry.'

'I'll see you again soon, I promise and meanwhile I'll call you as often as I can. I don't want to make your parents angry so please, I have to go now.'

He kissed her forehead gently. 'Take good care of yourself.' Giving a final wave to the others he left.

Mark moved towards her and curled an arm round her shoulder as they walked back in silence.

Mattie relived the poignant moments over and over again as they waited for their flight to be called.

She could understand Akina's pain but that would ease given time.

It had been an eventful holiday in every respect. She glanced at Mark and Adam, laughing together as they arm-wrestled fiercely on a small table. They had finally made their peace. Mair was playing with one of her new games, happy as ever with her own company. Mattie was happy too at having achieved what she'd set out to do.

An announcement over the intercom told them to go to the gate and she stood up, alerting the others.

Akina wiped a tear from her cheek but it didn't go unnoticed by Mark who smiled with compassion. 'I hated saying goodbye but I'll see Akio again before too long and when I do, he'd like to come with me to scatter Mum's ashes. I must have known subconsciously I had to hold on to them.'

'That's nice,' he replied but she was quick to spot a morose tone.

'Dad, listen to me please. I don't know what's on your mind but Akio's my father and always will be. I can't change a biological fact nor would I want to. He'll be a part of my life from now on because he's my flesh and blood.' She took his hand in hers and smiled. 'If it bothers you, it shouldn't because he'll never take your place. *Akio's* my biological father but *you* will always be my dad.'

That was what Mark needed to hear. His concerns had finally been laid to rest and as he tightened his grip on Akina's hand, tears pricked his eyes. Mark was deliriously happy, for in a bizarre kind of way, their holiday had brought them together as a loving and united family.